WILLO\ ⌐⌐ ⌐⌐⌐⌐K ONE

Live, Ranch, Love

EMMA LUCY

To anyone who has ever struggled to believe in themselves—it's time to start trusting blindly in who you are.

Because you are *magical*.

Author's Note

This book is intended for audiences of 18 years old and over.

Explicit sexual content can be found in chapters 23, 24, 25, 26, 31, and the epilogue, for those who might want to skip, or those who want to dive straight back into the spicy stuff.

There is on-page discussion of the death of a relative from cancer, and on-page minor panic attacks.

Official Playlist

1. Butterflies by Kacey Musgraves

2. Wide Open Spaces by The Chicks

3. Bless The Broken Road by Rascal Flatts

4. Meant to Be by Bebe Rexha ft. Florida Georgia Line

5. Heartbroken (Jessie Version) by Diplo & Jessie Murph

6. Stand By Me by Ben E. King

7. Blame It On Me by Morgan Wallen

8. Cowboy Take Me Away by The Chicks

9. Shivers Down Spines by Zach Bryan

10. Forever After All by Luke Combs

11. Man! I Feel Like A Woman! by Shania Twain

12. Wrong Turns by Old Dominion

EMMA LUCY

13. What Ifs by Kane Brown ft. Lauren Alaina

14. Good Girl by Dustin Lynch

15. Still Goin Down by Morgan Wallen

16. Right Now the Best by Zach Bryan

17. Golden Hour by Kacey Musgraves

18. Home by Phillip Phillips

19. Blessed by Thomas Rhett

20. The Other Side of The Door (TV) by Taylor Swift

ONE

Aurora

Whenever I watched my favourite Christmas film *Love Actually* growing up, I always hoped I'd end up like Keira Knightley, with a sweet Andrew Lincoln confessing his love for me on handwritten cards. Or maybe I'd be Martine McCutcheon, caught snogging the sexy Prime Minister, who hopefully looks like a young Hugh Grant.

But turns out, I'm bloody Colin Firth.

Catching my partner cheating on me.

How exactly does a positivity and wellness influencer whose entire career has been built on teaching people how to be happier, more successful, and have fulfilling relationships, spin that?

Rejection is just redirection! Sometimes you need him to cheat on you so you can move on and find the right one!

Apparently you run away to a different continent after a month in hiding at your mum's house. To the only place that you think might save you from your spiralling lack of self-confidence and inspiration. The two things that your career is riding on.

And as the taxi nears the wooden archway where iron letters hang, spelling out *Sunset Ranch,* while golden memories ease any leftover tension from travelling, I really hope I'm right.

I remember always loving the long drive from the airport to my great aunt's. Watching the city slowly turn into quaint towns and rolling fields with inky mountain backdrops. Driving up the long stretch of road from Willow Ridge, seeing the big wooden house up the dirt track, positioned so perfectly in front of two tall mountain peaks where the sun always set between them, bathing everything in an orange glow. Just like it is now.

It's how Auntie Grace came up with the name for Sunset Ranch. That and because her favourite saying was always *sunsets are proof that no matter what, every day can end beautifully.* A reminder I've been needing.

I have to push down the sob lurching in my chest when I realise I won't ever hear her tell me that again—she would've been the best person to cheer me up after everything with Jake. She always had a solution for everything, like a self-help book personified.

I guess I'll just have to find a way to be strong and tell it to myself instead. That's what she would've told me to do.

Still, I think this is the most relaxed my body has felt since I came back from the funeral we did for her in London. And all it took was a ten hour flight across the world. A bit excessive, but let's hope it's a good sign—that coming here to fix up and sell the place might give me a much needed mental reset.

If I want to keep my job, I'm going to need it.

Thick strokes of amber and saffron fade into the cornflower sky above, the last few deep golden rays of sunlight sweeping over the surrounding pastures from between the mountains. The taxi comes to a halt at the archway, sunlight glinting off the sign.

"Alright, Miss Jones. Here ya go," announces the driver. He's a middle-aged man named Luke, who spent most of the journey asking me what words we say differently across the pond—like chocolate instead of candy, or jam instead of jelly.

I didn't mind though, it helped to keep my mind off the fact that I didn't manage to come up with a single sentence for a new article or Instagram post during the whole flight. I can't even face checking my emails right now, knowing there's going to be one from the magazine with the editorial schedule attached, blank spaces by my name.

God, I *desperately* need this trip to help me find my passion for writing again, because even though I can take a cute picture or video for my feed, it's the captions that my followers want. They're there for the inspiring quotes and knowledge that have helped me build my business. That's what I do this all for, I love teaching people and sharing what I've learnt.

Aware I have two overstuffed, large suitcases to haul up to the house, which is about ninety metres up the road, I furrow my brow. "Oh, do you mind going up to the house, please?"

Luke unbuckles himself, leaving the car to open my door. Got to love a good old gentleman. "I'm sorry, Miss, but Mr Hensley prefers us to stay off the private property." He holds out a hand, encouraging me out.

I make a little huff. It might be private property, but it's technically *my* private property now. Though, I don't say that, as it sounds a bit too entitled in my head, and I still haven't quite comprehended the truth of it either.

Sunset Ranch is *my* ranch now.

I can't believe she left it to me.

Because it's more than just the big house I used to stay in every summer growing up. It's a whole bloody business, one my great aunt was struggling to manage in the economic climate. Hence why Auntie Grace had already started renovating a lot of the old buildings into guesthouses before I inherited it, to find some way of making up for the investment the ranch unexpectedly needed.

And now it's all down to me to sort it. The great niece who was always too nervous to learn to ride a horse.

I'm slightly concerned this trip won't be as relaxing as I thought.

Still, I climb out of the car, rummaging for my purse. "How much do I owe you?"

"No need, Mr Hensley settled up in advance the other day." Luke rounds the car to the boot, where he heaves out my two purple suitcases. He wipes his forehead afterwards. "Did ya bring the whole royal family in these with you?"

I laugh and put my purse away, surprised Mr Hensley, the head rancher who worked for my great aunt, didn't mention that. Though, he hasn't even replied to my earlier text letting him know I was in the taxi. Something tells me he's not a very tech-savvy old man.

"Haha, no, but I'm here for a few weeks, so I wanted to make sure I had enough."

Luke smiles and nods. "Well, if you ever need a cab into Willow Ridge, you got my number. Enjoy your stay, Miss Jones."

"Thank you, Luke. Have a great rest of your day."

I drag my suitcases out of the way and watch Luke drive off. Then, I turn to the dirt track ahead, inhaling deeply, readying myself to sweat profusely during the two minute trek to the house.

LIVE, RANCH, LOVE

Thirty seconds in and I'm already out of breath. I might have been slacking on my usual fitness routine the last few weeks, despite posting old yoga videos I luckily had saved to pretend otherwise to my social media followers, but I am by no means unfit. The jetlag probably doesn't help. Or it's because I've just never learnt to pack lightly and now I'm suffering for it.

I stop for a quick breather and admire the house ahead—it's all dark wood and long windows, thick wooden posts and stone chimneys, with a wraparound deck where my favourite porch swing sits hidden round the back. There was always something fashionably contrasting about Auntie Grace's style—the perfect blend of rustic and modern. Even inside, the kitchen and living area is all open-plan, with a few little rooms for an office and cosy bar tucked away behind doors. Yet, she just crowded that airy atmosphere with mismatched Persian rugs, colourful embroidered cushions, and an obscene number of plants.

God, I've missed this place. I wish I'd made more of an effort recently to visit. Then at least I might have known she'd been sick.

I don't know how I'm going to sell this place, seeing it again now. There's so many heart-warming memories here and—

No, I have to sell it.

I can't run a ranch from a different continent. Even if it would mean keeping a part of Auntie Grace going...

I will away the thought, letting my eyes trail along the porch, over the front door, which is opening and—

There's a man walking out of Auntie Grace's house... *My* house. And it's not old Mr Hensley. What the hell?

That suddenly kicks me into action and I'm racing up the dirt path, ignoring the way my muscles are screaming at how quickly I'm trying to lug my suitcases over.

Given that I don't really know anyone here, and we're on a ranch in the middle of nowhere, I probably shouldn't be thundering over to a strange man who may or may not have been trespassing in my house, but here I am.

The man notices me and leans against one of the posts beside the porch stairs, arms folded. He's just watching me.

When I get closer, breath ragged and body slick with sweat, he descends the steps. Dark jeans hug his thick thighs, and an open red flannel shirt encases a white top underneath, set against his light-brown skin. A cowboy hat shadows over his face and just about hides most of his dark hair, though a few curls peek out beneath.

"Um, excuse me," I barely get out as I try to catch my breath, bringing me and my suitcases to a halt. One of them immediately falls over and I drop my bag trying to pick it back up. "Shit."

This is not the best start.

Just breathe, Rory.

After composing myself, and my suitcase, I turn back to the towering man, who's still regarding me with folded arms and the darkest eyes I've ever seen.

God, now that I get a proper look at him, I'm stunned into speechlessness at how attractive he is—a wide angled jaw covered in dark stubble, high cheekbones, and a nose that tips up slightly. His shirt is barely containing his bulging biceps, the kind that could easily throw a girl about. Quiet, teenage me would've wanted to run away, and the impulse to do so is definitely stronger since my self-confidence was hit by the tall blonde woman whose legs I found wrapped around my ex-boyfriend.

LIVE, RANCH, LOVE

The man can't be any older than thirty, which would make him one of the ranch hands that work under Mr Hensley, and definitely gives him no right to be in the house. I almost feel like I recognise him.

He angles his head, giving me the once over, then says in a deep, faintly raspy voice with an evident country drawl, "Are you lost?"

I'm taken aback by the scowl he's shooting my way, immediately breaking whatever enrapturement his beautifully carved face held over me. I scoff, hands flying to my hips. "I should ask you the same thing—what are you doing in my-my house?"

He lets out a breathy laugh and twists his face. One thick brow quirks as he scans my body again. "*Your* house? I'd say you're a few thousand miles from home, darlin'."

I narrow my eyes. I think I'm going to struggle being my usual positive self today. I understand that I don't exactly fit in here—with my little lavender gym outfit topped with a white cardigan slung round my shoulders, and ginger waves pulled back into a high ponytail, as opposed to being clad in plaid and denim. But neither did my great aunt, and I doubt he had the audacity to question her.

"Yes, it belonged to my Auntie Grace. Is Mr Hensley about?"

"Wait." His mouth pops open and his arms drop. "*You're* Grace's niece? I was expecting someone... older." He wipes a hand over his face, mumbling, "Fuck my life."

What a nice warm welcome. I always remembered the Americans here being friendlier than us Brits, but clearly there was an exception.

"Well, technically I'm her *great* niece. Look, I'm not sure why you were inside my house, but could you please tell me where I can find Mr Hensley?"

"You're looking right at him," he deadpans, eyes boring into me, darker than the emerging night sky.

13

Does he think I'm stupid? I've met Mr Hensley before. I know my body is still on British Summer Time, and normally I'd be fast asleep by now, so my brain is working slower than usual, but I'm adamant that he's not the old man I last saw seven years ago.

"Um, no, Mr Hensley is like seventy years old. Tall, lanky old man with a massive moustache."

"He's eighty, actually, and hasn't worked here for four years." Crossing his arms again, the man smirks, a dimple appearing in the cheek where his mouth hooks up. "I'm his grandson."

My whole face drops along with my bottom lip.

So, I've been texting *him* this whole time?

Holding out a hand, somewhat reluctantly, he adds, "The name's Wyatt. But you're more than welcome to keep calling me Mr Hensley if you like, Princess." He finishes with a wink.

Now I'm the one mumbling *fuck my life*. He's got the whole cocky, brooding cowboy persona down to a tee, and it's grinding my gears. I'm not normally this touchy. I'm usually sunny, positive Rory—it's what I pride myself on. It's who I get paid to be.

But I think the tiredness from travelling must be getting to me. I know better than to judge someone straight away, and maybe I'm being too hasty with my assessment of him. Besides, it's not like my judgements of people have been on point recently—I never pegged Jake for a cheater, nor me as someone who would let a man's actions determine my self-confidence, yet here I am.

I reach my hand out and it's completely dwarfed by his as we shake. His calloused skin rasps against my palm, leaving a tingling sensation in its wake.

"Aurora Jones, but most people call me Rory."

He frowns, looking at his hand before shoving it in his pocket. "Isn't that a boy's name?"

The memory of teenage boys saying exactly that to my quiet self at school flashes into my mind. I take a deep breath and will the thought away, remembering that I've worked hard to grow into the secure, confident woman I am today. Or was.

And that those same teenage boys are now the grown men in my DMs failing to get my attention.

"It's gender neutral." I press my lips together, unable to muster a smile. Hasn't he ever seen *Gilmore Girls*?

"If you say so." Wyatt shrugs. His sharp features drop into a scowl again. "Anyway, to answer your earlier question, I was in *your* house to make sure you had all the necessities to tide you over for a few days. I guessed you'd be tired and wouldn't want to be heading into town tonight."

"Oh..." I stare back at him but struggle with the heaviness his dark eyes seem to weigh on me. "Well, thank you. I appreciate that."

"Just doing my job." He slips his other hand into his pocket.

"Right, well I'd like to get settled in tonight, and honestly just get into bed because it's *way* past my bedtime." I laugh, trying to break whatever unpleasant tension hovers between us, but Wyatt's face stays strained. "Um, but it would be fab to meet tomorrow and run through everything going on with the ranch so we can get this place sorted and sold, and I can get back home."

Hopefully with my inspiration and confidence back.

"Great, can't wait." Wyatt's eyelids flutter in what seems an attempt to hide his eye roll, though it's rather futile. He forces a half-hearted smile and hands me a key. "I'll leave you to it."

He spins on his heel and marches off down the dirt road, leaving me and my exhausted body to deal with my massive suitcases alone. How I wish Luke was here still.

I press my eyes shut, inhaling deeply for five seconds, before blowing out the biggest sigh—

"Hey, Aurora," Wyatt calls out, my skin prickling at the way he's using my full name. I turn to see him heading back up, rubbing the back of his neck as he huffs.

"Um, yeah?"

Wyatt closes the distance between us with his last few steps, my eyes directly in line with the broad expanse of his chest. I try to let the flutter in my stomach go unnoticed. Flicking my gaze up to where his dark stare peers down at me, I can't ignore how tight his jaw looks.

"What do you do for a living again?"

I go to reply, but almost start when he reaches around me to grab each suitcase. There's no mistaking the ease with which Wyatt lifts them and carries them up the porch, his shirt barely containing his flexing muscles. I suppose a couple of suitcases don't compare to the other kinds of hard labour he does on the ranch.

Once he's back in front of me, Wyatt crosses his arms, thrumming his fingers against his muscles.

"Oh, right, I'm a wellness and positivity influencer," I say with a proud smile.

"Perfect." He snorts out a laugh. Shaking his head, he then twists to leave again. My smile immediately drops.

In the distance, I hear him grunt, "Fuck. My. Life."

I'm predicting that working with this man is going to require lots of deep breathing sessions and stress-relieving meditations.

Two

Wyatt

I like to think I'm a good person. I work hard, I take good care of my family, especially my younger siblings and grandfather. I even give money to charity every month to support the Indigenous heritage initiatives my mom sometimes volunteers for.

Yet for *some reason* the world has decided to punish me by sending over a red-headed British princess to knock down the small bit of happiness I've managed to build for myself.

I mean, she literally shares the same name as one of the Disney Princesses—knowledge I've regrettably gained from my younger sister forcing me to watch those films.

My dad would laugh and say this is what I get for giving up everything to work on a ranch for someone else. The classic old *I told you so* lecture I've been dreading to experience again. It was soul-draining enough to hear after Holly left me, *because if I'd gotten myself a fancy job like my parents wanted or pursued my football career, that would never have happened*, apparently.

Even though I've known for a while now, since Grace got ill, that my future here was less certain, I really didn't expect it to be destroyed so soon. Especially not by a *wellness and positivity influencer.* Whatever the hell that is.

As I race towards my place—a cabin-like building just a short walk up the track from the main house—I realise my mom would also say that I was raised to be a gentleman, and in no way was I one just then with Aurora. I wipe a hand over my face, groaning, because I do feel bad for not being more welcoming.

But the way she barrelled up to the house, like she already owned the place, despite the fact that she likely has zero idea how to run a ranch, pissed me off.

And then she mentioned selling, and any patience I had—which is rarely much even on a good day—vanished.

It took every inch of self-control to force myself back to at least take her suitcases up to the front door. Even though it was mildly entertaining watching her try to tackle them, given that they looked about twice her size.

It doesn't matter how attractive she is either—with her freckled golden skin, wide hazel eyes, and striking copper hair—as soon as she started talking, that posh British accent coming out, my body buzzed with infuriation. Even if that little purple gym set she had on did cling to her figure far too distractingly.

It doesn't matter.

She doesn't belong here.

She won't understand how important this place is.

Aurora's out of sight by the time I reach my front door—I can only see the back deck from here.

I know if I go inside, I'm just going to sit and work myself up, so I head back down the porch steps and jump in my old red Ford F250. I turn the radio up loud, letting the lyrics of my favourite man Zach

Bryan drown out my thoughts. I take the truck up to the stables where my American Quarter horse, Dusty, is resting. She gives me the dirtiest side-eye when I tack her up.

I give her a pat as I lead her out. "Sorry, girl, I just need to clear my head for a bit. I'll bring you extra carrots tomorrow, promise."

Dusty offers me a brief huff in response, but I know she's a wild spirit at heart like me and can never resist a ride around the lake. As soon as I'm mounted, I give her a squeeze and she's off galloping through the fields happily, proving I know her too well.

I've run Sunset Ranch for Grace since my grandfather's stroke four years ago. It was never the most profitable ranch even when my pops was in charge, but I've kept it afloat the best I can, despite rising costs in the last couple of years. Grace gave me the freedom to make Sunset Ranch as much mine as it was hers—as long as I kept her safe haven running, that's all that mattered.

I think she knew I'd appreciate what it meant to her—given she left her corporate job in London to start it, going against everything her family wanted for her. I'll always remember the chat she had with me before I headed off to college, reminding me to make time for what I enjoyed, even if it didn't seem like the right thing to do.

And honestly, Sunset Ranch has become my safe haven too. Even if my family doesn't understand, it's the only place I've ever felt fully myself. The only place I've ever felt truly free. Able to roam and soar like an eagle.

It's why I gave up everything to be here. And it's why I'll do anything to make sure I don't lose it.

The world's shown me that I can't always have everything I want, but this is the one thing I'll forever fight for.

I don't know what I'd do without it.

I'm not naïve enough to pretend that I don't know what's been happening to other ranches, people selling out because the money we get for the work we do just isn't sustainable, and that anxiety is spreading into Willow Ridge.

But I haven't let myself even consider that yet properly, hoping it meant I wasn't speaking it into existence. Hoping I'd be saved from having to return to my parents' house, tail between my legs. Hoping I wouldn't have to be applying to jobs way below my experience level at other ranches, where everyone knows who I am, and will just echo the usual *peaked at high school* gossip.

I know that people will say I might be able to carry on working here when it's sold, but the likelihood of the ranch being bought out by another Grace is about zero. Yes, if someone buys the ranch and wants to capitalise on making it into holiday homes—like Grace expected since she already started renovating some of the old buildings—they might want to keep some of us on to look after the land, even without the cattle. However, there's no way they'll match the salary Grace gave us or let me stay in my house. I don't technically own it, it's just part of my contract, with a small rent to be paid. So that's extra upheaval.

The alternative is probably what most of the other ranchers around Willow Ridge are worried about. You're either going to be bought out by some rich-ass millionaire who just wants the land for themselves, maybe to do a bit of fishing and horse riding and pissing about, but never anything that requires employing all of us ranchers. Or, you'll get some company buying the ranch for the land, where they'll just end up splitting it up to sell it off or wiping any trace of ranching away by building some huge mall.

Basically, I'm fucked.

Usually, it only takes a few minutes riding before my mind returns to a more comforting emptiness, the whistling fresh air and glowing sunset kneading out any tension that's built in my body.

But today, there's an unshakeable feeling hovering over me. One that the thrum of hooves beating against the ground or amber sunlight glistening across the lake can't move. One that feels like a chapter has come to an end, and I'm not sure if I want to turn the page.

***

Aurora: Morning! I'd love to discuss everything that needs sorting out for the ranch today, so feel free to pop over when you get a chance! I'll probably be out the back when you get here! Thanks!!!

I can practically hear her sunny British accent chiming through with her excessive use of exclamation marks. Doesn't this woman realise that texting was created to reduce the amount we had to say to each other? One of my favourite inventions actually.

It's barely even late morning and my muscles are already aching. The lack of sleep probably didn't set me up well for today, nor did one of our ranchers, Josh, calling in sick, doubling my workload for the day. Still, while some might complain, the idea of getting to spend longer out in the fields or on the back of Dusty somewhat soothes me.

As I near the house, I notice a flash of copper hair shining in the morning sun on the back deck. I have to angle my head as I get closer, trying to figure out how the hell Aurora's body is contorting the way it

21

is without her screaming in pain. In fact, she's even smiling as one leg bends in front of her, while she reaches back over her head to hold her other foot.

A masochistic princess then.

Upbeat, classical music plays from a speaker at the top of her purple yoga mat which is decorated with little white butterflies. Her eyes are closed, so she hasn't seen me climb up the stairs. It gives me a chance to take a few deep breaths to calm my already tensing body at the sight of the woman who might be about to tear down my dreams.

It also gives me a chance to notice the tight, light-green sports bra and shorts she's wearing that show off even more of her toned body than her outfit yesterday. Mesh panels on her thighs reveal lean muscle, and another panel down the middle of her chest shows off an intricate tattoo of a butterfly on her sternum that's just a little bit too sexy for my liking right now.

There is something about tattoos on a woman that excites me. Especially when that said woman gives off the kind of innocent, sweet vibe that Aurora does. It's like they're a little window into the dark side she's hiding.

"What's with the butterflies?" I ask.

Aurora starts, letting go of her leg with a squeak. She opens her eyes, immediately gracing me with another smile as she shuffles onto her knees. She's too cheery for the morning, I don't like it.

"Good morning," she chimes. Her voice is much softer than yesterday, and less flustered. I'm guessing she probably got a good night's sleep after all that travelling—can't be hard to fall asleep though when you've just been handed an estate without having to lift a finger.

As she stands, sweaty skin glistening in the sunlight, I realise that everything about her is a pop of colour—the orange hair, the bright green outfit, and shiny lips the colour of strawberries. I'm so used to all the dark wood and shadowy mountains around here, it's almost blinding.

"Butterflies are my good omen."

"*Good* omen?" I wish I'd never asked. This sounds like some voodoo shit I don't want to know about.

"Like a sign that good is coming. If I see a butterfly, it means I'm on the right path." And I'm not even joking when I say a butterfly floats by at that very moment, making her beam.

I decide I no longer like butterflies. I don't appreciate them encouraging her to think she should be here.

"Hold on one second," Aurora says as she bends down to retrieve her phone that's propped up on a small tripod.

I get a glimpse of another tattoo of several butterflies cascading along the back of her shoulder, similar to one I have of birds across mine. How many more of these little tattoos does she have hidden? I bet there's another underneath those shorts somewhere.

"Sorry." Aurora stands and her nails tap across her phone screen as she frowns. "I was just filming my yoga routine. Better make sure I cut you out of the end."

I try to hold in a laugh. "Why the hell were you filming yourself?"

Her hazel eyes flick up to meet mine dubiously. There's a little bit of fire dancing in the pale brown, something she quickly tries to quell with another smile pushing up her freckled cheeks.

"For my followers." Aurora shrugs. Like it's silly for me to not know that, making me feel like an old man.

"Right, is this part of your whole *influencer* thing?" I make quotation marks with my fingers when I say *influencer*, because I still don't quite get how it's a profession.

23

When Grace eventually confessed that she was ill and didn't have long left, she'd assured me that the niece she was leaving her ranch to was capable and knew how to run a business. She even said she thought we'd get along well. I wonder if she's laughing in her grave right now.

Aurora rolls her lips in contemplation, eyes narrowing. Hands land on her hips as she quirks a brow at me. I've got the fire kindling again it seems.

"That *influencer thing* is my business where I help people transform their lives and become happier, more successful individuals. And part of that includes yoga videos to help them de-stress."

My eyes rocket heavenward, begging for the self-control that will stop me from ripping into that too hard. I mutter under my breath, "Yeah, I'm sure a few stretches will make me a millionaire in no time."

Aurora flicks her ginger waves behind her shoulder, hip popped. "Feel free to give me a follow on Instagram, you might find you'll learn something, like how to smile."

"Sounds awful," I grunt out, undeniably a little shocked at the sass. She looks all proper, but there's a feisty side for sure. If that's how she wants to play, count me in.

I cross my arms, leaning against the fence. "How does it work, anyway? Do you wave a crystal about, tell me to *live, laugh, love*, and all my woes disappear?"

Aurora's jaw tightens, before she takes a deep breath and drops to her knees to roll up her yoga mat. When she stands back up, she asks, "Is the folder for me?"

That brings me straight back to reality. Because there was a real reason I came over here, not just to spar with her.

I sigh. "I put together everything you need to know in there."

Hesitantly, Aurora takes the folder, our eyes briefly meeting when her cold fingers accidently brush mine. I immediately cross my arms again. I don't need to know what her touch feels like. The less I know about her the better.

Aurora flicks through the folder—everything I collated last night while I couldn't sleep—maps of the ranch, details and schedules for the ranchers, and the contractors doing the place up to make it sellable. Everything I've been sorting out for Grace since she passed. Hopefully, if Aurora has all the paperwork then she'll have less reason to pester me.

"Wow, this is super organised," Aurora observes, disbelief lacing her words. "There's a lot in here."

"Yep, and it's your problem now." I push off the fence.

Admittedly, I'm probably overloading her with a hell of a lot of information that even I would've struggled to assimilate all in one go when I first started here. But if she's so insistent that this is *her* ranch now, and hers to determine the future of so blithely, then she's going to have to learn how this all works pretty quickly.

"Wait." Aurora spins as I dash away. "You're not going to sit and go through it all with me?"

The gruff laugh leaves my lips before I can stop it. "Sorry, *Princess*, but I actually have a ranch to run. Unless you're planning on getting up on one of the horses and helping out?"

Strawberry lips pop open. "I... I don't ride."

I shake my head, smiling at how predictable she is. Owns a ranch and can't ride a horse. Just perfect. "Of course you don't, Princess."

25

Three

Aurora

What do my readers need to hear right now? I tap my pen against my notebook, leaving little marks of ink across the blank page I've been staring at for ages.

I knew that forcing myself to write as soon as I got here was never going to work. After my morning yoga yesterday, I spent a good couple of hours going through Auntie Grace's stuff, putting together bags of old clothes that I could donate. As hard as it was to do so, with all the memories playing through my head, I had to start the ball rolling somehow with sorting Sunset Ranch out. Otherwise, I'll end up staying in Willow Ridge for far longer than necessary, when I really need everything to just go back to normal as soon as possible.

Luckily, it took my mind off the unopened email from my agent waiting for me, asking after the outline for my next self-help book. It also helped me calm down after how snarky Wyatt was with me, which was totally uncalled for. He is *not* helping with my situation.

I even found some awesome red cowboy boots I never knew Auntie Grace owned, which I'm not ashamed to say I tried on. I could just imagine her wearing them, probably dancing around the house to an

Emmylou Harris song with her long white hair swishing behind her. She'd definitely have paired them with some bright red lipstick, that's for sure.

Then, in the evening, I finally plucked up the courage to dive into the folder Wyatt made me—to figure out where everything had been left off. Auntie Grace had already kickstarted converting some of the old buildings into guesthouses, so decorating is underway in most of them. I thought maybe giving my brain something completely new to focus on would be a good refresh, readying me to start writing today.

But I think there was just so much to comprehend regarding the ranch—whether it was the rancher's work, the different contractors doing up the guesthouses and any other conversions, or all my great aunt's finances—that my mind feels so lazy now. The cogs have been overworked and don't want to churn anymore.

That's what happens when you fall asleep with your face in a folder, I guess. Still, I do feel a little more confident about managing Sunset Ranch and getting it sold, which I'll take as a win.

Staring out at the lake ahead, I watch the late morning sun's reflection sparkle along the ripples and light up the ground beneath the surface, emphasising the clearness of the water. It's a short walk west from the main house and splits Sunset Ranch up from its surrounding land. Proud, emerald trees line the majority of its edge, save for a small stretch of shore where Auntie Grace always said she'd build a deck, but never got round to it.

I can almost hear her warm laugh beside me, from where she would sit with a book, watching as I splashed about. Her smile would always light up her surroundings, brighter than the sun.

Goosebumps cover my skin. I'm too aware that I'll never feel her warmth again. I hate that the more time goes on, the more I forget how it even felt, because I always thought I was too busy to make time to come out to Sunset Ranch. But now I'm here, blessed by the unadulterated sense of freedom and peace radiating off the leafy trees and expansive mountains, I can't think of a single reason why I wouldn't have visited.

Adulthood really does have a way of blinkering you.

Maybe I could write something about making the most of the time you have with the people you love... but considering that just feels a little too sore still, and my readers are so used to the positive, upbeat articles and posts I write, I'm worried that might be too depressing.

Fortunately, I get a needed shot of joy when my phone starts buzzing, and my best friend Sofia's beautiful face graces my screen when I answer. She's clearly at work late tonight because I can see the whiteboard of her classroom behind her.

"Hey, Sofia!"

"Hey, bestie! Wait, are you naked?" Sofia's tight black curls bounce as she angles her head.

"You wish. No, I'm in a bikini." I tilt the phone down to show off my white strapless bikini, then flip the camera to pan across the charming lake ahead. "Was going to reward myself with a swim once I got something written."

"Ooh, you look so fit. Still struggling to find inspiration?"

I just make a long whiney moan in response and rest my head against my knees.

The problem is, I *can* write. I can write tonnes about what I'm feeling right now. I've done that every morning and night in my journal since I popped by Jake's after the funeral.

I can write for hours about how the leggy blonde he'd been kissing left in tears, hurt that she'd been tricked into thinking he was single.

29

How he'd gone after her first, telling me to stay and he'd come back to explain.

I can write for hours about how even though I know I'm a great person, I still wonder what I did wrong, or where I didn't live up to the other girl. How could I have changed to fit what Jake wanted? Should I have toned parts of me down? Been more of something else?

All the questions and second-guessing of myself I'd worked so hard to stop doing since I was a shy teenager wondering why the boys at school talked to all the other girls instead of me. I guess no matter how hard you try, there's always a part of your younger self that stays with you.

But none of that is on brand. Grieving and jilted aren't exactly synonymous with successful positivity and wellness influencer.

It feels so silly to be ruled by that, but it's my job. That's the career I dedicated so much to and made into a beautiful business. One that made me feel excited to wake up every day for—and that's the dream, right? When I used to write letters to myself, as if they were from my future self—a manifestation technique Auntie Grace taught me—I'd always start by saying how amazing it was to spend each day writing about what I was passionate for.

But the only things I can write about right now are the things that make me sad. The people I miss. The heavy loneliness aching in my chest every day. That my favourite things to do right now are sit on the back deck and watch the sunset or listen to the nature chirping and whistling away around us, as opposed to doing an intense manifestation session. And none of that will get me paid by the magazine or brands or publishers.

I guess I need to find something that's going to spark that passion again and just hope it will keep the fire burning.

"Oh, Rory," Sofia laments. "Well, if it's any consolation, I've been sat here for an hour trying to figure out how to make the Public Health Act of 1848 interesting to a bunch of fourteen year olds, half of whom will probably laugh at the word *public* because it looks like *pubic*."

That makes me snort.

I think if anyone met Sofia and I separately, they'd have no idea how we were friends when our lives are so different—here I am, an influencer whose life revolves around social media, whereas she doesn't even have any socials anymore because of her job. One of her students finding her Instagram and sending her fire emojis in her DMs after a few weeks of teaching was enough to make her delete everything.

But seven years ago, we ended up in the same university halls at Exeter and the rest was history.

"Wanna swap?" I ask.

Sofia closes her eyes, a dreamy smile appearing. "I wish, but I have to teach this tomorrow, and I'm not sure you even know what the Public Health Act of 1848 is."

"A very valid point."

"However, maybe I can help you out and be your inspiration." Sofia's voice becomes hushed. "What would you say to someone who wants to quit their job but has no idea what else they want to do?"

My heart aches for her—she was so excited to become a teacher but turns out not all teenagers love learning like she did.

"Aw, Sofia, it's still shit then?"

"The worst. I had to send a kid out today for making sex noises every time I wrote on the board. He was *eleven*! What is wrong with kids these days?"

If I'm ever feeling down about life, I can always count on Sofia to make me realise it's not so awful because I don't have to teach adolescents all day. Next article idea: *Hey, life isn't so bad, at least you're not a teacher.*

"Honestly, Sofia, you know that you can always move in with me if you quit until you find a job, right?"

"I know, you're the best. Maybe you should just not sell the ranch and I'll come live out there instead? I'll find myself a pretty American girl to fall hopelessly in love with." She bats her lashes, making me chuckle. "And I go to the gym, I'm sure I can throw some hay about."

"Believe me, there's a lot more to running this place than just throwing hay, I had *no* idea. Plus, the head rancher is actually Mr Hensley's grandson and is super grumpy, so I don't think you'd wanna deal with him." I can't stop my eyes from rolling just thinking about Wyatt and the cheek he spoke to me with.

Sofia's face lights up. "Wait, the head rancher is like, our age? Oh my God... is he hot?"

"Sofia..." I groan.

"That's a yes!" She lets out a cackle, tipping her head back and spinning in her chair. "So, you're telling me that you've moved to a foreign country for a few weeks, newly single, and there's a mysterious, hot cowboy down the road? I actually hate you. You're living a movie."

"I'm really not. Besides I'm certain *he* hates me."

"Whatever." Sofia winks with a grin. "Anyway, I think I'm gonna try to finish this off at home. Just wanted to check in and see how things were going. Hope you find some inspiration to write, and maybe a cowboy to ride. Miss you, love you."

I shake my head, unable to conceal my chuckle. "Miss you and love you too, so much."

Sofia blows me a kiss through the screen before hanging up.

LIVE, RANCH, LOVE

I write her question into my notebook and dot a few bullet points beneath, ready for any ideas that might come. The cool breeze coasts along the lake and whispers through my hair, coaxing me towards the water. Perhaps a dip will clear my head, and then the ideas will come flowing. I tip toe along the rocks to the water's edge.

Sofia was right, really—I'm so lucky to be here. Sunset Ranch feels like a movie, just like it always did, and maybe this is my opportunity to have my main character moment. I always thought I was already having it—my career was advancing every day, the money in my bank account growing, my health and fitness at their peaks, and I was in what I thought was a loving relationship. It felt like the happy ending of the film. In the beginning, I'd started as a shy, insecure girl, and now I've blossomed into a successful, confident woman.

But maybe that was the prequel.

Maybe this is the start of my movie and I'm being given the chance to be reborn again. I just don't know how the movie is going to pan out, and that scares me.

Either way, I'm going to make the most of being here at Sunset Ranch. If it's my last chance to enjoy this place, what's left of Auntie Grace, then I'm going to run and dive into the water, not timidly wade in. And when a butterfly crosses my path, that's exactly what I do.

***

I floated in the water for longer than planned, but I couldn't remember the last time my body had felt so light in the past month. Once I convinced myself out of the lake and wrapped myself up in my towel, I actually managed to get some ideas down in response to Sofia's dilemma. I remember feeling that panic when everyone else around you seems to have their future sorted, whilst all you can see is hundreds of paths ahead, unsure which one to take.

It took time to build up the success I have now, and my parents required a lot of convincing when all my friends were getting jobs lined up for graduation, yet I was snapping selfies and writing blogs about my favourite manifestation techniques.

But I kept running Auntie Grace's reminder through my head—*do it for you, not them*—just like she did when she moved out to Colorado. That kept me going, because your life isn't your own if you always care what others think.

Damn, there's the Rory Jones I know.

Maybe that lake has special healing properties, because as I finish sunbathing and slip my sundress over my head, I feel revitalised. I'm ready to sort out this ranch, reset, and get back to reality.

On the way back to the main house, I decide to stop by the guesthouses where the decorators and plumbers are working today, to check in on progress. When I walked up to the lake this morning, all their trucks and equipment were outside, yet now they're all gone. There's no way they could be finished already. I know I took the scenic, longer route back, but when I check my watch it's still early afternoon.

Confused, I mosey inside, noticing that hardly anything has been done. Wooden panels are scattered about and some of the sinks still don't have taps, which I specifically remember one of the plumbers saying he was going to fix today. When I check, my phone is still on, so it's not like there was a problem and anyone called—which they should've done, as I made sure to give my number to all the contractors yesterday.

I march back out, phone still in hand as I scroll through my contacts to find the number for the decorators. I hear shouting in the distance and whip my head up to see three people on horses, one of them now galloping down towards me.

As he comes into view, I realise it's Wyatt. Thick, corded muscles tense as he rides, his light-brown skin slick and glistening in the sun. My pulse quickens, and when he slows his horse down as he gets closer, Wyatt knocks the brim of his hat up, bringing his chiselled face into view.

There's something so annoyingly sexy about the way he looks, high up on his horse, shoulders relaxed and confident as he saunters along. Just like when he leant against the fence yesterday, goading me.

God, Sofia would have a field day if she saw him right now. Masculinity literally pours off him, and my mouth is so dry, I wonder if he's what I need to quench my thirst.

Jesus, Rory. It hasn't even been that long since you last had sex, why are you thinking these things?

"Hey," I squeak out.

"All good, Princess?" he husks, and for once that name hits me in a whole new way.

I have to stop myself from gawking when he slings his leg over the horse and jumps off so casually, muscles rippling under his jeans. Wyatt ties his horse up before turning to me and leaning against one of the posts outside the guesthouses, arms folded. For the first time, I notice his forearm is covered in a tattoo that looks like a mountain range.

Ignoring the fuzziness in my stomach, I offer Wyatt a polite smile. "Do you know where the contractors have gone?"

Wyatt removes his hat and wipes his sweaty forehead with the back of his hand, making his bicep flex. "Oh, yeah, I sent them home."

My body tenses, reminding me of who I am dealing with. Of course he did. Because why would Wyatt want to make my life any easier? He made it clear yesterday that wasn't his plan.

I take a few deep breaths, blowing out the last as calmly as possible, wondering why the universe wants me to deal with this man. I'm already a patient person, so what else is he here to teach me?

"Um, why?" I question.

Wyatt shrugs, but something dances behind his dark eyes. "There was a fence down and we needed to move some cattle. I didn't want them getting in the way."

"Okay, well, I really would've appreciated it if you'd consulted me first. You could've rung."

"Hate to break it to you, Princess." Wyatt pushes off the post and stalks closer. "But calling you up for a nice chat was the last thing on my mind when I had cattle roaming the roads." One corner of his mouth hooks up, daring me to engage.

I suck my teeth, then take a step forward, removing the distance between us. I just know that he doesn't think I belong here.

"Look, I get that, but this is *my* ranch now, and I need you to run things by me first. I need this place sold, so I don't want anything getting behind schedule. Okay?"

Now I cross my arms and Wyatt throws me a sneer.

"Sorry, *boss,*" he pushes through gritted teeth, then holds his hands up. "God forbid you don't get your money on time. Must be so hard sitting on your ass all day wondering when those thousands are gonna drop."

Four

Wyatt

Aurora's jaw drops, shock plastering her freckled face. Redness creeps up her neck, the apples of her cheeks flushing.

Maybe that was a little harsh, but I'm too tired to play nice. I came over here to tell her to be careful because some of the cattle got out and there's a few unaccounted for—I'm not sure someone pint-sized like her would want to come up against them.

Sunset Ranch isn't the biggest ranch compared to some of the others around Willow Ridge, which means there's only ever been a few of us to manage and work it, so when something like this happens, it's all hands on deck. Me and the other ranchers have been busting our asses trying to round up the cattle, move them and fix the fence, all on top of getting our usual chores done. It was the last thing we needed given we're supposed to be moving some of the cattle this week to pastures we've leased off my friend Sawyer's family ranch—one of the largest ranches in Willow Ridge.

Aurora, on the other hand, looks like she's spent her morning sun-bathing and swimming, and still thinks she has the right to question my decisions. I have no doubt I'll be clearing out the stables late into this evening, while she'll probably be painting her nails or getting an early night. Nice for some, hey?

Of course I sent the contractors home. I didn't want them getting in the way. I didn't have the time or capacity to deal with any issues or questions they had because of everything else I was trying to manage today. It's one day.

If Aurora worked on a ranch, she'd know that.

I have to roll my lips together to stop the mocking smile from dancing along them at the way Aurora's crossed her arms, tipping her nose up at me to try to seem threatening. It only makes her face pinch even more.

There is something oddly entertaining about how easily I manage to get under her skin. How quickly I seem to be able to pull clouds over her sunshine, which I know is how she wants everyone to perceive her. Like when I call her Princess. I wonder how far I can push her, what might finally set her ablaze?

Call me immature, but it might be the only thing that makes having her at the ranch and dealing with the looming end of my time here partially bearable.

Crushing her arms against her chest tighter, Aurora sputters, "Is that—is that seriously what you think of me?"

I take in a deep breath, noting how Aurora watches my chest heave and release, then flicks her gaze back up to my face. If this was any other day—and any other girl—I'd give more time to consider that she might have been checking me out, but I'm too riled up.

"I think there's a lot more to this ranch than you realise, darlin'. That it's not just a lake to float in or a deck to film yourself rolling around on. It's our livelihood." I gesture behind me, trying to make this seem about more than just me, even though I know the other ranchers aren't as pissed off about the prospect of this place selling as I am.

The freckled skin across her nose crinkles. "Well, if it's so important to you, why don't *you* buy it?"

I have to smother my face with a hand to stop my laughter barking out in harsh disbelief. If only it were that simple—but I guess everything in her life probably is. "Because, *Princess*, some of us don't have trust funds to rely on and have other people to help take care of."

Aurora's forehead creases, a line appearing between her brows. "I don't have a trust fund. I don't even know what that is."

"It's fine. You're right, it's *your* ranch, you're the boss. I'll make sure to keep you updated with my every move from now on." I shove my hat back on my head, relishing in the shadows that fall over my face. It's too hot today. "I'm going to go get on my horse now and make sure all the cows are safe, is that okay with you?"

I wait, clasping my hands in front of me on purpose. With narrowed eyes burning into me, Aurora nods. I don't delay a second to jog over to untie Dusty and climb on up, racing back up the road where I'll find people who actually understand how to run a ranch.

***

"Are you trying to burn this ranch down?" I holler at Aurora, hurrying towards the back deck where she's currently wafting a burning stick around. My eyes are painfully trained on its every movement and the smoke billowing from it as I finally reach the stairs. Its familiar earthy scent hits me a second after.

Copper waves bouncing, Aurora pivots, face brightening with shock. She blinks her wide eyes at me, as if it's too early in the morning for her to be fully awake yet, then sucks her teeth as her expression begins to tighten, taking me in.

After a moment, she lifts her chin, like it took her a second to build the courage to do so, which is mildly amusing. She grimaces. "What are *you* doing here?"

Well, at least she's not pretending to be play nice this time. Maybe I've officially broken the positivity influencer. My bad.

"What are *you* doing setting sticks on fire and waving them around?" I counter, folding my arms firmly over my chest, trying to keep my heart from beating out of my chest with frustration from her proximity.

Aurora narrows her eyes at me. "It's called sage."

"You named your stick?" I tease, well aware of what it is and that, yet again, social media has popularised an Indigenous practice without considering its origins. But I don't want to go there right now. Plus, I can already predict that if I show any knowledge of these wellness practices she does, she'll start squealing or jumping about all happy. Not what I want to deal with this morning.

I can't keep my eyes off the wad of burning sage, the way Aurora's handling it so loosely in her delicate fingers, as if she doesn't live in a house—on a whole ranch, actually—that's practically made from nothing but wood. I guess at least if she burns the place down, she can't sell it to one of the too-rich-for-their-boots companies that have been sniffing around. Maybe I'll even get some insurance money from my own place being destroyed.

Silver linings and all that.

Aurora opens her mouth to speak, then stops to press her fingers to her chest, taking in a deep breath. Do I get a hint of pleasure at the way she has to calm herself around me? Well, it does make her distracting me from my work a little less annoying. I'd only popped back to my place to clean up a nasty cut I'd gotten while fixing a fence when I walked out to see the smoke filtering through the air.

"No, I didn't name it. This," she holds it out, "is a smudge stick made of herbs—sage. It helps to cleanse the energy of a space." Hazel eyes look me up and down twice, accompanied by a smug curve of her lips. Then she waves the smudge stick towards me a few times. "Just trying to rid the house of any *unwanted* negativity."

I grind my teeth, but manage to mumble out, "I should've used that before you turned up," with a roll of my eyes. They're going to end up getting strained if she sticks around for much longer.

"Though," Aurora muses, ignoring my comment and finally plopping the smudge stick into a bowl to put it out. *Thank God*. When she glances back, one of her brows perk up. "I'm wondering if maybe I should take it around the whole ranch now... Where have you been working this morning?"

It takes too much force to unclench my jaw. She's a fiery one today—and no doubt because of what I said to her yesterday. Not that I'd take any of it back, especially since it has awakened this snappier, intriguing side of her. She's bypassed the sunshine this morning, going straight for fire.

"Whatever." I shake my head with a sigh. "Just don't go wafting that thing around the rest of the place. The last thing I need is a fire on my ranch. I've got enough to deal with today."

"Oh." Aurora crosses her arms and takes a step closer, angling her head at me. Flames dance behind her hazel eyes. "It's *your* ranch?"

The sound that vibrates in my throat is practically a growl. "It ain't gonna be anyone's ranch if you burn it down."

Another sneer is thrown my way before Aurora unfolds her arms and moves away. She swipes her phone up from where it was sat on the swing, perusing whatever is on the screen like my presence is suddenly boring her.

I guess that's my cue to leave... but part of me kind of wants to stay for a moment longer, just to annoy her. I don't particularly like myself for it, but I also don't particularly like having her here. And as expected, Aurora flicks a glare up at me, hazel eyes tightening as I hold her stare, giving me a shot of satisfaction.

She finally lets out a squeaky huff, stuffing her phone into the back pocket of the denim shorts she's wearing. Incredibly *short* shorts, actually, that show off almost every inch of her toned legs...

Not that I'm particularly affected by them. Even if it does take me a second longer than I'd like to admit to tear my eyes away.

"Don't worry," she concedes, heading towards the back door. "I'm not planning on using the smudge stick anywhere else. I was only trying to cleanse the house for when the guy from Crestland gets here."

Alarm bells immediately blare in my head.

"No!" I basically leap in front of Aurora with my arm out to stop her without thinking. But where I was aiming to place a hand against the door, it ends up making contact with her, and before I know it my fingers are wrapping around her arm.

Face plastered with shock, Aurora gawks down at where I'm harbouring her forearm, dwarfed in my grasp. Her skin has suddenly prickled, as well as along my own arm, and the heat of her makes my palm tingle... like a warning that this girl might burn me.

She doesn't tug away though, just stares.

As do I, watching where I'm holding her.

Because I never expected to ever really hold her.

And neither did I want to know how it felt—

I suddenly notice how her chest swells and falls with deep breaths, and I realise what I've just done.

"Shit, sorry," I sputter, finally ripping my hand away. I take a good few steps back to create a comfortable distance between us. "I don't, um, usually grab women like that." *Or freeze when I do touch them...*

"I should hope not," Aurora half laughs, her British accent particularly strong as she speaks. Her eyes look like they're about to bulge out of her head, though. They're so wide, I can see for the first time how her irises are mottled with different hazel shades, some honey-like, others closer to brown—

"What was that all about?"

"I..." Letting out a groan, I swipe off my hat and run a hand through my hair.

I fucking panicked, that's what happened. I'm on edge—more than I've ever been in my life—because I don't know when my time on this ranch is going to end. Nor do I know how to stop my freedom from being taken away from me. And the last people I need to be responsible for that is fucking Crestland.

I can live with Aurora's presence for the next however many weeks she's planning on frolicking around here. But to stay in Willow Ridge knowing that a company like Crestland has made their mark here, I'm not sure I can handle that.

Hands now firmly placed on her hips, Aurora pins me with her hazel stare. She's rolling her strawberry lips together, waiting.

I sigh, shoving my hat back on. "Please don't sell the ranch to Crestland."

"Oh." Aurora's lashes flutter as her stance softens. "Why not?"

"Because they're a big corporation that doesn't give a shit about what this land means to people, or what ranching means to our town." I don't hold back from raising my brows at her, as if to say, *a little like someone else I know*. She barely rolls her eyes. "I know a place a few towns over—Crestland bought the ranch, promised they'd keep it going for the community, then bulldozed everything. Put a stupid mall down instead. We don't need that happening here."

I don't like the way I'm laying all my fears bare for her, especially when she's blinking up at me with something like pity behind her eyes. I clench my fists at my side. "And if you knew anything about this place, what you've gotten yourself into, then you'd understand that."

That makes her eyes narrow, and she shakes her head. "Um, you can't be mad at me for not knowing that. You could've gone through everything with me, but instead you shoved a folder in my hands and rode off."

I press my tongue against the inside of my cheek.

Aurora lets out a deep sigh. "Sometimes change can be good," she says, but it's somewhat mumbled, like she's almost trying to convince herself of such.

"I doubt it." I need to get back out in the fields. On the back of Dusty probably too given how tense my whole body has felt since the second I grabbed Aurora's arm. I'm wasting time standing around with her, thinking she might actually give a rat's ass about Sunset Ranch's future now Grace is gone. "If you gotta sell the ranch, just... at least try to choose someone who cares, yeah?"

Pressing her lips together, Aurora nods and opens the back door.

I turn on my heel and—

"Wyatt," Aurora calls over her shoulder, something scarily gentle in the way she says my name. I hold her hazel eyes. "I'll cancel the meeting with Crestland."

Relief washes over me like a crashing wave. I give Aurora one nod before heading down the stairs, not looking back. Even though I can feel the first flowers of hope faintly blooming in my chest, I know full well that whatever the future holds is only a few steps away from trampling them.

FIVE

Aurora

"**O**h, say it again," June, the sweet-faced elderly lady behind the counter of Willow Ridge's thrift store, Nifty Thrifty, coos at me.

Luckily for her, I'm still on a high from mustering up the courage to take Auntie Grace's old truck into town, despite it being seven years since I last drove on the opposite side of the road, so I happily oblige.

"I'm from London." Yep, that's literally all she wanted me to repeat, but apparently it's like music to her ears because she gasps animatedly, clapping her hands together in front of her face. Just like she did when I first started talking.

It definitely beats the stares I got from the locals when I first parked up and started walking along Main Street. Auntie Grace always did say it took Willow Ridge a while to get used to her moving here—a symptom of being a small town, I guess.

"Oh!" June exclaims with a big grin, beginning to pilfer through the bags of Auntie Grace's old stuff that I'd put together earlier in the week. Though, now that I've had a good look around the thrift store, I'm pretty certain my great aunt got most of her clothes from here, and I'm probably just returning them. There's several gaudy throws and rugs in here that I'm sure she would've adored too.

"I just love a British accent, you know? I remember when Grace first moved here—we couldn't get enough of her accent. The men especially liked it." June wiggles her brows at me. "I'm sure you'll have them quite enraptured soon too."

I have to force my smile out this time, aware that she doesn't quite realise that firstly—Auntie Grace was in her forties when she moved here, so unless I'm looking for a silver fox, I don't think I'd be attracting the same men she was, and secondly—I'm currently knee-deep in post-heartbreak self-depreciation, meaning meeting someone is the last thing on my mind.

What's actually on my mind right now is the fact that I've only got one scheduled social media post left before I have to start making up content again. One more post to carry on this façade that I'm still the happy, self-assured woman I've always claimed to be. And the biggest joke of it all is that it's one I made ages ago on manifestation techniques to attract the perfect partner. Maybe I should give it another read myself. Clearly I didn't do a very good job of it last time.

That's what forced me to finally venture into the main town of Willow Ridge today—to run some errands with the hopes of distracting myself, and maybe finding some inspiration in... a thrift shop?

Honestly, though, I wish I'd come into town earlier. I couldn't contain my laughter as I drove down the streets, realising that Willow Ridge hadn't changed a bit since I'd last visited. Local businesses still line the roads, some buildings all red brick, while others have different coloured wood-panelled fronts and awnings. Black iron streetlights are dotted along the pavements, and Auntie Grace's favourite café, Sitting Pretty, still rests on the corner of Main Street, its mint-coloured walls slightly faded now. I couldn't quite bring myself to stop by and grab a smoothie, though, my chest a little heavy at the memories of our summer afternoons sat outside.

Maybe next time I'm in town. Baby steps, right?

"This all looks great, Miss Rory. We'll make sure to find your great aunt's stuff a nice home." June piles the bag beside the others I brought in. "I hope you enjoy your time here—though, I'm sure Mr Hensley's grandson is looking after you."

I have to stifle my laugh. How is it that Wyatt is finding ways to annoy me without even being around?

"Oh." Another forced smile. "He really is."

"Enjoy your day, sweet." June waves me out the shop, the bell above the door tinkling as I leave.

I rub a hand across my chest where a strange pressure builds, knowing I've parted with the first belongings of Auntie Grace. Eventually it will be the whole ranch and... well, we'll get to that when we get there.

Right now, I've got some food shopping to do—the groceries that Wyatt got in for me when I arrived lasted longer than I expected, but I'm now down to a few crumbs and seriously craving my homemade granola. My hopes that Willow Ridge's small grocery store will cater for my usual food preferences are incredibly low, but I'll find a way to survive until I'm feeling confident enough to drive further to somewhere with a bit more choice.

Besides, spending an afternoon shopping around a quaint town with mountains for a backdrop and golden sunshine raining down on me isn't the worst thing in the world. In fact, as I dawdle down Main Street, I let myself romanticise this moment a little and close my eyes, basking in the sun's warmth on my face, the sound of soft chatter as I pass shops, and the occasional low hum of a truck driving by—

I suddenly whack into something solid.

Two thick, warm arms wind around my waist. My eyes shoot open, discovering a broad chest in a plaid shirt, a couple of buttons undone to reveal light-brown skin and dark chest hair. A steady scent of leather and pinewood encompasses me, and I let myself breathe it in, relishing in the way it seems somewhat familiar. For a second I consider just letting myself enjoy the view.

That is, until he speaks.

"You alright there, darlin'—oh, it's you." Wyatt's head rears back, brow furrowing as he gets a better look of my face. His cowboy hat blocks out the sun, casting a shadow down over his sharp, dark features in a way that has me unsure whether I want to run away or draw myself closer.

But then I'm alarmingly aware of the fact that he's still holding me, large hands now splayed over my ribs. His grasp on me is gentle, yet stable, like if I fell, he'd catch me in a flash.

I wriggle a little in his grasp. "Sorry, I—"

Wyatt instantly flinches, tearing his hands away. Something akin to disgust paints his hardening expression, accompanied by a subtle shake of his head. It takes him a second longer to also stop staring at me and push his face back into his familiar, casual scowl.

"Where did you come from?" I half-laugh, trying to muster up a smile as I peer around the corner from where he appeared. I'd assumed he'd still be on the ranch. Maybe June somehow summoned him when she mentioned him—speak of the devil and all that.

"You should watch where you're going," is all he says, his arms now folded, closing that chest off from me properly. Not up for chit-chat—I should've learnt that by now. If our interaction is about to follow its usual pattern, he'll be sighing and rolling his eyes at me in no time.

Maybe I should write a book about how to piss off a cowboy, because I somehow have a natural talent for that. I could even turn it into some sort of scientific experiment—try out a bunch of wellness practices in front of him and see which ones anger him the most. Oh, I bet he'd just *love* manifestation. I'm sure I still have my old research methods textbooks from my psychology degree somewhere. Not entirely certain that's the vibe my publisher and agent are hoping for though, sadly.

"Wow, thanks for the advice," I say with a saccharine smile, brushing out the creases from my white broderie sundress. "I'll be sure to post that quote on Instagram later—so inspiring."

Wyatt practically snorts, his arms tensing against his chest, barely contained in the rolled-up sleeves of his shirt. I get another quick glance of his mountain range tattoo. It's not far off the view behind Willow Ridge.

"Such a *positive* positivity influencer, aren't you?"

My next inhale is much longer than necessary—that struck a nerve Wyatt isn't even aware of. He regards me, mouth twitching into a smirk and dark eyes sparkling wide as he awaits my response. My retaliation. But what does he want me to say?

I might have only known him for a few days, but I can already tell the last thing he wants to do is listen to me vent about my chaotic thoughts and messed up confidence right now.

Even I'm getting tired of it.

So, instead I make a noise of contemplation, before replying, "And I thought you said you didn't usually randomly grab women."

He pokes the inside of his cheek with his tongue, angling his jaw. But then he brushes my comment off with a shrug. "I also don't usually have to deal with annoying little princesses strutting about my territory, but times have changed recently."

EMMA LUCY

His territory? I'm half expecting him to whip out two pistols and start going on about how *this town ain't big enough for the both of us.* Lord, give me strength. Maybe Wyatt's presence is just the universe's way of telling me to get my ass in gear and sort the bloody ranch out.

I take in a calming breath as I check down at my watch, realising if I want to get in a call with anyone from home—maybe my older half-sister, Sophie, if she's not on a night shift—then I need to get my shopping done quick.

"Well, see you around." I push off without even giving a wave or a smile goodbye, planning to cross the road so I'm far away from him. I check down the road for cars quickly and step out—

"Aurora!"

My whole body is yanked backwards, caged yet again by the same thick arms as a minute ago. But this time I'm even more crushed against Wyatt's chest, stumbling straight into him so that we both go flying back a few paces. The strength in his legs manages to keep us from tumbling all the way to the ground. I like to think the way my fingers are holding onto his shirt for dear life helped to keep him upright too, but really it's just because I'm bloody shaken.

Someone shouts from the road and a truck engine grumbles away as my head finally catches up with what just happened. But I can still barely hear over my suddenly racing heart. Over the heart pounding inside Wyatt's hard chest too, where my hand is now pressed against, able to feel every indentation and line of his muscles.

Tensed, solid muscles. Exactly how I imagined they'd be when I saw him chopping up wood shirtless yesterday for the bonfire he had later that night. Yes, the same day he'd had a go at me for supposedly nearly burning down the ranch.

I didn't let myself look at him for too long, only catching a small glimpse of a few more tattoos peppering his body, but his broad muscles were too obvious to not admire, all slick with sweat—

"Jesus, Aurora," Wyatt scolds me.

When I look up this time, his eyes are wild—pupils so blown out all I can see is black. They gleam with the same hints of desperation I noticed yesterday when he was trying to stop me from meeting with Crestland. Even if all his harsh, cold angles tried to hide how he felt, I saw it still. Felt it too, in his grip.

I've recognised that same desperation in my own expression plenty of times when I've been begging my reflection in the mirror to just find a way to get back on track. To be able to write and feel like the Rory Jones I used to be.

Wyatt's eyes flick over my face, quickly down to my body, lingering for a few seconds, then back again. His fingers pulse against my upper arms, where he's holding me, a little tighter than last time.

"I *just* told you to watch where you were going."

"I... I did. I checked—"

"The wrong way," he barrels on, voice gravelly and slightly too loud. I can't help but notice the way people have slowed as they pass us by. I'm going to be the talk of the town today it seems. "You're not in England anymore, Princess. You could've been seriously hurt."

Not that I think Wyatt would ever actively enjoy watching someone get run over, but I am slightly shocked by his concern at my almost-death. Unless maybe he was hoping to be the one behind the wheel and I was about to take the opportunity away from him...

But the fierceness in the way he's still staring down at me, the way his chest heaves against me like he was struck with as much fear as I was, says otherwise. It's all a bit overwhelming, trying to comprehend this sudden change in his behaviour, and the way my body is softening into that feeling of stability in his hands. His scent is everywhere again, overwhelming me, yet anchoring me too—reminding me of the ranch, a place of safety. I gulp it down with two long breaths to steady myself.

The only thing I can think of to say is, "You could've just let me get run over and then forged my will, saying I left you the ranch, you know?"

Wyatt laughs. He actually *laughs*. Not a sarcastic one, or the usual huff of frustration he gives me, but a full-on hearty laugh. My whole body vibrates with him, still locked in his embrace so that his muscles press even harder against me. Some kind of warmth puddles deep in my stomach.

"True," he mulls over the idea, a curve gracing his full lips, leftover from his laughter. "But then I wouldn't have the fun of getting to rile you up every day anymore."

And now I'm chuckling back, my shoulders bouncing in his hands, making his palms rasp against my bare skin. It's a sensation I don't think I'd complain about feeling again.

His eyes flash wider. Then he finally glances down at where he's harbouring me, yet again. A muscle feathers in his jaw, and this time he retracts his hands from me slowly, letting his fingers stroke along my upper arms, leaving just the gooseflesh covering them. Along with a strangely cold emptiness now I'm no longer fenced in by his warmth.

Wyatt bobs his head, looking practically everywhere other than me—apparently the sidewalk is incredibly interesting right now. "Please tell me you didn't drive in?"

I roll my lips together. "I might have."

He rubs a hand over his face. "Do you need to follow me home? I don't really want to get a call from the cops later because you've caused a seven-car pile-up by driving on the wrong side of the road."

I want to laugh again but something strikes a chord inside of me when he says *home*. I can't quite place my finger on the weight swirling inside my chest, winding it a little tighter. Maybe it's because when he said the word, it wasn't London that flashed into my head, making me want to correct him that Sunset Ranch isn't actually my home. No, it's more of a sensation that the word felt... right.

I look up and down Main Street, distracting myself from the feeling. From the rancher in front of me who reminds me that as much as I'd like to call this place home, I don't really belong here.

So, I settle for a soft smile instead, watching his bright expression fall back into its usual shadow. I'm already walking away when I reply, "Nope, all good. I'll try keep out of your way from now on."

SIX

Wyatt

"Wow, she's hot!" Cherry, my younger sister, calls out while I button up my shirt, then head out my bedroom to where she's lying on my couch, staring at her phone. She's been here all of two minutes and has already made herself at home.

Can't say I don't love having her back in Willow Ridge since she left for college a couple of years ago though.

"Who is?" I perch on the edge of the couch.

Cherry twists around, her long black hair falling over her shoulders. She holds out her phone to me, where a picture of Aurora mid-yoga pose takes up the screen. She's got that little green set on with the mesh panels, showing off her sternum tattoo again.

"Your new boss—there's loads more, look." She continues scrolling through what appears to be Aurora's Instagram, showing me countless pictures of smoothies, gym outfits, selfies of Aurora, and the cringiest positive quotes, all posted by the username *roryjwellness* for one hundred thousand followers. Her whole feed is so bright and cheery, it makes me uncomfortable.

"How the hell did you find that?" I ask Cherry.

She sits up and shrugs. "I just Googled her name and wellness influencer and voilà! The internet is quite handy, you should try it sometime, caveman."

I roll my eyes and give her a shove. "Whatever. I should probably let her know I'm gonna be out late tonight, anyway—in case she breaks a nail and can't find anyone to help."

"Wyatt!" Cherry tsks and raises her brows, looking scarily like Mom when she used to scold me. When I wave off her look and stand, she gets up too, hands on her hips. "I hope you're being nice to her."

I avoid her eyes, making a long groan to signal that I really don't want to get into this. I just want to jump in the car, head down to Duke's bar, and get nice and drunk with my best friends and sister. I've been looking forward to wrapping my hand around a cold beer all day.

"I haven't been *not* nice," I grumble, grabbing my denim jacket off the back of the door.

"There's a surprise," Cherry says sarcastically, using her phone screen as a mirror to top up her dark red lipstick. "You should go easy on her you know—she did just lose a family member. Plus, her Instagram had loads of pictures of her and this *really* fit guy for a while, and then he disappeared, so I'm guessing she's also had a breakup. The last thing she probably needs right now is you being your grumpy self."

I cross my arms, staring at Cherry, not wanting to admit she's probably right. Perhaps I have been a little short-sighted and not considered how big of an impact Grace's death might have had on Aurora. I was too wrapped up in what it all meant for me.

Damn, when did my little sister get so wise? Sometimes I think she's still eight years old, begging me to play with her and her unreasonable amount of My Little Ponies, as opposed to the twenty-year-old, grown up, beautiful woman who's probably breaking hearts left, right, and centre at college.

"Now, hurry up and go tell her, so we can get on the road." Cherry waves her hand, ushering me towards and out the door.

Walking along the road, as I get closer to the main house, music starts to hit my ears. It's not overly loud, but I soon realise it's *How to Save a Life* by The Fray, a gut-wrenching song if I ever heard one.

Then I spot Aurora—curled up on the swing in a blanket, knees to her chest, staring out ahead with tears rolling endlessly down her red, freckled cheeks. The sight of her stops me in my tracks.

Fuck, I've never seen her like this before. She looks so... *small*.

I've always thought of her as the overly sunny, well-spoken princess, who doesn't care what happens with the ranch. But right now, she looks like she'd break into a thousand pieces if anyone touched her.

Maybe Cherry was right after all. Maybe things have been pretty overwhelming for Aurora.

I have a scary urge to wrap her in my arms and hold her until she falls asleep. An urge I did *not* expect to feel towards *her*. But, having a little sister has always left me with this weird soft spot, despite what I do to conceal it. If this was Cherry crying, I'd do everything I could to make her feel better. And Aurora could be someone else's younger sister, but they're not here to help her.

Aurora obviously hasn't noticed me yet as she doesn't turn, she just lets out another loud sob which kicks me into action and I race up the stairs. Not that I have any clue what I can do to help.

"Hey, are you alright?" I ask. *But of course she's not alright, Wyatt, she's bawling her fucking eyes out.*

Aurora jumps at my voice and immediately wipes her face and nose with the sleeves of her pink sweatshirt. "Shit, sorry."

She brushes her hair behind her ears an unnecessary number of times and struggles off the swing. I grab the edge of it to hold it still.

"Why are you apologising?"

"Because you had to see me crying."

"I'm a grown man." I shrug, laughing a little, which does actually prise the corners of her mouth up slightly. "I mean, I might find any signs of emotion deeply uncomfortable, but I can deal with it."

Now she properly laughs, rolling her eyes playfully.

The shot of dopamine that making her smile gives me is a little alarming. I thought I liked dulling her sunshine, I didn't expect to enjoy igniting it too.

I should really ask her if she wants to talk about it—that's what Cherry would tell me to do—but I'm not sure that's what she'd want. Especially not to *me*. I haven't exactly been the friendliest to her since she got here, proven by Cherry. Plus, she's just looking at me right now, rubbing a hand up and down her arm, the silence a little awkward.

Maybe she wants me to go.

But I also feel like I can't just leave her alone now.

"Uh, I was gonna head out to my best friend Duke's bar with my sister and some others. Did you want to come? Meet some of the locals? We can put a bet on how many times someone freaks out over your British accent." I shoot her a grin, wiggling my eyebrows.

Honestly, Aurora looks a little shocked—hazel eyes wide and bloodshot—probably because it's the first time I've properly smiled at her. She nibbles at her thumbnail, looking around the floor like she's considering it.

"Um, yeah, okay. That would be nice." Aurora presses her lips into a soft curve. "Although—wait—it's not one of those line dancing bars or whatever, right? Because the only country kind of dancing I know is the Hoedown Throwdown."

"The Hoedown—what?" I ask, face twisted.

Aurora's eyes widen even further in disbelief. "You know—the dance from the *Hannah Montana Movie*?"

"Why would I—never mind." I shake my head, wiping a hand over my face. When I look back up, Aurora's biting her lip, reddening it under the pressure as she holds back a smile. "Don't worry, it's just a normal bar."

"Okay, good. Um, I need a little time to get dressed."

"Sure." I nod. "My sister's gonna drive, so come on up to mine when you're ready."

***

Aurora's knock comes exactly fifteen minutes later. To be fair to her, I was expecting to be waiting a lot longer. And thank God, because Cherry has spent the whole time deep diving through Aurora's Instagram, pulling up photos and reading out her philosophical captions that make me want to gag. I've also now heard about ten reviews of her book, which I had no idea she'd written. It's quite impressive, actually.

Cherry leaps up from the sofa before I can and runs to the door, throwing it open with a high-pitched, "Hi!"

"Oh, hi," Aurora says, tucking some hair behind her ear shyly.

Damn, she cleans up well.

As I stand, I can't stop my eyes from raking over her. Red waves run wild, lit up from behind by the evening sun's glow. A short denim skirt with frayed edges shows off her toned legs, and a white, cropped corset top pushes up her breasts, emphasising how they'd be the perfect handful. She's also wrapped in an oversized plaid shirt, one shoulder hanging off, a heavy dusting of freckles across the bare skin.

Topping the whole outfit off is a pair of red cowboy boots that there's no way belong to her. In fact, I swear I saw Grace wear some like them once. Regardless, I'm thrown by how well the whole country vibe suits her. How well she suddenly fits in with the ranch.

Like it was always meant to be hers.

Aurora holds her arms out and wiggles her hips. "What was it Shania Twain said? Man shirts, short skirts, right?"

It's then that I realise I've been ogling her, bottom lip dropped. I have to shake my head to snap out of it.

"You look amazing," Cherry gushes before pulling Aurora into a hug, showing me an overly friendly side I'm not used to seeing. Normally she's mocking or hitting me, our brother, Hunter, and my friends. To be fair, she's probably grateful to finally have some female company for once. "I'm Cherry, Wyatt's little sister."

"No, *you* look amazing!" Aurora eyes up Cherry's black waistcoat and flared jeans. "I'm Rory, so nice to meet you. Gosh, you guys really do look alike."

"Oh gross, don't say that. I don't want to look like a caveman." Cherry mimics sticking her fingers in her throat and makes a gagging noise, eliciting a hard scowl from me.

That's twice she's called me a caveman today and I'm starting to wonder if I need to work on my posture.

But Aurora laughs, a hand on Cherry's arm like they're already best friends. First the ranch, now my sister... I'm not sure how I feel about letting Aurora into this part of my life too. I had no choice over the ranch, it wasn't mine to control. But my family? My friends? They're parts of me that I can stop her sunny light from drowning.

Am I tempting fate by opening these up to her? Especially when I'm struggling to keep my eyes off her right now.

"Shall we go?" Cherry questions, a brow perked at me and a hand on her hip, while she swings her keys.

I clear my throat and nod, waving to encourage Cherry to head out. She points Aurora in the direction of her car, which despite driving along these dusty roads, always manages to look spotless.

I turn to lock up, assuming Cherry has headed down to the car too, when suddenly she's behind me, whispering in my ear.

"I'm glad you agree that she's hot."

Checking the door, I twist around, forcing my face to stay expressionless. "I never said that."

She shares a knowing grin. "Yeah, but your face did."

SEVEN

Aurora

"There's no way in hell I'm listening to this," Wyatt grumbles as the next song from Cherry's phone plays through the stereo. It begins with a quiet guitar solo, before a guy with a strong country accent starts singing about a girl's eyes, and the backing music builds.

"Why not?" Cherry protests but struggles to stop Wyatt from skipping through songs as she's navigating the roads. "It's actually a decent one of his."

"I don't know how you're not sick of hearing them yet."

Never did I think this would be how I'd spend my Friday night—sat in the back of a car with Wyatt and his little sister, on the way to the bar, whilst they bicker over music taste.

But then a month ago, I never would've thought I would be in Colorado, packing up and selling Sunset Ranch. Single and uninspired.

The universe does like to throw curveballs sometimes, doesn't it? And for some reason, it thought I needed this. Somehow I'll grow from it, and I look forward to meeting the version of me on the other side of it all.

I'd fully committed to feeling sorry for myself and listening to my sad girl playlist on the back deck until I got too tired and resigned to a bubble bath and bed. I mean, where else could I go? I don't know anyone here in Willow Ridge, and I still have enough dignity to not take my pity party to a bar alone.

But it seemed the universe also had other ideas for me there too.

In the form of an oddly kind invitation from Wyatt, who up until today I was certain despised me for no good reason.

I can't deny that it does feel good to be dressed up, even if I am reconsidering whether I've gone a little overboard on the country vibe. I couldn't figure out how to interpret the way Wyatt's eyes trailed over me. But donning Auntie Grace's red boots and old shirt felt like a tribute to her, like I was taking a part of her with me into town.

It also feels good to do something out of the ordinary for me and meet new people. God knows I've been lonely out here, and being around people always does lift me up.

Cherry's not stopped talking the whole ride, asking me tonnes of questions about life back in England, and admitting that she's Insta-stalked me. I've also discovered that she's halfway through college, doing an interior design course which sounds incredible. Her energy is so sweet and vibrant—*very* different to Wyatt—it reminds me a bit of Sofia, which instantly starts to fill that lonely void in my chest.

Leaning forward to catch a glimpse of the phone screen, I ask, "Who's the singer?"

"Our brother," both Wyatt and Cherry say in unison, though their tones are starkly different.

"You're kidding me—your brother's famous?"

"No," Wyatt grunts before finally choosing a song and setting the phone down.

"Yes, actually," Cherry corrects, her dark red lips grinning at me in the rear-view mirror. "Hunter Hensley."

I wasn't wrong when I mentioned her resemblance to Wyatt earlier—she's got the same light-brown skin and contrasting dark eyes, though hers leave a soft warmth on me, as opposed to the heaviness of Wyatt's. Her angled features and plush lips are framed by long, layered black hair. I imagine that Hunter's a mash up of the two of them.

"He's a country singer," Cherry explains, pride radiating. "Super talented. He scored himself an amazing record deal a couple of years back, moved to LA, and the rest is history."

"That's incredible!" I watch out the window as we finally hit the main town. The strings of lights between the streetlamps are lit up now, like rows of starlight. This place really does feel like it was taken straight out of a cosy book sometimes. We pass by Ruby's Diner, which used to do the best burgers ever.

Wyatt snorts. "Oh yeah, it's great that we can't go into town without being pestered for his autograph." Twisting round to me, a small curve graces his lips, the faintest dimples appearing amongst his stubble. "One girl once asked me if I had any of his old underwear. Honestly, what the hell?"

The chuckle rings out of me, making Wyatt's brows jump up. Midnight eyes flick across my face, like he's joining up my freckles, then he clears his throat and sits forward again.

I'm honestly still baffled that he's tolerated me for so long. Without mocking me too. I'm not sure if I like it.

"If you ever wanna go to a show, I'm sure we can score you some tickets," Cherry adds, already so kind. But I'll be gone soon, so I just smile my thanks, rather than accept the offer. Better not get too attached to anything here.

It's only a few more minutes before we park up alongside the curb, and Wyatt jumps out to open my door. He shoots me a look when I hesitate, because I'm shocked that he's suddenly being *nice*. Is this the same guy that basically called me stuck up the other day?

Still, I climb out, thanking him, and take in the bar ahead, admiring the black wooden panelling. I recognise the building but don't think I've ever been inside.

"Wait, your friend named his bar after himself?" I ask, noting the buzzing neon sign with cursive red letters spelling out *Duke's*, a white horseshoe as the backdrop.

Cherry answers before Wyatt can, hooking her arm through mine and guiding me towards the door. "It used to be his grandfather's, who he was named after. When he passed and Duke took the bar over, he decided to change the name in his grandfather's memory." She quickly adds on with a nervous smile, "I work here when I'm back from college, so I know the whole backstory."

"You're allowed to work here when you're under twenty-one?"

"Oh yeah." She waves it off. "The bartending age is eighteen here. But we keep any drinks I'm served on the down low, obvs."

When I glance back to Wyatt, I can't read his expression as his eyes are trained on our linked arms. But I don't miss the way his whole body relaxes and his face lights up at the sound of people cheering when we head through the swinging doors. I almost have to do a double take at the grin that's taking up his face, bringing out the dimples properly now.

Really cute dimples, actually.

Wyatt bustles forward, received by a group of three guys at the bar—all just as tall and broad as him. They clap hands and pull each other into hugs. Cherry releases me and skips forward, also being pulled into the embrace. Though, the guy who's wearing a black shirt and trousers seems to make his hug brief with her.

Now they all turn to me, and I swear the bar goes silent.

Because I'm a fish out of water.

Muscle clad in denim and wearing an off-white T-shirt that is tight in all the right places, a guy with sandy blonde hair and tanned skin steps forward. His twinkling brown eyes remind me of a golden retriever—energetic and eager for my attention—flicking between my outfit and face excitedly.

"And who do we have here?" His country drawl is thick, voice deep and inviting. "A friend of Cherry's?"

"Rory Jones." I smile, aware that other people in the bar are also staring at me now. I might have dressed the part, but my accent gives me straight away.

The guy's eyes immediately light up and he bounces on the spot, flashing his grin back at Wyatt. "Oh, *you're* the British girl we've heard so much about."

Wyatt stares at the floor when I glance at him, slightly concerned what exactly they've been told. But before I know it, the guy strides towards me and wraps me in a hug.

"Nice to meet you, Red. I'm Sawyer—Wyatt's best friend."

"Actually." The other guy with pale skin, messy brown hair, and a short beard shoves Sawyer out the way once he releases me, then also draws me into a loose hug, giving me a pat on the back. "I'm Wyatt's best friend, Wolfman."

I'm not going to pretend I don't enjoy the amount of muscles I've had pressed against me already tonight.

"Did you get that from *Top Gun*?" I ask.

"No, *obviously* I'd be Maverick." He furrows his brow, like I should know that, but still grins.

A hand lands on Wolfman's shoulder, tugging him back to make space for the last guy. His presence is too quiet for how gorgeous he is—dark skin, broad shoulders, closely shaven black hair, and umber eyes that glisten when his soft smile charms his high cheekbones.

"He's called Wolfman because he's the hairiest guy you'll ever meet. Like a werewolf."

Wolfman howls, making plenty of customers turn around. To be fair, his chest hair is peeking out the top of his green shirt. "Name's also Miles Wolfe, so reckon that might have something to do with it."

I nod, holding in my grin, returning to Wyatt's last friend. "You must be the *actual* best friend—Duke, is it?"

Duke glances to the floor then smiles, shaking my hand. "That's me. Nice to meet you, Rory. If you need anything just let me know. I'll be working tonight." Throwing a wave to the rest of the group, Duke heads behind the bar, laying three bottles of beer on the top for Wyatt, Sawyer, and Miles.

"What's your poison then, Red?" Sawyer asks, wrapping an arm around my shoulder to lead me towards the bar. I know a lot of people get thrown off by touching, but my family have always been like that, so I welcome the close contact.

"Um..." I really don't know my answer. I'm not entirely sure if they have the same kind of fruity cocktails I occasionally drink whenever Sofia comes to visit me in London. My knowledge of alcohol has withered away recently.

Still, I'm kind of excited to let loose. Not think about everything that's been going on. Just drink and talk and who knows.

Cherry chimes in, pushing Sawyer's arm off me, replacing it with her own. He covers his heart, like she's wounded him and frowns. "Do you like Pornstar Martinis? Duke makes the best cherry-flavoured ones!"

I nod, tensed shoulders releasing in relief that there are more options than whiskey and beer, like I was expecting.

Though, as I finally get a second to behold the bar, taking in all the dark polished wood, red mood-lighting and leather seats, I realise that Duke's has a slightly more sophisticated edge to it than anticipated. The western vibe is undoubtedly infusing the decor, with the country music playing on the jukebox and framed pictures of bull riding on the walls. Yet, there's an elegance laced through—subtle fairy lights along the rafters, candles on the tables, and glass shelves behind the bar.

Hearty laughter and clinking glasses echo throughout, adding to the feeling like this is the kind of place you make warm, unforgettable memories.

EIGHT

Wyatt

"**W**ait, so *that* is the British woman you've been moaning about all week?" Sawyer asks, tipping his beer bottle towards where Aurora and Cherry lean against the bar, chatting with Duke as he makes their cocktails. We're sat in our usual booth, waiting for the girls.

I just nod and grunt.

He shakes his head, eyes wide. "What is wrong with you?"

"Seriously, man, are you blind?" Wolfman scratches his dark beard.

I shrug and swig my beer. "I don't see her that way."

"Why?" they both ask in unison, complete bewilderment plastering their faces.

And I get it—Aurora's undeniably attractive. Even when she's not showing off her toned body doing yoga on the deck, which I won't pretend hasn't popped into my thoughts every now and again. But I can't let that get in the way of how she just waltzed onto the ranch without a care, ready to get rid of it. You don't sleep with the enemy.

"You know why."

"Oh right, of course." Wolfman holds his hands up. "She's getting in the way of you having your little happy ending."

"I don't know." Sawyer brings his bottle to his lips, already failing to hide his smirk. "I think she could give a pretty good happy ending."

Wolfman snorts out his beer, and Sawyer chokes on his when I kick him under the table.

Sometimes I don't think these two have grown up since high school, so obsessed with sex and women. I would've thought by now, with all the buckle bunnies Sawyer's spent his nights with since he started bull riding, he'd at least have grown a little tired of chasing women. But Sawyer seems to run off attention, while the rest of us rely on coffee. Though, I think whatever went on between him and his father when he was younger has made sure of that, so I'll cut him some slack there.

Wolfman has no excuse.

At least Duke is more mature.

It's not that I didn't go through my fair share of women when I was younger, but I like to think I know how to treat a woman properly. Having a little sister made me learn that earlier than most. I always try to make sure whoever I'm sleeping with is on the same page as me, whether it's a one-time thing, or more. Sawyer and Wolfman, on the other hand, have left a decent trail of broken hearts through Willow Ridge.

"Oh, come on, Wyatt. God has literally delivered you a no-strings-attached opportunity, and you're just gonna pass it up." Sawyer's not even trying to cover up the way he's ogling Aurora at the bar. I don't know why it grates on me. If she was anyone else, I wouldn't care.

Maybe it's because I know she's delicate right now.

It's clearly grating on some of the other girls in the bar too whose faces no doubt lit up when heartthrob Sawyer Nash waltzed in. Now their scowls keep flicking between him and Aurora.

Wolfman leans in. "You've gotta admit it though, she is hot."

The guys stare me down, raised eyebrows, until I finally sigh and admit, "Fine, yes, she's hot. Okay?"

"Who's hot?"

I start at Cherry's voice as she and Aurora approach the booth, dark-red drinks in their hands. Cherry lets Aurora slide in first next to Sawyer, then perches on the end.

Sawyer shoots me a shit-eating grin, then clinks his bottle against Aurora's glass. "Little Miss Jones here."

"Oh right." Cherry rolls her lips, holding in a smile.

Aurora flashes her eyes at me, redness creeping along her cheeks and neck, then quickly looks away, nursing her drink for an achingly long time. Great, now I probably seem like a creep. Bet she wishes she'd stayed at home.

"Don't worry, Cherry, we think you're hot too." Wolfman lounges back in the booth. "We just keep those discussions for when your brother isn't here." He ruffles my hair, knowing full well that mentioning my sister like that would grind my gears. I just let out a long sigh.

"Gross, Miles," Cherry responds, rolling her eyes.

That's my girl.

"Well, I propose we play a game so we can get to know Red a little better." Sawyer's vibrating with excitement, beaming at Aurora. "What do you say?"

He nudges Aurora playfully, making her chuckle. He's probably exactly her type—just like the pretty boy on her Instagram.

Not that I care.

She says back, "Sure, sounds like fun."

"Never have I ever it is then!" Sawyer announces and I'm already groaning. Even though Cherry's always been good at being one of the guys—she's had to learn to with two older brothers—this is not a game either of us particularly want to play in front of each other. In my mind, she's still a kid, even if I know that's naive.

Aurora scoffs, a brow perked accusingly. "God, how old are you guys? I haven't played that since I was at uni."

Sawyer leans in, smirking at Aurora as he sips his beer. She mirrors him, leaning closer, eyes narrowed. "Ah, see that's why we play it, Red. We've got more experience under our belt now, so we'll get drunk quicker." He winks. "How about the newbie goes first?"

The two of them remain in a stare-off that is too tension-filled for my liking, and Wolfman must clock it because he nudges me with his knee under the table, waggling his eyebrows at me.

I look away, because I don't really care, and take a long drink of my beer.

Aurora hums in contemplation, then says, "Fine, never have I ever done anal," and I spit my beer over the table.

***

"You're all just picking on me now. You're not playing this properly!" Aurora declares, huffing at me before she finishes the last gulps of her second cocktail.

She wipes a droplet of the cherry drink off her bottom lip with her thumb and I track the movement, noticing how the drink has stained her lips faintly darker.

In Aurora's defence, we've all been throwing in lines like *never have I ever been to school in England* and *never have I ever posted my yoga routine online* once the guys found out about her influencer status during one of the conversations that punctuated the game.

My personal favourite, however, was *never have I ever used the phrase* live, laugh, love *unironically* from Wolfman who, despite Aurora insisting she hadn't, managed to track down a video of her saying it from years ago when she first started blogging. I'm not sure I've ever cried from laughing so much before, thoroughly enjoying the way Aurora's face screwed up when she realised she's a walking cliché.

Though it feels strange to admit, and maybe it's the beer talking, seeing Aurora come out of her shell has been... nice. She's actually kind of fun, and she's fallen into place with Cherry and the guys pretty swiftly. The way her shoulders have slowly eased down, and that she's stopped flattening down her waves, proves that she's feeling more comfortable too. Her smile is so bright when she laughs as well, it baffles me how a tiny person like her can radiate so much happiness. Especially when she was crying only a couple of hours ago.

So, yes, we have been picking on her a bit, but it's all in good fun. Hopefully it's been a helpful distraction from whatever upset her earlier.

Besides, she's been goddamn ruthless too with her *never have I evers*. She's forced me to relive the time my mom walked in on me and my high school girlfriend going at it, and she uncovered that Wolfman has slept with a mom of a kid on the high school football team he coaches, which even Sawyer and I were clueless about. I thought British people were supposed to be all prudish, but Aurora seems to have no issue discussing our sexual experiences.

"Just because you made it sexual to start with doesn't mean we all have our minds in the gutter," I tease, biting down on the strong smirk I'm throwing her way.

Aurora sneers, hazel eyes boring into me. Under the mix of red mood-lighting and glittering fairy lights, her eyes remind me of the hazy morning sun. Or maybe soft bonfire smoke in the evening.

Either way, it's weird I'm even thinking that.

I haven't even finished my second beer. Jesus.

Cherry takes her turn, now sipping water as she's our ride for the night, and because she knows I'll get worried if she drinks too much with her epilepsy. Luckily, she's mostly focused on revealing anything she knows Sawyer and Wolfman have done, keeping me as comfortable as I can be.

"Don't worry, Rory, I'm on your side." Aurora grabs Cherry's arm and hugs her tight, mouthing *thank you*. "Hmm... okay, never have I ever had an orgasm."

Our simultaneous sharp intakes of breath could be heard from down the road.

"For fuck's sake," I mutter, wiping my face and letting out a loud groan. I really did *not* need to know that about my little sister.

I hate this game.

"What?" Aurora whips her head round to Cherry. "You're twenty and you've *never* had an orgasm?"

Just as she asks that, Duke arrives at the booth with some more glasses of water, and he almost stumbles. Cherry laughs nervously, a forced smile thrown at Duke before biting down on her lip. The tips of her ears redden as she tucks her hair behind them.

Aurora must struggle to read a room, and my pained face, because then she investigates further. "Haven't you ever tried a vibrator? I can't orgasm without one. I can give you some suggestions of my favourite ones if you like." She pulls her phone out of her pocket.

Honestly, kill me now.

"I need another drink," I announce, scrambling out of the booth and dragging a still stunned Duke with me. The other boys are creasing with stifled laughter as we march away.

***

"Game got a bit intense for you, huh?" Aurora slides next to me, leaning forward on the bar, where I've been taking a breather for the last couple of minutes and grabbing another beer. I'm going to need more alcohol if I'm going to make it through any more rounds.

"Sorry if the vibrator thing made you uncomfortable." Innocence paints her face—all wide-eyed and sweet smiling—but I can see the smirk trying to escape through. "I'm sure you've got plenty more *never have I evers* stored up to take the piss out of me with."

"Hundreds. But it's cool," I admit, turning around to relax back against the bar and people watch. "It's Sawyer I should blame anyway, he's the one who suggested the game knowing Cherry was there. Something was bound to come up."

Aurora orders another cherry cocktail from Duke, watching with sheer fascination as he shakes and pours. Once she's supplied, she twists round and takes a long sip.

I'm just about to suggest we head back to the booth when she hits me with, "Never have I ever chopped wood shirtless."

Okay, she's getting me back now, I get it.

What's wrong with chopping wood shirtless anyway? It's basically summer, and I didn't want to get my shirt covered in sweat and wood chippings. It was never a problem before she turned up.

"It was hot," I reply, narrowing my eyes at her as I drink from my beer. Her brows are raised smugly as she watches, stirring her drink with its swizzle stick, looking very conniving.

And I'm not one to turn down a competition.

Getting one over on her will definitely make my night.

I shuffle around so I'm properly facing her, having to tilt my head down. "Never have I ever... not ridden a horse."

"That's an awful one." Aurora's nose crinkles. But I just shrug and point at her drink, pressing my lips together as I watch her down a third of it. An unnecessary amount but it seems like she definitely needed a drink tonight.

"Never have I ever worn a cowboy hat." Aurora nudges my bottle up to my lips, not letting her fingers off the beer until I've taken a few gulps. I'm not sure how this will ever end, all I know is that I want to win. Even if it does mean getting too drunk.

I settle my beer on the bar. "Never have I ever created an Instagram business just so I can show off how great my ass looks in my tight little gym outfits."

Tipping her head back with silent laughter, Aurora closes her eyes. When they shoot open, her face melts into a far too menacing expression. She takes a step towards me, drink close to her strawberry lips as she bats her lashes.

"You think I have a great ass?"

Damnit, I just lost.

NINE

Wyatt

"You really didn't have to walk me all the way to my front door, you know? I haven't had that much to drink," Aurora says as she fumbles in her bag for her keys. Her voice is a little raspy from talking all night. And the whole car journey home with Cherry, who just left after dropping us off.

I have a key to the main house attached to my own set of keys that Grace gave me when she got ill, but I don't tell Aurora that in case it seems a bit creepy. I've already outwardly called her hot and said she had a great ass, neither of which she probably wanted to hear from me.

Instead, I try not to lose my patience as Aurora continues searching through her bag and lean against the wall. "Don't go thinking I'm a gentleman now. It's not exactly a trek back to mine, is it?"

Aurora flashes me a look that's half scowl, half smile, amusement dancing in her eyes.

"Gotcha!" she shouts, yanking the keys out of her bag, turning to smile at me like she's expecting a gold star for such an achievement.

I raise a brow at her. "Besides, I'm actually here to make sure you don't start playing The Fray all night while sobbing again. I'd like to get a few hours of sleep at least."

Aurora groans and leans her head against the door. "I was kind of hoping you'd forgotten about that."

She stays silent as she rests there, save for her soft breath, and I'm worried she's going to start crying again.

I'm not good when people cry. Growing up, we were always a *just got to get on with life* kind of family, not a *sit and dwell on your feelings* one. I think it's why I always go into solution-mode when people are upset, wanting to figure out how to make them feel better so the emotions stop.

Yet, even though I most certainly do not want to talk about it, suddenly I'm asking, "Do you want to talk about it?"

Aurora sniffs then turns, furrowing her brow. "To *you*?"

I should be insulted, but I totally get it. I wouldn't want to talk to me about how I'm feeling either. Especially if I was Aurora. Even if tonight has eased out some tension, it's not like we've got off on the best foot. Which, I will admit, probably hasn't made her feel better.

Hey, maybe I'm not so bad at this empathy thing after all.

"Yeah, come on." I cock my head and she follows me around the deck to the back of the house.

Tentatively, Aurora shuffles onto the swing beside me, dragging the blanket left there around her. The dim porch lights cast a golden glow over her, making her cheekbones shine and hazel eyes sparkle. She crosses her legs under her and then lets out the longest sigh. I didn't realise such a small person could hold so much air in their lungs.

"I'm Colin Firth," she admits. "And a massive failure."

I blow out a breath, partly because I'm incredibly thrown off by the Colin Firth comment, but mostly because the whole *massive failure* thing rings a little too close to home. "Well, there's a lot to unpack there."

She lets out a hoarse laugh, puckering her lips as she glances up at me. Since we sat, she's been leant slightly forward, not fully relaxed into the seat, but now she slumps back, the swing moving with her.

"Let's start with the Colin Firth thing."

Aurora smothers her face in the blanket. "I caught my boyfriend cheating on me."

Oh damn. Okay, maybe she isn't living the cosiest of lives right now like I first thought. I'm starting to feel even worse for being such a dick. Especially since I'm the poster child for heartbreak, so I know how awful she is probably feeling.

"Well, that's shit." It also explains the guy disappearing from her Instagram. "What's that got to do with Colin Firth, though?"

Her head shoots back up. "You know, like how he gets cheated on in *Love Actually*?"

"Never seen it."

"What?" Aurora's jaw drops. "It's one of the best Christmas films like ever. We will simply have to watch it."

I frown. "I was kind of hoping you'd be gone by Christmas."

When Aurora's mouth pops open again, I immediately regret saying it, because it was actually said in jest, though I doubt she would think that.

But then she jabs me with her elbow and laughs. "Um, rude. That's not going to make me feel any better."

I hold up my hands. "Okay, sorry. Please, *Colin*, do continue. Tell me why you're a massive failure."

Aurora narrows her eyes at me, mouth curving. I might not be that good at comforting people, but I've had her smiling multiple times already, so I'm taking it as a win.

"Ugh, it's just that I feel like I've built this whole career for myself on helping people to create happy, successful, fulfilling lives. I write social media posts and articles and books on attracting healthy relationships, on feeling positive all the time, on being your best self... Yet, now my life is a complete sham." The words are coming out her mouth quicker than I can keep up. But I don't miss the way her shoulders are also loosening with each sentence.

"Jake cheated on me, I'm only just starting to feel inspired to write again now I'm here, I don't know what I'm supposed to do with my life if I can't keep up with this wellness stuff, and the mean girl in my head that I've worked *so* hard to quieten is suddenly louder than ever. I feel like I'm questioning myself all the time because I'm feeling sad a lot since Auntie Grace died, when I pride myself on being a happy, positive person. All this work I've been doing to have a great life, what I tell others to do—it's a complete lie. *I'm* a complete lie."

Aurora's almost out of breath by the time she's finished. She hunches over and buries her head in her hands again. I'm not sure what I was expecting, but this is a little deeper than I usually care for.

"I guess dealing with a grumpy rancher hasn't helped either," I add, attempting an apologetic smile.

Her head flops back up with a raspy giggle, and I get a strange rush from making her smile like that. From pulling her out of whatever hole she lets herself spiral into. Her wide hazel eyes stare up at me, almost with too much hope behind them—like I might be the one with the solution she's been desperate to find.

I scratch my head, settling my arm along the back of the swing. "Look, no offence, but I think you might have actually been lying to your followers this whole time."

Freckled nose crumpled, Aurora's eyes then ignite with fire. As sunny as she may seem, that feistiness is always waiting just around the corner with her. Like the first day I met her.

And I like it. *That's* the real Aurora, I can just tell. Sweet *and* strong. Like my favourite kind of whiskey.

"I just mean that life isn't always perfect. It's full of seasons, good and bad. No one is happy *all* the time."

"I *was*," she mumbles, crossing her arms.

"Yeah, but your followers probably aren't. And as much as you might inspire them with your cliché quotes and woo-woo manifestation stuff," she shoots me daggers at that, "it would probably help them just as much to see that you have bad days too. That it's okay to not be okay sometimes, but there's things you can do to help you get through those difficult times."

Jesus, maybe I should take up this wellness blogging shit, I sound like a motivational speaker. Tony Robbins, move out the way.

Aurora sucks her teeth, regarding me. I can see the cogs working in her brain as her face softens, processing what I've said. I'm not usually one to find silences uncomfortable—if anything, I welcome them—but with the way she's staring so intensely at me, like she might actually discover where my soul is hiding, I find myself needing to fill it.

"Besides, if it makes you feel better, your failure has *nothing* on mine." Fuck, why did I say that? Now she's going to want to know.

Aurora's brows raise, her stare turning silkier under her dark eyelashes. I swallow hard when she shuffles a little closer. "How come?"

"Um..." I have to clear my throat again. "Well, my dad's a rancher too. Works on Sawyer's family ranch. And he's always worked so hard, my mom too, so that I could go to college and do something more than working on a ranch for someone else, like him." I have to stop to uncurl my fists, not realising at first I'd been clenching them so hard. My nails have dug into my palms. "See the irony yet?"

"Ah." Aurora gives me a sympathetic smile, lips pressing together. "So, the big burly cowboy has a brain after all."

"Hilarious." I throw a mocking smile back. "But surprisingly, yes. I was Valedictorian at my high school too, *and* on our champion football team. Had a 4.0 GPA that continued into college. Also had the opportunity to go pro with football, and if that failed, I had a place in law school waiting for me. My parents were so proud, said all the hard work and money they'd put in for me was finally worth it."

"Bloody hell," Aurora huffs. Her knee knocks against my thigh. She's too comfortable with touching people when I go out of my way to avoid it. "How exactly did you end up at Sunset Ranch then?"

"When I had such a great life set up for me?" I say it in the same tone everyone else usually does when they question my choices. The kind that makes it seem like you're so stupid for giving up.

"Because it didn't make me *happy*, Aurora. I finished college with all that success just waiting for me, with people telling me how well I'd done, but then my pops got ill, and Grace needed someone to take over. And I *loved* being on the ranch. I also had to have surgery on my knee in college, so that gave me a good excuse to stop the football, even though they said I could still play."

Now Aurora's shoulder brushes against me too, like she's slowly inching her way closer. I guess it is somewhat comforting...

"There's something about the hard labour and being surrounded by nature and animals that makes me feel alive, but also peaceful. And *happy*. So fucking happy." I look out at the peaks ahead, and the night sky between them splattered with stars. "But these days, success doesn't seem to equate to happiness, so people think you're failing when you're not. And that sucks."

"Success doesn't seem to equate to happiness," Aurora repeats under her breath, then lets out a scoff of a laugh.

I've probably bummed her out even more now with my sob story. But I can't pretend it doesn't feel good to let that all out after so many years of holding it in. After just grinding my teeth down, learning not to react to the comments people make. Old friends gloating about their city jobs or whispering about how they expected more from me after high school. My parents reminding me of everything they gave up for me, meaning there was less for my siblings.

It's why I've always worked extra hard to support Hunter and Cherry through college too. It's why I helped Hunter get gigs when he was younger, before he got his record deal. It's why I convinced Duke to give Cherry a holiday job so she could earn her own money too, and help him decorate the bar.

"Oh," I add, because the alcohol in my system decides that as I've gone so far already, I might as well confess all my embarrassing stories. "I also came back for a girl."

With an amused gasp, Aurora spins around, tired eyes lit up. "Wait, *you* have feelings? I'm so invested now." She wiggles forward, touching me in too many places. I track her tongue dart out over her strawberry lips, leaving them shining.

"Yep, my high school sweetheart, Holly Slade. We did long-distance for the whole of college, then she got a job teaching back in Willow

Ridge. It was even more reason to come work here. One month later, she left me for some fancy lawyer and moved to the city with him. Said she needed someone with more *ambition*. Still texts me every now and again to check if I'm still a rancher."

I hate the way Aurora's face drops. I don't need anyone's pity. I wouldn't have been happy with Holly anyway, always trying to be the person she wanted me to be, rather than who I truly was. I just forget to remind myself that sometimes.

Aurora makes a noise of disgust. "Wow, what a dick move from Holly Slade... If it helps, I get it. The happiness thing. I know *some people* make fun of what I do for a living." She nudges me, tipping her head up to raise an accusatory brow at me. Still, I appreciate the quick slide away from Holly because those wounds aren't completely healed yet. "But it makes me happy. I love talking and writing about wellness and positivity."

She lets out another long sigh and swings back around, resting her head against my shoulder. I tense, a few of her wild waves tickling my jaw, while all the nerves in my shoulder light up.

"This place makes me happy too. Even though it's been hard, I feel like I can be myself here. I feel... free. It's so beautiful and peaceful."

I sigh too. "It's the kind of place with views that make you realise how insignificant you and your problems actually are."

"Yeah. I'm sorry that I turned up and threatened it all," she admits, a faint quiver in her voice as she continues. "I don't really want to let this all go, but I just don't know what to do."

I don't know either. I'm pissed off at her for being here, taking the reins away from me and steering the ranch towards being sold. But what else is she going to do? She's not going to stay here in Willow Ridge, she belongs elsewhere. Even if I hate to admit it, selling probably is her only choice.

"And I'm sorry for acting like a dick."

Aurora huffs out a little laugh, nuzzling her head into my shoulder again. "You're forgiven."

We sit in silence as I move the swing gently with my foot, both staring out at our surroundings. It's a weirdly comforting feeling when someone else gets you. And it's even weirder when that someone is Aurora Jones.

I should probably get going, let Aurora sleep, so I shift to start moving when I notice her breathing has deepened. I look down and there she is, eyes closed, pink lips parted, the corners tipped up ever so slightly, asleep on my shoulder. Of course she smiles in her sleep.

She's still bathed in the orange glow of the lights, the freckles all over her golden-lit skin reminding me of the constellations I was watching seconds ago. Her waves are tucked behind her ears, save for a couple of loose ones that tumble across her cheek. I want to brush them away, but I also don't want to move and wake her up.

She looks so happy, so peaceful, so... beautiful, goddammit.

Instead, I sit back and continue staring out at the midnight-drenched valley ahead, until I drift off to the rhythm of Aurora's breath.

TEN

Aurora

My mouth is so dry, and my bedsheets feel as hard as denim. The morning sun is far too painful as I prise my eyes open.

Hold on... why am I outside?

It takes me a few seconds to register that my bed is in fact not a bed, and instead a body. Wyatt's body to be exact, and I'm lying across the swing with my face in his crotch.

And, unless he's got something very hard in his pocket, his morning wood is poking my cheek.

"Shit," I hiss as I scramble away from him, wiping the dribble off my chin.

Wyatt groans from the sudden wake up, the swing rocking until he digs his heels into the ground. He looks dazed, hair mussed, eyes a little glassy, as he also takes in the morning. In a strange way, it's almost sexy. But it's also Wyatt, so thinking that would be weird.

"Did we fall asleep out here?" I rub my eyes. The last thing I remember was talking on the swing together. Thank God I was wrapped in a blanket as there's a faint, lingering chill in the air.

Wyatt shakes his head and looks at me a little stunned, eyes flicking across my face. My hair is probably a mess right now, and no doubt my make-up is smudged. Plus, I can feel the pattern his jeans have left indented on my cheek.

Redness creeps up his neck before he clears his throat. "Must have."

An awkward silence lingers as we stare at each other. It feels like we've been caught doing something, but in reality we just drank a bit too much and fell asleep. We *literally* slept together. Never thought I'd be saying that about Wyatt.

Wyatt looks away first and stretches with another groan, arms up above his head, flexing his biceps. His T-shirt lifts, revealing the way his stomach softly tapers into a V towards his trousers.

Towards where he's definitely straining against his jeans.

And there's a wet mark from where—

"Oh God, I think I drooled on your dick," I say, brain not quite fast enough yet this morning to stop the words from leaving my mouth.

"I'm sorry?" Wyatt flashes his eyes at me, a muscle feathering in his jaw, then he checks down and immediately leaps up from the swing. "Oh shit." He turns around, trying to quickly adjust himself under his jeans.

I bite back my nerve-induced laugh. After managing to get the swing back under control, I stand up too, keeping the blanket around me. The movement sends my head throbbing.

God, they really don't lie when they say the hangovers get worse as you get older.

I rub my temples and take in a few deep breaths of the fresh air, which wakes me up a bit more. Out of the corner of my eye, Wyatt is still wiping his face, eyelids looking heavy.

"Not a morning person, huh?" I ask, attempting a smile.

He grunts. Guess we're back to the Wyatt Hensley I knew before we confessed our biggest insecurities to each other. Before we fell asleep cuddled up together. God, earlier this week I would've gagged at the image.

"Especially not when I've wasted hours this morning." Wyatt groans, turning to finally face me again, and takes a step back when our eyes meet, not saying anything for a few seconds. I try to pat my hair down—maybe it's crazier than I thought. "I have work to do. I'll see you later."

He doesn't even give me a chance to respond as he spins on his heel and jogs down the stairs, off towards his house.

Just before he's out of hearing range I call over, "Wyatt."

He halts, turning slowly, failing to suppress his scowl.

Really not a morning person, evidently.

"Thank you, for last night," I say, and he nods, lips curving ever so slightly, then he heads off.

I needed last night far more than he probably realises. I know he invited me out of pity, but it was better than wallowing by myself all night. Being surrounded by people who welcomed me in so easily made me forget about everything.

Plus, I needed that talk with him, or at least someone.

And since Jake and I shared some friends, the only people I feel like I can talk to right now are my mum, half-sister, and Sofia. But the time difference makes it difficult when you're upset at seven in the evening in Colorado, and they're asleep because it's two in the morning over in England. Sofia might have said she didn't mind a midnight chat if I needed her, but I also know she starts work so early, and needs all the sleep to deal with the hellraising teenagers she teaches.

I always feel better after talking things through with people, and since I've been at Sunset Ranch, I haven't been able to do that. Which is why all the feelings hit me yesterday—I was just overcome with loneliness.

There was a strange comfort to knowing Wyatt understood some of my feelings, too. Even if I thought he had *zero* capacity for emotions before that, except for grumpiness.

He was right as well. Annoying as it is to admit. Life isn't perfect, and I need to accept that. Maybe my followers will appreciate seeing that I have lows amongst the highs too. Maybe we can all be on this journey of healing together, I'm sure I can't be the only one recovering from a little crisis.

And screw thinking that I have to have everything figured out to be happy. I can still be happy even if I don't know what the future holds, even if I don't have the perfect relationship.

I grab my phone from my pocket and angle the camera at the beautiful scenery ahead of me—the mountain peaks, the sun rising up over them, cascading buttery sunlight across the rich green fields. I don't even consider sitting for half an hour to edit the photo, to try and make it look better, because it already looks amazing. The beauty of this place is so natural and unparalleled. So raw and unfiltered. It's everything I didn't realise I needed.

It's time for me to be the same.

Raw. Unfiltered. *Honest.*

I upload the photo to my Instagram, with the caption:

> *Who decided that running away to a ranch in Colorado to escape my boyfriend's infidelity and find some inspiration again meant I was unsuccessful? Whoever*

they are, I'm ready to prove them wrong. Better days are coming, my loves! Rory xo.

***

I honestly cannot contain my excitement as I skip up the steps to Wyatt's house. It's almost enough to drown out the dull ache in my lower back I get when I'm on my period. Loudly, I knock on the door, eager to explain what I've been working on for the past few days. I only managed to get one swim in at the lake over the entire weekend, too engrossed in all my planning.

When he doesn't answer, I knock again and call his name.

"Jesus Christ, I'm coming," he yells.

"Actually, it's just me, Rory."

A few seconds later Wyatt opens the door, sighing. "What do you want?"

He's dripping wet, a towel wrapped around his lower half, whilst the rest of his body is on full display, glistening in the sunlight. The sight of him makes me gulp.

His muscled body is thick and softly sculpted, built from hard, heavy work, as opposed to the slimmer, more sharply chiselled gym influencers I'm used to, like Jake. The way his hips taper in that same V shape I saw the other morning has my heart stammering. Muscles ripple through his legs too, and I can see a scar on his knee from the injury he mentioned.

I'd seen the mountain range tattoo around his forearm before, but he's also got a beautifully illustrated tattoo of an eagle mid-flight that spreads from one shoulder across most of his chest. When I'd walked past him chopping wood shirtless the other day, I'd been too riled up to pay him or his tattooed body enough attention. But now I'm seeing this up close, it's actually breathtaking—the detail that must have gone into it. God knows how long that took.

His dark chest hair is neatly trimmed, but still long enough for me to run my fingers through it.

Not that I want to do that.

Wyatt clears his throat. "Aurora? You good?"

I flick my eyes back up to his, and his face looks strained. Shit. I'm not sure there's any way I can pretend I wasn't just ogling Wyatt, so I just say, "Yeah, you've got a bit of water on you—just there," and point at his shoulder where the eagle starts, despite the fact that his whole body is soaking wet.

Just like how between my thighs will be in a second if he doesn't put some bloody clothes on.

Jesus, what is wrong with me?

He scowls. "I was in the shower."

"I can see." I give him a toothy grin, still holding the folded paper behind me. "Can I come in?"

Wyatt regards me for a second, jaw ticking. I know the other night doesn't make us best friends now, but the last couple of days since have been amicable. He's even not scowled at me when we've crossed paths, so I feel like we've moved forward.

Eventually, Wyatt concedes. "Sure."

I've never been in Wyatt's place properly before, only caught a glimpse the other night before going to the bar, so I'm intrigued to see what it's like. The interior mimics the rustic parts of the main house, thick wooden floorboards, and beams, despite it only being on one level. There's an open plan kitchen-diner and living room, with three bar stools that look custom-made beside the counter, and a long forest-green sofa on the other side opposite the television.

"I'm going to get dressed, hold on," Wyatt says, already heading down the corridor where I assume his bedroom is.

It gives me the perfect view of the rest of the tattoos down his back—five rows of Roman numerals, birds soaring across his shoulders like my butterflies, and a muscled man with wings falling. My fingers itch to trace them, find out what they mean.

But I get the vibe that Wyatt's confessions the other night were out of the ordinary for him, and I don't think he's likely going to be opening up to me again. He was only trying to make me feel better anyway.

Whilst Wyatt changes, I decide to snoop, placing the paper I brought with me on the sofa for later. Three big dark bookcases take up most of the wall space around the living area, filled to the brim with history books. Why does it make me smile knowing he loves to read?

I call out, "Did you study history at college?"

A grunt of confirmation echoes into the room.

In between the piles of books and on other surfaces, there's little ornaments, bowls, and vases with large colourful patterns on them or wolves and eagles. There's an eclectic vibe to his place, but it's clearly curated, with the odd pop of brighter colours dotted amongst the more natural and toned down ones.

Next to a red bowl is the only photo frame in the whole room, which has a picture of what I assume is his family, because there's a younger version of him and Cherry, and a boy that looks like a mix of the two of them, who must be the rockstar brother. They're standing between an older woman with long dark hair, and an older man with grey hair and a thick moustache. And they're all smiling, hugging. Even Wyatt.

The way he's looking at his two younger siblings like they're so precious makes my heart melt.

"Did you do that on purpose?" I ask loudly, running my fingers over more books, inspecting the spines. There's books on everything—the American Civil War, the French Revolution, Ancient Greece, even the Battle of Hastings. I try to pretend I'm not embarrassed that he probably knows more about British history than me.

Sofia would be ashamed.

"What?" Wyatt responds, his voice closer now as he saunters back into the room, finishing pulling a white T-shirt over his head. Dark, faded jeans hug his thick, corded legs, whilst the T-shirt complements his darker skin and does nothing to help me dispel the image of his body from my mind.

My stomach feels like it's filled with butterflies.

God, finding Wyatt annoying is going to be much more difficult now I also find him hot.

Licking my lips, I throw on a smirk. "Studying history? So you'd struggle to get a job and then you could just come back to the ranch."

Wyatt leans his hip against one of the bookcases and crosses his arms, looking at me pointedly. It gives me that weird rush of nerves like when you get in trouble with a teacher. Maybe if *he'd* been my History teacher I would've paid more attention.

"If I'd known you were running over here just to insult me, I'd have stayed in the shower."

I wave him off. "Yeah, well you didn't, so go cry about it to someone else." He sucks his teeth, the scowl returning. "I'm actually here because I have something exciting to tell you."

"You're leaving?" His eyes prick with amusement, and now I'm the one scowling.

"Hilarious, but no. Quite the opposite." At that, Wyatt stands up straighter, unfolding his arms. I perch on the arm of the sofa. "After our DMC the other night—"

"What the hell is a DMC?"

"Deep and meaningful conversation."

"Fucking hell," he mumbles, wiping his face.

"Don't worry, your secrets are safe with me." I sign crossing my heart over my chest, grinning whilst Wyatt just shakes his head. "Anyway, our DMC really got me thinking a lot about life and inspired me so much that I managed to actually write an article! It wasn't as positive as my usual ones, but I gave it a happy spin at the end."

The relief I felt sending that off to my boss at Thrive Magazine was unparalleled. I even posted about it on my Instagram, discussing creativity block and what might be causing it. The post didn't get as many likes as usual, but the comments suggested people really appreciated it.

"Well done—what was it about?"

"How success doesn't always equate to happiness, and why that's bullshit." I bite my lip to contain the beaming smile that follows when Wyatt's face lights up, softening all his harder features.

"I hope you gave me credit."

"Oh, of course. I made sure to reference *tall, grumpy rancher* in the footnotes," I say, meeting his gaze.

There's a palpable silence between us as his dark eyes lock with mine. A strange heat rises within me, but not the usual ire I experience with him.

It's too weird, so I cut the stare off first and clear my throat.

"But the inspiration didn't stop there. I've been thinking a lot this weekend about what I want to do with my life. I know I love helping and inspiring people, and it felt really good to be surrounded by people on Friday. And you're right about this place, how happy and peaceful it feels. So, I came up with a bit of a plan... one that means you can keep your job."

I reach behind me to grab my paper from the sofa, and when I turn back around, Wyatt's walked over, barely a couple of steps away. I have to tip my head up to him. The way he towers over me still has that intimidating edge to it, but it also gives me a little heady rush.

I unfold the paper quickly between us, creating some distance again.

"Ta dah!" Just seeing the collage of pictures I've put together gives me a thrill, like this could actually happen, like my body knows this is the right path. And I've seen two butterflies already this morning, so the universe must agree too.

Wyatt's expression does not reflect the same, however. "What is it?"

"It's a vision board." His quirked brow begs for an elaboration. "It's a collage of images that represent what you want. It's supposed to help you visualise your goals and future, which motivates you to achieve them."

I still have my first ever one I made at university somewhere at home, when I first decided I wanted to start blogging. And here I am, so they must have a bit of power to them.

Now is the part where I'm supposed to explain my ideas, but the thought of saying it aloud is scary. It will make it real, which sets it up for failure. But also, success. I could literally be about to speak it into existence.

"I want to turn this place into some sort of wellness retreat," I confess, stomach churning from nerves. I need Wyatt to be on board for this to work, and his blank expression isn't looking promising.

"Look, the buildings are already being renovated. This place needs money, and running the ranch alone isn't enough, we both know that.

But Sunset Ranch is so much more than just a ranch—the joy and serenity I feel here is unparalleled to anywhere else. Imagine sharing that with other people—helping them to feel happier, maybe even inspiring them to create too. I really think this could be a hit. And it could bring money into the town too with new visitors."

Wyatt rubs the back of his neck, opening his mouth to respond, but I'm too scared he's going to reject my idea, so I keep talking.

"And you'd stay here, be in charge of the ranch properly—everything ranch-related goes through *you* not me, because let's be honest, I have no idea how it works. Maybe you guys could do riding lessons and trails too. But basically, it couldn't work without you."

The silence that follows is deafening.

I know I'm impulsive sometimes, and don't always think things through, but with this, I really have. When I first arrived here, I was more than happy to sell this place—I knew I wasn't going to stay in Colorado, and there was no point in trying to run the ranch from across the world. There were people I could easily sell it to. The ranch was also a reminder of Auntie Grace no longer being around and how lonely I was, how I was struggling to get work done.

But now, I just feel called to stay.

Growing up, we moved around a few times. It never really disrupted our lives too much, and I quickly adapted to my new environment, but it meant I never had a place that I felt really connected to. I've never had a *home,* just lots of different houses. And even though I love living in London, that's not my home either. I know I won't stay there forever—I don't think anyone can truly stomach it for their whole lives.

Yet I always had Sunset Ranch growing up. That was always constant, until I got older. The joy and freedom I felt here growing up never disappeared. It's the same now. Every morning I have woken up, walked

101

out onto that back deck with my hot lemon water, breathed in the fresh air that smelled like freedom, and felt this thrumming in my chest that says *home, home, home.*

I know Wyatt must feel the same. I'm not going to pretend either that a small part of me doesn't also feel bad that if I sell the ranch, it's taking it away from him too. He doesn't deserve that.

Though I'll never say it aloud, maybe I did need Jake to cheat on me, to force me out here, so I could remember where I always felt like I belonged.

Everything happens for a reason, right?

Eleven

Aurora

"Aurora, I'm not sure..." Wyatt's forehead creases.

"Okay, listen to me." I grab Wyatt's hand and pull him over to the sofa where we sit. I put the vision board on the table in front, glancing at all the pictures to give me the motivation to fight for this.

My knee bumps against his as I turn to face him. He glances down at it briefly, then jerks his leg back.

Not cool with touching, got it.

"You were right—there are a lot of people out there who are unhappy, who are stuck living a life that doesn't fulfil them or bring them joy, because they're so focused on doing what they think they *should* do over what they actually want. But it's hard in this world to catch a break or find the time to sit and figure out how to feel better, let alone implement it.

"I mean, I literally had to fly all the way to Colorado to be on this ranch to feel better again. So, maybe I can help others do that too, with this retreat. Give them the opportunity to feel the peace and freedom this place offers and start focusing on prioritising their happiness."

My leg is bobbing as I stare back at Wyatt, hoping I've convinced him. Because I don't think I can do this alone, and I really don't want to leave yet. I want to stay here and help people.

He picks up the vision board to inspect all the pictures, face unbearably blank. God, I want to shake him.

Just tell me what you think, Hensley!

Then he grabs the paper underneath—a map of the ranch, where I've planned all the guesthouses and activities—including some changes in line with the seasons. It's all colour coded too, with different pastel colours for different areas and parts of the retreat, which was incredibly therapeutic to draw.

"It's a great idea, Aurora, but I don't think Willow Ridge really has the right people for this." Wyatt presses his lips together.

"I know that, silly." I lean forward, shuffling into him. Gooseflesh covers the bare arm that brushes against mine, causing him to quickly glance at where our bodies are touching. Dark eyes dart up to mine, then back to the papers.

"It'll be for anyone. We can do a trial run anyway to start with. I've got tonnes of contacts through my influencing who we could invite to test it out, give us feedback, and help to market the place. Once a few people with several hundred thousand followers start talking about Sunset Ranch, it won't be long before we've got people begging to come here."

"And what about money? To set it all up?"

"I have some savings from my influencing. It was for a house, but I have one now," I say, gesturing to the ranch out the window. Besides, using the abundance I've accumulated to help people *and* pursue my dreams sounds worth it to me. Sometimes you have to risk a little to get the reward.

Now he's nodding ever so slightly, and my body begins to buzz.

"You've really thought this through, haven't you?"

When Wyatt turns to me, I can't stop myself from wincing as a cramp hits. I'd been trying to push through, hoping I could avoid taking any painkillers, but this one catches me off-guard.

"What was that?" Wyatt freezes, eyes narrowing.

"What?"

"That face. You look like you're in pain."

"Oh, it's nothing." It's not like I'm about to discuss my period pains with him—most men normally get all weird about that kind of stuff. "Just a headache, that's all."

"Yeah, the way you're rubbing your back really suggests that." He eyes how I've been instinctually massaging my lower back with my thumb, where the cramps normally start.

I pull my hand away. "Really, it's nothing."

Wyatt gives me a pointed glare, then huffs and stands up, heading into his bedroom. I'm slightly concerned he's just got too annoyed with me being here and decided to leave, but then he comes back out and tosses me a packet of painkillers. He grabs a glass from a cupboard and fills it with water. Handing me the glass, he sits back on the sofa and nods to the painkillers.

"Take two of them, then give me your feet."

"Excuse me?" I raise my brows, whilst he just throws me his usual dark scowl. "I guessed you might be a little kinky, but I never pegged you for a foot fetish guy."

As his eyes widen, I can see him trying to work out which part of that to respond to first. "Correct, I don't have a foot fetish."

And correct that he might be a little kinky? Interesting.

Wyatt holds his large hands out, where I'm guessing he is expecting me to put my feet. I'm so confused right now. "Cherry used to get super bad cramps and, for some reason, massaging her feet helped."

He's offering to massage my *feet*. Who is this guy and what has happened to the Wyatt Hensley I was talking to just a second ago? And the painkillers, he's... taking care of me. This is so strange.

"I think your sister might have just been conning you into giving her free foot massages." I quirk an eyebrow as I swallow down the painkillers.

"No, I've definitely read up on it before. I don't know if it's just a mind over matter thing or a distraction, but apparently it helps." Wyatt shrugs. "Now, are you gonna give me your feet or sit there whining?"

I go to retort, because I haven't complained one bit, but another cramp spikes through me, shutting me up. Instead, I suck in a breath and slip my feet out of my shoes, hesitantly swinging them up into Wyatt's lap. I'm just glad I painted my toenails, so they actually look relatively pretty. If feet can ever look pretty, that is.

The warmth of his big hands instantly eases a bit of my tension as he grabs my right foot, kneading his thumbs gently into its arch.

"Jesus, Aurora, your feet are freezing."

"I have bad circulation, sorry," I say as I close my eyes, already feeling the dull ache in my lower back starting to dissipate.

"Is that good?" he asks, and I can feel the heaviness of his dark eyes on me.

"Yeah," I breathe out, because truthfully I want to groan, but I feel like that wouldn't be appropriate. God, this man knows how to use his hands—every stroke of his thumb sends a rush of bliss up through my legs and into my body.

I don't tell Wyatt that the pain has basically subsided when he switches to my other foot. Instead, I open my eyes and his flick down, like he doesn't want to be caught watching me. The corners of his mouth are tipped up slightly though, as if he's maybe enjoying this. Shocking as it is, he did say he used to do this for Cherry, and my heart warms just a little at the image of a younger Wyatt looking after his little sister. So maybe he does enjoy this—caring for people.

I just didn't expect him to care about *me*.

When Wyatt presses his thumb in deeper, a moan accidentally slips from my lips that sounds far more sexual than I would've liked. Wyatt's hands freeze and I have to smother the laugh that bubbles up with my fist. His eyes flash up at me, before he shoves my feet away from him.

"Well, you've made that weird now."

Now my laugh fully escapes. "I'm so sorry."

He shakes his head and shuffles a couple of inches away, displeasure suddenly written across his furrowed features. I guess that's all the nice Wyatt I'm getting today then.

I sit back up properly, still biting my lip. "Thank you, though. It really did help. I owe you."

"Yeah big time... especially if I'm gonna agree to this retreat."

"Wait..." I widen my eyes at him, the buzzing spreading through my whole body violently. "You'll do it?"

He shrugs. "I can't really say no, can I?"

"Oh my God!" I fling my arms around him, squealing. I almost feel light-headed from the sudden burst of excitement.

Wyatt groans and tries to wiggle free. "Aurora, please get off me."

"Sorry, sorry!" My cheeks are aching from how hard my grin is pushing them up. I clear my throat and try to compose myself, straightening up on the sofa before holding out my hand. "Business partners then?"

Wyatt rolls his eyes and reluctantly slaps his hand against mine, shaking it. "Business partners."

As his midnight eyes lock onto mine, the fluttering picks up in my stomach again. Butterflies are my good omen, right?

Twelve

Wyatt

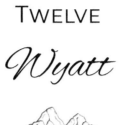

"It's just so big. I don't know how I'm going to fit my legs around it," Aurora whines.

"Heard that before," I snort, waiting behind her as she sizes up Scout, the palomino American Quarter Horse.

Twisting round to shoot me a scowl, she pops a hip. "Hilarious."

"Wasn't joking." I wink, then remove my hat to wipe my forehead, the sun beating down heavy on us today. "Now, are you gonna be a good girl and give it a ride, or what?"

Aurora's eyes flash wide, pink cheeks appearing rosier by the second. Any attempt to keep down her giggle fails, and her quick laugh rings out like silver bells. "You did *not* just say that."

"Yes I did." I don my hat again and cross my arms, taking a step closer to Aurora, only a few inches away. Hints of coconut from whatever sunscreen she lathered over her freckly skin earlier fill my senses. It's a pleasant difference to the mud, manure, and beer my life usually smells of. "I've shown you about a hundred times how to mount already. If you don't get on that horse right now, I'm gonna pick you up and throw you onto it myself."

Aurora learning to ride a horse was one of my conditions to agreeing to help her with the retreat. I'm still not one hundred percent confident in the idea—mostly because it's very different to anything I'm used to, and it means having to spend a lot more time with a girl who doesn't know how to keep the pitch and volume of her voice at a normal level. And I know a lot of ranches have been struggling economically over the last few years, but we've barely managed to afford all the vaccines and medicine needed for the calves this year, let alone prepare for unexpected costs.

So, if this is the only way I get to stay on this ranch and keep it going, then I'll run with it. Beggars can't be choosers, right?

Besides, Aurora literally handed over control of the ranch to me, which is more than I could've asked for. Not legally, of course—she still owns Sunset Ranch and can overrule any decisions I make—but I'm in charge of everything ranching related. As long as I keep the ranch running, and help get the retreat going, Aurora's happy. It's almost back to how it was when Grace was here—except, unfortunately, now I might have to interact with a few more people. But I think I can let that slide if it means Sunset Ranch gets to stay. Along with me.

I know it's only early days, and honestly, there's no saying the retreat will work at all. Though, I can't deny how thought out and detailed Aurora's plans were when I properly went through them the other night, which does give me a little confidence. Hats off to the girl, because she'd planned it all down to the tiniest details, and the passion radiating off her when she explained it all was inspiring. It was also kind of nice to hear that our talk motivated her.

And that she'd planned for me to stay.

The retreat could technically work without me and the other ranchers. She doesn't need the actual ranch aspect of Sunset Ranch to keep it going. Yet, she wants it to. She wants me—and the other guys, of course—to stay.

Still, it all feels too good to be true. Like I'm missing something. Somewhere in all those bright, colour-coded plans is a problem that hasn't been pre-empted.

Because that's how life works.

Just like when I was given the opportunity to run this ranch in the first place—to do a job that I enjoyed. There's always something waiting around the corner. Your girlfriend leaving you for someone more successful. Your dad being disappointed in you. Your ranch being handed over to some annoying British girl to sell.

Whatever it is that's waiting to remind me I can't always have everything I want, I just hope I get a little bit longer here before it arrives. Even another month will be more than I expected.

"Okay, okay!" Aurora holds up her hands to ease me back, before she turns to Scout, determination hardening her features. Taking in a deep breath and blowing it out slowly as she steps onto the stool I grabbed to help her get up, Aurora then whispers to herself, "My fear does not know my strength. I can do this."

"Jesus." I smother my laugh with my hand, but she still shoots me a scowl.

Shoulders suddenly straightened out, Aurora grabs the reins and the pommel, then pushes her foot into the stirrup and swings herself up. Realisation that she's done it so naturally dawns on her face as she shuffles in the saddle, and she squeals, strawberry lips breaking into a glowing grin. The midday sun reflects off her copper hair, casting a golden halo around it.

So high up, she almost looks angelic.

I rub Scout on the neck for being so calm with her and nod at Aurora. "Well done. Now, hold on."

She's still gleaming with pride when I step up onto the stool and reach out for the saddle—

"Um," Aurora's voice halts me. Her brows have pinched in. "What are you doing?"

"Getting on the horse. What does it look like I'm doing?"

Aurora swallows, my eyes drawn to the column of her throat. "Yes, but why?"

"Ain't no way I'm letting you ride on your own right away. I don't wanna be chasing after you because you've suddenly got the horse flying off."

That's why I chose Scout for her to learn on—he's the strongest and calmest horse on the ranch, so I know he'll manage with us both for a short time. Just until I'm confident Aurora has a hang of things. I'd rather not be spending my day in incredibly close proximity to someone who manages to get on my nerves so easily, but I also don't want to be responsible for Aurora being thrown from a horse. Taking her to the hospital would eat up far too much of my time.

Before Aurora can stall any more, I hoist myself up onto Scout, settling on the pad behind the saddle. Aurora's body tenses, and I immediately regret my decision because my senses are currently going wild. The strong citrus scent from what must be her shampoo fills my lungs as her wild waves tumble about. Heat also radiates off her body where her back almost touches me.

I'm trying not to press myself up against her too much out of respect, but my body is still getting more excited than it should. I honestly can't remember the last time I was this close to a woman...

Nope. Not going there.

"Right." I clear my throat and quickly reach around Aurora to place my hands on the reins, over hers. "Keep your feet in the stirrups, hands tight on the reins." I wait for her to do so, feeling her hands stiffen beneath mine, making me realise how small they are. "Okay, to get him going, give him a gentle squeeze with your legs."

"Woah!" Aurora goes even more rigid when Scout starts moving gently around the corral, and I can hear her breathing suddenly quicken.

Being up on a horse is so natural to me—calming actually—that the idea Aurora could be scared baffles me. But I've got years of riding under my belt, and I know that she needs to relax into the movements, otherwise she's not going to experience the bliss of being in the saddle. I can't let fear get the best of her now.

Taking one hand off the reins, I stroke her arm, trying to ease her back, and her skin prickles. "Hey, let yourself relax. It will feel more comfortable. I'm behind you, so I ain't gonna let you fall."

Briefly, Aurora glances back at me, hazel eyes searching mine. But she struggles to not keep her eyes ahead, and snaps back. Her hair flicks about as she nods, then she takes another deep breath, leaning back into me, shimmying slightly to get comfortable. Copper waves tickle my jaw, making it tighten, and her warmth diffuses into me now her back is flush to my chest. I ignore the gooseflesh on my arms as they brush against Aurora's.

I also ignore the way my stomach tumbles when she lets out a sweet sigh, tension visibly releasing as she softens in my hold. That undeniable shot of dopamine rushes through me again too. Just like it did when I made her smile after she was crying, and when I helped ease her pain with the foot rub the other day.

When did I get so motivated by caring for people?

Especially Aurora Jones.

"That's it, Princess," I say, returning my hand to where hers are on the reins. Even from behind, I can sense her smile widening, already brightening the world around us. I don't know why she'd ever doubt herself. She's stronger than she thinks.

I run her through how to steer Scout and slow him down, then get us trotting around the corral. Eventually, Aurora agrees to give it a go on her own, and before I know it, we're side by side on Dusty and Scout, heading up the dirt road, lush pastures and shadowy mountains surrounding us. Every now and again, I notice Aurora tense up or wobble, but then she mutters something to herself—no doubt another little pep talk—and eases back into riding, looking like the natural I knew she could be.

Like maybe she could belong here.

Whistles grab our attention when we pass one of the cattle fields where the guys are working and waving at us. They're still on a high from hearing that they'll get to stay on at Sunset Ranch, so didn't tease me too much when I explained I had to leave at lunch to teach Aurora to ride. Usually, I'd be concerned about the work I'll have to catch up on, but I can't remember the last time I rode with someone else just for fun.

Just two people, two horses, and a whole lot of beauty surrounding us. Not the worst way to spend a Wednesday.

***

"God, it's just so beautiful, isn't it?" Aurora gazes at the lake ahead. The hot sun leaves a haze in the air above where its golden light glistens along the lake's surface.

I've just finished tying up the horses to the fence, giving them both a snack I packed in one of the saddle bags to keep them happy while we take a break.

When I reach Aurora's side, she suddenly starts taking off her crop top, revealing a purple strappy bikini beneath. Her sternum tattoo is on full display, immediately grabbing my attention, and I can't help but notice that her breasts are barely covered by the thin fabric. I just know they'd fit perfectly in my hands.

"What are you doing?" I ask, shaking my head to snap out it.

"Going for a swim." Aurora plops her top on the ground and starts working her shorts over her hips, while I just stand there frozen.

The word *grateful* is written in cursive writing along her hipbone, just above where her bikini bottoms sit. Every one of her tattoos dares me to appreciate more of her body. And I'm a weak man who is easily convinced.

Aurora ties her waves up with a scrunchie then steps towards the water, giving me a shot of that great ass I admitted to thinking about the other night. But I'm not wrong. It is fucking great.

And I shouldn't be staring.

She looks over her shoulder, hazel eyes glistening with pure innocence, like she hasn't just undressed in front of me. "Want to join?"

"Uh, I have work to do," I respond, pulling my dropped jaw up.

Aurora waves a hand at me. "Well, as your boss, I say you can take the rest of the day off."

I cross my arms, raising a brow. "I thought we were business partners."

"Fine, yes." She rolls her eyes, tiptoeing closer to the lake's edge. "Then as your *business partner*, I say you can take the rest of the day off."

"I don't have my swimsuit," is my next attempt to avoid getting in the lake with her. I'm not even sure why. Sawyer and Wolfman would be screaming at me right now to get in the water with this goddamn beautiful woman.

But something is holding me back, like the lake is a line that shouldn't be crossed. I'm certain Aurora doesn't see me as any more than a business partner and neither do I with her, but I don't want to risk changing that dynamic by giving the wrong impression. We're going to have to work together to make this retreat happen, and I need it to if I'm going to get to keep my piece of happiness here at Sunset Ranch.

That's what's important to me right now.

I can't jeopardise that.

"Just swim in your underwear," Aurora suggests with a shrug. She dips her toes in the lake, shivering in response. Then, with a perked brow, she smirks at me, lacing her words with a terrible attempt at a country drawl. "Come on, let yourself relax. I'm right here, so I ain't gonna let you drown."

With that she winks and dashes into the lake, squealing before diving fully in. Her head pops back out of the water with a loud gasp, ginger ponytail flicking up behind her. A huge, liberated grin fills her face as she hovers in the water, waiting for me.

I push my tongue into my cheek, scowling at her. It's funny, I can't remember the last time I went for a swim in the lake. Things have been so hectic and busy, especially since Grace got ill, that the only times I let myself have fun these days is my Friday nights at Duke's. Then it's back out in the fields straight away the next morning.

That's just a rancher's life.

I sometimes wonder if that was also why Holly couldn't stand to stay with me. She had to share me with the ranch, when other guys could give her all of them.

The thought riles me up.

"Fine," I mutter to myself and whip off my T-shirt and jeans, receiving a cheer from Aurora like she's some bride-to-be at a Magic Mike show. It's interesting watching her slowly let more of her true self come out around me.

As I wade into the lake, the chill of the water electrifies my body, a stark yet welcome contrast to the beaming sun. Muscles I'd grown used to aching soften in relief as the water floats around them. The water's not as high on me when I reach Aurora, where it's around her shoulders, so I dip down to her height. Her eyes follow my chest down, staying on the water's surface for a moment before they flick up to mine.

"Why an eagle?" she ponders, hazel eyes surveying me.

It takes me a second to realise what she's talking about. I'm so used to my tattoos now, I forget about them. "Oh, it's just a reminder."

"Of?" Aurora raises her brows as she swipes her arms along the water's surface, creating gentle ripples. Everything around us is so still and silent, it's just the faint sound of water moving and our voices. Just the two of us.

"My mom always used to say that animals could act as guides throughout our lives—something she learnt from her heritage. She's a quarter Cherokee. I remember her saying, or maybe I read it once, that eagles represent freedom and courage."

Sighing, I let myself float back on the water and stare at the unbelievably clear sky above. Admiring the vastness of it, how I can't remember the last time I really notice of such. The water around me bobs as Aurora joins me on her back. The weightlessness has me wanting to float here for hours.

"When I was at college, realising that I didn't want to do what everyone else wanted me to, I kept seeing eagles everywhere. It was probably a coincidence, but I got the tattoo to remind me that I feel happier when I'm free, not caged. Then I took the job at the ranch."

"Oh my God, and you make fun of me for being a cliché!" Aurora cackles, flicking water over me. I lose my steadiness in the water and have to drop back to my feet before I go under. I shoot her a scowl as she stands in the water again too, still giggling.

That's the last time I'm telling her *anything* vulnerable again.

I splash a huge gush of water in her face, making her scream.

"Hey, that was so uncalled for," she sputters out, wiping the water from her eyes. Droplets cling to her lashes, sparkling. But a smile dances on her strawberry lips.

A mischievous, enticing smile.

"What are you gonna do about it?" I cross my arms, watching her bite down on her bottom lip, hazel eyes burning wild.

Before I can react, Aurora pounds her fists against the water, drenching me with the spray. I spit out the water that got in my mouth, opening my eyes just in time to see her go to do it again so I grab her wrists, yanking her forward to stop her.

Unexpectedly, Aurora's legs wrap around me almost instinctually as her silvery laugh chimes out, echoing across the lake.

I freeze at the contact.

At how well she seems to fit against me.

Aurora's eyes flash as she takes us in—me holding her arms up over my shoulders, her legs circling my waist, our stomachs pressed together, flimsy wet fabric failing to stop us feeling every bit of each other. In the cold water, the heat of her is even more intense, making my body burn at every point we're touching. If she sinks herself any further down my body, I'm going to be in a lot of trouble.

Shivers race through my bones, and I tell myself it's only because the water is cold.

Aurora's breath shudders out, the only sound filling the deafening silence that hangs between us for a beat too many.

"I should get back to the ranch," I suddenly announce. Instantly, we both pull away, eyes darting around at anything but each other.

"Right, yes." Aurora offers a thin smile. "Well, thanks for the ride—oh!" Her brows skyrocket up. "Not on you, obviously, haha. I mean the horses."

"No problem." Cool indifference laces my words as I stride away, trying to pretend that wasn't incredibly awkward. Trying to pretend an image of her riding me didn't flash in my head. "You alright to walk home? I'll take the horses back to the stables on my way back."

"Yeah, of course," Aurora says. "Oh, Wyatt?"

I pause in the water. "Mhm?"

"Would you take a couple of pictures of me in the lake? For my Instagram. My phone is in the pocket of my shorts. Please?"

I fight the groan bubbling in my throat. Not because I don't want to help her—I realise that I'm sadly part of this wellness blog now that it's linked to the ranch with the retreat. But because I don't think it's a good idea to let my eyes lay on Aurora for much longer. Not when I can still feel the warmth of her skin pressed against mine so clearly.

Huffing out a sigh, I say, "Fine. But only a couple."

"Thank you!" she chirps.

When I finally get out the water, regret hits me because I realise we have no towels. Aurora's probably going to sunbathe the water away, whereas I have to use my T-shirt in a futile attempt to dry off. I shuck my jeans back on, denim and wet skin struggling against each other, and rummage through Aurora's clothes for her phone.

When I turn back, Aurora's stood waiting, lake glistening around her like stars floating in the water. Ripples sparkle and cast a shimmer over her freckled, golden skin. Aurora loosens her hair from her scrunchie, letting the wet copper waves flow free.

I feel like I've stumbled upon some goddamn water goddess, honoured to have the opportunity to see such grace.

"Ready?" I ask.

She nods and smiles, trailing her hands along the water's surface again gracefully. I snap a few photos, fingers tightening around the phone as I try to will away the reminder of what it felt like being tangled up with her perfect little body.

Because that is a road I know I'll regret taking.

Thirteen

Aurora

"What the hell is going on?" Wyatt's voice echoes amongst the three ranchers that I've currently got in downward dog.

I flick my head up to see him marching towards us like he's ready for battle, muscles tensed and bulging, so at odds with the happy classical music playing from my speaker. I have to quickly push the reminder of what they felt like against me in the lake the other day out of my mind. He seemed so appalled by us touching, I couldn't let myself even consider he might have enjoyed it even a fraction as much as I shamefully did.

But who wouldn't want to have their legs wrapped around a handsome, muscly cowboy?

That's what Sofia said to me anyway when I video called her straight after to tell her what happened. Just to see if the overwhelming sensation of him would finally leave my brain and body if I confessed about it to someone.

Because the last thing I need right now is for my lonely, still-healing self to get distracted by the reminder of what it feels like to be close to someone again. I'm vulnerable still, and my wounded ego must have just wanted to feel desired, which I shouldn't give in to. If I need love, I can give it to myself. Besides, with the way Wyatt acts around me, it's clear he wouldn't think about me like that.

So, I've tried to keep things between Wyatt and I very light and neutral when he's been helping me with anything to do with the retreat so far this week.

Fortunately, the whole ordeal inspired me to write another article on giving yourself the time and space to heal after experiencing hurt like heartbreak. My boss loved it, surprisingly asking for more articles that feature the *raw honesty* I've been writing with recently. The magic of Sunset Ranch is real, ladies and gentlemen.

The photos Wyatt took of me also served as a great start to marketing the retreat—I could practically feel the happiness and freedom radiating from the picture when I posted it. Which is the exact approach I'm taking when discussing the retreat—a chance to experience freedom, clarity, and joy. A chance to get back to what makes you feel inspired and liberated and *happy*.

Plus, the brand whose sustainably made bikini I was wearing were super happy with the photos, and how the retreat matched their own core values. They've even sent me more to pose in. One of the great perks of influencing.

"Oh hey, boss." Flynn, the youngest ranch hand with a frantic eagerness to him that buzzes despite it being early morning, waves at Wyatt from his bent over position, grinning.

I lower down to my knees and the three guys follow, all shuffling into a crossed leg position whilst Wyatt makes his way over, huffing. Josh and Colt, the other two ranchers stifle their laughs as they watch Wyatt. They're both a year younger than me, apparently in the same school year as Wyatt's younger brother, which I learnt when Wyatt introduced us properly earlier in the week.

Once Wyatt finally reaches us, he crosses his arms, brows raised as he darts his glare between us all.

Josh lazes back. "You gonna join us, boss?"

"*We've* got work to do," Wyatt responds coolly.

"Come on, Hensley," Colt chimes in with a teasing grin, his country drawl the thickest. "You're always so tense. Might help you loosen up a bit."

Rolling dramatically, Wyatt's midnight eyes finally land back on me. There go the butterflies in my stomach again. "What are *you* doing up so early anyway? It's barely light out."

"Just wanting to get a head start on the day."

I press my lips together, feeling a bit like a school kid trying to explain to her teacher why she doesn't have her homework. But I also kind of enjoy the way that, for some reason, this has annoyed him. Probably because he thinks yoga is pointless, and I've got three of his employees proving him very wrong right now.

"The guys came over to say hello when they saw me doing my routine and I invited them to join."

Since the retreat idea got set in motion, I decided to start getting up at a similar time to Wyatt each day. He's working hard on the ranch hours before I even get started on any retreat related matters, and it makes me feel like I should be doing more.

Seven in the morning is my ideal wake up time usually, yet, at Sunset Ranch it's actually been refreshing to get up even earlier. Watching the golden rays of the sunrise bleed down the mountains and through the pastures makes a big difference, but I've also enjoyed the feeling of having so much of the day to go. I need to go to bed an hour or so earlier to compensate, but it's worth it for how much more productive I am in the mornings—especially with making up new social media posts to discuss the retreat in.

"It's been real fun, boss," Flynn admits, one corner of his mouth hooked up. "Miss Rory's *really* flexible. She's been showing us all kinds of positions."

A muscle in Wyatt's jaw ticks as Flynn talks, but he's still looking at me. Flynn's groan cuts his attention away quickly though, and we all gape as the nineteen year old pushes himself impressively into a crab pose, which I definitely did *not* show him how to do.

"See, imagine all the things you could do in this position. Bet you can't do it." Flynn's voice is strangled as he shows off, before he makes a pained noise and falls back to the ground. I have to bite my lip to keep in my chuckle at Wyatt's twisted features.

"I don't *want* to do that," he grunts, angling his jaw.

Colt moves himself back into downward dog and looks at Wyatt. "Don't knock it 'til you've tried it, Hensley."

When both Josh and Flynn share a grin and also return to their downward dogs, Wyatt scowls at me, eyes constricting. It's quite a sight, three muscly cowboys with their asses in the air on a Friday morning.

"See it as a test run for the yoga sessions I'll do at the retreat." I shrug at him and get on my knees, then nod to the space next to Josh. Wyatt's eyes rocket heavenward before he sighs and shocks me by getting down on his knees too. His scowl never leaves his face, though. I wink at him, wetting my lips. "I'll go easy on you, don't worry."

"That's it, boss," Josh snorts, and Wyatt whacks him on his rib, almost knocking him over.

He widens his eyes at me impatiently. "Let's get this over and done with then."

"Right, get into tabletop." I move onto all fours and wait until Wyatt does the same. I show him how to push up and back into downward dog, which he can't do without grunting. I'm so pissed off that I don't have my phone nearby to get a picture of this right now.

All four of them watch as I show them how to bring their foot forward and lift up, then stretch their arms out into a warrior two pose. Their attempts are plagued with wobbles and a lack of balance, yet they all manage it eventually in one smooth sweep, and now they try it with their left leg. Flynn's astounded at himself for how easily he does it this time, beaming.

"Excellent boys." I jump to a stand as I walk around, inspecting their warrior poses and adjusting their posture slightly.

When I reach Wyatt, I hesitate until his eyes catch mine, a flicker of dark wildness still behind them. I don't know why but my breath catches, fluttering picking up in my stomach.

He perks a brow at me, no smile. "If this is what you're spending your days doing while I'm busting my ass off working on the ranch, we need to rethink our business plan."

"Arms up a little higher," I say, gently setting my fingers against his arms, lifting them. Wyatt flinches faintly as gooseflesh covers his skin but tries to keep his composure, following my directions. "Actually, whilst you've been supposedly *busting your ass off*, I've already got four of my influencer friends on board for the trial run."

Even my ex's friend, Rowan, reached out asking to come, saying he condemned Jake's behaviour, and offered to help with anything if I needed it. People are lapping up all the posts I've been sharing about the retreat and my excitement is buzzing.

Wyatt's face lights up, whatever disdain he had for me this morning wiped away. He eases into his position more, shoulders dropping. "Seriously?"

I flick my hair behind my shoulders. "What can I say? I'm amazing."

"Yeah..." Wyatt angles his head. "Something like that."

A softness fills his eyes now as he regards me, gaze flicking about my face. He doesn't counter me, insult me, or whatever he would usually do—instead, it feels like he's actually *looking* at me properly, for the first time. Like he's finally noticed the real me... and it feels far too vulnerable.

Snapping myself out of it, I pull myself away, raising my voice to speak to the whole group again. "Right, um, shift your weight forward a little for a good stretch, and hold it there for a few seconds. Remember to breathe through it."

Whilst they're all facing away from me, I use it as a chance to go grab my phone from the deck and take a few photos of them all. Wyatt's huffing and tries to check his watch from where his arm is stretched out ahead of him.

"Is there a prize for the best warrior pose?" Flynn questions, mischief lacing every word. "Maybe a date with the yoga teacher?"

"How about an extra day shovelling horse shit for asking stupid questions?" Wyatt retorts, all sour-faced as he glares at the back of Josh's head. It's the perfect distraction for me to creep around him.

"Smile!" I shout, jumping in front of Wyatt and snapping a selfie of me with him doing his warrior pose behind.

"You little—" He lunges for me and the phone.

Squealing, I manage to duck away and run, but my legs are no match for his, and in a few seconds one big arm hooks around me.

My back is suddenly crushed against his chest, feeling the outline of his muscles again, like when we were riding together. Heat and rapid breaths encompass us as I try my best to lean forward, holding the phone out of his reach.

"Give it to me, you menace," Wyatt demands.

"But... it will be... such a good... promo for the retreat," I wheeze out, scrambling and laughing in Wyatt's grip, fighting so hard to get away, whilst also secretly revelling in the way he grips me, a hand splayed across my waist. Even a few laughs rumble from his chest as he struggles to get the phone.

"Rory, over here!" Josh calls out, just in time for me to lob the phone through the air to him before Wyatt spins me around and pins me against the deck.

Wrists held above my head, Wyatt presses me up against the fence. All the breath whooshes out of my lungs—not from the impact, which he surprisingly manages to keep gentle, but from the way his body is now inches from mine, head dipped, dark lashes lowered as he stares down at me.

His gaze has darkened to a point that all I can see is two pools of molten and wild midnight. It lingers over my face, touching my lips once, making me swallow.

There's not enough space to avoid my chest from rocking against his with our racing breaths. I try to wiggle in his grip, but it just brushes my breasts against him, and his eyes drop down, noticing exactly that. I'm encompassed by the scent of leather and pinewood radiating off him.

Why do we keep getting ourselves in these positions? And why is my stomach fluttering like a thousand beating butterfly wings?

"Yoo hoo!" Josh whistles from behind.

Wyatt turns to see him waving the phone about. He curses and tears back to me, confliction painting his face as he rakes his eyes up my body to where he's still clasping my hands.

"You are a pain in my ass, Aurora Jones. You know that?" Wyatt rips himself from me, though he's not looking quite as repelled by the idea of us touching as he did the other day.

"At your service, sir," I giggle and pretend curtsy.

"You better delete that photo," he says, crossing his arms.

Josh jogs over, a toothy grin meeting me when he winks and hands me back my phone. Wyatt's already started walking off, throwing a vulgar gesture at the other two ranchers laughing at him.

"And what if I don't?" I call out to him, still riled up by the challenge in his eyes.

He halts, broad shoulders tensing. Lazily, Wyatt glances over his shoulder, making my insides melt with the darkened gaze that still lingers in his eyes, daring me. "Oh, I'll find a way to ruin you, Princess."

Ruin me.

My whole body tightens at the words, breath catching.

Then he announces, voice booming, "Right, the ranch needs us, boys. Let's go."

"Same time tomorrow?" I shout after them, biting down on my lip as they all give me a *hell yes* in response, except for Wyatt, who just shakes his head.

Fourteen

Wyatt

"**P**inch my cheek one more time, Aurora, and I'll take back my offer to help with the retreat," I grumble, freezing just inside the door frame to try and cool down my irritation.

I don't know whether to put Aurora's frantic energy this afternoon down to her being excited that the meeting we just had with the council went well or nervous that it didn't. Although we'd sorted out most of the legalities with shifting the ranch into a partial retreat, the Willow Ridge council had to sign off on the change—nothing happens in this town without going past them. Luckily, Wolfman's mom is on the council, so she was already singing our praises in advance to soften the famously tough crowd. But honestly, Aurora smashed it. We'd spent the last few nights prepping for every possible question or concern they might have had, and even talked about ways local businesses could get involved once the retreat is fully up and running.

Assuming it all works out and that's even what she wants.

Either way, whatever has got Aurora in this mood where she enjoys annoying me too much, I need to make her snap out of it because she's pushing me into a corner of irritation that makes me want to touch her so badly. Especially after that day in the lake. I don't know why but I just can't get the way she felt against me off my mind. I'm itching to grab her perfect little body and make her shut up with my mouth.

I was seconds away from caving the other day when I had her pressed up against the deck after I chased her because she took that stupid selfie with me in the background doing yoga. When her breasts were heaving against me, lips parted and inviting—

Quit getting carried away, Wyatt.

"But then you wouldn't get to work with me every day, and I know how much you'd miss that," Aurora counters with a daring grin, and flicks her sneakers off. They land lopsided, so once I've taken my boots off I nudge our shoes around making them sit side by side, nice and neatly. I look up to catch her perking a brow at me, hands on her hips.

I frown. "That's debatable."

She waves me off with a giggle—the kind that seems so at odds with the crying girl I found on her deck the other week. "You just looked like you enjoyed it *so* much when Mrs Wolfe pinched your cheek, I thought you'd want to experience it again."

Aurora skips off into the open-plan living room. She begins filtering through some folders on the coffee table, humming and checking up at me with a mischievous glint in her eyes.

I let my eyes flutter closed as I take in a breath, begging for patience before my sigh rumbles out. "Firstly, I clearly did *not* enjoy it when she pinched my cheek in front of the *whole* council—I literally told you that. And secondly," I find my way to the coffee table, her breath hitching when she spins around, inches away, "even if I did enjoy it, you then continuing to pinch my cheeks *seven* more times in the span of the twenty minute journey home ruined that."

She snorts, too amused by herself.

"But you're such a *big, grown up boy with a big, grown up business* now," Aurora teases, attempting an accent as close to Mrs Wolfe's as possible. She bites down on her lip straight after, a menacing smile held back.

"Have you found those paint swatches from Cherry yet?" I ask, changing the subject back to the real reason I even came into her house.

Getting Cherry on board for decorating the guesthouses, given her interior design background, was a no-brainer. It's the perfect opportunity to get expert advice on how to make the guesthouses feel as relaxing as possible, while also offering Cherry experience that'll give her a competitive edge when it comes to applying for internships and jobs in the next year. Knowing I could help both Cherry and Aurora out at the same time made me feel useful.

"I thought they were down here." Aurora's grin disappears and she scrambles through the folders again, huffing when her search appears futile.

I flop down onto the cream couch, shuffling into the patchwork throw that's draped over the back. It might be the first time I've properly sat down all day, apart from driving. Despite that, my shoulders feel oddly at ease in comparison to normal. I don't feel the usual need to roll them about to loosen the tension. I can hear the reason why blaring in my mind, but even if it's silently, I'm not ready to admit that the yoga Aurora's roped us into doing every morning now might actually have helped.

"Maybe they're upstairs. Come on."

It takes me a second to realise Aurora's waving at me to join her on her continued search upstairs. I make a whining noise, hoping I could stay sat here for more than ten seconds but apparently not. When I don't move, she whines back and waves even more wildly. I concede and follow her upstairs with a deep sigh.

"And you said you thought I was kinky," I comment, nodding to the tripod and camera set up at the end of her bed when we reach her room. Aurora spins, brow furrowed until she notices what I'm staring at. I don't hold back my smirk as I lean in the doorframe. "Is wellness and positivity influencer code for something else?"

"You wish." Her eyes roll, a subsequent sneer thrown my way, but I don't miss the way her cheeks take on a rosier flush. "I was filming myself meditating *actually*. My followers sometimes like to do live sessions with me in the morning."

"Wait." I push off the door frame further into the room as Aurora starts rummaging through a bag. I'm trying really hard not to stare at her ass right now as she's so blatantly bent over in front of me. "People literally watch you sit in silence on your bed? And you get paid for that?"

"Well, I get paid to do posts for brands, but I have done some live sessions with different companies' meditations playing, so yeah, I guess so. Ah ha!" Aurora jumps up, paint swatches in hand and she fist pumps the air. She hops over to me. "Here you go."

"Thanks." I pocket the swatches. I guess I should probably go, maybe pick up the paint or check on some of the cattle—actually do my job—but something makes me want to stay... "So, what is so great about this meditating? I don't get it."

Aurora lets out a breathy laugh, the corners of her mouth twitching. "Get on the bed."

I freeze. That wasn't exactly where I was expecting this afternoon to go. "Excuse me?"

"Get on the bed and I'll show you how meditating works."

I run my hand along my angled jaw. "Once again, I feel the need to ask—is wellness and positivity influencer code for something?"

"Oh, shut up and do as you're told," she retorts.

Offering back a sneer to mirror hers, I cross my arms. "I thought we established you're not my boss, I don't have to do as you say."

Aurora tilts her head at me, brows raised. "Wyatt, you can't do this retreat and not have a clue what meditating is. Just do this once."

"Ask nicely."

With a roll of her eyes, fire beginning to dance behind them, Aurora scoffs. She glances away from me for a few seconds, then snaps her gaze back. "Fine, *please* get on the bed."

Fuck, that wasn't quite how I was expecting her to phrase it. The way my body suddenly zapped to life with her words is also not ideal. The room in the edges of my vision seems to darken, all the light pooling around her.

Suddenly, her hazel eyes catch me, glistening as she steps forward slowly, forcing me backwards until the back of my legs hit the bed. I drop down onto it, my legs spread out with Aurora practically standing between them. The whole position makes me swallow now that I'm the one staring up at her. Sunlight radiates through the window behind her, giving her a golden glow that feels too angelic with the way she's towering over me.

"Close your eyes," she instructs next, nothing given away in her expression for me to decipher what the hell she's thinking.

I'd actually rather have the annoyingly excitable Aurora back from earlier just because then she'd give me some daring grin to tell me she was up to something. But no, instead I've just got two big hazel eyes twinkling at me, waiting for me to abide. I huff out a sigh when I finally do and a few seconds later some calming music begins to play.

I shift about trying to get comfortable and my leg brushes Aurora's, making me freeze again at how close she is. It's really the last thing I need right now when I'm trying to focus. My mind is anything but clear when her body is on it.

"Just let yourself relax. Focus on breathing in through your nose and out through your mouth." Aurora demonstrates and I try to match the pace of her long, slow breaths and—

Her hand covers my chest making me start.

"You're breathing a lot through your chest but if you focus on breathing through your stomach it will feel deeper."

"Right, okay," I say through gritted teeth, aware that I actually haven't let out a breath since she touched me. And then when her fingers trail down my chest to my stomach, my whole body tightens. I don't know how I'll get the memory of her long nails tracking down my abs out of my head now.

"Wyatt," Aurora whispers. She must lean closer because I suddenly get a hit of her bright, citrus scent.

"Yep?"

"You're not breathing."

"Right," I finally sigh out, shaking my head a little. I'm practically panting now as I take in a few more gulps of air to compensate. Heat crawls across my skin, over the back of my neck, as I try to push the embarrassing fact that I literally forgot how to breathe because a woman just touched me from my memory.

And that I can hear Aurora's breathy little snigger at such.

She must think I'm such an idiot.

I'm about to open my eyes and end this uncomfortable moment when whatever meditation she's playing starts talking, telling me that I am capable of anything I put my mind to. Sure.

"I didn't think people spoke in meditations."

"Only some, but I prefer them. I find it helpful to have someone's voice guiding me and reassuring me."

It kind of makes sense for her really—the number of times I've heard her give herself little pep talks, like when we were riding for the first time the other week and before the meeting we had today, suggests she likes to talk things through. And like that time when she confessed everything she was feeling on the porch swing after our night at the bar. Watching her face brighten and body soften as the tension disappeared with each sentence was pretty relieving.

"I'll keep that in mind," I find myself saying.

The meditation pauses and when I open my eyes, Aurora's still stood between my legs, looking down at me with promising hazel eyes and copper waves tumbling over half her face. It's going to take a lot more effort than I first thought to remove myself from this position with the soft energy holding us so close together.

"I'm surprised you haven't got your phone out, snapping secret photos of me," I jest, trying to change the mood.

Aurora rolls her lips with a bashful smile, bringing my attention to where they're all shiny from her strawberry coloured lip gloss. Damn, I wonder if they taste like strawberry too?

Nope, I shouldn't be thinking about that.

"Anyway," I laugh, "you've missed your chance because believe me, that's the first and only time you'll ever catch me meditating. I think I'll stick to riding."

She tucks some of her hair behind her ear as she asks, "Riding?"

"Yeah, that's how I clear my head." And it's exactly what I plan on doing once I leave this house, because there's no way I'm going to be able to focus for the rest of the day when all I can think about is her hands against my chest, trailing down my stomach.

Fifteen

Aurora

"I know I've already thanked you, but I'm so grateful for this!" Cherry squeals, wrapping me in a tight hug, swathes of black hair almost suffocating me. Though I just tighten my arms around her because I'll happily lap up the love.

"You do realise I was the one who suggested you to her, right?" Wyatt scoffs from where he's carefully pouring creamy peach paint into several trays for us.

Honestly, it was kind of sweet how Wyatt immediately thought of Cherry, looking for ways to help her out. Even if he likes to play his usual act of indifference, I see how much he cares for her. I hadn't realised until she told me the other day that he helps pay for materials for her college course when her money doesn't stretch far enough.

It makes me realise even more why having the ranch is so important to him. No wonder he was so annoyed about me wanting to sell the place.

Still, Cherry's plans for the guesthouses are a bit more complicated than whatever Auntie Grace quickly put together, so to keep everything on schedule, we're all chipping in when the contractors aren't here.

Like painting the walls that were going to stay wooden but have now been plastered. But we've kept some with feature walls of the original wooden panelling, to create a light yet rustic feel.

And that means spending my weekends and evenings with Wyatt, as well as my daytimes.

Not that it's a problem, really.

It's just that I'm having to work a little bit harder against my healing ego, and not look too far into each time Wyatt smiles at me, flashing those dimples, instead of his usual scowl. Or give too much thought to the way my core heats each time he accidentally touches me. Or let the deep, husky voice saying *I'll find a way to ruin you, Princess* stay in my head for too long.

I'm sure it's just another challenge the universe is sending me—a test to see how well I'm concentrating on what really matters.

Like healing and focusing on me.

And getting that inspiration back.

And building an amazing new business venture.

As opposed to falling for another guy who will undoubtedly break my heart when I'm still fragile.

But I'm not falling for Wyatt. At all. I just mean that it's easy when you're healing from heartbreak to be led astray.

And to prove that I'm not interested in him, I've made myself look extra resistible this evening with a baggy white T-shirt which pretty much covers my old, washed-out gym shorts. My waves are messily shoved into a low bun, half of them hanging out to signal I'm not dressing up for anyone here tonight.

Besides, as Cherry's not working at Duke's tonight, she's helping out and can act as a buffer for any unwanted tension. The kind that felt electrified between Wyatt and I when he had me pressed against the deck last week. The kind that seems to still linger whenever we're together, which feels like most of the time. I kind of regret roping the ranchers into morning yoga every day now, because it takes me a while to cool off from the way my body buzzes aş Wyatt watches me stretch with eyes full of dark wonder.

Once Cherry releases me, she waltzes over to her brother and grabs one of the paint rollers beside him. "Yes, brother. Don't worry I appreciate you too. Does your ego feel better now?"

Wyatt sucks in a long breath, eyes closed before glancing at me, ignoring Cherry. "I reckon we'll get just as much done without her here, you know?"

Gasping in fake pain, Cherry knocks Wyatt on the head with her paint roller, eliciting a curse from him before he shoves her. I can just see one of them putting their foot in a tray of paint and slipping or getting paint over the newly fitted kitchen counters. In hindsight, maybe we should've covered those with plastic as well as the floor.

"Children!" I holler, failing to hide my amusement.

Wyatt's just about to give Cherry a second shove after she swung the paint roller at him and missed, but he halts, sighing and stepping away. He crosses his arms with a pout, midnight eyes seething at me, like I'm some killjoy.

"I hate to imagine what you're like when Hunter's around." I just shake my head at him, a bemused giggle escaping.

Cherry holds her hands up in surrender, paint roller swaying. "Okay, okay! How about I get out of the way and start on the bedroom while you guys do in here? Happy?"

The usual shrug and grunt comes from Wyatt before he picks up another paint roller and dips it in the tray. Cherry takes that as a yes and gives me a wave, then grabs a tray and the sage green can of paint she picked for the bedroom and heads out the living area.

There goes my buffer.

It's fine. I'm a strong, independent woman who can separate herself from her distractions, so that they don't separate her from her goals and the life she wants.

Bolstered by my internal pep talk, I pick up the last paint roller and smother it in paint from the tray, watching the grey material soak up the peachy liquid. The sound of it splattering and squelching against the wall as I roll it on is oddly satisfying.

In fact, watching the paint strokes slowly cover the walls, white plaster melting into early evening sunset peach, is incredibly therapeutic. Whatever acoustic music Wyatt's playing through his speaker only calms me more, and I fall into a blissful rhythm of spreading paint across the walls, unaware of the time passing.

I think Wyatt must feel the same way, because he's been silent too the whole time, dark eyes locked intently on the roller as he finishes off the wall he's working on. I try not to let my eyes linger too much on the way his muscles shift under his thin grey T-shirt—

Wyatt's phone chimes loudly over the speaker making me yelp and almost drop the roller. That'll teach me for staring.

"Jesus, Aurora. Calm down, it's just a text," Wyatt scolds me, angled face all pinched before he whips out his phone.

"It was loud," I retort, not liking the way his face hasn't softened since he unlocked his phone, ignoring my reply.

The screen's light reflects in his eyes, only highlighting the discontent lingering in them. It makes me wonder if the text is from his ex, the one he said sometimes checks in on him. But when something almost akin to realisation descends on his features, mouth curving, cheeks and brows lifting, I stupidly hope it's not her.

"Everything okay?" I ask, worrying my lip.

"Yeah," he laughs, pocketing his phone and running a hand through his loose dark curls. He waits a second before finally looking at me, making me feel so on edge for no reason. Why is my heart suddenly beating so fast now his midnight eyes are locked with mine? "The council said yes. The retreat can officially go ahead."

If I thought my heart was already racing, then now it feels like it might explode.

I knew the meeting on Monday had gone reasonably well—the six middle-aged Willow Ridge residents that made up the council seemed far more receptive to the idea than Wyatt had prepped me for. Especially now I've had twelve influencers interested in visiting, so we've decided to do a second trial two weeks after the first.

I think I've been so caught up on everything else that I hadn't realised what the meeting actually signified, though. I'd been following my usual advice—to focus on the small steps, as opposed to the whole staircase. Market the retreat, get friends to come and trial it, plan out activities, decorate the guesthouses, organise the decking to be built by the lake for lakeside yoga sessions, order in extra horse-riding gear for lessons and trails, and so on.

But now I'm staring up, overwhelmed by the length of the ascent. This feels bigger than the nightshade mountains encompassing the ranch. If the retreat happens and it's successful, then it could become permanent. And so would my time here at Sunset Ranch.

I'd be living in Willow Ridge. Permanently.

Is that why Wyatt looked disappointed?

But then he smiled?

I'm not sure if I'm ready for—

"Aurora? Did you hear me?" Wyatt steps forwards, brows drawn in with concern. His eyes keep flicking between mine, but I'm struggling to move.

I haven't frozen like this since I caught Jake.

"Yeah, I..." I'm clutching the paint roller so tight, my knuckles hurt. There's so many thoughts swirling through my head right now all I can do is try to concentrate on keeping my breathing steady, despite the fact that my heart is rattling against my chest again.

Wyatt quickly drops his paint roller back in the tray and returns to prise mine from my hands, his leather and pinewood scent diffusing through the smell of paint. He unfurls each of my fingers from the roller gently, keeping hold of my hand as he lowers it to the ground and stands back up. The heat of his skin against mine draws my attention to where we're touching.

Where his thumb is gently stroking over my knuckles.

Back and forth. Constantly.

"What's going on in that head of yours?" His voice is like distant thunder, a deep rumble that reminds you that you're safe and warm inside. I really appreciate the way he's not just asked if I'm okay, giving me an easy way out by just saying *yeah, I'm fine.*

I take in a shallow breath. "I'm suddenly really scared."

Wyatt's fingers pulse against my hand.

Searching charcoal eyes behold me. So still and focused. Opposite to how my mind feels right now.

"That's understandable," he admits, lips twitching into a brief smile. I think he's going to leave it there when silence drags between us—I know he's not usually into discussing his emotions and all that unlike me—but he squeezes my hand again. "What's scaring you in particular?"

I almost miss the way he glances at my lip when I bite down on it. "If this all works, then I might stay here. It's a big change, and I don't... I'm not sure if I can do it. I've never run a retreat before. A trial run is a lot easier than a full blown business. What if it's all too much?"

Wyatt steals another inch of space between us. I can feel the warmth radiating off his body now and I have to stretch my neck up to keep my eyes locked with his, completely encapsulated by them.

When we've been this close before, I've felt daunted, nervous, exhilarated. But today, I feel safe.

No anxiety, just security.

Like Wyatt is this shield blocking out the rest of the world. Slotting himself between me and the enormous mountain peak that is my current dream, so that its looming shadow doesn't seem as frightening.

"If it's all too much, then you'll find a way to get through it. Just like you have before," Wyatt insists, grabbing my other hand in the process, bones tingling in response. "You're smart, Aurora, and probably the most passionate, determined woman I've ever met. You're the kind of person who takes adversity by the reins and rides it. If anyone can succeed in this, it's you."

Every word embraces my heart, calming it. I want to lose myself in the swirling night skies of his eyes, in the smoky timbre of his voice.

"Besides," Wyatt shrugs, letting his smile fully play out, coaxing mine from its hiding place too, "you're not alone. You've got me to help you out when things get difficult. We're in this together, right? Business partners?"

And with that I'm reminded that I can't get lost in him like part of me wants to. He's right—he's here to support me, yes, but as friends.

Business partners. Which is how it needs to stay if I want things to run smoothly. It's going to be a lot harder to run away again if things get messy, because I'll have a retreat that needs me.

And a home I'm not sure I want to leave just yet.

Plus, I need to be able to support myself. I need to pull myself out of any spiral I've gone into, just like I used to be able to do when I evidently believed in myself more. Even if Wyatt's words and soothing touch have made me feel safe, if I get too used to that, what happens if he leaves? I can't always expect him to be my shoulder.

Pressing my lips together, I give him a nod and loosen my hands from his. "Thanks, Wyatt, really. I know I'm just being silly. I just get in my head sometimes."

"Right." His hands stay in front of him for a beat before he runs them through his hair robotically and clears his throat. Wyatt picks the paint rollers back up and hands me mine. "Anyway, I'm scared too."

My face scrunches. "You are?"

"Oh yeah." A playful smirk flashes as he spins to dip his roller in the tray beside him. "The idea of having to see you every day with no end in sight is just terrifying."

"Such a dick," I say under my breath.

I don't know what comes over me next, but in one quick swoop, I shove my roller in the paint and slide it down his back, paint dripping off every inch of him.

Wyatt freezes mid-motion and I smack my hand over my mouth with a gasp as I process what I've just done.

Painfully slow, he spins on his heel to face me, eyes molten black. Maybe he's finally calculated his way to ruin me—

My vision is blocked by a spongy roller and coat of paint covering me from head to toe. I let out a scream, but it becomes a sputter when paint gets in my mouth, which makes Wyatt howl with laughter. I hate that even though he's done this, hearing him laugh makes my legs go a little weak.

Finally wiping enough paint out of my eyes to prise them open, I immediately see Wyatt's creased face and swing my roller at him.

He catches it whilst also trying to jump out of the way. There's a loud squelch as his foot lands in the paint tray—

And then we're both falling, paint rollers flying.

Wyatt plummets to the floor with a thud, groaning when I then flop onto him, headbutting his chest. Pain rackets through me from the impact against his solid body, but all I can do is laugh.

Uncontrollably. Wyatt too.

His arms wrap around me, one hand sifting through my hair, the other seeking the small of my back. Shaking with the tremors of both our laughter, I tip my face up to see his dazed grin. Either he hit his head super hard, or he's enjoying this way too much.

"Are you okay?" I question, aware that he definitely felt the brunt of the fall, with the extra weight of me landing on him.

He lightly strokes the back of my head, lips curving higher. I have to fight the urge to close my eyes and sink into him. Partially because I don't want to get even more paint on him.

"Never been happier," he admits, fingers trailing from my hair to my painted jaw and—

"What the hell is going on?" Cherry's voice startles us both as she marches into the room. Shock sparks in her eyes when I turn and she gets a good look at my face, plastered in peach paint. I'd almost forgotten what a mess I must look like, because Wyatt definitely wasn't regarding me like I was.

And he still hasn't let me go yet.

"Um... we were fighting, and then, well, we fell," I confess.

"You two are so weird," Cherry chuckles, rolling her eyes. "Just glad I wasn't walking in on anything more."

Part of me wonders if she'd have been a few minutes later, even a few seconds later, whether there would've been *more* to walk in on. But I can't let myself consider that. So instead, I reluctantly peel myself away from Wyatt to carry on painting.

Emphasis on the *reluctantly*.

Sixteen

Wyatt

"That's actually incredible," Aurora admits, hazel eyes wide as she watches the video on her phone of Sawyer's most recent bull riding win. "But also terrifying. I don't get how you stay on."

Cherry's working at the bar tonight, so it's just Aurora with us three guys in our booth, while Duke is behind the bar. I expect he'll join us for a drink later. You wouldn't think Aurora's only been hanging out with us for around a month now with the way she slots so naturally into our group.

Sawyer stretches his arms behind his head, relaxing back in the booth with a smug grin. "Years of practice, baby. If working with Hensley doesn't drive you away before December, you can join the guys when they come watch me win the PBR world championship."

I almost miss the way Aurora gives me a side glance because I'm struck by the reminder that she might not be here forever. It feels weird given how she's become a part of my daily life. December is still months away, and there's a heavy possibility she could be gone before that—her panic the other day when we were painting was a sobering reminder that she's not one hundred percent keen on living in Willow Ridge permanently.

Even if the retreat works, I have no doubt Aurora will miss England eventually. I know I would if it was the other way around. Yet, the idea of her no longer being around the ranch, making my life more difficult, makes an emptiness hang in my chest.

A very *unexpected* emptiness.

I mean, for God's sake, I've gotten so used to being forced into morning yoga with her and the other ranchers now, it would be weird to suddenly just wake up and head out to work without her shouting different positions at me.

I just don't like change, that's all.

"Sounds great." Aurora nods, a soft smile gracing her lips. Sawyer beams even at her faint consideration. "Did you always want to do bull riding, or did you want to pursue football, like Wyatt? I just assumed as that's how you guys said you lot became friends."

Sawyer shakes his head. "Nah, I always had it planned that I was gonna run off with the rodeo. Football was fun, but never endgame for me." What he doesn't say is he didn't even consider college because it still meant coming back home to his dad for the holidays. The rodeo gave him an all-year opportunity to get away.

"Hey, Sawyer." A curvy brunette struts past the booth, giving Sawyer a wave, completely oblivious to the fact that she's walked right in front of Cherry who was heading over with a tray. It's enough to dim the agony that was creeping into Sawyer's eyes, immediately perking him up as he waves back, twisting to watch her.

She settles in a booth with a few other women I recognise from high school, who are all smiling and batting their eyelashes our way. One of them, Lyla, mouths *hey* to me, and I immediately look away, checking if Aurora has seen, but luckily she's facing Wolfman now.

Not that she'd care.

The way she jumped away from me when we fell in the paint the other day made it clear she doesn't plan to spend any more time on top of me. Which is exactly how I should be feeling too... it's just hard when every time we're together we seem to end up all close, the little space between us a mix of her bright scent and our hot breaths.

Cherry rolls her eyes when she reaches the booth, mumbling, "I'm gonna make Duke ban these buckle bunnies one day."

"And what about you?" Aurora asks Wolfman.

He grins, as if it's a silly question. "Oh, I still like to play, but being a coach means I get to shout at kids and tell them what to do as opposed to actually doing it myself. It's great."

"I thought you did it for the hot moms?" I jab.

He runs his fingers through his hair. "I forget you guys know about that now. It was a low point in my life, but to be fair she did have massive—"

"Oh my God!" Aurora suddenly yells, thankfully cutting Wolfman off, bouncing in her seat. Cherry almost drops the tray of glasses she's been stacking. "Oh, this is like my favourite song! *Please* can we go dance?" She tugs on my shirt, eyes bright and imploring.

I cock my head to listen out for the song, expecting it to be some silly pop number, but it's *Stand by Me* by Ben E. King, which immediately humbles me. Still, I don't budge even when Aurora's climbing out the booth, humming along to the intro. She holds out her hands to us all.

"Sure, Wyatt loves dancing," Wolfman declares, nudging me with an elbow. I shoot him a scowl before turning back to Aurora.

"Not a chance," I laugh and pick up my tumbler, taking a sip. There's a reason the dance floor in Duke's is practically non-existent in size. This is a drinking bar, not a dancing bar, save for the odd night with a bit of live music, but even then rarely do people feel compelled to start jumping about.

And that's how I like it. Chilled. Not making a fool of myself.

Aurora pouts, pressing her fists to her hips. That childish little face she makes always has my eyes rolling. "Fine. Cherry, you'll dance with me right?"

"Girl, I would if I wasn't working," she says, bumping her hip to Aurora's.

"Hmm..." Aurora looks behind her, towards where Duke is at the bar. She cups her hands around her mouth as she yells across the room, making the rest of the customers turn to her. "Hey, Duke! You don't mind if Cherry dances with me for one song, do you?"

Duke's eyes widen as he freezes mid-wiping a glass. There's no way he's going to say no—he's way too reserved to get into a shouting match with Aurora across the bar, and I honestly don't think he'd care enough whether Cherry was working or not. She seems to get away with murder around him.

Duke darts his eyes between the two girls, then he shrugs and shakes his head. Cherry bites her lip, holding in a grin as Aurora grabs her hand and drags her off towards the dance floor, leaving the tray of glasses on our table.

Sawyer shoots me a wink, then knocks back the rest of his whiskey, sliding out the booth as he shouts, "I'm coming too, Red!"

Once they're on the dance floor, Sawyer holds both girls' hands, spinning them about. Taking in turns, he lets each girl roll into him, giving them a little sway before swinging them back out. There's so much joy radiating off them, and it's all down to Aurora. Just like the rising morning sun, she has a beautiful way of lighting up everything around her.

It should piss me off, the fact that Sawyer's touching my little sister. But truthfully, that's not what's got my blood rushing, or my knuckles whitening around the tumbler I'm clenching way too hard. No, it's the fact that he's also touching Aurora. And up until now, I'd been the only guy in Willow Ridge blessed to know how she feels in my hands. Even if it has been accidentally.

I can't stop focusing on every time their bodies brush, every time they smile at each other, every time Aurora places a hand on his chest. I can't stop gawking at how goddamn sexy Aurora looks when she dances—even when she's just being silly, because she's so bright and golden when she's being her true self. The way her tight black dress shows off her ass as her hips sway, the muscles in her legs working as she moves, her copper waves shining under the lights like a flickering bonfire. It's all too much.

I don't even care that it's Sawyer, it wouldn't matter who it was dancing with her—and that's the problem. A few weeks ago, I would've done anything to get rid of her, happily palm her off into another guy's arms so she'd maybe leave me and my ranch alone. But now, my whole body is tense. I'm unable to rip my stare away from them, and my stomach is churning—

"You should go dance with her," Wolfman suggests nonchalantly, not even looking my way.

"Nah, I'm good." I pick up my whiskey, trying to relax back into the booth so it doesn't look like I'm being a jealous, glowering idiot. I focus on the alcohol burning my throat, hoping it will chill out whatever feelings are surfacing right now. Whatever feelings I don't really have a right to feel.

"Funny," Wolfman perks a brow at me, "I just assumed you'd want to, given it looked like you were about to pop a vein scowling at them."

I clench my teeth, then retort back, "Maybe it's because Sawyer's got his hands on my little sister."

Wolfman just shrugs and eases back into the seat, but he's failing at hiding the shit-eating grin plastered across his face. "You don't really care about that right now, though, do you?"

I sigh and wipe my face. I need new friends who don't know me so well that they can figure out everything I'm feeling before even I do. No doubt that's why Sawyer winked too.

Goddamn. Have I been that obvious?

Does Aurora know too? I thought I'd fought back these feelings well enough.

Taking in a deep breath, I shoot a look at Wolfman, and he angles his beer towards the dance floor. I make it seem like it's taking every ounce of effort to lug myself out the booth and over to the dance floor, when really my pulse is racing the nearer I get to her.

They pause when I reach them. Cherry's eyes widen before her face settles into a knowing smirk at how I'm offering my hand to Aurora. Sawyer lets go of Aurora, giving her a soft nudge towards me, and her eyes sparkle as they meet mine. The dim lights make her cheekbones glisten, and her cheeks flush pink.

Aurora's hand slips into mine, electricity sparking from the touch. I pull her towards me, sliding one arm around her waist, noting Sawyer do the same with Cherry beside us. But I don't give another thought to my sister when Aurora's warm body presses into mine, and her hand trails up over my shoulder, fingers brushing against my bare neck, leaving fire in their wake.

Honey-brown eyes twinkle up at me and her fingers pulse in mine as I start to sway us from side to side. I have no idea how to dance and probably look like a goddamn robot, but I think I might be able to endure it given how brightly Aurora is beaming at me right now. I think I might be able to endure a lot more for her.

"Hi," she whispers.

"Hi," I say back, eyes dipping to where she's caught her bottom lip between her teeth. I shouldn't be looking at her lips for so long.

Sparks dance behind the hazel eyes staring back at me. I'm not even sure I can hear the music anymore, just my heart rattling in my chest. I thought coming over here would rid me of all those feelings, yet now I'm just drowning in even more of them.

I abruptly spin Aurora around, breaking the contact between our bodies briefly, giving me a second to compose myself. She gives a little squeal of delight, before stumbling back into me, hand returning to my neck again, this time brushing up and down.

"Thanks for dancing with me."

"Thought I'd save you from Sawyer's terrible dance moves."

"Right." Aurora nods, rolling her lips.

And then she does the worst possible thing and rests her head against my chest. Right where my eagle tattoo spreads out. The reminder that I'm happier when I'm free is torturous, because if I truly let myself do what I wanted right now, then I'd be dragging Aurora back to the truck and straight to the ranch, so no one else can touch her but me.

I can barely move from how tense my body goes. What if she hears how hard my heart is beating?

My hand is splayed across the small of her back, thumb stroking the delicate curve of her waist. I've never felt so much of her for so long before, pressed against me everywhere, and it's overwhelming. The citrus scent from her hair takes over my senses, giving me that same shot of dopamine that her silvery laugh does. I want to nuzzle my head into her, but that would be weird, because she's barely my friend. She's my business partner. Who is going to leave eventually.

It's then that I see a flash of familiar blonde hair enter the bar on the arm of a man in a suit. My gut twists as it's just another reminder that I can't be greedy with my happiness. That nothing lasts forever. That, realistically, I'm not the kind of guy someone as accomplished and ambitious as Aurora would even consider.

I'm just Wyatt Hensley.

I'm barely her friend.

I'm her business partner.

Who panics and leaves before the song ends.

Seventeen

Aurora

"**I** need to go," Wyatt abruptly announces and races off to the bathroom.

All the tingling in my body starts to disappear, no longer kindled by the warmth of his body holding mine.

Oh God. I must have overstepped a line resting my head against his chest. It's just that being in his arms felt so oddly calming, like being wrapped up in your favourite blanket.

There was both desperation and softness in the way he held me, his clutch so demanding, but also gentle in the subtle stroke of his thumb over my waist. His midnight eyes were so wild when he marched over and offered to dance with me too, like if I didn't say yes the whole bar would burn down. Yet, it felt so right to slip my hand into his, feel his rough skin rasp against mine.

And then I was too rebellious and stole the chance to feel more of him by laying my head against his chest, drinking up the leather and pinewood scent that radiated off him. The scent that is so entrenched in my memories of Sunset Ranch now. But he immediately seized up, stopped dancing, and then left me like a jilted bride.

Not that it matters—I was just letting my vulnerability get the best of me once again, making me take advantage of any attention Wyatt was giving me.

I don't like Wyatt that way. He doesn't like me that way either. In fact, I'm still not one hundred percent certain he even *likes* me—*tolerate* might be a better word.

When Wyatt disappears, Sawyer and Cherry stop dancing and shrug at me, faces twisting like they're just as confused as to why he stormed off. Sawyer wraps his arms around Cherry's and my shoulders, guiding us back to the table, where Cherry finishes clearing off the empty glasses.

I'm incredibly grateful that my full drink is still waiting for me and I down it, receiving a cheer from Wolfman and Sawyer, before asking Cherry to bring another. Anything to numb the annoying sting in my chest.

***

"Who has Wyatt been talking to all night?" I shuffle closer to Sawyer and gesture my glass towards where Wyatt stands at the bar with the couple. Ever since he came out the bathroom, he's been chatting to them. Hasn't even looked my way once.

Not that I care, I've been happily conversing with Sawyer and Wolfman, but... it's just weird.

"That, my dear Red, is Miss Holly Slade and her hot shot lawyer boyfriend," Sawyer laughs.

"Nah." Wolfman shakes his head. "My sister told me they're engaged now."

Sawyer blows out a breath. "Shit, well, don't tell Wyatt."

I snap my head round. "*That's* the infamous Holly Slade?"

I'm not entirely sure what I was expecting when he told me about her, but it definitely wasn't someone as devastatingly beautiful as this woman. She's got long, shiny blonde hair, and she's wearing a sweet-looking white linen dress that shows off all her feminine curves, whilst deep-red paints her lips. Not ideal for Wyatt to know he lost *that*.

Also not ideal for me that there's a quick pang of something that feels a lot like jealousy in my stomach... but I shake it off and turn back to Sawyer. It's probably just reminding me of the blonde girl I caught Jake with.

He raises a brow at me. "How do you know about Holly Slade?"

I sip my drink, unable to stop myself from taking side-eye glances at Holly and Wyatt, thinking about how good they would've looked together as a couple—she's all innocent country beauty, whilst he's all dark and mysterious. I also notice how she's covering her left hand, like she doesn't want Wyatt to see the ring.

I immediately dislike her.

"Wyatt told me about Holly Slade the other week."

"Wait, what's her name again?" Wolfman grins.

I roll my eyes and twist in closer to Sawyer, who is laughing in what seems like disbelief. "Jesus, he *never* talks about Holly Slade, even to us. All we get is a grunt if we bring her up in conversation."

Taking another long sip of my drink to try and hide how much I'm glaring at the three of them, I study the guy who's got his arm around Holly's waist. He's also the complete opposite to Wyatt—he's got the pretty city boy look locked in, his whole image evidently curated. He's shorter and a little slimmer than Wyatt, with perfectly coiffed light-brown hair, and is wearing a flashy tailored suit. He's what Wyatt could've been, I guess.

It all makes sense now. Why Wyatt's stood so closed off, arms crossed tightly, those goddamn mouth-watering biceps bulging. Seeing him look so defeated doesn't sit right with me, and with the vodka that's coursing through my veins, it riles me up more than I'd like.

"It must suck seeing her move on when he's still... here." Even though I know he's happy, that *here* is what he wants. But I can tell he's still bothered by what she said about him, that he wasn't ambitious enough. Even though I think the fact that he's found what makes him truly happy is the most successful thing ever. Inspiring too.

"Yeah well..." Sawyer sits back and nurses his drink, flashing a raised brow look at Wolfman, who just shakes his head. "It's not like he hasn't moved on himself, but he doesn't get to parade that in front of her like she does with her guy because of his weird rule."

Wolfman scoffs. "The fucking rule."

"What's the rule?" I ask, attention darting between the two guys who are rolling their eyes animatedly.

Sawyer's strained smile seems almost pitiful. "He's always had this rule that he has to make sure any girl is aware of his intentions before anything happens between them, whether it's serious or not. He says it's because he has a little sister and wouldn't want anyone being dishonest with her."

Jesus, that was not what I expected. I've seen the way girls gawk after him—like the women a few booths down from us earlier—so I kind of thought he'd take more advantage of that.

"Essentially, the idiot won't go home with a girl without telling her beforehand that he either wants to just fuck her, or marry her,"

Wolfman chimes in, chuckling. "As you can imagine, it doesn't always go down well, and means less girls to show off to Holly Slade."

Sawyer tips his drink towards Wolfman's with a wink. "More girls for us though, so we don't discourage him."

And they call Wyatt the idiot.

I spin back around and lean on the table, circling my drink as I watch Wyatt and Holly again.

No, I'm not having this.

I down the rest of my drink, slamming the glass on the table, making the guys jump. I'm too far past the level of intoxication where I still care what people think now. Unless, of course, it's Holly Slade. And there's some weird protectiveness that's rearing its head inside of me and wants to put an end to all this.

Because Wyatt is my friend... it's what I'd do for any of my girl friends at home.

"Well, I wonder if Holly has heard that Wyatt's bagged himself a hot British girlfriend?"

"Hmm," Sawyer's mouth hooks up on one side, "you know, I don't think she has. Maybe someone should go tell her."

"That is a great idea." Wolfman holds his bottle up to me, grinning.

"Wish me luck," I say as I climb out the booth and head towards Wyatt. On the way, I quickly adjust my dress, pulling the top down further so what little cleavage I have is more on show, and I ruffle up my wild waves. As I get closer, everything about Wyatt seems dimmed—there's no glisten in his dark eyes, no cheeky smirk that makes you melt, no rich warmth that reminds me of an evening bonfire radiating off him.

For a heartbeat, I realise how deeply he's entrenched in my new memories of the ranch, in my new *home*. How Holly's presence here is threatening that.

It makes it a whole lot easier to fling myself at him once I reach them, not giving him a chance to react. My hands wrap around his neck, tugging him down to me, lips barrelling towards his. Our mouths meet in a crash, his crossed arms press against my chest whilst he's frozen in understandable shock. I half expect him to push me away when I weave my fingers through his hair...

But he doesn't.

His arms uncross, hands accidentally brushing my breasts in a way that sends a shock of heat pulsing between my legs, and then they slide around my waist. Being wrapped up in him again sends sparks along my skin, and his lips give, kissing me back. He lifts me up closer to him, and my head tips back, mouth opening for his tongue. Stubble rasps against my cheeks, sending shivers down me.

God, he tastes of whiskey, all smoke and vanilla, and it's enough to make me groan a little. Even more when he grabs my hips, pinning them against his, where I swear he's hard. There's no gentleness now in how he's taking me, and it makes me feral.

I'm shocked at how much I love it. How much my body seems to be screaming *finally* at the sensation. Despite denying it, I always knew I found Wyatt attractive, but this is so much more.

This doesn't just feel hot.

This feels *right*.

I think I can hear cheering in the background, but the noises around us seem to drown out, all my senses too focused on the electricity skittering through my body. Deep down in my core. It's enough to let myself get lost in it...

But I can't.

This is Wyatt.

This is just an act... even if it feels scarily like more.

I rip away from him. Wyatt just stares at me, blinking hard, cheeks and neck all flushed. My eyes dip to his swollen red lips once, watching how his tongue darts out over them, and I'm hit with the reminder of how fucking good they felt. With thoughts of how good they'd feel all over the rest of my body...

Nope. Can't go there.

Jesus, I must be drunker than I realised.

Quickly, I turn to where Holly and her fiancé are stood, gaping at us, and force out the poshest British accent possible. "Oh gosh, I'm *so* sorry to interrupt, I just couldn't be away from him for another second." I slip my arm around Wyatt's waist and nuzzle into him. He's rigid as a rock. "I'm Rory Jones, Wyatt's *girlfriend*."

Wyatt makes a strangled noise.

Because I feel like being an absolute bitch, I hold my hand out to the two of them, but turned over, as if I'm expecting them to kiss the back of it. Their faces are still twisted as they behold Wyatt and I, and I don't miss how Holly's mouth turns down. My plan is working.

The fiancé shakes my hand awkwardly but offers a soft smile still. "Easton Brooks."

Holly's face has completely soured—which makes me want to turn and give Sawyer and Wolfman a massive thumbs up—but she attempts to push a smile through it. "Holly... I didn't realise you had a girlfriend, Wyatt."

Before he can answer, I cut in, throwing out a fake laugh. "Oh, that's probably my fault. He barely gets any time outside since we met, always in the bedroom, deep in that honeymoon stage, you know." Wyatt stiffens even more when I reach up to caress his face. "I'm sure you and Easton had it the same, right, *Polly*?"

Fuck, I'm so mean. And I love it.

"It's Holly." She presses her lips together, giving me a shot of adrenaline.

"Oh, my bad." I squeeze against Wyatt again, running a hand down his chest, allowing myself to relish in the feel of his muscles. "Now, I'm awfully sorry, but I need to steal Wyatt away because I turn into such a horny little cowgirl when I've had a few drinks, and I can't wait for my big boy any longer."

Then I slap Wyatt on the ass and pull him away, leaving Easton choking on his drink and Holly scowling.

Eighteen

Wyatt

"What the hell was that?" I ask once I'm in the truck, voice cracking. My legs feel like jelly. I only had one glass of whiskey but I'm not sure I can drive right now.

"What?" Aurora has strapped herself in, one leg crossed over the other, with an alcohol-induced, blissful glow to her face. As if she's completely oblivious to what just happened. How she just *kissed* me. In front of Holly Slade.

And the problem is, it might have been the best kiss I've ever had. It might have completely turned my world upside down, might have made me question every single decision I've ever made in my life, wondering why the hell I've never kissed Aurora before when it felt so fucking *right*.

I've felt fireworks before. I know what a good kiss is like. But that was something else. That was a thousand shooting stars racing through my body, lighting up every single inch of me. My whole body was on fire.

If she hadn't pulled away, I would've let it carry on, tasting as much of her strawberry lip gloss as possible. I would've let the heat of her touch devour me. I would've spun us around and pressed her against the bar, no fucks given about who was watching, as the feel of her body dragged me into oblivion.

I didn't give a single thought to Holly and her boyfriend. All I could focus on was the bright, sugary taste of Aurora, wondering if she tasted just as sweet everywhere else...

But I need to stop thinking about that because I'm getting hard again. Shit. How am I supposed to suppress my stupid feelings now? I'm in goddamn trouble.

I can't quite get any words out at first, sputtering. My eyes bulge. "Horny little cowgirl? *Big boy*?" I'm not proud of how high-pitched the last bit comes out.

She cackles, tipping her head back, the column of her throat shining in the moonlight. I want to run my tongue over it.

"Oh yeah, that. I just couldn't stand seeing you sulk like a little lost puppy dog in front of Holly whilst she looked down at you."

In the two seconds my brain wasn't spinning from shock, I'd guessed Sawyer and Wolfman had put her up to it. But *she* was the one who just decided to do that. She cares enough about me to try and make me feel better in front of Holly. Warmth climbs into my chest.

"Wait, so you were doing something *nice* for me? Jesus, how much have you drunk?" I smirk and start up the truck, hoping the chug of the engine might overpower the sound of blood rushing in my ears.

"Enough that I'll feel it tomorrow." She flashes me a playful grin which I struggle to pull away from. The way she bites down on her soft pink lip afterwards makes me want another taste. And to find out I what her mouth would feel like on the rest of my body... but I shouldn't be imagining that.

LIVE, RANCH, LOVE

I shake my head as we drive away from the bar. I don't know what to say, because *I want you so badly right now* doesn't seem appropriate. So, I settle for, "Well, thank you."

"Ah, don't mention it." Aurora waves me off, closing her eyes and snuggling into the seat. Cheeks all rosy, she looks so sweet and innocent, even though she tried to stick her tongue down my throat and slapped my ass not even five minutes ago. "Always happy to help out a friend."

The word hits me like a tonne of bricks. *Friend*.

That's what I am to Aurora. Just a friend. My stomach bottoms out, an impossible heaviness kindling where my heart sits.

Of course, I'm just a friend. That's why she just *pretended* to be my girlfriend and kissed me. That wasn't real. She's not looking for anything more. She's still hurting from her ex. And I didn't think I cared. At least that's what I've been trying to convince myself.

But as I drive the truck along the road, knuckles whitening from how hard I'm gripping the wheel, I can't help but glance over to where she's gazing serenely out at the passing hills and fields, looking so goddamn beautiful.

It's Aurora Jones. The wildfire of a woman who came to destroy my dreams. But now I'm afraid she might be here to set them ablaze and bring them to life instead.

No, I need to snap out of this.

It's just because I'm worked up from seeing Holly and because I've been going through a dry spell for the last year. I'd be feeling this way about anything touching me that wasn't my hand. Right?

Besides, I can't fuck up whatever we are. The dynamic we have right now works—when we're friends, working on the retreat together, it means Aurora stays, and so does the ranch. As long as she's here, the ranch doesn't get sold. I can't risk all that based on one kiss.

Nothing lasts forever, and I don't need another woman leaving me to remind me of that.

That's why I got my Icarus tattoo, to remind me to not get carried away and fly too close to the sun. And with the way Aurora's always brightening up my days, I'm worried I've already let myself soar too high.

My phone suddenly chimes, filling the silence and making us both start. Taking one hand off the wheel, I fish my phone from my back pocket, taking a quick glance at the screen—after Aurora's little stunt, I'm expecting plenty of messages from the guys. It wouldn't even surprise me if they took pictures.

A small part of me kind of hopes they did because then I could look at them again later.

But before I can check, Aurora lunges and snatches the phone from my hand. "Oh no! Eyes on the road, Hensley."

I shoot a scowl at her and make a futile attempt to get my phone back, but the way she's grinning at me, laugh chiming like silver bells, melts away any disdain. I huff, and struggle against my responding smile as I over-emphasise placing my hand back on the wheel.

From the corner of my eye, I can see the screen lighting up Aurora's face, her long eyelashes casting shadows over the apples of her cheeks. "Ooh, you've got a text from Holly."

"Really?" My body tenses.

"Want me to read it?" Aurora offers, voice laced with mischief.

I shoot her a narrowed look. "Only if you don't reply and call her Polly again."

Aurora throws her head back in a fit of laughter, which elicits even a chuckle from me. I swear every emotion is doubled in Aurora—if something is funny, she's cackling, if something makes her happy, her smile is brighter than the morning sun. It makes me feel like I've been missing out on life sometimes.

"The password is 031570."

Aurora taps away. "Someone's birthday?"

"Mom's. Mine is November seventh."

"I knew you were a Scorpio! So brooding and mysterious." I haven't a clue what she's on about, but the way Aurora's voice deepens in a sultry way when she says *brooding and mysterious* is far too sexy.

"Okay, it says 'Was so good to see you tonight. Best of luck with your new friend'. Oh my God—*new friend*—that's so funny. I'm dying. But I'm also so proud because clearly we riled her up." Aurora does some weird-ass little wiggle that I'm guessing is her attempt at a victory dance in her seat.

Another laugh bubbles out of my chest, warmth following it. My cheeks ache from how she keeps making me smile. My face isn't used to it. I normally limit myself to one smile a day.

That went out the window once Aurora turned up, though.

Damn.

"Oh my God, you even have me as Aurora Jones in your phone. That's so formal."

"Stop going through my phone, Aurora." I swipe out to try grab it again, failing when she scoots out of my reach, giggling.

"Too slow! Why don't you call me Rory?"

I shrug. Originally, it felt too friendly, and we both know that was not how things started off between us. "You said most people call you Rory."

"Yeah? You don't want to be like most people?"

I don't want to be like most people *to her* anymore. But I can't say that. I'm still grappling with the truth of that which I've evidently been trying to hide even from myself. And that's even harder to do when she's sat across from me. It makes me incredibly grateful when we finally hit the last stretch of country road home.

I grunt in response.

Then Aurora gasps and bobs her legs excitedly. "I know exactly what we need to do. We need to make it Instagram official." Suddenly, she's shuffling around in the seat, twisting to lean on me, and holding the phone out in front of us. "Smile!"

I try to duck out of the picture. "You just had a go at me for looking at my phone while driving and now you want me to take my eyes off the road for a selfie?"

"Oh, Wyatt, come on." Aurora rests her head on my shoulder, pouting while her big hazel eyes glisten up at me. It takes far too much self-control to rip my gaze away from her, so that we don't veer off the road. Otherwise, I think I could stare into those golden pools of honey, so sweet and enticing, forever.

"Fine," I grumble, because her smile that follows lights me up.

Aurora counts down from three and I quickly flash a half-smile at the camera, while she throws up a peace sign and a toothy grin. Giggling to herself, Aurora slides back into her seat properly, my body sagging from the loss of contact. She's typing furiously at the screen as we pull through the arch to the ranch, then makes a little hum of satisfaction and shoves my phone in the drink holder of the centre console.

Once we reach the main house, I help Aurora out of the car, walking her to the front door. Her eyelids look heavy, blinks getting slower as she opens the door and leans against the frame.

"You gonna be alright?" I ask, struggling to keep in my laugh at how adorably sleepy and drunk she looks. I hate that I can't go in and cuddle her into a slumber.

"Oh yeah, I've got Pinky to look after me anyway."

"Pinky?"

Her cheeks flush and her eyes widen. "Um, yeah Pinky is my... bedtime toy."

Of course she has a fucking teddy bear. It wouldn't even surprise me if she's one of these adults with twenty stuffed toys in her bed, or all lined up on shelves.

"Right..." I narrow my eyes. "Drink some water, sleep well."

"Will do! Night, Wyatt!" And with that she closes the door.

I'm shaking my head again, trying to comprehend everything that has happened tonight as I jump back in the truck to drive it up to mine. Before I go though, I take out my phone. Old Wyatt would pull up that text from Holly and lament over it. Wonder if it really was good to see me, or if that comment is laced with the usual pity she seems to look at me with.

But instead, I'm going straight to Instagram and looking at that photo of me and Aurora, where she's tagged herself and captioned it *LIVE LAUGH LOVE <3*. I cringe over the amount of people that have already seen it and might think I chose that caption myself.

Yet it doesn't really bother me, because truthfully I can't stop rewatching the story, staring at how fucking good Aurora and I look together. Remembering how amazing that kiss was. Wondering if that manifestation stuff she talks about really works, because if it does, I'm going to be imagining us together a lot.

Nineteen

Leaning my elbows against the counter, I watch Wyatt hang the painting of a lake up—the finishing touch for this guesthouse that Cherry picked out. I'm totally not checking out the way his back muscles shift under his thin T-shirt, though.

Because I promised myself I would try to fight these thoughts. The alarming reminders that make my skin burn like a bonfire. Like the lick of passion that ripped through me as his tongue slid against mine the other night. Or the solid press of his warm body, ensconcing me in his scent—

No, Aurora.

You're trying to stop thinking about that.

Even if it has been playing on my mind all weekend, I have to remember that the kiss was fake. *I* was the one who instigated it, who did it to make Holly jealous, not because I actually like Wyatt that way.

I was just being drunk and reckless.

And I swear he's been quieter with me ever since. I've clearly made him uncomfortable and need to set things right. To reinforce that we are *friends*—business partners mostly—and I'm not just planning on

171

running around kissing him like that all the time. Because that would make our whole situation with managing the ranch and retreat together very awkward, especially so close to the first trial run.

Plus, he's clearly not over his ex-girlfriend yet, which last Friday confirmed.

"Do you like it?" I ask, trying to fill the silence as Wyatt finally decides he's got the painting hanging straight with a proud nod. He didn't have to help with any of the decorations today—he always has plenty to do on the ranch—but he insisted.

"Yeah." He turns, stretching to scratch the back of his head, gorgeous bicep flexing—*no, it's just a regular bicep that has no effect over me.* God, I'm such a liar. "I'm just glad you don't have *Live, Laugh, Love* banners all over the place."

I roll my eyes. "Why do you hate that phrase so much?"

"I don't know... it feels kinda reductive."

"Yeah but that's the point," I chuckle. "How a successful life is about living well, laughing often, and loving much. I would've thought that matched your outlook pretty well Mr *I Don't Need a Fancy Job to Be Happy.*"

Every inch of his face drops. Those dark eyes pierce into me, eyelids slightly narrowed in a way that has me swallowing. I hear his words from the other week run through my mind, *Oh, I'll find a way to ruin you, Princess.* It takes a lot more willpower than I'd like to admit to stop myself from just getting down on my knees in front of him right now, hoping to hear exactly how he'd like to ruin me. Especially after experiencing the euphoria that kissing him gave me.

Bloody hell, I need a cold shower.

"Anyway... what are your plans for tonight?" I press on.

"Probably gonna get the bonfire going and read a book. You?"

"That's so cute and wholesome," I snicker, finding the image of Wyatt reading by a fire, maybe with a little blanket over him like I saw him with the other night, so contrasting to the dark, brooding impression he likes to give off.

"Cute and wholesome?" Wyatt angles his jaw, stalking towards the counter. Two hands land on the surface, making me shoot upright, still captured by his dark, challenging glare. His lips entertain a faint curve. "Two words every guy dreams of being called by a girl."

I perk a brow at his sarcasm. "What would you rather I called you, then?"

Wyatt's gaze narrows on me, smirk spreading higher, letting his dimples deepen. He wets his lips as he leans in ever so slightly closer, and his leather and pinewood scent compels me to inch forward too.

Opening his mouth to speak, he then tugs his bottom lip with his teeth, his hesitation evident in the way he wipes his playful expression away. Cold indifference is barely nudged by the quick smile he offers. "Just business partner will do."

Loud and clear, Mr Hensley. I'll try my best to ignore the stab of rejection wedged in my stomach.

"What about you? Any *cute and wholesome* plans for tonight?"

Maybe a night in with my vibrator because clearly I've got some pent up tension that needs releasing... But I don't say that, obviously. And I'm just about to describe another boring night alone with a self-help book when an idea pings into my mind, bright and enticing.

"Actually, I was thinking maybe we put that bonfire to an even better use. How do you fancy helping each other move on from our exes?"

"With... fire? As much as I enjoyed pissing off Holly the other night, I'm not down with arson." Wyatt's forehead creases. He stares at me like he's slightly concerned for my mental state. But my mind is laser-focused on how he said he *enjoyed* pissing off Holly, which was achieved by kissing me...

I shake my head, waves bouncing and a little matted from sweating with today's work. "Neither am I. I'm talking about something else that won't get us tossed in jail, don't worry. I'll explain properly later." I round the counter, readying to leave. "But for now, just get together anything of Holly's you have still and have the bonfire ready."

"I don't have anything of Holly's." Wyatt is quick to respond, the words barely finished leaving my lips.

"Sure," I elongate the word with clear incredulity. "Then just find something that reminds you of her still. It can be anything."

When I open the door, I notice Wyatt is still cross-armed, sloping against the counter, features strained.

"We don't have to if you don't want to," I hurriedly add, realising that he hasn't actually agreed to hang out yet, and maybe the way he insisted he didn't have anything of Holly's was him trying to find a way out of my suggestion. It's just me, embarrassingly lunging at any opportunity to be around him.

But then everything in his face flashes, and he jolts towards me, as if he's worried I'll run away. "No—I mean, yes, I want to spend the night together." He wipes a hand over his face. "As in, the *evening* part of the night. Not the whole night. I'm going to shut up now. Just tell me what time to have the fire ready."

Wyatt winces whilst I smother my laugh, pretending to chew on my thumbnail. Redness creeps across his cheeks, and if I didn't know better, I'd say that I make Wyatt Hensley a little flustered. And I didn't have to even kiss him this time.

***

The pep talk I gave myself before I left the house about being a strong, *independent* woman who doesn't need attention from a guy goes to absolute shit when I reach Wyatt's place.

The dancing amber firelight casts streaks of glowing orange across his angled face, which is all brooding and strained with concentration as he reads his history book. His light-brown skin is almost golden under the last remnants of the sunset too. But the worst part is, he's swapped his usual dark jeans and T-shirt for a thin navy fleece with *Michigan Ann Arbor* embroidered in yellow thread, paired with my ultimate weakness—grey sweatpants. I have to hold in a whimper as my whole body twinges at the sight of him lounging.

There's a beer in the arm of Wyatt's camp chair and a soothing man's voice sings a chilled country song from a speaker, just loud enough over the rhythmic crackle of the flames. Cool grey and pale brown smoke cascades towards the emerging starry sky. I'm disappointed I don't have any marshmallows because that would be the cherry on top.

"Is that Hunter singing?" I ask, pulling my cardigan a little tighter around my body.

Wyatt immediately slams his book shut and shoots to his feet like a soldier standing to attention. He doesn't even try to fight his smile, dimples blazing. Coupled with the grey sweatpants, I'm in trouble. My heart has never raced so fast.

"Oh, no." He gestures to the camp chair next to his and waits for me to settle into it before sitting back down himself. "It's Zach Bryan. He's, uh, my favourite singer."

"Nice, I didn't think it was Hunter, anyway. Not quite as upbeat as his usual stuff."

Wyatt throws his head back and groans. "Please tell me you're not a fan of his music now?"

"One hundred percent." I grin, biting down on my bottom lip as Wyatt peeks out of one eye at me, disdain written across his face. "His voice is *so* sexy. In fact, you don't happen to have any of his old underwear around do you?"

"I hate you," he deadpans.

"No, you don't, you love me," I tease, gulping when Wyatt's face doesn't move, save for a small twitch of his jaw, proving me very wrong. Abruptly, I snag Wyatt's beer from his chair and try a sip, grimacing as I hand it back to him. "Yep, still hate beer. God, why do you drink this?"

Shrugging, Wyatt jibes, "It helps me get through having to deal with you every day."

"Always a charmer."

I throw Wyatt a sneer, then smack my hands down on the notebook sat on my lap. The one that's full to the brim with paragraphs of emotional word vomit about Jake's infidelity. If my agent wanted a book about how awful it feels to be cheated on, our upcoming meeting would be a *lot* easier.

"Anyway, have you got the stuff that reminds you of Holly?"

Wyatt sighs and reaches down beside him, picking up a folded black T-shirt. He holds it out for a few seconds, revealing that it's a worn Simple Plan band T-shirt, like the kind I sometimes sleep in.

"Oh my God! I like Simple Plan. They did a song for one of the *Scooby Doo* movies!"

"It pains me that that's what you remember them for." Wyatt holds the T-shirt to his chest, like he's trying to cover a stab wound. "Why do I need this anyway?"

"We're gonna burn shit tonight, that's why, Hensley." I jump up and beckon Wyatt to join me. There's clear apprehension in his expression, face all dark, sharp lines, but the flames flicker in his eyes, lighting up the intrigue.

"When I was younger, my Auntie Grace used to say that we create connections with people and events in our lives that will continue to affect us until we purposefully cut those metaphorical cords. And she reckoned the most cathartic way to do that was using fire."

I open my notebook and rip out the first few pages. The ones where the ink is splodged and has run down some of the pages, disfigured by the tears that fell as I scrawled all my hatred down.

"You're supposed to admit your feelings, and then say you'll let them go. Then you throw whatever it is into the fire so those connections can burn."

Wyatt's arms are folded, T-shirt screwed up tightly in his hand as he smirks at me. "I should've known at some point you'd drag me into doing some weird ritual."

I choose to ignore him and hold out the ripped pages. "This is everything I wrote down after I found Jake half-naked with a tall, beautiful blonde woman on his lap when I came back from my great aunt's wake."

Tightness winds in my chest, breath struggling to leave as all the memories flood back and lay themselves bare for me to experience yet again. The stab of betrayal, the emptiness of loss, the heaviness of doubting my worth.

But when Wyatt's hand finds my arm, fingers pulsing, warmth floods my body, reminding me that I'm still standing. I made it through that cold spell of broken trust, and I'm stronger now. Especially now that I have this ranch—including Wyatt—to anchor me back down.

"I am letting go of this betrayal so that it doesn't hold me back." Briefly meeting Wyatt's midnight eyes, which are glazed with unnecessary apologies, I turn to the fire and toss in the pages, watching the flames devour the heartbreak as my body begins to buzz.

It's not going to be an overnight cure, I know that, but I can already feel some of the lingering unease washing out. Because I'm choosing to release it, as opposed to hoarding onto the pages of messy emotions. This is progress, I know it.

"Your turn, Hensley."

Wyatt's head bobs when he eyes the top in his hands. "Holly never came to any concerts with me, always judging my music taste, I think. Then one day she got me tickets to Simple Plan, who I loved growing up. She spent the whole time texting, which I realise now was probably to Easton. She left me for him the following week."

God, I think I hate that woman even more now.

"Burn that shit!" I shout and point at the fire.

Wyatt chuckles, all hearty, warming every inch of me. Awakening those butterflies.

Teeth tugging on his bottom lip, he balls the T-shirt up, passing it from hand to hand. A moment passes, and I question whether he'll actually do it, then he lobs the top into the fire and yells, "Fuck you, Holly!"

"Yes, Wyatt!" I cheer on, bouncing on the spot as he lets out a hoot, features suddenly brighter. Freedom pours off us both, tension dissipating into the smoky air.

"I am letting you go," Wyatt continues, voice raised as he berates the charred top in the fire. "You don't have a hold over me anymore. I don't care about you because you never cared about me."

Wyatt turns and high fives me, buzzing and proud. Spurred on by him, I rip out a huge wad of pages, the ones that represent the hardest part of Jake's infidelity. "I don't even care anymore that he cheated on me. I just hate how long I spent torturing myself over why I wasn't enough for him to only want *me*. Why he chased after the girl he cheated on me with when I found them, rather than trying to fight for me. I'd worked so hard to be sure and confident in myself, yet the last couple of months have made me question my worth more times than I'd like to admit. But no more!"

"Yeah, fuck that—he's a fool, Aurora. Now, burn that shit!" Wyatt hollers with a giddy, almost maniacal smile. His tall frame shakes with mirth, laughter loud enough to echo through the mountains when I fling the pages and then the whole notebook into the fire.

"Hold on one second." Wyatt dashes up the stairs and into his house, leaving me for a couple of minutes to watch the notebook crumble into cinders.

It's funny because even though talking about Jake still makes me feel raw, I realise that it's been on my mind far less than I expected recently. Like the last wounds are starting to seal.

When Wyatt returns, he's got more clothes in his arms. He hands me a shirt that screams white collar, and then proceeds to launch another top into the fire. Deeper shades of orange flames and ruby sparks frolic in response, hissing with celebration.

"These are clothes Holly once bought me that I hate and have never worn, but always felt bad for throwing out." He nods towards the shirt I'm holding. "I mean, when would I ever need to wear that? It's literally designed for some city boy office worker, like she was trying to slowly morph me into one. Like who I am wasn't enough for her—but I say *fuck that.* No one, not me or you, should have to question our worth. So, help me out and *burn that shit*."

Uncontrollable laughter waves out of me as I chuck the shirt in and watch Wyatt throw his arms out in release, letting the other clothes fall into the fire. I couldn't ever imagine how anyone would want to change this man in front of me—he might be full of dark, sharp edges, but lurking in the shadows is passion and kindness I don't think I've ever found in someone before.

Suddenly, the flames spit up in a rage and Wyatt pulls me back, my body hitting his chest.

But neither of us move.

We just stand, beholding the fire, Wyatt's hot breath against my hair, fingers still on my arms, tracing lines up and down. If I was letting myself be reckless again, I'd sink back into him further, allowing the intense heat of his body right now to diffuse throughout me. Or maybe I'd grab his arms and wind them around me so I'm completely in his embrace, like when we were dancing.

"God, this feels good," Wyatt admits, assumedly talking about burning everything in the fire. His head dips closer to mine, and I swear he inhales slowly. Then, voice deep and hushed, like he's telling me a secret, he says, "*You* make me feel good, Aurora Jones."

All my self-control melts away and I can't stop myself from confessing out loud what I've known for too long. "You make me feel pretty good too, Wyatt Hensley."

TWENTY

Wyatt

I hate it but I'm spending another evening scrolling through Aurora's Instagram instead of reading the book I'd picked up. I always tell her I'm going to sit by the fire or on the couch diving into some history, but I barely get through a few pages without checking my phone, just to see her face.

Today was tough. I'd had enough to do on the ranch including tending to a sick heifer which always gets me down. Especially when you know you can't afford the best medicine for them, and are basically just trying to keep them as well as possible until the infection gets them. Then Aurora confessed she'd been distracted by planning for a meeting with her agent tomorrow that she was stressed about and hadn't got anywhere with finishing the last guesthouse. So, despite my splitting headache, I obviously jumped at the opportunity to help her, buzzing at the relief that swept through her eyes, knowing that was my doing.

As soon as we were done, Aurora announced she needed a long, hot bath. The image that flashed into my mind had all my blood rushing down south, making me feel like a stupid, horny teenager. After that, I

181

hurried straight home, had a long, *cold* shower in contrast, cooked some food, and settled down with a whiskey and a book to distract myself.

But I am a weak, weak man these days.

And though I hate to admit that her silly wellness stuff works, after burning the clothes that reminded me of Holly the other night, I feel like my mind is completely free to think of nothing but Aurora.

It's weird seeing this side of Aurora on her Instagram, which is so perfectly curated, but omits all the beautifully vulnerable parts of her. There's more of the ranch on there now, including pictures of us ranchers doing yoga, regrettably. But there's no evidence of the crumple of her freckled nose when she laughs and gets annoyed at me, or the way she nibbles her thumbnail when she's thinking, or how she does a weird little dance when she's happy about something.

Jesus. When did I become so obsessed with Aurora?

I should just go to bed.

I do one last check of my home feed, when Aurora suddenly posts a new photo.

And she's holding a goddamn vibrator.

I have to do a double take, but I'm not mistaken—it's a photo of her posing with a hot-pink bullet, beaming. Her hair is a little messy, and there's a golden glow to her skin that screams post-orgasm. She's obviously done that on purpose, and it turns me on far more than it should. I want to be the one who makes her look that way.

The caption reads:

> *Self-pleasure is a form of self-care! Whatever your relationship status, devoting time to your pleasure is proven to reduce stress and improve your self-confidence. And what better way to take care of your mental health than*

with an earth-shattering orgasm? I know Pinky here has
definitely helped to ease some of my tension whilst I've
been working hard in the States on the upcoming retreat.
Rory xo.

My eyes run back to the name *Pinky.*

I thought that was the name of her teddy bear.

Has she been using Pinky up in that empty house, all alone, while I've literally been next door?

Hold on.

She told me about Pinky looking after her on the night she kissed me... Fuck, did she go and play with herself after kissing me? Was I sat on my bed that night, fisting my cock, imagining it was her lips around me, while she was finishing to the thought of me too?

God, my cock is straining against my sweatpants—

No.

I need to stop being so hopeful. That's never helped me before.

That kiss was fake. She told me I was her friend.

Or... was that just a cover up? Because if she asked me what she meant to me, I'd lie and say a friend too. To save face. Just like I've been doing this whole time, pretending I'm not obsessed with her.

It's that exact thought that has me tucking my boner up into my waistband and marching out the door, over to hers. The rational, sensible mind I pride myself on has been thrown out the window by my throbbing cock and wild, racing thoughts. By the agony I've felt around her, suddenly aware of how badly I want her when I have to be professional and just a goddamn friend.

I have no idea what my plan is, but I need to see her. Need to speak to her. I rap my knuckles on the door and lean against the frame, waiting.

There's a period of silence before I hear the shuffle of Aurora's feet coming down the stairs. She opens the door, a phone in her hand, eyes widening as she takes me in, dropping down my body and slowly back up. Her tongue darts over her lips, wetting them.

Aurora's dressed in a pair of silky purple pyjamas, with an oversized, chunky white cardigan hanging off her shoulders, bringing out the pink of her strawberry lips and flushed cheeks. The pyjamas do nothing to hide her figure, hugging every soft curve, and I can faintly see the peak of her nipples through the fabric. I have to rip my eyes away.

Her hair is slightly wet, making her waves all frizzy, but it looks exactly like I imagined when I thought of her in the bath.

She's goddamn delicious.

"Wyatt?" Aurora asks, bringing me back from eye-fucking her.

I take in a deep breath, jaw tight as I struggle to keep my gaze *just* on her face. "You said Pinky was a teddy bear."

Aurora bites her lip, cheeks reddening more intensely, realisation hitting her. But her honey eyes are wild. I can't stop myself from glancing down to where her chest is heaving, her breaths coming out louder, faster.

"No, I didn't," she counters, glancing at my lips. "I said it was my bedroom toy."

Her eyes rake over me shamelessly, and it burns. It's like she's daring me to do the same to her again, because she's so obviously less clothed, and the way she's now smirking makes me feel far too vulnerable—

"Are you going to carry on talking about your sex toys or are you planning on introducing us?" A woman's voice suddenly rings from her phone. Aurora's gaze snaps back to the screen, the blush spreading up her neck now too.

"Sorry, Sofia!" Aurora grimaces, then looks at me. "I'm on Face-Time to my friend from home."

The phone coughs and corrects her, "*Best* friend, actually. Now, spin me around so I can see if he's as hot as you said he was."

"Sofia!" Aurora squeals, pulling the phone to her chest as if that would stop me from hearing what had already been said. Her eyes shoot heavenward in a plea. I don't even try to suppress my proud smile, letting the thought of Aurora finding me attractive bolster my ego.

Eventually, she mouths to me, *sorry*, and turns the phone around so I'm faced with a girl who has curly black hair and knowing eyes that are too eager to meet me.

"Hey, Wyatt, I'm Sofia. Hope you're taking care of my girl whilst she's out there." Her raised eyebrows make me feel like I'm suddenly being interrogated, and I have to remind myself that she's just a face on a phone screen.

"Nice to meet you, Sofia. Don't worry, if you should be concerned about anyone, it's me. Your girl's a feisty one."

Aurora sneers at me and yanks the phone back, but I catch a glimpse of Sofia's approving grin before she's gone.

"Well, it's the middle of the night here, Rory," Sofia adds with a yawn. "And I only love you a little bit more than I love my sleep, so now Wyatt's here, he can keep you company instead. Bye, love you."

"Wait, Sofia!" Aurora's shaking her head, but it seems Sofia hangs up before she can argue. She sighs, and rolls her lips together—they're shiny, and I bet she's got that strawberry flavoured lip gloss on like the other night. The one I'm craving another taste of.

Once Aurora pockets her phone, those hazel eyes glance up at me, seeking. "Did you... want to come in for a drink, Wyatt?"

God, why does the way she says my name make me want to get down on my knees for her? What the hell is happening to me?

I've already had a drink tonight. I probably shouldn't have another. My parents are coming over tomorrow. I've got a lot to do. And she's got that meeting tomorrow. She probably needs to sleep.

I should leave.

There's no reason for me to be here.

Still, I say, "Sure."

***

We're sat on the swing, sipping on our drinks, staring out at the sun setting between the peaks. These views would usually make me feel peaceful, but right now I feel like I'm drowning under the palpable tension that's thickened the air around us.

We had a brief conversation about her meeting tomorrow over some old, cheap whiskey I assume belonged to Grace, before we dropped into the silence that's hit for the last couple of minutes.

All I can think about is the way that Aurora's knee is resting against my thigh, where she's pulled her legs up onto the swing. My whole thigh is tingling, begging for my sweatpants to go so that I can feel that skin-on-skin contact. And although I know I've never exactly been much of a talker, that feeling coupled with the vibrator picture flashing in my mind, has me speechless.

I'm just about to down the rest of my drink and announce I need to go home when the song playing on the speaker changes to one of my favourites by Zach Bryan—*Shivers Down Spines*. It's one of his older ones, so I'm surprised she's been listening to it.

"If I didn't know any better, I'd say you're a bit obsessed with me, Aurora." I nudge her, feeling so silly for trying to touch her any way I can.

"What? Why?" Her eyes flash wide, and I watch the column of her throat work as she gulps. She glances around my face, genuinely looking concerned—no retort or insistence that I shouldn't flatter myself like I expected.

My lips twitch. "Zach Bryan? You've started listening to him. I told you he was my favourite singer."

"Oh," she says as she blows out a breath, relaxing back into the swing again. She bites her lip and shakes her head. "Though I hate to admit it, you've got good taste. His songs are... beautiful, really."

Aurora shuffles around to face me, and the remnants of the setting sun's amber rays dowse her in golden light, making her freckled cheek-bones gleam and her honey eyes even richer. The way her messy waves tumble over one of her cheeks, shining like rivers of fire, is too divine.

The shivers that race down my spine just confirm how holy her beauty is. And that I might need Zach Bryan to write the soundtrack to my life.

Aurora's lips hook up into a mischievous grin as her eyes brighten. "In fact, this is the perfect song to finish that dance you owe me from last week."

"Um, I—"

I don't have a chance to protest because Aurora takes my glass away and settles it with hers underneath the swing, then grabs both my hands and yanks me up, giggling. I'm panicking because I'm not sure I'll survive this—her warm body pressed against mine, barely any material separating us as I'm able to explore the curve of her waist, hips, back. All with the thought of her and that vibrator in my mind.

Yet here I am, not saying no, because once again, I am a weak, weak man.

Aurora slips both arms around my neck, lifting onto her tiptoes. One finger slowly strokes the back of my neck, while she inches close enough that her breasts press against my chest, causing me to inhale sharply. I can feel her heartbeat racing. Biting her lip, she watches me, not smiling until I take her in my hands, letting them splay over her hips, treading the fine line of how low down I can touch her.

I never let myself indulge.

I know the universe doesn't reward those who are greedy, that if I let myself get too carried away, something will come to humble me.

But maybe tonight can be an exception.

Because the way Aurora's staring up at me as we sway to the music is like I've hung the moon. And I'd do anything to have the way she looks right now tattooed into my mind.

Aurora Jones. Forever.

The shivers resurface when she stretches up so she can rest her head in the crook of my neck, hair tickling my jaw. Her breath is hot against my shoulder, coming out in heavy shudders. I rub my thumbs up her hips, caressing the soft curve of her waist, hating the thin barrier of satin. When her breath hitches, I let my fingers dig into her skin just a little, wanting to make her gasp like that every morning. Every night.

My whole body aches with need, blood feeling unbearably thick as it rushes through my veins along with the whiskey, pulsing with my unsteady heart.

"Wyatt," Aurora whispers against my shoulder.

It's all I need to pull me from my silly daydream. I've had my fill, and now I need to come back to reality. I can't fuck this up, no matter how badly I want to.

I yank my hands away, taking a step back, and announce the first thing that pops into my head incredibly loudly, "My parents are coming over tomorrow so we're not going to the bar."

"Um..." Aurora's forehead creases as her arms slowly lower. She mumbles, "That seems totally relevant."

I shuffle back until I'm leaning against the porch fence, putting plenty of distance between us. But it doesn't stop the words from spilling because now I'm suddenly really nervous and I don't like the way Aurora's glaring at me. I feel too hot.

"Cherry will be there too. They want to see what we've been working on. I'm gonna cook us all dinner if, um, if you wanted to join?" My laugh comes out all nervous. "I'm sure they'd love to meet you—because you're my boss, technically—"

"Wyatt?" Aurora waves. "Are you alright?"

Definitely not. I've never been this flustered around a woman.

"Yeah, why?" I shrug.

She shakes her head, laughing. "Because you had total verbal diarrhoea then, when normally you communicate in grunts."

I sigh, the whole verbal diarrhoea phrase helping to dispel any still-roaming wild thoughts in my head. "Sorry, yeah. Too much to drink, ha. I should probably get going. We've both had a long day. I expect you want to get some beauty sleep before your meeting tomorrow."

Aurora's face drops, and she jumps forward as I go to head off. "You could do your meal here."

"What?"

She tucks some hair behind her ear. "I mean, your place is great and all, but there's more space here for everyone to sit and eat. You can take advantage of the bigger kitchen too."

"I wouldn't want to inconvenience you."

"You wouldn't be. I want you here—um, your family here. It would be nice to make use of all this space for once. It feels a bit empty and lonely when it's just me." Aurora worries her lip while her honeyed eyes glisten up at me.

The thought of her being lonely up here makes my chest twinge. I want her to know that I'm here. That she's always got my shoulder to fall asleep on if she needs it.

That she always got... well, me.

But I'm not sure how to put that into words without completely crossing the healthy boundaries we've set any more than I already have tonight.

The boundaries that keep this ranch, and my job, intact.

"Please." Aurora widens her eyes even further. I feel like I could fall straight into them. I can't stand the idea of her being upset now.

"Fine, yes."

Squealing with delight, Aurora shakes her hips in a little dance towards the back door. My eyes are glued to her ass the whole time. She spins around too quickly, catching me.

With a smirk, she waves and says, "Goodnight, Wyatt."

Twenty-One

Aurora

A fternoons in Sitting Pretty, my great aunt's favourite café, were always saved for sipping sugary drinks and discussing dreams like they were inevitable.

What would you do if you knew you couldn't fail? Auntie Grace would ask me, admiring the buttery sunlight glazing over the mountainous backdrop to Willow Ridge. I wonder if she posed the same question to herself when she was burnt out in her corporate job. If it was the catalyst to her starting Sunset Ranch.

Throughout my teenage years, there were plenty of dreams that now I wouldn't be interested in, but I'll always remember the time I admitted that I wanted to write a book one day.

Marvellous, and so you shall, she said, clinking her glass of sweet tea against mine. Like it was as easy as that—declare what you wished for, knock some drinks together, and it would happen. It's not too dissimilar to the manifestation techniques I like to follow, I suppose, but even I know dreams need action as well as desire to come true.

Still, she wasn't wrong. I wrote that book. It became a bestseller in the self-help sphere, and now everyone is expecting me to write a second. Especially my agent, whose video chat should be popping up on my laptop screen imminently. I might have managed to delay meeting with her since Jake cheated on me, but there was only so many excuses I could make up. That's one of the downsides too when it comes to influencing—everyone knows what you're up to, including your agent.

I've already devoured two berry smoothies, hoping the sugar will give me a rush of energy. Yesterday was supposed to end with a chilled, early night that consisted of purely a bubble bath, a quick FaceTime with my best friend, and reading a motivational book. Yet, instead, I found myself dancing on the deck, wrapped in the thick arms of Wyatt Hensley, who once again ruined me with the sight of him in grey sweatpants.

I struggled to sleep all night because every inch of my body was overheating with lust for Wyatt and the memory of him digging his fingers into my hips pooling too much need between my legs. The desperate glisten to his dark eyes when he frantically knocked at my door to discuss the revelation of Pinky was etched in my mind, making me wonder how I could make him look at me like that again.

But then, every time I let myself get too carried away with those thoughts, that stab of rejection would come through, reminding me how he pushed me away when we were dancing.

Again.

And there wasn't even an ex-girlfriend to worry about this time.

Even if Wyatt does find me attractive, it doesn't necessarily mean he wants anything more from me. I remember what Sawyer and Wolfman said about his rule, how he always makes it clear to girls about what he wants. I can't help but feel like if he really did want me in that way, he would've told me. Right?

Either way, I shouldn't let myself worry over a guy right now when there are so many more important things happening. Like the retreat. Like my blogging, where my followers are drinking up the new perspective shift I've been taking. Like my writing for the magazine, which seems to be flowing with inspiration, unlike my book—

"Rory!" My agent's face pops onto the screen, her white-blonde bob razor sharp, alongside a bright, welcoming smile that instantly coerces out mine. "You are glowing. How is Colorado?"

"Hey Krissy, thanks so much! Yeah, Colorado is great. Super peaceful. It's been good to come back after all these years." I quickly glance around the café, taking in the mint-green, tiled walls lined with black and white photographs of Willow Ridge and its residents. Warmth climbs into my chest at how it still looks exactly the same as when I used to visit with Auntie Grace.

"I bet!" Krissy beams again. "It sounds like you've really needed it with everything that's been going on. But I have to say, I absolutely love the slight shift you've taken with your socials and articles. It feels so much more *raw*. Like you're giving people the real Rory, and that's great."

Krissy has always been so supportive of my work—she was the one who sought me out after following me for years and proposed the idea of writing a book, unaware that I'd already started planning one. She gave me the opportunity to combine all of my learning into one beautifully bound hardback and championed me the whole way. Just like she's still doing now, which I'm so grateful for.

"That means so much, thank you. The ranch has really given me the space to reflect and tap into that version of me."

"On that note." Krissy's voice takes on a more professional edge, making me know what's coming next. "Has it also given you the space to tap into the best-selling author version of yourself?"

"Um, well..." I nibble on my thumbnail.

"Because the editors at Quartz are asking and—"

"It's just that I've been struggling to think of any—"

"—they want you to write about your ranch."

I adjust my headphones, wondering if I didn't hear her properly. "Wait, what?"

Krissy claps. "I think it's a great idea too. It can be a book about how you managed the grief and heartbreak through tapping into your creativity and transforming the ranch into a retreat. Quartz says the real life example of what you've gone through will really sell."

"But—"

"Look." Krissy presses me with another enthusiastic smile. "I'd really like you to think about it. We can brainstorm after the first trial in a week's time, yeah? I'm here to help, and together I know we'll get another bestseller on the shelves, don't you worry."

I'm speechless. This was not how I expected this meeting to go. Part of me is relieved, flattered too, that everyone seems to be supporting me and the retreat, but I'm also a little overwhelmed at the unexpected interest from my publishers.

"I'll leave you to consider it, Rory, and I'll send you a meeting invite. Good luck with starting the retreat, I can't wait to hear all about it!" With that, Krissy signs off, and I drop my head into my hands, staring at my laptop keyboard.

A few seconds later, another berry smoothie lands on my table, making me squeak. I whip my head up and find Wyatt towering over me, grinning. I swear the sight of him instantly loosens all the muscles in my tense shoulders. Particularly since he's wearing a backwards cap that makes me want to melt on the spot.

He drops into the chair opposite, sipping a coffee.

"What are you doing here?" I blurt out.

Wyatt's brows draw in. "Firstly, you're welcome for the smoothie." I bite my lip with regret, hoping the sweet smile I offer back will make up for my abrupt greeting. "And secondly, I was in town to pick up stuff for dinner tonight."

Right, because I suggested he do it in the main house so I could learn more about him and his family. To take advantage of every moment I could to dive deeper into Wyatt Hensley.

"Thank you," I say, before easing the smoothie towards me and taking a long slurp. The sudden brain freeze makes me wince and Wyatt snorts.

"Anyway, your face suggested you could use a pick me up."

"What's wrong with my face?"

"How much time have you got?"

Wyatt tries to hide his smirk with his coffee, which almost spills when I kick him under the table.

"Ow, fuck! Calm down, I'm only joking. There could never be anything wrong with your face, Aurora," he says so nonchalantly with a shake of his head. When his eyes catch mine, he quickly clears his throat. "I just mean, you seemed concerned during your meeting. How did it go?"

"I don't know…" I swirl the smoothie around with my straw. "My publisher wants me to write my next book about the ranch and the retreat."

"And that's a problem because?"

"It's a bit pre-emptive, don't you think?"

Wyatt just raises his brows.

I groan and rest my chin on my fist. "What if the retreat doesn't work out in the end? What, I'm supposed to write a book about how I overcame heartbreak by starting up a new business venture only for it to fail? That's not gonna sell, and I don't like that my author career is basically riding on that."

To my surprise, Wyatt just laughs. Then he snatches my smoothie from me. "You don't deserve this anymore."

"What, why?" I pout, failing to stop him.

"Because you clearly don't trust my judgement, and that hurts." He shrugs, and then has the audacity to drink some of the smoothie, watching me with dark eyes and a crooked smile.

Afterwards, he licks his lips, and I have to look away before I'm hit with memories I really don't need right now. I'll *definitely* have to leave out any mention of my stupid feelings for the head rancher in the book, that's for certain.

Chapter Four: How I Became Embarrassingly Desperate for the Cowboy Who was Still in Love with His Ex.

"I've told you multiple times that I believe in you and this retreat." Wyatt leans forward, resting his hands achingly close to mine.

His little finger gently brushes against my knuckles, and I have to suppress a shiver. I hate that I want so much more of his touch than this.

"If your publishers want you to write about it, then they clearly believe in it too. And I just know that if Grace were here, she'd be cheering you on."

My chest constricts. Wyatt's eyes dart between mine, as if searching for my thoughts, and his fingers reach out, resting on top of my hands. Calm begins to slowly flood my body, and once again, he's saving me from my self-doubt. How long will it take for me to be strong enough to save myself?

Regardless, he's right. Auntie Grace wouldn't let me second-guess this book idea. She'd already be marching down the street announcing to everyone about it.

What would you do if you knew you couldn't fail?

I'd start a retreat on a run-down ranch. And then I'd write a goddamn book about it. That's what I'd do. Just like how Auntie Grace gave up her job to run a ranch, as if she knew it would be worth it.

I just need to find that same belief she had.

"You know she told me something once, before I went off to college," Wyatt begins again, voice rumbling with warmth. There's a faint curve to his lips, eyes sparkling with memories. I forget how much time he must have spent with her as well.

"She said that sometimes the hardest thing we can do is trust blindly in who we are. I think she knew even before me that I'd end up wanting to leave everything for the ranch. And honestly, those words helped me make that decision, which, despite everything, was still the best decision I ever made."

"Because you got to meet me, obviously," I jest, pushing out a smile and a wink.

Wyatt scoffs, eyes rolling, but still says, "Obviously."

Our eyes lock and linger for a few tender beats. The constant buzz of the café around us has disappeared, and all I can focus on is where he's harbouring my hands. Where my skin tingles in response to his touch. Where I feel like I'll always be safe.

"So..." Wyatt pulls away, and all the surrounding noise rushes in—the whir of the coffee machine, the clink of cups, and the soft chatter of the customers. Wyatt finally hands me back my smoothie.

"I'm gonna need you to start trusting in yourself, please. All these goddamn DMCs are ruining the whole cool, unemotional reputation I've got going."

Right, and if I'm not careful, all these DMCs full of locked eyes and stolen touches are going to make me fall for him. Hard.

Twenty-Two

Aurora

Hearty laughter, the clatter of cutlery against bowls, and eager conversation fills the open dining room. Early evening sunlight shimmers through the large glass panes, casting everything in a soft honey glow. The warmth of family surrounds us, and I drink down the sense of tenderness and connection as Malia—Wyatt's mother—gushes about Hunter's upcoming tour with evident pride.

I can immediately see where Wyatt gets his caring streak from based on the way Malia pours over her children with raw affection. The same quiet, brooding energy Wyatt usually emits is mirrored in his father, Beau, too. I wonder who he got his cooking skills from though, because the chilli con carne he made us tonight is bloody delicious. I'm already on my second helping.

The whole evening reminds me of dinners with Auntie Grace—especially when my parents were visiting too. Almost every night would bleed into the early hours of the morning, everyone too blissfully unaware of passing time, encapsulated by the conversation. Smiles and laughter have a funny way of drowning out the ticking of clocks.

"Oh, Wyatt, I almost forgot," Malia adds on. "I bumped into Holly and her mother the other day in the grocery store."

Wyatt tenses and glances at me across the table, quickly shovelling some chilli down.

"Oh nice," he basically grunts through his mouthful. It's not hard to notice how rigid he's gone. Shoulders hunched. I remember that his parents gave him a hard time for his career choice, but I wonder what they thought when Holly left him.

Under the table, I shuffle my foot along and find his. He starts a little, then moves his leg forward, letting me stroke my foot up and down his shin for comfort. I half-expected him to pull away, just like he did last night when he was grasping my hips and all I could think about was how badly I wanted his hands over all of me.

But it's fine. I'm over it.

We're just friends.

And he's so closed usually, yet I was lucky enough to be let into that healing part of his life for some crazy reason, so the least I can do is support him on it. Show him that I'm here for him, like he did for me earlier in the café.

Because that's what friends do, right?

We go on pretending like I'm not currently rubbing his leg and continue eating our chilli.

There's a smirk on Malia's face though as she continues. "Yes, I was quite surprised to hear about your new British girlfriend who," she turns to her husband as Wyatt and I freeze with mouths full of food, "what was the phrase?"

Beau clears his throat. "Climbs him like a tree."

Mine and Wyatt's eyes meet, widen, and then we're both choking on our food, coughing back the shock. But also, the hilarity of it—because

I can just imagine how pinched Holly's face must have been when she said that.

Cherry's absolutely beside herself with laughter, tears already streaming down her face. She holds her hands up, barely getting an apology out for how loudly she cackled, trying to compose herself.

The whole time, Wyatt's just looked at me, biting back a grin that I bet his family doesn't see often. He coughs once more, taking a sip of his drink to help. "Well—"

"That's my fault, sorry to disappoint you. I just thought it might make Holly stop parading her man around and finally leave Wyatt alone." I give Malia and Beau a nervous smile. "I also definitely did *not* climb him like a tree."

Wyatt rubs his face with a muffled groan.

"Oh no," Cherry mumbles quietly next to me. "You just stuck your tongue down—ow! Wyatt, don't kick me!"

To be fair, even I heard the thud under the table. That must have hurt.

"Wyatt, don't kick your sister." Malia gives him a tap on the arm, causing him to pout like a massive baby and shoot daggers at Cherry. She sticks her tongue out in response, whilst I struggle to hold back my smile at how heart-warmingly childish they are, despite being grown adults. Even Beau shakes his head and laughs before we settle back into a content quiet.

But then he has to go and ruin it all by saying, "Maybe if you'd gone to law school like Easton, it wouldn't be him that she's parading around."

The whole room goes still. A cloud passes over the setting sun in perfect timing, its shadow bleeding through the windows. The silence

201

makes my skin prickle, but it's the way I can feel Wyatt buzzing from here that worries me.

He lets out a long breath, then carries on eating, as if nothing was said. I don't get why he isn't saying something back.

Unless he's too worn down already by it.

I slide my foot under the table to try and stroke his leg again, but he's moved them back so I can't reach. He won't even look at me now. My whole body aches to be able to touch him, to hold him, to tell him that I'd do anything to get to parade him around to everyone I know.

Because, God, he's so fucking perfect.

Even if I've been trying to deny it.

Aside from the fact that he might be the hottest guy I've ever met with his messy black curls and those dark, soul-reaching eyes, he also makes me smile so much my cheeks are constantly aching.

And I've never known anyone to *care* so much before. About everything. The ranch, the animals, his family, his friends... me. He literally pours every inch of himself into the work he does and the way he tries to be a good person for those around him. Without ever asking for much back. He deserves so much more than feeling like a disappointment.

God, I feel like there's fire burning in my bones. I didn't expect to be so protective of him. So easily riled up by Beau's words.

"Beau." Malia glares at him. "Not tonight, not when Wyatt and Rory have cooked us such a lovely meal." She turns a gentle smile back onto me which I struggle to return.

Beau sighs, shaking his head. "I'm just saying, he can't still get upset that she chose someone else. Come on, Malia, it's not like you go around showing off how I work for pennies on Jack's ranch. We both know there's nothing to brag about there."

Malia just presses her lips together. Cherry sighs and digs her spoon around in her leftover chilli. Auntie Grace would never have dreamt of letting such a conversation play out in her house.

So, neither will I.

I suddenly stand, my chair scraping loudly, and say, "If you're going to carry on talking like that, Beau, then I'm going to have to ask you to leave. We don't put people down in this house."

Everyone just blinks at me, stunned. Honestly, I'm shocked at myself too. I'm not normally this fiery, but right now I'm seeing red.

So, I just smile and start clearing up, stacking Cherry's bowl on mine, along with her cutlery. I place it on the counter behind us and head back to the table.

"Excuse me?" Beau raises his brows, running a hand over his moustache.

As I reach to grab Wyatt's bowl, I brush my fingers along his neck, making his breath hitch. I just want him to know I'm here. I'm in his corner, even if it doesn't feel like anyone else is.

Because that's what he's done for me.

Acting like I'm not two seconds away from arguing with Wyatt's dad who I've only just met, I smile and take Malia's bowl too. "I think you heard me just fine."

"Rory." Beau's voice deepens with warning, and he settles back in his seat, almost pretending like everything is perfectly swell. "I understand you might disagree, but I don't appreciate being told how to speak to my children."

"Well." I grab Beau's bowl, pushing out the politest smile possible, as if I'm not about to unleash the fury inside of me. "I'm afraid I'm going to, because it pisses me off that you don't see how bloody special your son is. He's probably the most hard-working man I've ever met—I

203

threw this idea of a retreat at him, and he just took it by the horns and brought my dream to life without even a complaint. He works his ass off here, and he gives all the reward away so that the rest of you stay happy. So that his siblings don't have to deal with the same soul-crushing words you throw at him."

Beau's face is as red as a hot poker, his hands scrunched into fists on the table. He goes to open his mouth, but I hold a finger up as I drop the stack on the counter, because I am *not* finished.

"And have you ever stopped to think that maybe he chose to work as a rancher because it made him happy? I mean, isn't that every parent's dream, that their child is happy? Would you really rather he hated his life, barely living because he's drowning in paperwork and meetings, just because it sounds better when you tell your friends?"

Beau's jaw is taught, eyes raging and enlarged.

I turn to Wyatt, locking onto his eyes, which are currently molten black. They may be fierce, but they anchor me back in the moment. Back to him. His brows drop, but he doesn't look away.

"Because I sure as hell would rather watch him feel as free and happy as he does when he's riding around this ranch, knowing that his mind is full of nothing but joy."

The corners of his mouth lift faintly.

"Now, can I get anyone another drink?" I place my hands on my hips, finally taking in a breath to steady my rattling heart.

"Some fresh air will do," Beau grunts.

I point to the door that leads outside and he abruptly stands, glancing at each person around the table, before heading out.

Twenty-Three

Wyatt

Hunter will be gutted that he missed tonight. Never in my life have I ever seen anyone stand up to my dad like Aurora just did. Especially not for *me*. In fact, I can't remember the last time anyone ever really stood up for me. Ever fought for me...

Leaving the women inside, who have managed to fall back into pleasant conversation once we all helped clear up, I head out to the back deck. My dad leans against the fence, just staring out at the glorious sunset, the sky set ablaze. He briefly checks over his shoulder when I shut the door quietly behind me. The corners of his mouth twitch, not even managing a smile.

When I join him against the fence, he lets out a long, hard sigh. One that sounds years in the making. "Are you really happy here?"

"More than you'll probably ever understand."

"Probably," he snorts, then rubs a hand over his moustache.

We rest there in silence for God knows how long. My dad's never been much of a talker, which is likely where I get my own disdain for unnecessary social interaction.

He probably didn't deserve quite so much of a public berating from Aurora because I know he does care about me—it's evident in the way he clearly wants the best for me and has strived to give me as many opportunities as possible to achieve that. But I don't think he's ever taken the time to understand *me*. To realise that we value different things in life. Possibly because he spent so much time working to be able to give me what he thought I wanted.

And I just silently accepted, nodding along because I wanted to make my parents proud. Still, there's only so much pretending to be someone you're not that you can do before it wears you down to the bone.

Dad's voice suddenly cuts through the silence, slightly strained. "I do care more about you being happy than how fancy your job sounds. You understand that, right?"

"I do now that you've told me."

"Well, then I'm sorry that I haven't told you that before." Dad flashes me a smile—a quick press of his lips. He begins to lift his hand, hesitates, then finally lands it on my shoulder, giving it a squeeze. It's not much, but it's a lot from him. "All your mom and I want is for you to be happy. I guess we just didn't expect this to be what did that."

I let his hand stay there, secretly relishing in the gesture. "It was enough for Pops, why can't it be for me?"

Dad chuckles, closing his eyes for a long moment as he pulls his hand back. Probably thinking about his own father. I wonder if my grandfather ever gave my dad a hard time for ending up doing the same thing as him too. "I guess it was. I think he would've been even happier working with a firecracker like that, though."

He gestures behind us, and I glance back, catching a glimpse of Aurora in a fit of giggles with Cherry on one of the couches through the window, Mom laughing beside them. God, she looks like she's been a part of the family for years.

I can't stop the smile that follows. "Yeah, can't say it's been the worst thing in the world."

***

Cherry gives Aurora a tight hug before launching herself at me. Dad has already said his goodbyes and is waiting in the truck. Fortunately, no one else locked horns this evening, and Dad actually managed to make conversation with Aurora, both of them pleasantly smiling the whole time as if their previous exchange hadn't even happened.

Cherry always wraps her arms around my middle when she hugs me, reminding me of when I had a huge growth spurt in my late teens, and she was still just a little kid.

"You know I appreciate everything you do for me, right?" Her dark eyes blink at me, a sincere smile following.

"Of course, kiddo." I give her a squeeze, then pull her into a headlock and ruffle her hair because I'm too uncomfortable with my sister being so nice.

"Get off me, you caveman!" she yells, slapping me until Mom finishes saying goodbye to Aurora and intervenes, reminding us both that we're in our twenties. Cherry huffs, trying to tidy her hair, but she can't hide the way her mouth twitches. "Ugh, I take back what I said. Bye."

And then she's out the door, leaving me with Mom and Aurora, who says she'll meet me out the back once I've said all my goodbyes. Mom waits for Aurora to be out of earshot before she smiles at me, eyes crinkling at their corners.

"I like her. I think she's good for you, Wyatt."

"Ma, you know we're not actually together, right?"

She waves my comment away and pulls me into a hug, scrambling like always to hold me as tight as possible, as if it's the last time she'll see me. "I just think it's nice to see you're moving on now that Holly has, with the engagement and all."

Engagement.

Holly's... engaged?

I expect my body to tense up, like it always does when I see her or hear about her. I expect my heart to start thrumming as the reminders of how far behind I am come racing into my thoughts, along with the memories of her leaving me.

But I feel... nothing.

Even when Mom mentioned Holly at dinner, I froze, but more because I didn't want my ex being brought up in front of Aurora. I didn't want to remind Aurora that I might not be totally open to her, even though nothing will ever happen between us. I was also hoping to not have to revisit the fake kiss for my own sanity.

I feel nothing about Holly for the first time.

Because of Aurora.

Who ripped into my dad to defend me.

Holly would never have done that.

A lot of girls would never have done that.

"Yeah, yeah, whatever, Mom. Let me know when you guys are home safe." I give her one last squeeze and then walk her out the door, waving the truck off once it heads down the dirt road into the distance.

***

"Thank you, by the way," I say to Aurora as I join her, leaning against the fence.

She's still got a drink in her hand as she admires the deep orange sky fading into the looming night. Her eyes are a little glassy when she turns to smile softly at me.

"For sticking up for me to my dad." Aurora looks down, cheeks flushing, before she drags her sparkling gaze back to me, a small crease between her brows. I turn to face the scenery ahead, rubbing the back of my neck. "It was weird... but in a good way. No one's ever done that for me before."

Aurora worries her lips, then takes a sip of her drink. "Well, someone should've. I meant what I said... But I honestly don't know what came over me. I felt *so* angry." Her laugh comes out all breathy. "I think it's just all the pent up anxiety about this week."

"Anxiety?"

Aurora rolls her lips together. "With the retreat. It starts in less than two days, and I think up until now, there's always been something to work on or create, so it's distracted me. But now that we're basically done, I can just feel all these nerves buzzing under my skin. Even more now I'm supposed to be writing a book about it all."

Sounds like what I feel when I'm around her.

With a sigh, she turns and leans back against the fence. "I mean, who am I kidding? I've never run a retreat before. I have *zero* idea what I'm doing here, and I'm scared it's going to show. I'm supposed to do a session on building confidence, yet I'm here doubting myself, ugh."

I hate it when she does this. Talks herself down.

The loose edge the alcohol has already given me means I can't stop the words leaving my lips after thinking them. "You're so annoying, you know that?"

I register the quick flash of pain in her eyes before it disappears and her lips curve into a smirk. "Of course. Getting under your skin is my sole objective in life. The wellness blogging is merely for passing time."

It's the perfect opportunity to steer the conversation back to our usual vying, away from the vulnerability, that even I would usually be too uncomfortable with.

But not when it's her. For some reason, Aurora has this unfathomable power over me that makes me want to bear the depths of my soul to her. Especially after she fought for me tonight.

"No, Aurora, I'm serious." That wipes her smile straight off her face. I take her glass away and settle it on the table behind us before returning, standing closer than I was before. She doesn't move back, but there's a hesitancy in the way she watches me. "It seriously annoys me that you don't realise how fucking perfect you are."

Aurora's breath hitches. The remains of the setting sun peek out from behind the mountains, showering her in golden light, the deeper red tones of her hair glowing like fire. She looks like a goddamn angel.

Her lower lip quivers. "You... you think I'm perfect?"

I hadn't really thought about what I was going to say next. I've never been good with words. But I know that *yes* isn't the response she needs.

I swallow down my pride, eyes dipping to her lips once, then to how her chest is suddenly heaving with her ragged breath, pressing against her dress. "Actually, I think you might be the most perfect girl I've ever met."

Aurora sputters, "But—but you don't like me."

"When did I ever say that?" I get that we didn't exactly get off on the greatest start, but the last couple of weeks have been... different. I mean, I've been doing goddamn yoga with her every morning and buying her smoothies.

Though, now I'm slightly concerned she hasn't felt the same.

Aurora's mouth is working like she's talking, but no words come out. Her big hazel eyes are so wide. I just know what her head is doing right now—trying to come up with all the reasons why I wouldn't like her, why I must be mistaken when I think she's perfect.

"Fuck it. If you don't believe me, then I'll show you."

"Wh—"

I slide my hands into her hair before she can finish the word and pull her towards me, our lips crashing together. Electricity sparks through me, my blood singing in response to the taste of Aurora again. I hadn't realised how starved I'd been.

Aurora stays frozen for a second, and I start to pull away, but then she grabs my T-shirt, fisting the material and dragging me closer as she steals another kiss.

It's like a thousand shooting stars again.

My skin is covered in gooseflesh and sparks dance underneath. We stumble back against the fence, fighting to taste more of each other. A whimper escapes her lips when I pin my hips against hers, and the sound makes me even harder.

Hands now under my shirt, fingers burning as they feel out my muscles, Aurora opens her mouth for me so our tongues collide, and I can't stop the groan that rumbles out of me. I grasp her hair tighter, angling her head back so I can kiss her deeper. The way she drags her nails down my back lights a fire deep in my core.

I drop my hands to her waist, and she lets out an irritated groan when I break our kiss.

"Fuck, I've been dying to kiss you again," I admit, making her eyes light up. "Is this what you want, Aurora?"

"God yes," she breathes out with a heart-shattering smile.

"Good, now turn around."

Aurora furrows her brow, but my hands are already guiding her around. I keep my body close to hers, lapping up the heat radiating off her, the way her ass brushes against my cock.

"Let's start with taking this tease of a dress off, so I can worship this perfect little body."

I hear her mouth pop open, and I grab the zip at the top of her purple dress. I'd noticed the easy access that would give me when she opened the door in it earlier. I plant kisses down her spine, following the zip, each connection making her breathe harder. I help slide the straps down her arms, letting the dress fall to the floor. No bra, and a bright red lace thong baring her perfect ass for me. My favourite colour. *Fuck.*

Silence echoes around us.

Brushing her hair out of the way gently, I bring my lips to Aurora's neck, just above where the trail of black butterflies lies, kissing and sucking. Her back arches, ass pressing back into me more, the friction making it even harder to not lose control just yet.

I wrap my hands around her, bringing one up to caress her breasts, which are the perfect handful, like they were shaped to fit so naturally in my hands. Exactly like I expected.

Even though blood is pumping through me at an alarming rate, I don't rush with exploring her body, feeling every inch of her freckled, golden skin. Perfection needs to be appreciated.

Slowly, I slide my other hand down her stomach, waiting for permission.

"Wyatt..." Aurora whispers, almost in a gasp.

It sounds similar to when she cautioned me while we were dancing, but now I realise it wasn't a warning at all. If the way she's pressing back against me right now, whimpering, says anything, then it's an invitation.

"Tell me what you need, Princess."

Her breath shakes. "I—I need you to touch me."

Thank fuck.

Without hesitation, I slip my hand under her thong, eliciting another sweet whimper from her. I hiss at how soaked she is.

For me.

I think my brain actually short circuits and I freeze.

"Um, Wyatt?" Aurora asks.

I flip her around, ushering her back. Her body is just unbelievable. Small, perky breasts pushed forwards, that little butterfly tattoo sitting between them. Round hips that are just begging to be grabbed and rolled against me. And her toned legs lead up to where that pretty little pussy of hers is dripping for me. The sunset frames her again, and if I needed a sign right now that I'm on the right path, I know this is it.

She's it.

I take Aurora's face in my hands, brushing my thumbs over her jaw. "You are divine."

Again, she's watching me with raised brows, but there's a trust in her expression, in her obedience, that makes me feel far more worthy than I deserve. I kiss down her beautiful body, nipping at her peaked nipples as I work her thong down her legs. I drop to my knees, grab the back of her thighs, and look up.

"Hold on to the fence, Princess."

Her eyes flash and she grips the fence, then I hoist her up, settling her legs on my shoulders.

Slowly, I drag my tongue up her centre, kissing her clit, and she immediately moans, one hand sifting through my hair. Fuck, she tastes so good. My cock pulses for her.

I work her clit with my tongue and bring one hand away from where I was grabbing her ass to stroke a finger through her centre.

"Is this all for me?" I ask, almost growling.

Aurora makes an innocent noise of confirmation, gripping my hair tighter. I plunge my finger into her, curling it and stroking inside gently as I return to licking her clit. When her body relaxes more against me, I slip a second finger inside and increase the pace. She's breathing so heavily above me, moaning louder when I suck on her clit and her body twitches. I can't get enough of the taste of her.

I can't get enough of *her*.

Saying she was the most perfect girl I'd ever met was an understatement. There are no words strong enough to do the beautiful existence of Aurora Jones justice.

I'm not even sure how long I've been down here, so lost in the way my body buzzes from the feel of her. From finally getting to devote myself to her pleasure like I've been dying to.

As I start to feel Aurora tense above me, she goes quiet. Her fingers are gripping my hair so tight, frozen in their hold. Then she whispers, barely getting the words out, "Jesus, Wyatt, I think I'm gonna..."

I keep up the exact same rhythm in everything I do, even as she gasps and shudders, crying out as her orgasm hits her, my name leaving her lips. I want to drown in the way her eyes roll back in her head and her copper waves fall over her face.

Still, I can't help but smirk—can't finish without a vibrator, hey?

Gently, I lower Aurora to her feet, though her legs are shaking. I have to stay on my knees for a few seconds longer as I look up at her, realising that I could get used to worshipping her like this far too easily. She cradles my cheek as I stand and then pulls me in, kissing me deeply.

Her lips having barely left mine, she whispers, "Thank you."

I don't think anyone's ever thanked me for an orgasm before. But she doesn't need to thank me, I'd happily experience the euphoria of Aurora Jones coming apart for me any time.

"Oh, we're not done yet, Princess." I can't stop the laugh that escapes as I take her hands and start leading her towards the door. "Now, show me where Pinky lives."

215

TWENTY-FOUR

Aurora

I have no idea how we got to this point. I'm following Wyatt up the stairs, completely naked, after having the most mind-blowing orgasm I've ever had in my life. I've *never* finished from oral before, but everything Wyatt did was heavenly.

And don't get me started on the way he called me *Princess*. I don't think I'll ever hear that in the same way again.

I think you might be the most perfect girl I've ever met.

I'm still dumbstruck that this is all happening with *him*. That he *wants* me. The way he kissed me shattered everything I thought about him. About *us*. There was a clear hunger in his kiss, a roughness I expected, yet it was so at odds with how gentle and ardent he was with my pleasure. Like he was trying to prove something. Like he'd happily get down on his knees for me a thousand more times.

There's a heady rush of empowerment that comes from that which I'm afraid I might just keep chasing.

Wyatt's fingers are interlaced with mine as we enter my bedroom, and he leads me to the bed. He takes hold of my face, molten midnight eyes staring into my soul before he kisses me again and I lose all control, slackening in his grip.

When his tongue sweeps over my lips, I can't stop myself from pulling his top up and over his head. I know I've seen his body before—even touched it—but God, feeling it like this is something else. Being held in his thick, muscled arms. Running my hands through his chest hair, down the faint ripples of muscles that carve up his torso.

Wyatt eases me up the bed and then... he pulls away, lips curving into a smirk when I moan from the loss of him.

"Where is it?" he asks, one brow raised. It takes me a second to remember what he'd said. He wants to use my vibrator. He's not intimated by it.

Where has this man been my whole life?

Voice a little shaky, I nod to the bedside table drawer. "There's condoms in there too."

"Perfect." He smiles, kissing my cheek as he climbs off the bed. He pulls my vibrator out of the drawer and tosses it over to me, eyes darkening as they trail over my body. "Show me how you like it."

I swallow, that hollow feeling of desire building inside of me again. Pleasuring myself in front of someone is new territory for me, but there's something about Wyatt that makes me feel so open, whilst also *safe*. Jake was always more guarded when I suggested using my vibrator during sex, probably not even realising the shame his reaction created for me.

I turn on the vibrator and press it lightly against my still-sensitive clit, circling. I'm not sure I've ever had two orgasms in one night, so I don't know if I'll get off again, but then I never thought I'd finish without my vibrator, so who even knows anymore.

Wyatt's chest heaves as he watches me, slowly walking back to the end of the bed. His throat bobs when I let out a little whimper. I'm suddenly rubbing my clit faster as he takes off his jeans, and I can see him straining against his boxers. All those inches.

Oh God, I want Wyatt Hensley inside of me so fucking badly. This is absolute torture.

Wyatt finally pulls down his boxers, eyes never leaving me, then rips open the condom with his teeth and rolls it down his impressive length, making my mouth water.

I swear the thought of feeling him inside of me already has me close. All the muscles in my thighs are clenching like there's no tomorrow. I wet my lips with my tongue, then bite down. He watches every movement.

Steadily, Wyatt climbs up the bed like a predator stalking his prey and kneels before me, thick thigh muscles bulging. He takes the vibrator, keeping it pressed against my clit and mimics the motions I was using. "Like this?"

"A little to my left," I respond, and he follows my instructions instantly. I moan to signal when he's hit the right spot. He's watching me with something like raw wonder, and I rather imagine I'm mirroring his exact expression, because I can't believe this is happening right now.

He shifts himself so that he's leaning on one arm over me and settles himself between my legs, somehow managing to balance whilst still stroking me with the vibrator. He nudges at my entrance, the first contact making my body scream to *finally* feel all of him.

He slides his cock against me, teasing me. I whine, not even ashamed of how desperately I need him.

Bringing his lips close to mine, his pinewood scent and the whiskey on his breath filling my senses, Wyatt rasps, "Ask nicely."

Oh Lord. I swallow hard. "Please, Wyatt."

His eyes widen, then his lips capture mine, stealing away my moan as he slides into me. Every nerve in my body is suddenly exploding, pleasure rippling through me with his slow thrust. It takes a few long strokes for Wyatt to finally ease all of himself into me, filling up the emptiness that's been longing for him.

"Fuck, Aurora, you feel so good," he breathes into my neck.

Wyatt picks up the pace, pleasure building inside of me at the combination of his cock and the vibrator—

Then he abruptly lifts himself up, dropping the vibrator.

He holds up a finger when I go to protest. "Patience, Princess."

I bite down on my grin. Wyatt narrows his eyes, then grabs a pillow and props it under my hips. He settles my legs on each of his shoulders and grabs the vibrator, resuming in the same spot. Raising his brows at me in silent question at the positioning of the vibrator, Wyatt awaits my nod. When he receives it, he grabs my hip and plunges into me again, both of us swearing in response. At how deep and intense it feels.

The new angle coupled with the vibrator brings me desperately close, the prospect of release rising as Wyatt's thrusts get quicker. Rougher. I dig my nails into his back, scratching down. He wraps his hand around my neck, leaning over me further so that he's fucking me harder and deeper than I thought possible.

My head feels light, all sensation in my body rushing down to my clit. I lose all awareness of time. I can't even think.

All I can focus on is my cresting orgasm and then I'm suddenly crying out, calling his name like it's the only thing that matters.

"Fuck, you're so beautiful when you come, Aurora."

The stars haven't even left my vision when Wyatt flips me over onto all fours and slides back inside of me, my body tightening from the intense pleasure of being filled by him again. Fuck, it's such a good angle, I can't help but arch my back to take more of him.

I'm lost in every stroke of pleasure rocketing through me, forcing myself back onto his cock to meet every one of his thrusts.

"Yes, Princess, that's a good girl. Take what you need."

My body shakes, lapping up the praise. Wyatt's thrusts get messier, and he fists my hair, body slapping against mine until he's groaning from the release of his own orgasm, sheathing himself to the hilt with one last thrust.

He leaves a trail of kisses along my shoulder as he pulls away, letting me flop down against the bed, head spinning, not quite able to comprehend the last hour.

Wyatt bloody Hensley.

Falling for Wyatt was *not* the plan. Albeit he's the painfully hot, brooding rancher who knows exactly how to get under my skin. And make me come harder than I ever have before. *Twice.*

Forget the fact that we're supposed to be keeping things professional to avoid any awkwardness when working together. The real problem is that he lives *here*, in Willow Ridge, where he told me he wants to stay, and I will eventually have to go back home, to England. I know the retreat will keep me here, but that's indefinitely, and who knows if its success will be long-term.

I realise I've been in my head for far too long when Wyatt is suddenly lying on the bed next to me, pulling me over so my head is on his chest. I freeze in his arms at first but quickly melt into him, relishing in the way my body seems to curve so perfectly to his. His heart is rattling in his chest still. Because of *me*.

And so is mine.

Maybe, just for tonight, we can pretend the future doesn't exist.

"That was…" I breathe out.

"Incredible," he finishes, fingers pulsing against my skin.

"Yeah… I know you only live like literally two seconds away but, you can stay, if you'd like." I twist around and meet his smile. It's not his usual smirk or smug grin when he's trying to rile me up, instead, it's a soft curve that almost suggests relief.

God, I can't get over the way he watches me so devotedly.

"I would. If that's what you want too?" Wyatt asks in a more hushed version of his usual deep voice.

"Definitely." I snuggle back into him, squeezing tight.

Wyatt's arms wrap all the way round me, and he traces lazy circles on my back. It feels so warm and safe to be enveloped in him and that familiar leather and pinewood scent. I can't imagine I smell anything as nice, some of my hair plastered to my face with perspiration.

"Although, I also want to shower before I sleep, so you'll have to entertain yourself for a little while."

"Probably a good idea. I didn't want to say anything but…" He grins, bringing a hand up to cover his nose and stifle his laugh.

"Um, rude." I jab him hard and push away, kneeling on the bed, hands on my hips. "Is that what this is gonna be like now? You fuck me senseless and then insult me?"

Wyatt grins and pulls me over to him so that I'm straddling his hips. I try to ignore the rush of desire slicing through me at the contact of him against me. Especially since he's hard again. It takes everything to not start rolling my hips. To not lean forward and guide him back in.

"Firstly, it was a joke," he sneers, hands running up and down my hips. "And secondly, I'm sure you could get used to the occasional insult if it means getting *fucked senseless* every day."

Scarily, I think I probably could.

TWENTY-FIVE

Wyatt

I wake up to a mess of copper waves in my face. And I fucking love it. Because that hair is attached to Aurora Jones, who's currently naked in my arms. Who screamed my name as she came all over my cock last night. And my face.

I nuzzle further into her hair, breathing in the citrus smell from her shampoo. Her scent is so invigorating, making me feel alive, just like when I'm around her. She lights up my life in a way I never expected. In a way I didn't think anyone could.

Aurora shifts against me, starting to wake, and the slight movement of her bare ass against my already hard cock has it throbbing even more. I trail my hand up her stomach, tracing lines and circles over her until I reach her breasts, nipples already peaked. I palm one of her breasts and she sleepily groans, arching her back so that her ass presses into me harder.

It takes every ounce of my self-control to not flip her over, lift her hips, and fuck her right now. I ended up joining her in the shower last night, unable to deal with the thought of her being in there naked, without me beside her. And yet I'm still craving the feel of her pussy

223

clamping around my cock again. The sound of her whimpers against my neck.

But it's also only four-thirty in the morning, and though my body clock might be hard-wired with the rancher life, I know Aurora could probably use the longer sleep before people start turning up for the retreat tomorrow. So, I stop touching her and tuck my hand around her waist, curling around her more, hoping I can lull her back into her slumber.

Another groan leaves her lips, and she starts rubbing her ass against me slowly. At this rate, I'm going to finish before she's even opened an eye.

"Go back to sleep, Princess," I whisper, pressing a kiss against her shoulder. I also realise that I need to get up soon, because I've got a ranch that needs me, and I said I'd help Duke out this morning with some big delivery for the bar.

"No." Aurora just keeps circling her hips, speeding up.

I grit my teeth.

My attention keeps going to where my cock is sliding between her cheeks. Where I'm already on the verge of barrelling into re-lease.

Fine. If she wants to lose sleep, I'm not going to complain.

"Do you want me to touch you, Princess?" I nip her earlobe, making her shudder. "Does your pretty little pussy need me again?"

"Mhm," she whimpers. Her breath has picked up, pulse quick-ening in her chest where I'm massaging her breasts. I roll one of her nipples between my fingers. She lets out another whine and grabs my hand, dragging it down between her thighs, forcing my fingers into the wetness pooled there.

Jesus fucking Christ, she's absolutely dripping.

A growl vibrates in my throat. I don't hesitate a second before plunging two fingers into her. My patience isn't good in the morning, and it seems hers isn't either.

She gasps and reaches out to grab the bedsheets. I use my thumb to circle her clit, causing her body to twitch a little like before. I fucking love the way she squirms and can't keep control over how her body responds to me, like the pleasure is too much for her.

I'm rubbing my cock harder between her cheeks, using my arm to pin her against me while she practically rides my hand.

"God, Wyatt," she moans, tipping her head around to me. I lean forward and catch her mouth, the angle meaning I can take her deep, tongues instantly sliding against each other. Hearing her say my name in this context stirs up a primal part of me I didn't even know I had.

"Is fucking my hand enough for you Princess, or do you need my cock too?" I mumble between kisses.

She nods wildly, waves bouncing. "I need it so badly." Her eyes have been closed this whole time, but now she opens them, flashing that sparkling hazel at me. She gives me a sleepy smirk. "Please."

I curse and tear my fingers away from between her legs. "Condom and vibrator. Now."

She giggles and scrambles through her drawer, pressing back into me as she hands me both. Frantically, I cover myself with the condom, then lift her leg and position myself so that my cock is just touching her entrance.

I hold back though, relishing in the way she starts moving her hips, sliding herself along it, trying to get as much of my cock as she can. But as hot as it is, knowing how much she needs me right now, even I can't deny us the feeling of when we're joined.

I always thought Aurora Jones might be my undoing, but *never* in *this* way.

Thrusting up into her, I groan into her hair as she gasps. I love the way her pussy has to slowly ease to take all of me, but when I'm finally fully in she fits around me so well. She clamps around me, making it even harder to ensure this lasts. Still, I'm not letting go unless she's falling with me.

"Keep your leg up, Princess," I tell her, moving her foot so it's on my thigh.

One of my arms is pinned under her shoulders, but my other is free to reach over and rub the vibrator against her clit. I brush it over her breasts first, biting down on her shoulder, then trail down to the apex of her thighs.

"Fuck, Wyatt. Don't stop that," she immediately moans when I start circling. I try to mimic the same motion I used with the vibrator yesterday, keeping in tune to what her body likes, and I'm rewarded when she breathes out, "More. Fuck, I need more."

"More? What a greedy little cunt you have, Aurora," I whisper to her, buzzing at the way her skin prickles across her neck and shoulders as she gasps, but then starts moaning again as I'm driving into her. "Good thing it takes me so well, because I'll happily reward it with more."

I slide my other hand across the sheets to where hers is fisting them and our fingers interlock, squeezing hard. Meanwhile, I'm thrusting into her as hard and deep as I can and pressing even harder as I rub her clit with Pinky.

Her moans start to get quieter, and her body tenses beneath me. Anyone else and I'd wonder if it wasn't enough, but I know this is her calm before the storm. The quiet before her shaking orgasm, which waves through her in shudders along with my name that she can't stop breathing out.

And then I'm flipping her over and doing exactly what I wanted to earlier. I wrap her red waves around my fist, relishing in how silky they feel against my skin, and lift her hips up from the bed while her chest stays down. Parting those toned ass cheeks, I discover her glistening pussy, all wet and satisfied and inviting for me.

Leaning down to where her ragged breaths are still heaving out, I murmur in her ear, "Do you still need more, Princess?"

"I don't think I'll ever stop needing more of you, Wyatt," she responds, voice raspy from moaning. There's almost a surprised edge to the way she says it.

I suck in a breath and try to ignore the wholeness filling my chest. Because I'm slightly scared I'll never stop needing more of her either. Not now I've let myself free to fly with these feelings.

***

"Will you quit smiling so much? It's making me uncomfortable," Duke grumbles as he settles one of the boxes beside me.

"What? I'm allowed to smile." I furrow my brow and head out of the stockroom, towards the back door where the rest of the boxes are piled waiting.

Duke's my oldest friend, and we've both always appreciated how well we can get along in silence, so I assumed the fact that I've hardly said anything because all I can think about is Aurora would go relatively unnoticed. Guess I hadn't realised I'd been smiling silly in turn. It does make sense why my cheeks are aching.

"Yeah, you're allowed to smile, but you never do." Duke catches up with a few long strides. "Except on Fridays when you've got a beer in your hand, listening to Sawyer and Wolfman chat shit."

Well, he's not wrong there.

I just shrug and head out the back door, giving the rock keeping it open a quick kick to make sure it's in place. "Maybe I'm thinking about all the free beers you're gonna give me for helping you out today."

I joke, even though I know that assisting Duke with his deliveries is my way of saying thanks for him helping out at the ranch when we need him, particularly during calving and branding season. He'd never admit to it, but the guy's a hell of a rider, and can rope calves better than me most days.

"Fat chance," Duke laughs, and grabs a box just as I do. We carry them back inside, silent until he heaves his box up onto another with a sigh. Then he twists to me, leaning an elbow against the stack. He raises his brows. "Though, come to think of it, you've been smiling a lot more for the last month or so."

The smug grin he's barely holding back elaborates enough.

"Oh yeah?" I ask, feigning ignorance and folding my arms.

"Yeah." Duke mirrors my stance. "Especially when there's a British redhead around."

Silence hovers between us, Duke still staring me down with a knowing smile. I'm not sure why I don't want to admit what happened between me and Aurora. I'd love to say it's because I'm a gentleman, and we all know a gentleman doesn't kiss and tell. Particularly since me and Aurora haven't discussed what happened between us, and what it meant. Though, that's mostly because we were a little preoccupied with doing something other than talking last night and this morning...

Besides, she might not want people knowing, which is a wish I'd want to respect. But, if I'm being totally honest, that's why I'm nervous to say anything. What if it didn't mean anything to her? What if I'm just a way for her to feel better after being heartbroken by her ex? It's not like I didn't do the same with my share of women after Holly left me.

Damn, how has she got me suddenly feeling all these... *feelings*? This isn't like me. I'm either content or pissed off. My emotions don't exist on a long spectrum like Aurora's clearly do. I learnt that life tended to be easier that way.

I don't get nervous. I don't get giddy. I don't get excited.

Except, apparently for Aurora, I do.

Funny thing is, I think there's a lot more I might be willing to do for her too. More than I thought I ever would.

"Fine, I slept with Aurora," I admit with a long exhale, one that has my mind easily slipping into a daydream of all the things I wish I could be doing with her right now. It takes a lot of strength to pull myself out of it. "Are you happy now?"

Duke lets out a whistle. "Well, I'll be damned."

Suddenly, he starts searching and scrambling along the shelves around us, then hooks down a pretty expensive bottle of whiskey. He cocks his head to usher me out of the stock room and towards the bar, where he grabs two tumblers and fills them.

And he's smirking the whole time.

He nudges one of the tumblers towards me and picks up the other. "To celebrate you finally letting yourself have what you want."

"What do you mean?" I scoff, eventually clinking my glass against Duke's, where he's been holding it out, waiting.

Chuckling, Duke sips his whiskey, a blissed-out look passing over him as he savours the taste. He sets the glass down and leans against the bar. "It means, ever since Holly left, you've had it in your head that you don't deserve good things. It's like you completely forgot what your tattoo meant. And I sure as hell didn't let you convince me to get that wolf on my shoulder so you could forget all about the point of us having those tattoos."

Right—I take a long drink of my whiskey to let Duke's words settle in—because I'm happiest when I'm not caged.

Like right now, when I've finally stopped suppressing my feelings and let myself indulge in the sweet honey that is Aurora Jones. And good God, did she taste phenomenal.

So much so, I might genuinely be addicted. I check my watch, wondering how long it's been since I last touched her. Last ran my tongue over her golden, freckled skin—

"And Aurora? She's definitely good for you. You seem, I don't know..." Duke shrugs, pondering over his drink as he swirls the tumbler. "Lighter around her."

Lighter.

I couldn't count the amount of times Aurora's had me smiling and laughing, even if a lot of that laughter is directed at her and the silly things she comes out with sometimes. Without Aurora, I wouldn't have thrown away and burned all the clothes that reminded me of Holly. That reminded me of the man I always thought I should've been, but now realise would've just made me a desperately unhappy man who could never be his true self.

Without Aurora, I wouldn't be letting myself indulge in midday lake swimming sessions, care-free horse rides, or even goddamn morning yoga under the sunrise.

Lighter might just be the perfect word to describe how she makes my life feel. And brighter, there's a whole lot more sunlight when she's around, that's for sure.

"I think that's the most you've ever said in one go," I tease, trying to pretend that his words haven't hit me so hard.

"Yeah, well, someone had to say it, and I am your oldest friend, so it should probably be me." Duke grins, finishes off his drink, and slaps a hand on the bar, the bang echoing through the empty haunt. "Besides, we all know Sawyer and Wolfman are just going to ask you weirdly intimate things when they find out—like what noises she makes. One of us has to be mature."

I almost spit the whiskey back in the glass. *Note to self—don't tell Sawyer and Wolfman about Aurora.*

Duke claps me on the shoulder as I down the last of my drink, relishing in the whiskey's smoky undertones. "Now, let's finish off this delivery so you can get back to your girl."

TWENTY-SIX

Aurora

"**I** think that's the fourth time you've counted those reins, you know?" Wyatt's voice startles me. I whip around to find him with his arms crossed, leaning against the open door to the stables, a stupid smirk plastered across his face.

My body tightens at the sight of him—the way the golden sun lights him up from behind, emphasising the solid lines of his muscled torso and thighs, clad in dark jeans and a white T-shirt. He's got that cowboy hat on again which casts shadows over the mischievous sparkle of his midnight eyes.

It's been all but a few hours since he left this morning to go help Duke. Yet, the way my body is begging for him, my core already ablaze with the memory of how he made me finish twice this morning, is like I haven't seen him in weeks. I don't remember ever feeling this turned on before. I'd thought the same even before anything had happened between us, but now I know how incredible it feels when we're together—my arousal is in overdrive.

"I'm just making sure we have everything before everyone turns up tomorrow," I state, propping the reins in my hand back on the hook

EMMA LUCY

with the others. I throw my hands to my hips. "How long have you been watching me?"

"Quite a while." Wyatt shrugs, glances tracking down my body and up again, leaving heat in their wake. "You see, now that I know what you look like without clothes on, it's even more fun to watch you."

I perk a brow, trying to pretend I'm not racked with heat at the reminder of our hot, bare bodies together. "So, you were just imagining me naked then?"

Wyatt's lips curve, dimples flashing. Dark eyes lock onto mine. "Oh, Princess, I've been imagining you naked all morning."

"Oh my," I inhale sharply, almost forgetting to breathe out again. The way he says *Princess* immediately gives me flashbacks to him using that name whilst he was thrusting into me from behind this morning, fingers digging into my hips.

I am *aching* between my thighs.

Trying to snap myself out of his spell, I wipe my forehead and let out a chuckle at what has unfolded in the last twenty four hours. "God, this is so strange."

"Hmm?" Wyatt pushes off the door frame and stalks towards me, one corner of his mouth still hooked up. He knows exactly what he does to me.

His strides eat up all the space between us, save for a couple of inches. I'm suddenly staring at his broad chest, racked with silly, horny thoughts of how I want to run my tongue over that eagle tattoo that I know sits beneath his top.

I tip my head up to him and point between us. "This. You hated me like a month ago and now I can't stop thinking about last night... This is going to be difficult with everyone arriving tomorrow. I'll be so busy

234

for the next week, and you'll have the ranch to look after when you're not doing the trails and riding."

Brows drawn in, Wyatt nods in contemplation for a few seconds, then instantly pushes any evidence of concern from his face. He suddenly swipes off his hat and places it on my head. "I guess we'll just have to make the most of today then, won't we? I've waited far too long for you, Aurora. I've got no patience left."

He's been waiting for me? For how long?

Wyatt doesn't give me a second to respond, though, before he bends to grab the back of my thighs and lifts me up, making me squeal. Instinctually, my arms wrap around his neck, legs circling his hips, locking my feet together behind his back. Wyatt spins and presses me back against the wooden stable walls, lips crashing against mine.

Hips pin me in place, pressing his hardness against me, and I can't help myself but roll my hips, needing to feel as much of him as I can, as much friction as possible. I've never been happier that I'm wearing a light summer dress right now, grateful the skirt is already hitched up, meaning it's just a barrier of my underwear and his jeans that's keeping me from him.

God, I need to get him out of his clothes now.

But I'm completely powerless to him, trapped between his solid body and the wall, overwhelmed by the scent of him and the burning inside of me. Yet, I wouldn't want it any other way. Even last night and this morning, he took total control of everything, giving my mind the freedom to just float away in the pleasure. I didn't realise how badly that was what I needed.

Hot breath races against my jaw as Wyatt trails kisses along it, then over the sensitive skin beneath my ear, gripping my ass in his hands. He rips a hand free and cups my face, tugging lightly on some of my hair when his lips return to mine. Groans vibrate in his throat, and when I open my mouth for him, the primal need that's driving such sounds is evident with the way his tongue lashes in, trying to taste as much as me as possible.

"Fuck, Aurora," he moans between kisses, quickly stopping to press his forehead against mine. Warm, racing breaths fill the space between us. "I can't get enough of you. I've needed you so badly."

I clench my legs around him harder, body screaming with impatience. "Me too."

Wyatt presses another hard kiss against my mouth, then pulls us away from the wall, finally settling me down. I'm a little confused when he starts walking away. But then I realise that's he's heading to the wall where loads of equipment is hanging, halting his steps just before.

Over his shoulder, Wyatt's darkened eyes rake over me, a smirk playing on his lips. "Don't worry, I'm gonna give that greedy little pussy everything it needs."

"The words that come out of your mouth, Hensley!" I gasp.

His shoulders shake with a silent chuckle. "You love it."

"Maybe." I narrow my eyes as Wyatt runs his hand over all the reins and ropes hanging on the wall. When he finally lifts one of the long leather leading reins, my breath shakes out, butterflies awakening in my stomach. There's no doubt that I'm nervous at what's to come, but honestly, I'm more excited. I've never dabbled in anything like bondage before, and I like how wickedly smutty it feels.

Wyatt swivels, not even trying to conceal the way he's straining hard against his jeans. My mouth is already watering. "Now, be a good girl and face that post with your wrists together."

His molten eyes flick to the nearest wooden post and I quickly abide, trying to bite back the nervous giggle that's bubbling up my throat. I don't want to seem juvenile when this is clearly something he's experienced in.

But then Wyatt's fingers are suddenly brushing my waves away from my ear, his lips dipping close as he rasps, "Laugh all you want, Princess, I love the sound. And remember," he starts wrapping the leather rein around my wrists, "all I care about is making you feel good. You tell me what to do. If you don't feel comfortable with something, you just say, and we stop." He knots the leather above my wrists, giving it a tug. "You got that?"

Letting the giggle slip out this time, I nod and grin. Wyatt's wild eyes home in on where I bite down on my bottom lip. He groans before ripping his gaze away and wrapping what is left of the rein around the post, fixing it through the leather already around my wrists. One more tight tug and I'm secured. A quick wiggle of my wrists confirms there's no way I'm slipping out of this.

The prospect that I can't run from whatever pleasure Wyatt has in store for me sends thrilling shivers along my skin.

"Aurora," Wyatt purrs my name, tipping my head up with a finger so he can take my mouth. This time, his kiss isn't rough or starved, it's gentle, tender, and warm. It builds the heat inside of me again slowly, like he's gradually adding kindling to the fire with each touch of his lips against mine.

Wyatt trails his kisses along my neck, then down my back as he positions himself behind me. I half expect him to revert to the way he was scrambling for me earlier and lift my dress up, but his mouth continues brushing down my legs, only pushing my dress up slightly. Planted on his knees, Wyatt kisses the back of my thighs, devoting his lips to every inch of my skin. His fingers trail softly higher with every achingly long second, but never far enough to give me what I need.

I go to reach for him, to beckon him up to where my need is pooling between my thighs, when the rein tugs against me, reminding me that I'm completely at Wyatt's mercy. Which is exactly why he's doing this. Teasing me.

I groan out with the realisation.

"Something wrong, Princess?" Wyatt laughs a breath out against my thigh, the tips of his fingers just grazing my centre. I groan again in response, trying to savour even that slight touch.

"Use your words," he insists, nipping at my inner thigh, and I can just imagine the smug grin plastered across his gorgeous face.

"Please touch me," I beg, not even ashamed. Because how could I be? The hottest man I've ever met, a dark, muscly cowboy, is sat between my legs, promising to do whatever I need.

"Gladly," Wyatt growls, standing up and flipping the skirt of my dress up over my ass. He yanks my panties down, helping me out of them, and then adjusts my position, bringing my hips back so that I'm slightly bent over, baring more for him. He reaches under me, running a finger through my slick centre. I swear he hisses in response. "I love how soaked you are for me."

Leaning over, Wyatt continues to torture me by just sliding his finger through my wetness, occasionally circling my clit, whilst his other hand palms my breasts. He presses a hard kiss against my neck when I force my hips back against him, wanting more than just teasing from his fingers.

"You only told me to touch you, Aurora," Wyatt states, then tugs on my earlobe with his teeth, sending chills racing down my body. "If you want more, you only need to say."

I grit down my teeth, aware of how much he must be loving having me like this—completely helpless, unable to give him the fire I might usually throw when he taunts me. Like when we first met. Something sparks inside of me, the flames of my passion blazing.

"Fine, Wyatt, I want you to take total control of me. Fuck me rough and hard against this post until I'm screaming your name and seeing stars."

God, that felt liberating to say.

"Jesus Christ, Aurora. That sounds fucking heavenly."

The zip of his jeans sounds and he shifts around behind me, before he's lifting my hips higher and running the head of his cock through my centre.

Every cell in my body sings with delight at the feel of his thick length against me, and I can't help myself from angling my hips up to try and make him slip inside. So I can finally get what I desperately need.

But then he pulls away, and the sound of a foil packet tearing has me twisting round to see him covering himself with a condom. Which is good because at least one of us is prepared.

Still, I shake my head, rolling my eyes. "As if you brought a condom with you, that's so presumptuous."

Wyatt's brows lower in challenge, a muscle in his jaw ticking, then he unexpectedly slides two fingers inside of me. My eyes roll again, this time in pleasure. "Says the girl who just told me to fuck her until she sees stars. Maybe I was only planning on a bit of foreplay."

The pace of his fingers picks up, stroking me faster, increasing the pressure in which they glide against me. I can already feel myself getting lost in the ecstasy of it, but I force myself to stay alert, enjoying the way trying to spar with him has made him rougher in how he's handling me.

"Yeah well I'd appreciate it if you got to it." I purposefully push my hips back, rein tightening around my wrists, forcing his fingers in deeper. "And before you tell me to ask nicely—*please*, Wyatt."

Wyatt inhales sharply, ripping his fingers away. But he doesn't give me another second before he drives into me, hands sinking into my hips to yank me closer. Pleasure bursts inside of me, shattering my awareness of our surroundings as my body rushes to adapt to his size. He knocks my legs further apart with his feet, providing him with a deeper angle as my back naturally arches.

Giving me exactly what I asked for, his thrusts are delightfully punishing. I wrap my hands around the rein binding me, pulling on it to offer me some sort of stability amongst the waves of pleasure crashing through me. Wyatt leans down, reaching both arms around me—one hand brackets my throat gently, giving me that lightheaded rush of bliss, whilst the other plays with my clit.

"Is this what you needed, Princess?" Wyatt asks, almost growling. His hot breath blasts against my neck.

"Yes, yes, yes," I cry out.

With our bodies so flush, every thrust is unbelievably deep, hitting the right spot in a way that increasingly makes my legs shake. My moans are coming out more like screams. I don't even care how I sound—I'm just letting my body respond how it wants to. I never thought I'd feel so free during sex. But right now, I'm so lost in the pleasure and the way Wyatt fits so perfectly inside of me, that I don't know if I ever want to come back from this.

"Fuck, Aurora, you are just so perfect," Wyatt groans as he forces us forward, pressing me against the post and knocking his hat off my head. His hand is trapped between the post and my clit, putting even more pressure against it.

As soon as I feel my body twitch from the pleasure, I know I'm closing in on my release. I'm still stunned that Wyatt's even managed to get me this close to orgasm without my vibrator, but I don't let myself worry too much from fear of losing it. Instead, I focus in on the cresting bubble of pleasure low in my stomach as Wyatt continues driving into me, still rubbing my clit. I'm more aware of him grunting against my neck now I've gone quiet.

"That's it, Princess," he encourages, pressing a kiss to my shoulder, stubble rasping against my skin. The pressure builds between my thighs, stealing my breath away—I can't let it go until I'm coming. My whole body begins to tingle as I feel the euphoria readying to surge through me. "Be a good girl and come for me."

I cry out, his deep, commanding voice sending me over the edge. My whole body seizes up from the ecstasy throbbing through my core as Wyatt carries on thrusting into me. My vision is nothing but silver and starlight. Bliss sparkles through my veins. I'm entirely weightless.

I'm barely recovered when Wyatt groans and thrusts harder than ever into me, a shiver running through him as he finishes too. Pants dissipate through my hair where Wyatt rests his head against mine. Three soft kisses are trailed down my neck as he stands up and pulls out of me. My body is racked with the shakes, barely managing to stay up, when all I want to do is collapse onto the hay-covered floor tangled up in Wyatt's gorgeous body.

The speed in which Wyatt manages to tuck himself away and unbind me from the post is impressive. I arch a brow at him as he saunters back over from returning the rein to its rightful place. I'm not sure I'll ever be able to use that one for horse riding now.

"What?" He asks, eyes all dark and dazed. "If I left you tied up for any longer, looking so goddamn delicious, I wouldn't have been able to stop myself from going for another round."

I'm delicious? No, *he* is. With his slightly swollen, still too damn kissable lips, and a sex-induced messiness of his hair. How the hell am

I going to make it through the next week surrounded by people all day when I just want to be naked with him twenty-four-seven?

"I wouldn't have complained," I admit, biting down on my lip and relishing in the way his eyes flash, darting straight to the movement.

Wyatt slips his fingers between mine without hesitation, like we've been holding hands for years. The way our hands fit together feels so right, as if the spaces between our fingers were made for each other. It seems silly to think that something as small as holding hands could feel so intimate when he was literally inside of me a minute ago, but the moment still makes my breath catch.

Because holding hands does feel intimate. And the things he's been saying, calling me perfect, beautiful, incredible... it feels deep. Enough to make my heart skip every time he does.

"I'm not saying there ain't gonna be a second round, Princess." Wyatt tugs on my hand, leading me outside. "I'm saying there's a whole ranch out there to make use of instead of fucking in a stable all day."

Twenty-Seven

Aurora

The sound of chirping birds and soft piano keys wake me with a smile on my face. Tapping my phone alarm off, I roll over to where Wyatt's shoved his head under the pillow and lets out an enormously loud groan.

Wyatt Hensley stayed the night in my bed. *Again.*

What is happening?

"Five more hours," he grumbles when I try to pull the pillow away, giggling. In his defence, we did exert a lot of energy late into the night, and definitely did *not* get the eight hours of sleep I had originally planned for. Though, I got plenty of stress relief in a different way, so I think I'll survive today.

"You're a rancher, you get up early all the time, why are you being such a baby?" I finally manage to rip the pillow from him and toss it to the bottom of the bed. He tears his head around, dark eyes leering at me beneath the messy curls that have flopped over his forehead. I swallow with anticipation.

But tiredness makes his eyes flutter closed again and he puckers his lips. "You can't call me a baby when you're younger than me, and the height of a twelve year old."

"Oh, shut up and go back to sleep." I give him a playful shove and sit up, reaching for my phone out of instinct because listening to my meditation would usually be the first step of my morning routine. Except... I've got a naked man in my bed.

"Um... I'm gonna pop downstairs for a bit."

Wyatt twitches, his eyes shooting open as he reaches for my thigh before I can slip out the bed. "Why?"

His thumb brushes over my skin, edging faintly higher up my leg after every few strokes. I have to close my eyes to try and force the already searing desire coiling within my core from his touch. Any other morning and I'd allow it, but today is too important.

Our first guests arrives today.

"Uh, I like to meditate in the morning, and I'm pretty nervous about today, so I'm gonna need to do a *long* one. But you can stay up here, I'll come back once I'm done."

Shuffling about, Wyatt sits up, letting the covers pool around his hips so that his rugged torso is on full display. I inch closer and run my fingers across his chest, tracing the edges of the eagle.

"Do you usually do your meditations downstairs?" he asks, covering my hand with his so it rests against his chest, eyes dotting across my freckles.

"No... I normally do them in bed."

"Then stay up here and do it," he suggests, and rolls his lips. "Maybe I could, um, do it with you?"

I can't stop from laughing, which sounds much more like a howl if I'm honest. I have to wrench my hand away to cover my mouth.

I know I showed him how to meditate briefly before, but he seemed so uncomfortable with the experience, I thought he'd never want to try it again. It is Wyatt Hensley we're talking about, after all.

"What?" Wyatt's features cave in and he crosses his arms, like a toddler who's had his favourite toy confiscated. God, he's so funny, my cheeks are aching from smiling. "Maybe I'm nervous too."

"Why would *you* be nervous about today?"

"Because you're forcing me to let six random people on my precious ranch *and* you're probably expecting me to talk to them when I usually reserve Sundays for silence only. Although," he gives me a lopsided grin, "you moaning my name is allowed any day."

I snort. "You're such an idiot."

"Whatever." He shrugs, dropping his arms so he can reach for my hands. "I should probably make an effort to do more of this wellness stuff now that we're doing the retreat. Besides, if it's important to you then... well, I'd like to be a part of it."

I'm not sure my cheeks can take it when my smile widens even further. I've never had a guy want to meditate with me before. It's never bothered me because I don't expect other people to believe in everything I do. But the fact that it's Wyatt, who seemed so repulsed by all my wellness practices when we first met, well that just feels extraordinary. It makes me feel... worthy.

Nodding, I bite my lip and search through my meditation app for a session on reducing anxiety and building confidence. Meanwhile, Wyatt props up the pillows so we can sit back against them.

Studying me as I get into a crossed-legged position, hands slack on my knees, he then mirrors my stance, relaxing back.

"The meditation is a guided one, so just close your eyes and follow what it tells you to do," I explain, quickly pressing play to let the soothing music begin. Just as I lean back and take in a relaxing breath, Wyatt threads his fingers between mine, my skin responding with sparks and gooseflesh.

If it's important to you then... well, I'd like to be a part of it.

As the meditation plays, I struggle to focus, those words of Wyatt's ringing through my mind every time I manage to quieten it. But knowing Wyatt is here with me, along for the ride of whatever my current path will bring, seems to anchor me more than any meditation has. One day, I'll get all my self-belief and strength back, but until then, maybe it wouldn't be so bad to let him hold my hand along the way.

***

I think my attraction to Wyatt has hit an all-time record high. Watching him be so assertive and serious as he guides the group of guests around the ranch, running over safety procedures and rules, has my mouth watering. Especially when he's wearing a bloody cowboy hat, playing the perfect part of the strong, brooding rancher. Exactly what made me fall for him.

But on top of that, feeling the pure joy radiate off him as he tells stories about his time working on the ranch, answering questions about the cattle and rancher life for him and the other guys, makes me want to melt into a puddle right here. I can practically feel the love he has for Sunset Ranch pouring off him, and I swear it's brightened up every single person he's been leading around on this tour of the ranch.

If only Beau could see him.

It's only day two of the retreat, but it's already taking a lot of self-control to not be skipping beside him right now, wide-eyed and awestruck by how I just can't get enough of him, despite the fact I got to wake up to him again this morning. So, I'm doing my best to stay at the back of the group with Anna and Lola, twin sisters who run their own fitness app and a Pilates studio in London that I used to frequent before coming out here.

It's not that I'm in any way trying to keep whatever has blossomed between Wyatt and I in the last few days a secret. Honestly, I want to run to the top of the mountains and shout about it for everyone to hear. Because, I mean, look at him. It's Wyatt Hensley.

But it's also so *new*.

I'm not going to be foolish and assume I know what he wants from me, especially since his rule dictates he would've told me he wanted more than just sex from me by now... even if he has been meditating with me and telling me how beautiful I am when he wakes up to me in the morning.

Still, there was a reason I held back from letting my feelings for him get the best of me for so long. If this gets screwed up, then how are we supposed to run the retreat together? There's more riding on whatever we have going on than I'd like to admit. I don't know if I have the mental capacity to consider it all right now—this week is about the retreat, not us—so I'm not going to let myself think too much on it.

I'm also super aware of the fact that our guests this week are a group of influencers, who constantly have phones in their hands to capture everything going on. If I'm not careful, Wyatt and I will accidentally end up in the background of someone's post, letting the whole world know that something is going on between us before we ourselves even know what that is.

So, I'm just going to keep reminding myself that *I am exactly where I need to be right now*. That whatever is kindling between Wyatt and I is meant to happen and is all part of the divine journey planned out for me. I just need to accept it and not overthink.

Luckily, everyone's so enraptured by Wyatt's tales, listening with sparkling eyes and wide smiles. Ryan, a Canadian wellness influencer friend of mine, has been walking with Wyatt up at the front of the group, reeling off so many questions like he can't get enough.

It's the perfect start to the retreat.

And I'm so grateful to have Wyatt by my side.

Even yesterday, once all the guests had arrived, Wyatt joined us in the main house for a group dinner to settle everyone in, making more effort than I expected to get to know each of the guests. I know that the retreat means keeping Sunset Ranch going, and that's important to him, but part of me also thinks all the effort he's putting in is for me, too.

"I feel like you understated how gorgeous this place is, Rory," Anna says, taking my arm in hers. Wide blue eyes scour our surroundings, an idyllic sparkle in them. She releases a long breath, one that shows she's finally relaxing. "I can totally see why you want to stay here. I feel so at peace."

"Agreed," Lola hooks her arm through my free one, making us into a chain of three, blissed-out influencers. "I have such a good feeling about this for you."

Me too, I think, biting my lip.

I just need to see some butterflies today, and I'll be one hundred percent convinced this is all going to work out. That I'll have saved Sunset Ranch and Wyatt's job and I'll have a successful retreat to write my next bestseller about. That I'll have done Auntie Grace proud.

Though the plan is to start every morning this week with yoga by the lake on the new decking after breakfast, we began the retreat officially with a tour of Sunset Ranch today, ending at the lake. I'm going to miss not having Wyatt, Colt, Josh, and Flynn stretching with me like I've gotten so used to, but it will be good to put myself out there and actually lead a proper class again. As opposed to doing yoga with guys who purposefully make fart noises when they're getting into new positions and blame it on one of the others.

When we finally reach the lake, the sun is high and shining in the crystal clear sky. Rays of golden light glisten on the water's surface, just daring us to jump in. Luckily, wild water swimming is planned for later. The guests thank Wyatt for the tour and head over to the deck, getting their yoga mats set up and ready for our first session.

I find my way to Wyatt's side, giving his hand a brief, soft squeeze. Not enough of a touch to grab anyone else's attention though. "You know, for someone who acts like he hates socialising, you sure seemed in your element this morning."

Arms crossed, Wyatt tilts his head down to me, letting all his smugness shine with his lazy smile. "Yeah, well, they're not so bad for a bunch of fitness freaks and hippies."

"Don't be a dick." I give him a jab with my elbow, but he only laughs, barely moved by the force. "You do realise that would make *me* one of those hippies."

He shrugs, a smirk playing on his lips. "Maybe hippies are my type."

"Then maybe I should be worried about letting you spend too much time around these lot," I tease, biting my lip to hold back the beaming smile that wants to escape. Because he just told me I was his type, and suddenly I'm a giddy schoolgirl.

"*You* should be worried?" Wyatt's brow skyrocket. He shakes his head. "And what about me? Knowing you're spending all week with these ripped guys. That Nathan dude gave you far too long of a hug when he arrived yesterday too."

The zing of satisfaction from Wyatt's possessiveness is too delicious. It also makes me feel better that I haven't felt that threatened by any of the women in the group, which I'd expected given my last boyfriend dropped me for another pretty blonde influencer. Maybe I'm healing better than I thought.

"If I didn't know any better, I'd say you were jealous, Hensley."

Wyatt quickly schools his features into something like indifference, returning his tensing arms to crossing over his broad chest. "I don't know what you're talking about."

"Sure," I say, chuckling afterwards. I swear Wyatt's lips soften into a momentary smile at the sound too. "Anyway..." I nod to him, as opposed to pulling him down for a long, hot make out session like I'd really prefer to do. "Have a good day, Mr Hensley. Thanks for the tour."

"You too, Miss Jones." Wyatt nods back, but then quickly grabs my wrist when I turn to walk away. When I pivot to meet his stare, his midnight eyes flick between mine as he worries his lip. Damn, I really wish I could be kissing that mouth right now. A few beats of silence play out before he finally says, "I know you want to keep things professional, but... just remember that I'll be thinking of you. All day. You're gonna smash this retreat, Princess."

He lets me go and tips his cowboy hat in goodbye, giving a wave to the group as he walks off, the encompassing lands of Sunset Ranch a backdrop to this cowboy who might be the end of me. And honestly, even if he is, I think I'd enjoy every second of my demise.

TWENTY-EIGHT

Wyatt

I don't think I've ever been so in awe of a person before. She hasn't noticed me yet, but I've been eavesdropping on the current workshop Aurora's leading for the last ten minutes. My plan was to just drop in when I saw the backdoor wide open, mostly because I wanted to see her sunny face, to get a shot of her warmth when I've had to spend the first half of the day without it. Especially since me and the guys have been baling hay since the early hours of the morning, keeping our fingers crossed that if the weather stays good, we might get another cut this year.

But as soon as I heard Aurora talking, I was captivated and haven't moved since. It was the exact same on Tuesday and Wednesday this week when she hosted her workshops on defining success and harnessing your inner strength. Even yesterday, when I popped by the vision board making workshop she was holding in the main house, I couldn't pull myself away from listening to her talk about manifestation and the power of visualisation.

It felt odd to think about the future, though. Almost traitorous. Since I took over on the ranch, I've been living life only focusing on the short-term. When you think about the future too much, you start making promises to yourself about what you'll do, putting your faith in something that might never happen. Especially when you're expecting multiple things to be in that future—like assuming that your job and relationship would always work together, as opposed to being mutually exclusive.

And when it doesn't happen, you're just disappointed. Bitter. Angry. At yourself, really, for getting too excited over something you had no proof would work out. So, the only thing I've allowed myself to consider long-term has been working on the ranch, and even that got disrupted when Grace passed.

Yet the way Aurora spoke of the power we hold inside ourselves to decide our own future with such conviction, such intense belief, made me question my ways.

It wouldn't be the first time she's done that either.

I don't like change, but there's parts of me Aurora's somehow managed to start opening up and letting in a little more light than usual.

I'll never admit this to anyone, not even Aurora, but I might have cut out some pictures from some old magazines later that day while waiting for her to finish the evening meditation session with the group. Ones that symbolised the life on the ranch I want to keep. Deep down inside of me, wherever I'd pushed the ability to get excited about the future, something began to flicker. I'd be lying too if I said imagining a beautiful redhead by my side when choosing those pictures hadn't helped to spark that flame.

Still, I didn't let myself dwell on it too much—I was getting too ahead of myself. If I pretend like whatever has happened between Aurora and I is forever, I'm only going to put too much pressure on it and set it up for failure. Besides, she's only going to stay as long as she's happy with the retreat.

I feel guilty though for not having realised how compelling Aurora could be when she talks about the wellness things she's into. I've prowled through her Instagram more times than I'd like to admit, yet never really paid that much attention to the videos of her talking. I didn't think I was interested in learning about how to tap into my inner child or how to balance my masculine and feminine energy, whatever that even means, so I'd just glossed over them. Her speech when she was trying to convince me to agree to the retreat was incredibly persuasive, yes, but watching her right now, speaking about facing fear, I'm completely enchanted.

Maybe it's because the heat of her passion ignites every word she says, her copper waves a dance of bouncing flames from her enthusiasm. Maybe it's because she's practically glowing as she speaks, brightening up the whole room and the eyes of each guest as they watch her, just as engrossed as me. Or maybe it's because I can feel the confidence radiating from her, the energy in the room lifting in response, as if her own words are building back up the layers of self-belief she once had.

I've been trying hard this week to remind her of how much I believe in her and the retreat whenever she gets slightly anxious, but I'm not sure she even needs me to. Each time she seems to be able to come out of her worries quicker and quicker. It's a wonder to watch Aurora flourish more each day, spreading her wings wider. Like she's finally climbing out of the cocoon of self-doubt she'd been trapped in, not so afraid to let herself fly.

"Everything you want will always be on the other side of fear. It sucks, I know," Aurora laughs, the group's chuckles ringing in response. "But it's because your dreams are on the next level of your current life. In order to achieve them, you have to level up yourself, you have to evolve and become the person who is capable of winning that next level—"

Aurora cuts herself off when she finally notices me. A rosy flush paints the apple of her cheeks as she tucks her hair behind her ears several times. She does that when she's nervous, I've noticed. It's cute.

But I don't want her to be nervous, not because of me, when I'm literally here cheering her on mentally. The six guests twist subtly, following where Aurora's eyes are locked on me, and all give me a quick smile before turning back.

You're doing great, I mouth, nodding to encourage her on.

Her shoulders drop from where I hadn't realised they had tensed up. Toning down the beam my words had elicited, Aurora rolls her strawberry lips together, taking a deep breath.

"Sorry, I got distracted by a wild rancher." She bites her lip when she gives me one last glance, a mischievous one this time, the kind that says *I'll make you pay for this later,* and has me thinking, *I sure hope so.* "So, you need to become the person who is capable of winning that next level. That means you have to evolve and develop parts of yourself for the good, and that's actually where a lot of the fear comes in. It's scary to change who we've become so comfortable being..."

I tune out from Aurora's speech, readying myself to leave. As much as I would love to stay there and listen, I want her to feel comfortable and as confident as she seemed before she noticed me.

Just as I head to the back door, I spy something on the kitchen counter. Trying to be as inconspicuous as possible, I shuffle over, hoping not to disrupt the session any further. Aurora's motivational words about *not letting the fear of what could happen make nothing happen* echo through the open-plan house. My skin prickles when I finally behold the vision board covered with photos of mountainous landscapes and vast pastures, bonfires outside of cabins and horse riding, candlelit picnics by lakes, and best seller book listings.

It's everything I could've ever imagined in my own future, including for Aurora with her books.

It's everything we already have.

This is all she wants?

I was expecting to see pictures related to the ranch and retreat, but alongside plenty of other things too—a London townhouse maybe, or holidays in some trendy place like Bali, or new brands she'd like to work with through her influencing.

But this... *I* can give her this.

This doesn't require me to be someone I'm not. It doesn't need me to be that *ambitious* guy Holly expected from me. It just needs me to be... well, me.

Wyatt Augustus Hensley might actually be enough.

Finally.

Because I can keep this ranch running, I can support Aurora through the retreat, I can help out with any errands when she needs time to write her book, I can take her on all the romantic dates she wants. I would *happily* do all of that.

If someone told me that was my future, I'd sign myself away to it without a second thought.

Don't let the fear of what could happen make nothing happen.

But if I let myself consider this and don't try and hold back from how I feel for Aurora, I could jeopardise everything I've worked for. She could decide that she only wanted me from a purely physical standpoint—the classic getting under someone to get over someone, a natural step in healing from a breakup, right? Even if she did want more, after

255

some time, she might finally see that I'm not like these other hustling, ambitious gym influencers she seems to surround herself with.

I'm just Wyatt Hensley. Rancher.

And when she realises that she might decide this ranch life is too small for her. It might have worked for Grace, but Aurora's still young, with vibrant dreams she wants to soar as high and wide as possible for, as opposed to settling down in the middle of nowhere. Then I'll be back to the same position as when she arrived—having to give up my ranch. Except this time, I'd also be giving up my heart.

So then, what? I just let nothing happen? Let this fizzle out?

Out of fear.

Everything you want will always be on the other side of fear.

You have to evolve and become the person who is capable of winning that next level.

It's scary to change who we've become so comfortable being.

The only version of me who can get past that is the Wyatt who lets himself root for a better future. The one who finds a way to believe that he might just be enough for a girl like Aurora Jones. Here I've been, wondering why Aurora can't believe in herself the way I do, yet I'm just as bad as her.

But *she* believes in me. I can feel it. In the way she's never judged my decisions in the past, the way she accepted my desire to do nothing but ranching for a living without question, the way she automatically made me a part of this retreat, undoubtedly happy to leave the ranch in my hands.

The way she stood up to my dad for me. Her fierce belief in me shone so brightly that evening.

Tightness pulls across my chest. I rub my hand over where my eagle tattoo sits, attempting to knead out some of the tension.

I'd managed to stay oblivious to what Aurora had been saying, until a familiar sentence leaves her lips, echoing behind me. "Sometimes the hardest thing we can do is trust blindly in who we are."

A faint shiver racks my body, her voice sounding eerily like Grace's the first time she told me that, just before I went to college.

I just need to trust blindly in my worth.

That I can be the person who can give Aurora this future.

And maybe I can do that, especially if I know Aurora is going to be by my side. Maybe I can try to make myself start hoping that she'll stay, start believing that I'm enough for her, that this could actually be... long-term.

I'll find a way to level up. For her.

And then I'll give her everything she could ever dream of.

Twenty-Nine

Aurora

Ryan gives me a massive hug, then shakes Wyatt's hand, thanking us both before helping Luke heft his suitcase into the boot of the taxi. He waves goodbye and climbs inside the car with a huge smile on his face, just like the other five did when they headed off throughout the day. I'm hoping that's a testament to everything they've learned and worked on this week.

That's the last one to leave, which means the first trial run of the retreat is officially over. I can't rip my eyes away from the car until it finally disappears in the distance, beyond visibility, because I'm still kind of stunned that I managed it all.

Taking a long blink and a deep breath to steady all the excitement and nerves and just overwhelm from the whole week, I turn to Wyatt, taken aback by how brightly he's beaming at me. I'm so bloody grateful to have had him this week—he's been so helpful and supportive throughout it all, anchoring me back down whenever I needed it, like I knew he would. He even gave me another foot rub the other night whilst I scrawled down all my thoughts about what I could write in my book. I don't know what's gotten into him.

259

Every time he's told me he believed in me I think I've started to more as well. Part of me is beginning to wonder if maybe I don't have to do this healing all by myself.

"We did it," I breathe out in a laugh of disbelief.

Wyatt takes my face in his hands, midnight eyes sparkling down at me. "No, Aurora, *you* did it. You were amazing!"

Suddenly, his hands drop to my waist, and he lifts me up, spinning me around above him until I'm squealing. His laugh is a warm, thunderous rumble, rousing the butterflies already waking inside of me. When he finally stops, he lets my body slowly slide down his, keeping his grasp on me close and tight, every inch of his warm, solid body flush with mine. My feet hit the ground and I lean my head against his chest, knowing he won't pull away this time, listening to his steadying heartbeat. The one I've loved listening to every morning as we've cuddled in bed, readying ourselves for the day.

I've always wondered if there was something missing from my morning routine, and I'm finally realising it was him.

Fingers run through my hair, stroking the back of my head as softly and rhythmically as the summer breeze. My arms tighten around Wyatt's neck as he presses a kiss on my parting, then whispers, "I'm so proud of you. I knew you'd smash it."

"We really did smash it, didn't we?" I peel myself an inch or so away—enough to gaze up at the dark angles of his face, but still close enough to smell his warm, pinewood scent. The smell of home. "Everything went so well, Wyatt. I really think this could work."

That we could do the retreat permanently.

That maybe, I could stay.

Damn, that's a big deal.

Wyatt's grip pulses, his eyes flashing momentarily. I wonder if he's thinking the same, considering the eternality of my words.

But then he quickly pushes out another smile, turning us away from the main house. One hand seeks out mine, fingers lacing together with the usual ease.

"Agreed, but let's talk about that properly later," Wyatt suggests, leading me towards his place, across the grass. After all the mental and physical capacity this week has taken, I was kind of hoping to jump in a bubble bath now everyone has gone, to properly relax. "Let's give everything some time to sink in, and in the meantime, I owe you a proper date."

"A date?" My brows shoot up and I halt, but Wyatt tugs me on, directing me over to his truck. "I'm very intrigued what a proper date with Wyatt Hensley entails. Chopping up some logs whilst we brood over all the problems with the technology-obsessed youth?"

His face hardens, smile disappearing.

Catching me off guard, Wyatt spins me and takes my hips, backing me up until I'm pressed against his truck door. All the breath escapes my lungs, his solid, hot frame leaning over me. His eyes track my throat as I swallow, then flick back to mine, pinning me in place harder than his body is with how dark they are. Being at someone else's mercy was never something I expected to drive me so wild, but when that someone is Wyatt Hensley, all gorgeous light-brown skin and dark features, I'm consumed by the feeling.

"Yes, Aurora, a date." Wyatt brings his lips down to my ear, brushing them over the sensitive skin just below. Shivers race across my chest. "Because even though not being able to have you whenever I've wanted all week has been driving me crazy." He nips my earlobe, exhilaration rushing through my bones. "I... I want you to know that this means more to me than just sex. I want to get to know as much as I can about you. I want all of you."

Now he's staring straight into my eyes, flicking between them like he's searching for something as he steps back. A layer of exhaustion from this week is immediately swept away with a wave of relief at his words—one I hadn't realised had been weighing me down. I'd been trying to force myself to focus on the retreat, as opposed to what was happening between me and Wyatt, causing me to ignore the worries that were clearly burdening me.

Because he hadn't stuck to his rule. He hadn't told me straight away what he wanted, like the guys said he normally does.

But now he has.

He wants all of me.

And I've never been more certain about something than I have about wanting all of him too.

The corners of Wyatt's lips twitch, and God, I thought I was in a vulnerable position, but I swear he might be shaking a little. I think he's nervous. Do I seriously make Wyatt Hensley nervous?

"That sounds wonderful," I manage to get out over my fluttering heart, the one he seems to have some weird control over now.

Wyatt nods and grins, then opens the truck door for me once I shuffle out the way. "Plus, I can't keep calling you Princess without actually treating you like one, can I?"

***

I'm honestly speechless when we pull up to the lake. If the golden blanket thrown over the mountains and water from the beginnings of the setting sun wasn't enough to make this place feel magical, then the myriad of tea lights dotted around the decking, surrounding the cosy quilt and blankets, might just do it. Words continue to fail me as Wyatt leads me down the deck to where our date night awaits.

Now we're closer, I can see the wrapped plates full of yummy cheeses, meats, breads, and veggies, alongside flasks of drinks.

This is almost identical to one of the pictures from Pinterest that I'd added to my vision board in the week.

"When did you do this?" I ask, barely able to get the question out in my breathless, awe-struck state. There's a lot of things I hadn't expected from Wyatt over the last month, but *this* has got to be the most shocking. He's a bloody romantic, isn't he?

Maybe the universe *has* been listening to me all this time. Maybe everything I've been working through, all the heartbreak and healing, was leading me here.

To... him.

Wyatt shrugs and waits for me to make myself comfy amongst the plentiful cushions before joining. He sits so his knee is touching mine, then leans back, one arm behind me.

"I had a bit of time in between people leaving."

"It's perfect," I confess, gushing over the whole set up, the effort that's gone into it, and our amber-lit, serene surroundings that have added the finishing touch. I don't think I'll ever tire of this. The beauty, the warmth, the nature. I could watch it all for decades.

When I turn to Wyatt, it's me he's watching instead, midnight eyes melting into dark golden pools from the lights around us. Like I'm more beautiful than anything Sunset Ranch could have to offer, and I don't even question the idea, because... maybe tonight I am.

A soft smile graces Wyatt's face before he leans in and kisses me gently. "Not as perfect as you," he whispers against my mouth, sealing the words with another brush of his lips.

Although part of me wants to run my hands through his hair and make out with Wyatt all night under the sunset and twinkling lights, I hadn't realised how starving I was until I saw the food, and we're quick to tuck in. We swap stories of our childhoods—favourite subjects at school, our dream jobs, friendships that came and went, and argue for far too long over whether it's easier being the youngest or oldest sibling.

Trying to figure out how British secondary school years match up to American high school years also proves to be far more complicated than it should be when we finally move on. I sip a fruity smoothie from one of the flasks—the closest flavour Wyatt could find in the shops to the berry one I like from Sitting Pretty—and relish in how animated he seems telling me all about his friendship with Sawyer, Duke, and Wolfman, how they bonded over football.

He almost pushes me into the lake when I ask if he had to let one of the guys get with Cherry, who he'd pick.

Every second of conversation, we're touching. Whether it's a knee against a leg, feet crossed over each other, or fingers drawing lazy swirls against arms and hips. I remember back to a month ago, when Wyatt would flinch or freeze at any contact we made. But now, it's like he can't get enough, like he craves the sensation of my body against his. And honestly, I feel the same.

It's like when we're connected, everything feels stronger, brighter, safer. Like we were two broken currents that are finally able to flow free.

I'm elated to discover that one of the flasks has hot chocolate inside, and Wyatt rummages around for another cup so he can pour it out for us both. Once we're both served, we huddle closer with a blanket wrapped lazily around us, even though the summer evening isn't that cool yet. I lean my head against Wyatt's shoulder, its curve supporting my neck as if it were designed for us to fit.

The water ahead is almost the same shade of Wyatt's eyes as night finally paints the last patches of the sky with glittering darkness. My heart feels so full, just like it used to when I was younger and would sit out here, my great aunt beside me. Part of me wonders if Auntie Grace didn't just leave me the ranch because she thought I'd want it, but because she knew I'd *need* it.

That maybe she knew how tumultuous your twenties could feel sometimes, how easily you could get lost even when you thought you were taking all the right steps. And that I would need the ranch to ground me again and remind me of what life is truly about.

Like romantic lakeside dates with a handsome, kind cowboy.

Sometimes Auntie Grace would do things, or tell me things, like she already knew they'd happen. Telling me to pursue my passion for blogging and wellness seemed so easy for her, she didn't even consider any other options, as if she'd seen the future and knew it would work out. Or maybe she just knew that everything always works out, so no matter what road you take, it would bring you to the right destination eventually. I wish I could tell younger Rory that.

"If you could go back in time and give your younger self one piece of advice, what would it be?" I ponder aloud.

Wyatt chuckles, and I peek up to see him worrying his lip, brows knitted in contemplation. Then he laughs again, this time his frame shaking, making me straighten up. I raise my brows, hoping for an explanation.

"It's funny, because if you'd have asked me that a month ago, I think my answer would've been *very* different."

265

"How so?"

"I used to think I'd tell myself something along the lines of sticking with football or pursuing the ranching career earlier to avoid disappointing people. I know what I chose to do made me happy, but I ain't gonna pretend that I haven't wondered about all the what ifs. What if I'd pursued football? Would I have been drafted to a good team? Or what if I'd gone to law school? Would I have been ambitious enough for, well, Holly then?"

Would we even be sitting here if he had done any of that?

Wyatt shakes his head, pushing some loose curls back. As he's been speaking, his eyes have stayed glued to the lake, yet now he slowly twists to face me, blinking before clearing his throat.

"But now, I don't care about any of that. I'd just tell younger me to do what felt right in the moment. I wouldn't tell him to do anything different, because no matter how broken my road ended up being, I know now that it was the right one, as it still led me here..." Wyatt's throat bobs. "With you. All those difficult decisions and wrong turns, all those losses and broken hearts, were just guiding me to where I am now. To home. And to you, Aurora."

The smile that appears as he says my name is pure hope. If he kissed me right now, I'd taste new beginnings, budding dreams, and shimmering promises. Everything I didn't realise I'd needed.

To be chosen.

Yeah, Auntie Grace definitely gave me the ranch for a reason.

I shuffle onto Wyatt's lap and take his face in my hands, letting his stubble rasp against my palms. I desperately want to let myself get lost in his midnight eyes, so full of wonder. His hands settle on my hips, fingers stroking just above where my shorts sit, brushing the exposed skin of my waist.

"I wouldn't change a thing either, you know? I'd do it all again, despite knowing I'd have to feel scared, lost, and heartbroken, because it would be worth it. Even just for this night." I trace the edge of his jaw with the tips of my fingers, and he leans into the touch, dark lashes fluttering down over his eyes. "I don't know what the future holds, but I do know that I was meant to come back to Sunset Ranch. I was meant to meet you."

When Wyatt kisses me this time, it's everything we've said repeated with the press of lips and the twist of tongues. It's desperate yet tender, impassioned yet soft. It makes me feel like every time I ever doubted or questioned myself was so silly, because right now, wrapped in Wyatt's embrace, I feel invaluable.

"Oh, there's one more thing I'd tell my younger self," Wyatt interrupts our kiss to say. He presses his lips to each corner of my mouth before explaining. "I'd tell him that if he ever gets a gorgeous, crazy redhead by the lake at night, he should definitely invite her to skinny dip with him."

I'm already jumping up and pulling my top over my head as I run down the deck, yelling, "Last one in has to clean all the guesthouses!"

Thirty

Aurora

"And this one?" Wyatt asks, rubbing his thumb over where the word *grateful* is tattooed across my hipbone, above my bikini bottoms. His head rests against my stomach, my fingers playing with his silky curls rhythmically as the afternoon sun beats down on us.

Perfection would be the best word to describe this moment. The world around us is so still, save for the occasional whisper of the breeze between the blades of grass in the pasture and the odd whinny from the horses grazing nearby after our ride. But I also can't wait for when we head back to the stables and can give the horses a brush down—one of my favourite little peaceful activities to do these days. I've started spending more time with the horses now I feel more confident riding, and I hadn't realised how soothing being around such majestic, strong creatures could be.

I don't even try to hide my glee when I see butterflies pass by, reminding me that this is exactly where I'm supposed to be. I feel at utter peace, just me, the beautiful ranch I live on, and the man who somehow has managed to help me feel strong over the last month or so.

The man who has helped me build a home here.

I honestly couldn't imagine being anywhere else. Sometimes I forget that I've only been at Sunset Ranch for almost two months. The past week, since the last trial run of the retreat ended, has just felt so *natural*. Waking up to the brush of Wyatt's lips against my forehead before he heads out to work on the ranch. Getting sun-kissed from our lunchtime horse riding sessions together. Even my writing has been flowing, words and ideas coming to me so easily as I describe the way Sunset Ranch has helped me believe in myself more.

I've always tried to romanticise life as best as I could, exactly how Auntie Grace taught me, but doing so comes so easily here on Sunset Ranch. The picnic blanket providing us comfort feels like we're floating on a cloud and the warm rays of golden sunlight bathing me make me feel weightless. Without a care in the world. I'm almost tempted to say that I feel like old Rory again.

"Princess." Wyatt pokes me in my hip, twisting his head around to face me now. "You better not be falling asleep on me there."

"I'm still here, don't worry," I chuckle, even though our ride together did tire me out more than I expected. I lift my head slightly to catch his midnight eyes for a moment. They look all glazed and blissful, just like they usually do when he wakes me up in the morning, peppering my body with kisses.

I let out a content breath. "That one is to remind me that there are always things to be grateful for in life, no matter the situation."

"What are you grateful for right now?" Wyatt mumbles into my skin, sounding far too close to sleep for someone who just made a jab at me for possibly dozing off. Though, in his defence, he has been working out in the hay meadows all morning.

I stroke my fingers over his hair softly, admiring the dark lashes lying over his shut eyes, the strong angle of his jaw covered in stubble, and his solid body, half-naked beside me. Everything about him speaks strength and toughness, yet I know where his softness lies. I can see it in the gentle brush of his fingers against my skin, the subtle curve of his lips, and the way he's purposefully taking some of his weight on his folded arms, not leaning it all on me.

"I'm really grateful that I got to meet such great friends like Sawyer and Wolfman."

One of Wyatt's eyes shoots open.

"And Duke?"

He frowns.

"What?" I laugh, biting down on my lip.

"You're supposed to say *me*."

I roll my eyes and poke his back. "Don't be so full of yourself... Besides, that's obvious, isn't it?"

"Yeah, true. You're obsessed with me." Wyatt grins too proudly and wraps his arms around me, hugging me overly tight. Even if he's right, I can't be the first to admit it.

"If you say so." I shrug, a pretty pitiful attempt at nonchalance considering how much I'm smiling at him. But he's grinning back, and that just makes me powerless. "Okay, your turn now, I've told you about mine."

I purposefully ruffle his hair to wake him up a bit. He's been resting on me in just his jeans, toned back glistening under the sun, baring those mysterious tattoos I've still yet to decipher.

"Fine, fine. Which one first?"

"I'm guessing the Roman numerals are birthdays or something?" I surmise, running my fingers down the list. His skin breaks out in goosebumps in response.

"Yup, the whole Hensley clan."

God, I just love how much he cares for his family. Even if he does shove Cherry about most of the time and complain about his parents, there's an undeniable undercurrent of love for them in everything he does. I'd be honoured to call him family.

"That's cute."

"Aurora," Wyatt almost growls, the combination of his breath against my bare stomach and the scrutiny of his dark eyes makes my body tighten. "You know what I think about you calling me cute."

"Sorry, sorry—I mean that's super manly."

"Much better." He nods and nuzzles back into my stomach.

I snort and tap his other tattoo—the one of a man with wings falling. I'm certain I've seen some similar artwork before, but I can't quite figure it out. "And this one?"

A slow sigh leaves Wyatt's lips before he explains. "It's of Icarus falling. It's supposed to be a reminder to not fly too close to the sun."

"Why?" I trail my fingers back up his neck and run them over his curls again, noticing the tension that's started to ease into his body, making him more rigid.

"Because I need a reminder to not let myself get carried away with dreams..." He opens his eyes, but they're cast downwards, as if his mind has travelled someplace else. Somewhere I can't go with him. "Because nothing lasts forever. Things always have to come down eventually."

"Wyatt." I shuffle so that I'm sitting up, forcing him up as well with another sigh. "Why would you want to remind yourself of that? That's not nice."

He runs a hand through his hair, avoiding eye contact. "No, but it is... or was, realistic."

"But... but you're always telling me that I can achieve whatever I want. You're always cheering me on to go after my dreams." I don't think there's been a moment when I've been worried about the retreat or my influencing or whatever my anxiety has fixated on in that moment that he hasn't told me he believes in me. He's talked me back into believing in myself more than I can count. Why won't he do that for himself?

Lightness sweeps across his face, his expression suddenly brightening as he turns to face me properly. He threads his fingers between mine, pulsing once they're intertwined. "Yeah, because you deserve nothing less, Aurora. I want you to have everything you could ever dream of."

"Well, you deserve that too." I pull my hands away and settle them against his jaw, shuffling onto my knees so that I'm closer. So that I can properly look into his midnight eyes. So that I can see the shimmer of fear in them, the kind that reminds me we're both healing. Together. "Wyatt, you're such a damn good person, you deserve everything you could ever want in life. Come on, if you could have anything in the world, what would it be?"

Wyatt glances down, his hands brushing up my thighs. I watch as his touch makes its way up my hips, hands settling around my waist. Reminding me of where I feel most stable. Then a small smile tugs at the corners of his mouth, eyes crinkling with an easily missed chuckle.

"I think I've got everything I could ever want right now."

My chest flutters when he catches my gaze, his smile spreading out softly. I have to force myself to breathe when the way he's looking at me with such wonder makes my whole body freeze. "Yeah?"

"Yeah... and I know I'm not wired to think as positively as you, but I'm trying, Aurora. I want to be the version of me who doesn't think this is all gonna come crashing down. Who doesn't worry you're gonna decide this life isn't enough for you. That *I* might not be enough for you, because even though it's hard to believe, I really think I could be."

Now my hands are locked around his neck, and I bring my forehead to his, relishing in being so connected to him, staring deeply into his dark eyes.

My anchor. My home.

"Well, I believe it. I know you're enough. I don't want you to be anyone but yourself, Hensley. Because I like you a hell of a lot as you are."

Wyatt's eyes flash with surprise, and what seems like hope—the kind of hope I don't think he's let himself have in years. "Good, because I like you a hell of a lot too, Princess, and I don't plan on letting you go."

THIRTY-ONE

Wyatt

This might be the first night Duke's bar has ever been graced by the voice of Hannah Montana. Or Aurora and Cherry's attempt to remember as much of the Hoedown Throwdown as possible.

I'm not sure how Aurora managed to convince Duke to let her play the song, but given that he's decided to actually take some of the night off with us guys for once, I don't think he cares. Besides, he seems to be enjoying watching the two girls make fools of themselves as much as the rest of us.

Still, the whole bar feels more vibrant than usual tonight, nothing but contagious laughter and ecstatic conversation flowing around us. Maybe it's always been this way, but all I know is wherever Aurora Jones is, life seems a hell of a lot brighter.

Just like the last two weeks have been since the first trial run ended. I've never been so stupidly excited knowing I don't have to make excuses to see her or touch her anymore. Instead, I get to wake up to her beautiful, glowing face some mornings, and finish work on other days knowing I can come back and listen to her beam about her day before making her come apart screaming my name later that night.

The best thing about Aurora is that she reminds me there are more than enough reasons to wake up smiling each day. Not just because of her, because I know what can happen when you base your entire happiness on one person. Though, she's definitely ninety nine percent of those reasons, especially when I've got my face between her legs, or she's on her knees for me.

But because of the way she lives every bit of her life to the fullest. Like how she savours every mouthful of food and can't wait to tell me about how delicious it was. Or how every time she jumps into bed, she loves running her hands over the soft sheets, relishing in how they feel. Or how she always stops to watch every sunset while listening to me tell her all about my day. And how she's constantly finding ways to touch me, even if it's just a brush of fingers against my back, like she's making sure to appreciate any time with me.

It makes me feel... worthy. More than I ever have before. It gives me just a little bit of hope that perhaps I've been wrong all these years. That maybe some things can last forever.

When I'm with Aurora, the self-doubt that creeps up on me when she mentions long-term goals for the ranch, wondering if she'll really want this life forever, is a little bit easier to bat away. It makes the road ahead look slightly straighter, as opposed to the rocky path behind me. And it makes trying to be the version of me who lets himself dream about our future without fear easier.

I'm shaking my head at Aurora dancing as I sip my beer, but I know right now she's so consumed with joy that she doesn't care what other people think. Which is exactly how she deserves to live her life, because her soul is goddamn golden, even if sometimes her brain doesn't always remind her of that.

Even if I didn't realise it at first either.

Still, I can't help but notice since the first trial run of the retreat went well, I haven't had to help talk her out of as many small attacks of anxiety like she's had before. She's been eager to tell me every time she's managed to get some new ideas down about her book, not so afraid of it anymore.

Breathless from dancing and the endless silvery laughs ringing from her strawberry lips, Aurora flops into the booth beside me, Cherry jumping in next to Duke on the other side, immediately dropping into conversation with him and Wolfman.

Aurora doesn't hesitate to press up against me, her heat spreading over me, scorching my skin. I don't like that it makes me freeze for a second, aware that there's so many other people around us. People I went to high school with that like to talk and haven't even tried to hide the way they've been eyeing up Aurora all night. Probably wondering what she's doing with me, how long she'll stay around before—

Wait, no. That was the old version of me.

I'm supposed to be next level me who believes in myself.

For her.

Aurora's hand slaps down on my thigh, pulsing against my muscles. So blatantly and unashamedly marking me as hers as she bats her lashes at me. Then she brushes her fingers along my jeans, making me flinch when they trail just a little bit too high.

I shoot her a wild glare, feeling the heat creeping into my cheeks, and other places. I don't need her teasing me when we're surrounded by people. When I'm already wound up because I've been seething every time a guy has checked her out tonight. Which has been a lot, since the ripped denim shorts and lacey white crop top hugging her body are leaving very little to the imagination right now.

And that's torturous for me, given that I know *exactly* what lies beneath. The paradise that just a few layers of clothing could reveal...

Aurora bites down on her grin, reddening her lip as mischief dances brightly behind those hazel eyes. Fuck, I want to be the one biting her lip. Her neck too. And breasts. Which I've realised I'm now staring directly at—

"At least have the decency to not eye-fuck each other in front of his little sister." Sawyer's head pops between ours, knocking me out of whatever lust-filled trance Aurora so easily had me in.

I throw my scowl over to meet his shit-eating grin as he arrives at the booth with a dark-haired woman he must've picked up on his trip to the bar. He lets her slip in first next to Cherry, who seems to recognise her, and they start chatting.

Aurora's fingers dig into my thigh once more before she announces, "Be back in a second, I need the loo," and bounces up from the booth.

I watch her walk away for all but five seconds before I'm also climbing out, stating that I'm off to the bathroom too. No one seems to take much notice, all in that perfect state of inebriation when their awareness doesn't spread far beyond whatever conversation has them enraptured.

Except for Sawyer, who perks an accusatory brow, beer bottle at his mouth as he jests, "Wow, so subtle."

"Can you really blame me?" I admit as I pass, knowing he's only goading me because this is the kind of thing I'd be ripping into him about. God knows he's done it in his fair share of bathrooms.

Luckily, it doesn't take many strides to catch up with Aurora.

"Hold up, Princess." I grab her wrist as we round the corner towards the bathrooms, spinning her into my clutch. Her hands land on my chest and quickly wind round my neck, rosy cheeks framing a dreamy smile. One that says she knows exactly why I'm here. One that makes me second guess who the mastermind behind this plan actually is.

Damn, I think I might have met my match.

"You took your time," she teases.

I don't even care who is looking when I steal a kiss from her before edging us further down the corridor. We slip inside the end toilet, and I thank God that Duke decided to put individual unisex toilets into the bar when he refurbished it.

The lights flick on, raining fluorescence over Aurora's golden skin, making it gleam where a light perspiration still clings to her from dancing. I plan on making her shine even more. I want her glowing with sweat and orgasms.

Hands clasped behind her back, pushing her chest forward, Aurora backs up into the door, watching me with anticipation of when I'll strike. But I'm still taking my fill, drinking in the sight of her, despite my aching cock straining against my jeans.

Licking my lips, I perch myself on the edge of the sink. "Take off your shorts."

Aurora lets out a one of those breathy giggles that I adore. It's a little slip of the innocent side of her, but the sparkle in her eyes that accompanies it tells me that she's excited. Eager to dip into that dark, sensuous part of her. The one that shows its face in each of her hidden tattoos. Tattoos I plan on running my tongue over tonight.

She starts to unbutton her shorts, but turns around, bending over as she drops them, giving me the perfect view of her ass. I barely hold back a hiss when my body tenses with agonising arousal. When she snaps back up, she flashes me a smug grin over her shoulder. Eyes stay locked with mine even when she shimmies her black thong over her hips, letting it drop to the floor.

"Such a little tease." I stalk towards her, gooseflesh covering my skin when her giggle escapes again. But there's trouble behind it this time, the tone slightly deeper.

Keeping my touch light against Aurora's skin, I trail my fingers over her hips, up the sweet curve of her waist, until they're tucked beneath her top. I lift it over her head, letting the floor swallow up her clothes as I cup my hands around her breasts. She presses her ass up against me, starting to grind with a sweet moan.

The heavenly sound forces me to spin Aurora around with sheer desperation. I want her delicious whimpers drowning out any other noise. Crashing my lips against hers, I haul her up into my arms, her legs instantly circling my hips when I force us back against the door. She angles her head so that I can take the kiss deeper, letting my tongue sweep in, lapping up the sugary taste of her luscious mouth. Her teeth skim my bottom lip in between kisses before sinking into the flesh, tugging until I'm groaning with shuddering pleasure.

"Condom?" I ask in a breathless whisper.

"My bag," she barely manages back.

Hands sunk into her soft ass cheeks, I squat down to grab her bag then move us over to the counter where the sink sits. Legs still draped around me, barely letting me push my jeans and underwear down, Aurora grabs the condom. While I pull off my top, she wraps her fingers around my length, giving it a few unbearably slow pumps before working the condom over me. I'm going to have to really hold it together if just her tight grasp is already driving me crazy.

With another urgent kiss, full of brutal hunger, I ease Aurora back, giving me the space to run my cock between her wetness, letting her need coat me. I press the head against her clit, making her body jolt and eliciting a gasp when I circle it around. I want to tease her more, coax her into begging for me, but she looks so goddamn divine right now, freckled face drawn in with irresistible need, hazel eyes ready to roll. All I want is to make her body soar.

So, I snake my hand around her waist and slide my cock through her centre, groaning at how soaked she is, gently easing myself inside of her.

"Oh my God." She sucks in a breath, and I don't think I'll ever get tired of the sound of her gasping for me. The feel of her slick heat as she stretches for me. The sight of us joined like this.

"God, you fit around me so well, Princess," I breathe out, reaching to rub my thumb over her clit. The pace of my thrusts increases, invoking louder whimpers from Aurora each time.

She's taking it so well, hands braced on the sink behind, breasts on full, delectable display. But I want to feel more of her.

"Hands around my neck," I demand, and Aurora quickly obeys. I wind my arms under her legs, allowing me to take her at an angle that feels so goddamn deep, I might just fall into oblivion. Especially when Aurora moans out my name against my neck, her hot breath making my skin tingle. Every one of my senses is lost in her—her reviving scent, her quickening breath, her fingers digging into my shoulders as I thrust harder and deeper.

"Play with yourself for me," I command, my voice hoarse from my shuddering breath and feral groans of pleasure. "I want you trembling around my cock."

She nods frantically as she licks her fingers then starts circling them around her clit, immediately moaning louder. The hot slap of skin against skin echoes through the bathroom with each punishing thrust I unleash on her, frantically desperate to soak up as much ecstasy from her tightness whilst pleasuring her to a point of no return.

Fuck, I can already feel my release racing towards me. I'm so addicted to being inside of her, I'm not sure I can stop. Not when her eyes are fluttering and her legs are shaking around me.

She's the kind of high I'd chase for eternity.

"God, Aurora, you're so fucking incredible," I say, pounding into her harder.

Her eyes shoot open, locking with mine as her face quivers, strawberry lips parting to let out a heavenly whimper. It's all I need to let go, and my orgasm hits me, making me drive into her brutally one last time, pressing my forehead against hers as I groan.

We're both trying to catch our breath, lips inches apart when I lean in to kiss her, slipping myself out. I trail my lips across her jaw, her neck, sucking on each tender spot, before I'm dragging my tongue down her chest. I take one of her nipples in my mouth, rolling my tongue around it. Then it's running over her butterfly tattoo, down to where *grateful* is scrawled on her hip, until I'm at her clit. Gently teasing and sucking, I thrust two fingers inside of her, curling them so I can stroke exactly where she needs it, the responding twitch of her body telling me I'm there.

Aurora's fingers sift through my hair, grasping and pushing my head down until she's basically grinding against my face. Knowing how badly she wants to come, how free she feels to demand it from me like this, is so fucking hot.

"Fuck, Wyatt, don't stop," she lets out in a broken whisper. Her mouth stays open, silent moans escaping, eyes scrunching closed harder by the second. I can feel her sweet body tensing around me, even her fingers are tightening in my hair.

Her legs start to shake around my shoulders, and then she's calling out, back arching up. She's trembling as I continue to devour her through the orgasm, wanting her to know that I'll give her every ounce of pleasure she could ever ask for. And that I'd give up everything for the opportunity.

Thirty-Two

Wyatt

"Hey, Princess," I call over to Aurora as I make my way to the stairs of the back deck. "Everything's set in place and ready."

She's curled up on the swing, engrossed in her phone, copper waves casting shadows over half of her crumpled face, until she hears me and perks up, glowing features softening. An excited, beaming smile follows, the kind where she has to bite down on those strawberry lips, the grin almost overwhelming.

Because she's happy to see *me*.

Sometimes I wonder if I've been living a dream for the last few weeks.

"Hey, Hensley," she purrs.

Lightness sweeps through my body as I near her, easing the usual tension I build up over a week's work. It's like she's my reward for working hard, a reminder that everything I'm doing is worth it. That trying to be this more hopeful version of me is the right choice.

There's no doubt that Aurora looks good in everything she wears, especially when it's one of my T-shirts to bed. But there's something about her when she's in her gym wear like today that has me stopping in silent wonder. Maybe it's because she wears it so casually, like it's just her boring, everyday clothes, oblivious to the way they highlight every beautifully sculpted curve of her body. Oblivious to the way the bright colours of all her gym sets make her stand out, like a beacon of hope in my dull world.

"Did that meditation help you feel better in the end, or do you need to calm your nerves by sitting on my face?" I ask, stalking over to the swing. The midday sun shines down, circling the house with golden light.

Her lips pop open with an innocent giggle as she bats her wide, glistening eyes up at me. "You have the dirtiest mouth I've ever heard, Hensley."

"And yet you let me do whatever I want with that mouth, so it can't be that bad," I retort as I settle onto the swing. I hold out my hands for her legs so they can rest over my lap, and she spreads out, her warmth seeping into me.

Locking my eyes on hers, my head angled just a little, I trail my fingers up her leg as slowly as possible, relishing in the way her body reacts to me as I drift further up her thigh. The flush of her cheeks, the prickling of her golden skin, the shuddering of her chest. Every inch of her body is burned into my memory, I feel like I could navigate it with my eyes closed, just like the back roads I always take into town.

The only thing in the way of where I really want my fingers to be is her phone, sat resting in her lap. I tap it, asking, "What were you so focused on?"

It takes Aurora a couple of seconds and blinks to snap back to reality. Oh, how I would love to know what was running through her mind just then, but I'm sure I'll get to find out later when all the guests have arrived and are in their lodgings.

"Just a post for tonight." Aurora giggles again as she finds the photo and presents her phone to me. And there I am riding Dusty, leading the trail on the last retreat. I don't even know how she managed to take that. I'm just glad it's not that darned one she once took of me when she forced me into yoga.

"Thanks for asking for my permission," I snort, shaking my head. There's no point in me trying to make her take it down. Even if I like to think I'm strong, I know I'll never win in a battle against Aurora—all she needs to do is flutter her lashes and I'll be on my knees. And I'm not even ashamed to admit that now.

I have always said I am a weak man when it comes to her.

Aurora waves me off and wriggles closer so we're more intertwined. "You looked so hot, up high on your horse, riding like a true cowboy. I couldn't resist. Though," she crumples her freckled nose, "it seems I'm not the only one who thinks that. I've had to remind myself multiple times that I can't blast my followers in the comments telling them to back off because he's mine."

"All yours." I kiss her forehead, not even thinking twice about saying it. I don't miss the slight shock that flickers in her eyes when I pull away, but it's true—I am completely and utterly hers.

I'm uncertain how I got to this point, considering two months ago I would've done anything to see her leave, yet I can't imagine existing without her now. She's so entrenched in this ranch, in my life now. It's a little scary.

But then Aurora snuggles her head between my collar and jaw, arms winding around mine to tug me closer.

Right. This just feels so goddamn right.

"Besides," she hums, "I probably shouldn't waste my strength on my followers and keep it for the next time I have to battle Holly."

I shake my head. "Don't be silly. Honestly, I doubt she even cares now that she's engaged."

Aurora stiffens slightly. "Wait, you knew Holly was engaged?"

"Yeah, my mom told me after they came around for dinner... How did you know about it?"

"Oh." Aurora rears her head back abruptly, features all pinched. She completely ignores my question, eyes fixed over my shoulder, somewhere scarily far beyond me.

It's an effort to try release the tightness winding in my chest. Something feels off, the air suddenly heavy. Everything begins to dull, the light in Aurora's hazel eyes dimming. "Is that... a problem?"

"Oh, um..." Her gaze flashes back to me, and the smile she attempts is pitiful, barely even a stretch of her lips. That's not the Aurora Jones I was just talking to. Neither is the uncomfortable breath of a laugh that follows. "It's just a little disconcerting to hear that you kissed me straight after finding out your ex was engaged."

Fuck.

Right, yeah that doesn't sound great. But *I* know that Holly being engaged has nothing to do with how I feel about Aurora—if anything it just proves how much I care about her because it didn't even bother me to hear about the engagement.

Alarms begin blaring faintly in my head as Aurora slithers away from me, tangled limbs disconnecting.

Say something, Wyatt!

"Me kissing you had *nothing* to do with Holly, I promise."

Her eyes dart back and forth across the floor. Save for that and her chest lifting faster by the second, she's pretty much frozen. I've seen her like this before, and it usually means she's starting to spiral. That she's doubting the confidence she has in herself. Even though she'd been on such a high this week and this morning about the next trial run.

I need to get her out of this. Doesn't she realise how much she means to me?

"Hey." I shuffle towards her, taking her hands from where they sit in her lap. "What are you thinking?"

"Sorry, I... I'm just finding it hard to not put a link between those two things. After everything you and the guys had told me about your relationship—"

"Look." I squeeze her fingers in one hand, and bring the other up to cradle her cheek, cutting off whatever nonsense she was about to spew. "When I found out about Holly being engaged, I didn't care—because *you* were all I'd been thinking about." Aurora nods furiously, like she's trying to force her mind to listen to her. "You—"

"Rory?" A man's voice echoes, followed by a loud knocking sound. We've still got at least an hour before any of the guests are supposed to turn up yet.

Aurora's face pales, whatever remnants were left of her golden glow draining away instantly. The sweet body that was finally starting to soften in my grip becomes rigid once again. I swear a faint tremor even rushes through her.

"Rory? Are you in?" The man shouts again, forcing Aurora to shoot to her feet. She runs her fingers through her hair frantically.

I go to ask, "Who—"

"Please just stay here," she barks at me. I don't even try to protest, shocked at the venom lacing her words as she disappears through the house. Who could possibly have pissed her off so badly in Willow Ridge?

I blow out a breath, trying to process the last minute or so, when I hear Aurora's voice raise. I don't like the sound of it—so at odds with the usual sunny, blazing charm she radiates. I know everyone has the propensity for all kinds of emotions—I'm learning that about myself—but Aurora's anger usually comes out in feisty ire, not the snapping of teeth and snarling of words.

Whatever is happening right now, she shouldn't be alone. Not when she had herself in such a positive mood ready for everyone to turn up today.

My instincts take over and I rush back through the house, the sharp edge of anger in Aurora's voice getting clearer as I near the hallway. The front door is open, so I head out onto the porch, to find her stood, arms crossed painfully tight, scowling at a familiar-faced, tall guy with short blond hair. There's a weekend bag at his feet, looking too stuffed for my liking, especially since he's not any of the guests Aurora showed me would be coming today.

When he sees me, he flinches, flicking his glare between Aurora and I, then lets out a breathy laugh. "Bloody hell, Rory, I didn't think you'd move on *that* quickly."

"Wyatt works here," she snaps back, and I push down the responding sting. Because Aurora hasn't even looked at me yet, but I can see her tense even more—which I didn't think was possible right now seeing as she's practically shaking from being so strained.

Fuck, I don't like seeing her like this at all. She's *hurt*. How could anyone ever want to break something as precious as her? I feel an overwhelming need to protect her.

She's mine.

No one hurts what's mine.

Then it suddenly dawns on me why I recognise this guy. From the Instagram photos Cherry once showed me.

This is her ex-boyfriend.

The one that cheated on her while she was at Grace's funeral. The one that's made her question her worth, when even her soul is made of pure gold.

And he has the audacity to comment on her moving on quickly.

What the fuck is he doing on our ranch?

A feral side to me starts to bubble up. Talons trying to claw through the calm demeanour I've assigned myself to.

Still, I force a smile into my cheeks and turn to him. "Ah, you must be the ex-boyfriend."

He looks warily at me, but I keep my body loose, unthreatening, and my smile pleasant. Eventually, he extends his hand. "Jake Thomas."

I lift mine to shake his. Then I punch him in the face.

THIRTY-THREE

Aurora

"Jesus, Wyatt!" I yell as I watch Jake spin from the punch and stumble straight into the fence.

I can't deny the deep satisfaction that threads through me, though, and the slight heat in my core in response to Wyatt's over-protectiveness. The way his eyes are as black and molten as eternal darkness, whilst his solid frame tenses, every muscle even more defined, is unnervingly mouth-watering.

That he'd do that for *me*.

But when Jake manages to steady himself and I see the cut across his cheek, blood already oozing, reality comes crashing back down. How hard did Wyatt hit him?

"What?" Wyatt shrugs, but he's gritting his teeth, jaw clenched hard to hold back whatever other violence wants to escape. "He tripped and fell into my fist."

I don't know whether to laugh or shout at him. Absolute idiot.

"What the fuck, mate?" Jake marches back over, fists clamped and ready. I slot myself between the two men, though I doubt my below-average-height self would do much to get in the way should this escalate.

God, this is a mess.

This is not what I need right now. Not when people are going to start arriving in an hour.

"Jake, let it go," I demand, ire seeping into my bones again at the sight of him. That the last time I actually saw him was when he left me to run after the girl he'd been cheating on me with. It's taking a hell of a lot of mental strength to not let those memories flood in right now. To not let them overwhelm me anymore than I already am.

"Honestly, *mate*," Wyatt growls. "You deserved it."

"Wyatt!" I snap around, my eyes practically bulging with the way I'm glaring at him. A faint throbbing pain starts to build behind my temples. "You are *not* helping."

"Yeah, well, I'm not leaving until he does," Wyatt declares, folding his arms as he steps closer to my side.

"Oh yeah?" Jake laughs, squaring his shoulders up.

I pinch the bridge of my nose. Well, that's going to be a little bit difficult since Jake just told me he's here for the retreat, because Rowan offered him his space without telling me. So, he's here until I convince him to get on another plane home.

Jesus, this is the last thing I need right now.

I was feeling so confident and excited for the next trial run today, and now...

A cool layer of indifference veils me. It's my only other option—there are so many emotions swirling through me that I think if I let myself feel any of them, I'll drown.

Especially since I hadn't fully worked through the heart-wrenching anxiety that hit me when I learned that Wyatt kissed me the same night he found out Holly was engaged.

I shouldn't care. I *really* shouldn't care. But I can't deny that the past months with him have felt so liberating. Wherever I go, whatever I do, I feel like there's a part of him with me, his voice in the back of my mind always cheering me on. Almost as if our souls are slowly intertwining just as naturally as our hands.

But that also means I'm growing more anxious about what we are, because the more days that pass, the deeper I feel myself falling for him, worryingly close to a point of no return. And for a split second when I found out Wyatt knew about the engagement the word *rebound* flickered through my head, even if I wish it hadn't.

Part of me feels like neither of us want to touch the conversation of where we stand yet, because realistically, isn't it all riding on whether this retreat actually works? And if it doesn't... then what?

But I'll deal with all these feelings and whirring thoughts later, because right now, I need to get through this without breaking down.

I am strong. I can do this.

"It's fine, I can handle him," I respond, crossing my arms to mirror Wyatt, ignoring the way Jake huffs behind me.

"Aurora." Wyatt's eyes gleam with the laugh of disbelief he releases. "You were about to have a *meltdown* back there, and now this, I don't think you're okay to be left alone with him."

Meltdown. I hate that it reminds that I'm still not fully healed, that I don't have all my strength back. It makes me feel like a burden. And I hate that he might see me that way.

I suck my teeth, taking in a deep breath, as calmly as possible, through my nose. "Yeah, well I can't always rely on you, can I?" Wyatt's eyes flash, his jaw growing tauter. "Please, I think it would be best if you just leave us to talk for a bit."

He just shakes his head. "No, I don't want him on my ranch."

"It's not *your* ranch, it's mine." I can't stop myself from snapping. Because my mental stability is currently hanging by an incredibly thin, fraying thread. But I don't miss the way Wyatt rears back, brows drawing in sharply.

I sigh, rubbing my trembling fingers across my forehead. "I'm sorry, I... I just need you to let me sort this out by myself."

Midnight eyes flick between mine, searching. Then they close, defeat washing over Wyatt's face as he drops his arms and sighs. He walks past Jake, who entertainingly fails to hide his flinch when Wyatt stops and points at him.

"If you make her cry, just know that I have a shotgun."

And then he trudges down the steps, off towards his place, leaving me with Jake and a past I don't want to face.

***

"Do you think it will need stitches?" Jake asks, tentatively pressing the ice pack to the cut along his cheek that's luckily looking far less bloody now we've cleaned it up. Though, I can still see the surrounding skin gaining more of a purplish tinge by the minute.

"No, I think he got you good, but not *that* good." I sit across from him at the dining table, arms crossed, just staring.

I can't believe he's here.

Jake lets out a breathy laugh. "I didn't realise you were employing bodyguards now."

I'm not sure if his subsequent wince is from his wound or because my face remains as cold as it has been since he arrived.

"Why are you really here, Jake?" I sigh. *Why did you have to turn up and disrupt this perfect little world I've created?*

"Right, not the time to joke." He worries his lip then sets the ice pack on the table. "I thought it would be good for us to get some closure. You just disappeared, I... I never had a chance to explain."

"Because you left me there alone... Besides, I don't need closure." I've already had it, from burning everything that reminded me of him. "It doesn't matter why you did what you did, what matters is that you did it. It wouldn't make a difference."

"I just thought it would be good to at least apologise. You blocked me on everything, how else was I supposed to speak to you?"

I'd kind of hoped that blocking him made it clear I didn't want him contacting me, but I also thought our conversation about exclusivity meant he wouldn't cheat on me, so I guess I can't assume he understands me at all. "I'm sure you could've found a way that didn't involve lying to me, *again*."

"I know, I know." Jake holds up his hands in surrender. "Look, I am sorry for all the deception, coming here had never been my plan. But when Rowan told me about what you were doing, he thought it might be a good opportunity to come out and talk, and maybe learn to be a better person whilst I'm here."

My eyes narrow. "What do you mean?"

"I've... been feeling lost for months, Rory, even when we were together. I haven't been the best version of myself for a long time. I think that's why I did what I did—because I felt like I wasn't really good enough, and I needed more than just you to make me feel that way—I know!" He quickly pushes on when I try to protest at his futile excuse. Rage flickers inside of me. "I know that's not a decent reason... But maybe doing this retreat will make me realise what I need to do to be a better person. To feel like myself again. Isn't that the whole point of what you're doing here?"

Genuine belief lights up his eyes, as if he really thought this was a rational idea. I lean my elbows against the table, fingers massaging my temples to try and comprehend it all. One of the deep grooves in the old wooden surface bites into my skin.

"I could really help too," he adds in quickly, but I don't bother to look up. "You know how many followers I have, probably more than whoever else you've got coming. Imagine how many people the retreat could reach through me. I'll do so many posts. To make up for it all."

As much as the quiet arrogance lacing Jake's words makes me want to roll my eyes, he's not wrong. Even before I blocked him a few months ago, he already had more followers on Instagram alone than the combined followers of the other guests coming.

Everything is supposed to happen for a reason—I try to believe that because it makes things like this more digestible, gives meaning behind the tough and weird times, and a little hope that something good might come out of them.

Though I would've rather not gone through the confidence-crushing hell of Jake's infidelity, I'm not sure I would've ended up here, spending my days in the stable arms of a handsome rancher if I hadn't. Like the universe needed to give me one last big, albeit traumatic, push towards the right path. The one that would lead me to the right person.

To... Wyatt.

God, I shouldn't have been so mean to him. I have a lot of making up to do.

Maybe I have to just trust that the universe has sent Jake here for a reason. Maybe even just to make use of his huge social media following so Sunset Ranch can survive. For Wyatt.

I knew I'd bump into Jake eventually one day, but I had hoped I might have had at least six months to get over everything first. Though, I am surprised at how confident I've been so far, able to stand up to him and not run away like last time. That's progress worth recognising.

Maybe, just maybe, that's the point. Here I've been, so intent on healing and gaining my confidence back, learning to believe that I am enough again, that perhaps the universe wanted to send me a test to prove it. Make me face Jake, show the world that I am that strong, confident, independent woman I'm always affirming to myself about. And use this retreat as an opportunity to ensure Jake never makes a girl feel unworthy again, whilst also taking advantage of his influencer status for the retreat.

I can't preach in the workshops I've planned for the retreat about getting comfortable with being uncomfortable and not step up to the challenge myself. If these last two months haven't been proof that pushing through the uncertainty is what makes you grow, then I don't know what is.

Thirty-Four

Aurora

A soothing wave of ease washes through my legs as I run through some warm-up stretches, awaiting the group to get themselves set up and ready for our morning yoga. Amber sparkles softly along the lake's surface beside us, a few rays of sunlight reaching my skin, heating it up along with the landscape around us. I decided to let the faint songs of awakening birds be the soundtrack to our session today, the sense of calm it fills me with so blissful.

While sunsets were always Auntie Grace's favourite time of the day, mornings have always been mine. They're a reminder that it's a fresh start. Whatever happened yesterday can be left in the past, replaced by the crisp new day beckoning you to do your best.

And as a familiar broad-shouldered, dark-eyed man strides over from where he's tied up his horse, I really hope that I'm right. That we can leave whatever disagreement we had yesterday behind, that he'll stay at mine tonight, as opposed to flopping into his own bed, exhausted after spending most of the evening riding Dusty to calm himself down. That he won't leave for work before I wake up tomorrow morning.

EMMA LUCY

When I told Wyatt of my plans to let Jake stay, he was expectedly pretty pissed off, which didn't bode well for my subsequent attempt to apologise for shouting at him. And this time, he didn't stay and talk it through with me like he usually would any time I've been upset. No, because this time he was upset too, and his way of dealing with that is riding. Getting out in nature.

Getting away from me.

For the first time in a long while since I came to Willow Ridge, I felt empty. Deflated. It made me see far too clearly that it's not just the beautiful scenery that makes Sunset Ranch liberating. It's him.

I finish my stretch and stand as he approaches, but he stops just short of the edge of the group, muscles tensing as if he wants to come closer. Because I sure wish he would, but no doubt he's following our rule of making our relationship seem professional in front of the guests, which feels even more pertinent with Jake around. Considering that he's found a way to worm his way into the retreat, I want to keep one thing out of his reach. And if that means keeping my hands, and eyes, off Wyatt as much as I can during this trial run, then I'll find a way to survive.

Our eyes meet as I offer him a hopeful smile, and his responding one—full of the warmth and tenderness I needed from him—tugs at my heart. But it's quick and disappears when he clears his throat.

"Colt isn't here, is he?" Wyatt asks, glancing around the group gathered on their yoga mats.

"Nope." I shrug, furrowing my brow. "Haven't seen him, sorry."

Wyatt scratches his head. "He's late for work. Thought he might be missing his morning yoga sessions and ran off to find you."

Scanning the mats once more, Wyatt then cocks his head when he spies the remaining empty mat waiting for Elio, a health and wellness

302

LIVE, RANCH, LOVE

influencer who is yet to arrive. I'd assumed the jet lag might catch up with some of the guests, so guessed he might be running a little late because of that. But then I catch a glimpse of movement over Wyatt's shoulder, where two distant silhouettes saunter down the track towards us.

When they come into view, I can't stop the smirk that spreads across my cheeks. Elio and Colt, looking a little exhausted—likely not from jet lag—eventually find their way to Wyatt's side, a faint blush reaching their cheeks as everyone turns to them. It appears Colt's still wearing the same clothes I saw him in yesterday too.

Colt shoves his hands in his pockets and throws a wobbly grin at Wyatt, who's now scowling at him, arms crossed. "Morning, Hensley."

"Something more important than work today?" Wyatt chides.

The whole group, even Elio despite being in the thick of the exchange, is struggling to bite down on their grins as they watch. Colt's jaw drops as he flicks his stare between Wyatt and Elio, cheeks reddening, the usually cocky rancher struggling to find words.

So, Elio saves him, patting Wyatt on the shoulder. "Sorry, man—I'm afraid that's my fault. I'll make sure he's up earlier next time." Then he winks and nudges Colt with his elbow, before making his way over to the yoga mat that's waiting for him.

"Next time," Colt mouths to Wyatt with a wiggle of his eyebrows and a too-proud smile considering that his boss is still throwing the kind of dark, cold stare at him that would make anyone's knees quake.

Wyatt just shakes his head and gives Colt a light shove to start walking away, towards the ranch that needs them. Without even so much as looking back at me. Something tells me this week is going to be more of a test of my strength than I realised.

***

"Hey there, Hensley," I shuffle up next to Wyatt, leaning on the fence beside him, as close as I can get without drawing attention.

His dark features have been pinched throughout the whole lesson, arms tightly crossed, watching Flynn have a go at teaching the group how to ride. After the last trial, he'd been pretty enthusiastic about getting involved, and Wyatt was more than happy to offer up the chance. Especially since he's refused to talk to Jake this whole time, so I'm not sure how he would've made it through instructing him. His daggered stare follows Jake as he trots around the corral.

"Hey," is all I get back, blunt and quick, not even a glance. Like he's so concerned that if he takes his eyes off Jake, the guy will steal me away or burn down the ranch.

The few inches between us makes my body ache, craving his touch since he's still been off since I told him I was letting Jake stay. I miss the way he'd always find an excuse to touch me.

"Still annoyed at me?"

Wyatt sighs, dropping his arms. He stares at the ground for a beat before talking. "I'm not annoyed at you, Aurora. I'm just waiting for you to get out of whatever daydream you've mustered up thinking having him here is a good idea. I don't care if you think the *universe*," he makes sure to use quotation marks to emphasise his disbelief, "sent him here. Tell the universe to take him back."

Jaw angled, locking in frustration, I take in a deep breath. "I've explained it to you before, Wyatt—he's trying to be better and it makes me feel good to help him, knowing I'm less affected by him as the days go by. I just need you to trust me on this. Please."

Even if it is killing me to see him so bothered by it. To feel his walls back up. But I just want to prove to myself, and to him, that I'm strong, that I can grow from this. Imagine how invincible I'll feel when I've made it through the week and sent Jake off, knowing that if I can survive him being here, in my new safe haven, then I can do anything. That has to be why the universe sent him here.

Wyatt's nostrils flare as he finally looks at me, eyes widening. "And I need *you* to trust *me* that he's bad news. You don't see the way he smirks at me every time he catches me watching the two of you talking, or how he glares at us when we're together."

I shake my head, chuckling. "I think that has more to do with you punching him in the face than it does him trying to get me back." Especially since Jake's now sporting a nice purple bruise across his cheek, having to make up some story every time he's asked about it. "You made it pretty clear how you felt about him and I. He's just goading you."

"I told you—he tripped and fell." Wyatt shrugs. He snaps his stare back to the group ahead.

"Besides," I add on, "he's been going above and beyond with showing the retreat off on his social media. The amount of traffic he's brought to both my account and the one we've set up for Sunset Ranch is amazing. At least we'll make money off him being here when we open this place up properly."

"Whatever," Wyatt huffs like a petulant child.

For some reason, despite his moodiness annoying me, it also makes me smile. I bite down on the inside of my lips, trying to pretend otherwise. But the truth is, I'm head over heels for him, and I don't think there's anything he could do now to make me run away.

I should be getting more involved with this riding lesson, yet here I am, unable to stop myself from gravitating towards him.

And when I check his expression, there's a small twitch of his lips too. A softening of his features and a stare now cast off in the distance, beyond the riding lesson ahead, as if he's been lured into an enticing daydream. One I'm hoping is the same as mine, where we might actually get to carry on this venture together.

Where I feel strong enough to do this.

Especially when he's by my side.

After a few beats of silence, Wyatt's fingers suddenly brush against the small of my back, making small circles from behind the fence. Just like I'd been craving. I'd be lying if I said my tears didn't well a tiny bit. My shoulders instantly drop too, even though I was unaware how tense they had been.

He lets out a long sigh. "You know it's okay to rely on other people sometimes, right? I know you want to be able to feel strong by yourself, Aurora, but it's okay to have some help."

"Old Rory never needed to rely on others to feel strong," I say, letting his touch soothe me. I press my back against the fence, trying to give him as much of me as possible.

"Maybe that was old Rory for a reason." Wyatt's hand spreads out across the small of my back. It rests there, like he's holding me up. "What if levelling up to the next best you is all about letting yourself lean on others occasionally?"

I flash a glance up at him, letting myself indulge in the thought momentarily. "Maybe."

"Either way, Princess, I want you to know that I'm always gonna be here to hold you up if you need me." Just like he has throughout these past months. God, what did I do to deserve this man?

Wyatt clears his throat. "Anyway, want to know a secret?"

"Go on..."

"I tacked up Jake's horse with the reins I tied you up with."

My lips pop open and I have to smack my hand over my mouth to quickly fight the cackle emerging out. A strangled noise gurgles in my throat instead, grabbing the attention of Priya, a breathwork instructor who I met at a wellness festival a year ago. I throw a thumbs up to encourage her on with her riding.

"You are terrible, Hensley." I perk a brow up at him and bite back my grin. He flashes me a smug smile, giving me a shot of hope that he's not as pissed off at me as he might seem.

I close my eyes, listening out for the soft summer breeze whispering through the grass and the distant calls of fluttering birds in the sky to ground me again. We just need to get through the second half of this week, and then Jake will be gone. It can go back to being just the two of us again, exactly how I love it.

And then, well, as daunting as it sounds, maybe it will be time to start considering my permanent position here at Sunset Ranch.

Just a few more days.

"*Terribly* handsome, I think is what you meant to say," Wyatt jibes and then squeezes my waist, making me squeak and whip around to jab him back—

"Hey, lovebirds!" Flynn suddenly shouts, knocking down the professional image we'd been trying so hard to maintain. Guess we forgot to mention that to him. "You two done flirting and ready to head out for a ride with us all?"

As we head on over to mount our own horses, I don't miss the way Jake glares at us.

Thirty-Five

Wyatt

"It's nice of you to entertain her little daydream," Jake's hushed voice tumbles down the porch stairs as he descends them. Every muscle in my body grows tauter. An oily, slimy energy follows him.

I don't bother to look his way, staying leant against the fence, watching Aurora and the rest of the group say their final goodbyes to Elio, who is the first guest to leave. I'm smirking at the fact that Colt is also here bidding him goodbye—though not for long, something tells me.

Even though I've enjoyed hanging out with the guests and getting to talk so freely about my passion for ranching and riding, a huge weight has finally lifted from my shoulders knowing it's the final day. When it finally becomes just Aurora and I again. Nothing more standing in our way.

"Hmm?" I try not to sound too interested, hoping maybe Jake will just walk straight past me.

He chuckles, the smug, breathy kind that already has my skin crawling. I've done my best to stay out of his way this week, respecting Aurora's baffling desire to want to prove she can be strong when he's around. I'd be lying if I said it didn't piss me off. I'd also be lying if I said

I didn't aggressively chop up a tonne of wood the night after she told me her decision to let him stay, choosing to give her the cold shoulder instead of sitting and talking like she probably wanted.

Because what Aurora said hurt me.

It's not your *ranch, it's mine.*

When all I want is for it to be *ours.*

Heavy storm clouds darkened my mind for a while after that. But when she mentioned opening the retreat up properly once Jake's gone the other day, bright white hope finally kindled in my chest.

Because she does want to stay—and that's what I keep reminding myself each time I get annoyed. That even if it irks me every time she talks about the goddamn universe sending him here, she made the decision for us. Because she thinks we can only be strong if she's strong. Personally, I think she's the strongest fucking woman I've ever met in my life.

"This ranch, the retreat," Jake gestures around us, "going along with whatever silly, impulsive idea she's latched on to for the time being to make herself feel good. Until she realises that there's bigger and better back home."

My chest heaves almost to a point of pain with the deep breath I try to take in. No wonder Aurora's confidence took such a hit from this guy—it doesn't sound like he ever gave her the belief she deserved. I flex my hands beside me, because as much as I'd like to, I really can't punch him again. Not in front of everyone.

"This isn't just a silly idea." I turn, eyes narrowed, and step forward to emphasise the few inches I have on him. "She's built something incredible here and everyone knows it. Besides, if it's such a *silly* idea, why did you bother coming?"

"Hey." Jake holds up his hands, still looking far too relaxed for my liking. "I'm only warning you. It won't last."

I'm not sure if he's talking about the retreat or me and Aurora now, but either way, ire starts to seethe in my bones. My words come out through gritted teeth, rumbling loudly. "Just because it didn't last with you, doesn't mean it won't with me. With Sunset Ranch."

"What makes you think you'll get any longer with her than I did?" Okay, so the little snake *is* talking about our relationship. The rush of blood in my ears starts to drown out our surroundings. "What do you have here that me or someone else can't give her back home, where she belongs?"

I don't know, is the first answer that pops into my head, because that's always been my response.

I don't know what else I could've given Holly to have made her choose me over Easton, when he had so much more to offer. I don't know why Aurora chose me... but I'm determined to give her everything she wants in life, every single picture on that vision board she made, so if I'm part of that, then I'll give every inch of my soul to her. Forever.

And I won't let anyone get in our way.

"Don't be blind, mate." Jake pats me on the shoulder.

Wrong decision.

"Well," I growl louder than expected, and give him a shove with one hand. "One thing I am certain of is that at least I'm not a massive cunt like you."

"Wyatt!" Aurora's voice rips across the road, followed by a cacophony of gasps from the others.

Jake's features slide into an unexpected, superior satisfaction. His eyes sparkle with amusement. "Nice one, mate. You just got caught on video shoving me and calling me a cunt."

Nodding to behind me, I catch how Priya has her phone pointing at us, one hand smacked over her gaping mouth. The rest of the group, including Aurora, all stare at us wide-eyed. Even Luke's paused midway through hefting Elio's suitcase into his cab, arms trembling.

But my eyes immediately seek out Aurora again as she marches towards me, hazel eyes lit with golden, thunderous fire.

She pulls me away from Jake, tugging me by the bottom of my T-shirt. Her voice comes out like a whispered shout, cheeks blazing red. "What the hell, Wyatt?"

"I'm sorry." I run my hands through my hair. "I shouldn't have called him that... or shoved him. He just riled me up, saying that this retreat was a silly idea, that it wouldn't last, that *we* wouldn't—"

"It doesn't matter what he said, Wyatt," Aurora cuts in. Her brows are drawn together, and she lets out a shaky breath. "All that matters is this retreat. That people say good things about this place *and* the people working here. And when you let your anger get the best of you, you're jeopardising *our* future."

That makes me wince.

She's right. I said I would give her everything she wanted, the glorious future she deserves, but if people start saying that I'm rude or violent, or if that video gets out, then making those dreams of hers come true will be even more difficult. And I can't lose her.

I really, really can't lose her.

"I'm sorry," I concede with a sigh. "I should leave you to finish the goodbyes. It's probably best if I'm not around him anymore. I'll be at mine, promise you'll come by later?"

Aurora gives me a soft, exhausted smile. "I promise."

***

The knock at my door is music to my ears, especially since it's earlier than I expected. But when I yank the door open, ready to embrace my favourite girl, she's not there.

Instead, it's Holly.

What is it with exes turning up out of the blue this week?

"What are you doing here?" I blurt out, immediately grimacing at the way Holly's brows draw in, hurt registering across her face. "Sorry, you just caught me off guard. Is everything alright?"

Brushing some of her blonde hair behind her ear, Holly pushes a wobbly smile out. "Um, not exactly. I could really use someone to talk to right now."

She worries her lip, hand rubbing up her arm. I know that tick of hers too well from all the years we spent together—she's nervous. I remember it from when she admitted she was leaving me for Easton. A couple of months ago, I would've been triggered by seeing her here, wondering why the universe was taunting me. But now, I feel indifferent.

"And you thought *I* was the best person to come to?"

Holly lets out a soft chuckle, angling her head. "Well, we were together for all those years, and our families are friends, so I'd like to think we're still friends too."

Clenching my jaw, I regard her for a second, noticing her bloodshot eyes and red cheeks. She's been crying. Considering she barely showed any emotion when we were together, it's a shock. Something must be pretty wrong.

313

"Please, Wyatt," Holly begs. "I feel like you might be the only person who understands what I'm going through right now."

"Fine," I sigh, stepping back from the door and gesturing for her to enter. I don't hesitate to shut the door as quickly as possible once she's in. The last thing I need is someone seeing Holly and blowing her visit out of proportion.

Holly heads straight to the couch, settling in like she's been over a hundred times, as opposed to the two times she stayed when I started working here, before she left me. It doesn't even look anything like it did back then—it was just a cabin with a few pieces of furniture. Now it's my *home.* And I'm suddenly so grateful that she never had any part of making it that to me.

"Can I get you a drink?" I head towards the kitchen.

"Do you still buy that honey flavoured whiskey you used to drink?" Holly spins to watch me, brows raised. She hated whiskey.

"I actually meant like a coffee." Not really sure how close to get, I just lean against the counter. "Things are that bad, huh?"

"Coffee would be good thanks. And yes." Holly lets out a long sigh, slumping back into the couch. She rubs a hand along her forehead.

I get working on the coffee, and neither of us say anything until I'm handing it over to her, plopping myself at the other end of the couch. With narrowed eyes, Holly stares at me for a few silent seconds, then at the space between us, corners of her lips turning down.

"So, what's up?" I ask.

"I'm worried I'm making a mistake marrying Easton."

"You've got to be fucking kidding me," I groan, pinching the bridge of my nose. "Seriously? You want to talk to *me* about whether you should marry the guy you left me for?"

"I'm sorry, Wyatt. I don't mean to make you uncomfortable," Holly presses on, voice quivering. "But out of everyone in this goddamn town, you know what it's like to question the path you've taken and wonder if you've just been doing what everyone else wants, as opposed to what you truly want."

She sets her mug down on the table and twists to face me better, pulling a leg up onto the couch. "And I just thought now that you've *clearly* moved on with your new girlfriend, we might be able to talk about this like friends."

My head hasn't stopped shaking, but I don't miss the way my heart rockets, beating *yes, yes, yes,* when she says *girlfriend*. Because for God's sake, what I wouldn't do to make that a truth. Aurora Jones, my girlfriend, has a rather nice ring to it.

"How long have you felt this way? You seemed pretty happy last time I saw you guys together." The last sentence comes out more genuine than I expected from myself.

"Yeah, see that's the thing..." Holly trails off, worrying her lip again. When she catches me glaring, trying to goad her to continue, she shuffles forward slightly. "That's when it started. When I saw you with Rory, and saw the way you both looked at each other, like you were so in love, it made me realise."

Like you were so in love.

But that was weeks ago...

Holly continues, "You were looking at her with so much passion and intensity and sickening love, and it reminded me of how you used to look at me. How I used to look at you. We used to have so much fun, be so happy. But I don't think Easton looks at me that way. I don't think we have that passion like you two. Like us."

Honestly, everything she's saying right now is going over my head because the only word my brain is latching onto is *love*.

Is that what this is? Is that why Aurora's a never-ending thought in my mind? Why I always wish I could stop time with her around? Why even when she's doing the weirdest little happy dance or rambling about something wellness related I'm not the slightest bit interested in, I'm still so enraptured by her?

I haven't been in love in... years. I think I'd forgotten what it felt like. Maybe even stopped myself from considering it because last time... last time it got shoved back in my face.

But somehow, I don't think that's going to happen this time. For some bewildering reason, with the comments Aurora's been dropping about our future here, a part of me does actually believe that we might be able to make that vision board come true.

Damn, I think I might be in love with Aurora Jones.

I should tell her, right?

"Wyatt?" Holly snaps me back to reality, and she's even closer, leaning towards me like she's trying to figure out what's going on in my head. All I know is I need to get her out of here, so I can go find Aurora. Nothing else matters right now.

"Sorry." I shake my head. "Look, Holly, everyone gets doubts about big steps like this—it's natural. You and Easton are good together, otherwise you wouldn't have said yes. And you can't compare what you have to what Aurora and I looked like that night because it was all for show—"

"So, you're not together?" Holly's blue eyes flare.

I sputter—because no, I guess we're not technically together yet, but I'll be damned if I spend another second with that as the truth.

I'm just about to stand and suggest Holly leaves, but a knock comes at the door. It's enough to distract me when Holly lunges forwards, grabbing my face and crashing her lips against mine.

Just as the front door swings open.

Thirty-Six

Aurora

White hot rage burns through me. I can't move. Not even as that rage continues to pound at my heart until it shatters into a million pieces.

I feel like I'm in a nightmare, reliving the worst parts of my life. Walking into his place, blissfully unaware of what he'd been doing whilst I was away. The beautiful blonde girl wrapped around him. The one that I couldn't possibly compare to and instantly destroys the walls of self-confidence I've been building.

But this time it's worse, because she's not just a girl he follows on Instagram, she's *the* girl he's been heartbroken over for years. The one I stupidly thought I might have helped him move on from and actually believed he'd left behind, for me. I should've trusted myself last weekend when I found out he kissed me after he discovered that she was engaged.

I'm completely frozen, every inch of me seized up, unable to let go of the door handle. Partly through the fear that if I'm not holding something then I might crumble.

Why does this hurt so much?

It never felt like this when I caught Jake. It was painful and heart-breaking, but never like this. This feels like the betrayal has ripped me completely apart, torn me to pieces, gutted my soul. This feels like something that can never be undone.

I'd come here to apologise for getting so worked up about how he acted towards Jake. That it's only because running the retreat is just an excuse to be able to stay here with him, even though it's scary that I want that so soon. To tell him how grateful I was for him trusting me when I let Jake stay.

I'm such a fool.

I'm such a *bloody* fool.

This is what I get for jumping into bed with the handsome cowboy when I clearly wasn't fully healed from my own heartbreak. When I'm lonely and lost. I should never have trusted the butterflies.

Wyatt shoves Holly away from him, yelling, "What the fuck do you think you're doing?"

Then I'm finally in his eyeline. His eyes lock onto mine, flaring as his face pales and he jumps to his feet.

"Well, this feels an awful lot like déjà vu," I laugh and immediately head back out, ready to slam the door—

"Aurora, it's not what you think." Wyatt grabs the door before I can shut it behind me, and I stumble a little as I whip back around. I've heard those words before. They mean nothing.

"You mean you weren't just kissing your ex-girlfriend?" I snap, each word pushed through gritted teeth. My jaw is aching.

"*She* kissed *me*—not the other way around, I promise," Wyatt insists, wild black eyes shining. He goes to step forward but halts when I shuffle backwards against the fence, needing something to support me whilst everything else starts to fall apart.

Because he said he'd always hold me up, but now it feels like he's pulled the rug from beneath my feet.

I don't know what to think. I don't know what to say. I trusted him, and he could be telling the truth, but all I can see right now are the torturous flashes of Holly on him and the girl on Jake. Everything's so mixed in my mind, I try to shake my head, to see if it can separate the two instances.

"Tell her, Holly," Wyatt demands, almost growling as he turns to his ex who just stands there and shrugs, opening her mouth but never confirming, or denying.

"Seriously?" he shouts at her, the word a thunderous rumble.

Fuck. I rake my fingers through my hair, clawing out the knots. Would he actually do this?

I knew how he felt about her. The way the guys made it seem like he would never get over her. The way she clearly still had a hold over him, keeping onto those clothes for so many years. We're technically not even together. Not like him and Holly were for years. How could I expect the couple of months we've known each other to trump years with his high school sweetheart?

Especially when neither of us know how long I'm going to be around. For all I know, this was always going to be ephemeral for him.

The blood rushing in my ears is almost deafening.

I'm letting myself spiral. And I can't rely on him to help me out of it this time.

I need to get out of here.

When I make a dash for the stairs Wyatt jumps out to try to stop me. "Aurora, please, don't go. Please, Aurora."

"No!" I throw my hands up to ease him back from me, to clear my escape route. "You don't get to call me that right now. You can call me Rory, like everyone else."

Wyatt flinches, jaw ticking, brows drawing together. I try to ignore the way whatever is left of my heart breaks again at the pain flushing through his expression. Slowly, I can see the fire in his eyes start to extinguish, a consideration to give up cresting. I use the moment as an opportunity to run and head down the stairs, trying my best to hold myself together by wrapping my own arms around my body.

I can make it to the main house without crumbling.

I can do this.

"Get the fuck out of my house, Holly," Wyatt's bark echoes behind me. I hear him calling after me, and I try to pick up my pace. I'm only a short distance from the deck.

"Aurora, please," his pleas are getting closer, and suddenly they're ringing from right behind me, his running footfalls thumping with them. The next thing I know, Wyatt's taking my arm, twisting me around to face him.

I want to yank myself away, but his touch instantly warms me, reminding me of all the times I was encompassed in his tender embrace, wrapped up in him and his pinewood scent. The smell of *home*.

But now, maybe also heartbreak.

Please tell me this isn't happening again.

My eyes stay locked on where he gently grips my arm, strained muscles moving under his mountain range tattoo. With all the tears brimming in my eyes, I'm scared if I look anywhere else, they'll gush out like a waterfall. So, even when he lets go, fingers stroking down my arm, I don't move.

"Aurora, please." Wyatt's deep voice is barely above a whisper, like a racing river in the distance, ready to sweep me away should I step too close. "Jake might not have chased after you, but I will. Because you are worth it. Because you mean more to me than Holly ever has. I promise, with all my heart, that *she* kissed me."

You will not cry, Rory. Not yet.

"But why was she there, Wyatt?"

"She said she wanted to talk. She was having doubts about her engagement and... Fuck, look, I realise now I shouldn't have let her in. I'm sorry, but please, don't run away from me."

One lone tear streaks down my face. Wyatt watches it, redness seeping into the whites of his eyes. I know he's breaking right now too—it's obvious in the way his breath is shuddering, the way his fingers twitch at his sides, unable to touch me, the way every dark angle of his face is strained, trembling.

But every time I think of moving to hold him, I just get another flash in my mind of bodies tangled in a kiss, blonde hair swaying. I just need to get away for a second. To think and pull myself together.

For God's sake, I said I'd take Jake to the airport in a couple of hours as well, as he forgot to book a taxi and Luke is busy. I can't be a blubbering mess then because I sure as hell don't want to go into the details of how his infidelity has clearly traumatised me to not be able to trust even when I know I should.

Reluctantly, I start easing backwards, checking over my shoulder to the house. "I—I just need some space right now. I'm not in the right headspace to talk about this properly. Please, I... I'll come find you when I'm ready. I promise."

***

"I think you're supposed to drown your sorrows in alcohol, not tap water," Duke's voice startles me.

I whip my head up from where it has been buried between my arms, leaning against the booth table. He settles a glass of some colourful orange concoction on the table, nudging it towards me as he slides into the booth.

"Not that I'm trying to encourage alcoholism or anything, but it does help when you own a bar." Duke's smile is light, a gentle press of his lips that manages to still ease my tension.

He steeples his fingers in front of him, just watching me. There's never anything forceful about his energy, never vying for attention, always just effortlessly bringing a sense of calm and quiet to his surroundings. My mind welcomes it with everything spinning around.

I didn't know where to go.

All I knew once I made it into the house, leaving Wyatt behind, was that I couldn't stay on the ranch. Not with him across the road. Not with Jake nearby. I waited until I watched Holly's car disappear in the distance and then I pegged it into my own truck, speeding off up the road towards Willow Ridge.

I just needed somewhere to hide. Somewhere to work through all the emotions racking my body, making my heart race and blood pump faster than it has in a long time. Not like the steady beat that's graced my days on Sunset Ranch, any spike soon soothed by the fiery sunset pouring between the mountains, or the summer breeze through the luscious pastures. Or the gentle, stable touch from Wyatt.

Truthfully, I'm not even here because I'm upset with Wyatt. I should trust him enough to know that he wouldn't have kissed Holly. Whatever reaction he had to the kiss seemed genuine, and I can't pretend how grateful I was that he chased after me, even if I only pushed him away in response.

I'm pissed off at myself.

For letting this affect me so much. For immediately questioning how much I meant to him, trying to convince myself that I'd been stupid enough to think that a couple of months by my side was worth more than years with Holly. I'm angry that was my automatic response. That I didn't even try to bolster myself like I would've had this been any other situation.

Because over the last few weeks, I've gotten so much better at believing in my own strength again. I felt worthy of Wyatt's time. I felt deserving of my influencer status, of writing a book about my experience with the ranch and the retreat.

I felt like me again.

But why does this make that all come crashing down?

"I have to drive later," I admit, rubbing my thumb along the rim of the glass.

Duke might not be offering to talk, but I can feel it in the way his dark eyes regard me, in the way he patiently waits. "It's barely even got a shot of vodka in it, you'll be fine. Besides, it was your Auntie Grace's favourite drink."

My eyes shoot up at that. "You knew Grace?"

Duke scoffs. "Everyone knows everyone in Willow Ridge."

"Right." How long will it be before word gets around that Wyatt's fake girlfriend is sat in a bar on her own, mascara probably running down her cheeks?

"But yeah," Duke adds, clearing his throat. "She used to come in every Thursday evening for one drink only. Would sit in the corner booth over there," he nods to it, "and just people watch. Pretty certain she knew my grandfather when he owned this place."

I wonder why I never knew she came here. Even though she wasn't a big fan of the rules, I suppose I was always too young to drink when I visited, so I don't even know if I'd have been allowed in. I wonder if she ever sat in here when the guys and Cherry were about, and if she ever imagined me being a part of their close-knit group. I wonder if she knew I'd find my way here alone one day, whether all the motivational things she'd tell me were meant for this moment.

The drink reminds me of a sunset, the liquid almost blood orange at the bottom, fading into a pale amber as it rises. One sip makes my mouth sparkle, the drink as sweet and glittering as dreams.

Of course this was Auntie Grace's favourite.

"Have you told him I'm here?" I ask Duke.

He shrugs, reminding me far too much of Wyatt. "No, but if he keeps blowing up my phone, I'm gonna be forced to. Normally our conversations consist of thumbs up and one word answers, so it's freaking me out to see so many messages."

The chuckle escapes out of me before I can stop it. One word answers, yeah, sounds just like the Wyatt Hensley I first met.

Duke's eyes brighten when I smile back. "So, if there's any way you could maybe make him stop, I'd really appreciate it."

"I walked in on him and Holly kissing," I blurt out, noting the way Duke flinches at my confession.

"She kissed him," he insists.

"That's what he said."

"Then that's the truth. There's no doubt about it." Every word Duke says holds permanence, his tone becoming intensely serious.

"But how do you know?"

"Because I know Wyatt. He wouldn't do that. And unless he's given you a reason to not trust him, then you should believe that he wouldn't either." Duke's shoulders rise, his chest broadening as he sits up straighter, ready to fight me on this. A fierce loyalty blazes in his adamance. A loyalty that I should be trusting blindly myself, just like Auntie Grace would've told me. Like Wyatt probably would too.

"But she's *Holly*. The girl he's been heartbroken over."

"Yeah," he laughs. "And you're *you*. That should be enough."

Something wedges in my throat. It should be enough, he's right. But why doesn't it feel like enough to me?

Every single thing Wyatt has said or done has been a promise to me. That we were inevitable. Like night and day, our lives would always lead into the other.

Why can't I just believe that without question?

Immediately softening, Duke lets out a sigh. "As far as I can see, Wyatt hasn't so much as *looked* at another woman since you guys started working on the retreat. And he smiles, like a lot now, when you're around. It's actually kind of creepy."

I struggle to bite back my responding grin.

"Look," he shuffles forwards again, back to leaning on the table, "I've never really liked Holly, even when they dated, I struggled to warm to her. She's always wanted what she can't have. She's probably panicking after seeing you and Wyatt kiss that night, because she's realised she's finally lost him. That he's in love with someone else."

The word hits me like a tonne of bricks.

Love.

Something squeezes my heart, tightening with every second.

"But... but that kiss was fake. He wasn't in love with me."

The look Duke gives me, his head tilted to the side, makes me feel like I've been the stupidest girl in the world. That he can't believe I've been so clueless...

Have I been that clueless?

I know I've been trying to ignore my own feelings, scared that they've been too strong for such little time spent together. That I couldn't possibly be ready to love again, but... Auntie Grace did always say that sometimes the best things come to us when we aren't even looking for them. I was never looking for Wyatt, in fact, I was ready to write off guys for a good few months when I came to Sunset Ranch.

But there he was.

The plot twist to my movie.

He's been there for me, given me whatever side I needed, both soft and strong. And now his arms have felt like home to me more than any house ever has.

Every song I hear reminds me of him. Every hazy morning reminds me of his sleepy eyes and messy curls when he wakes up next to me, groaning. Every sunset reminds me that it was another beautiful day, because I got to see him smile.

Oh my God, I... love him.

I love Wyatt Hensley.

And I think he might love me too.

The butterflies were right!

I shake my head, smile beaming, making my cheeks ache. I need to tell him. I'll drop Jake at the airport, so that my mind can be completely free and all that can be put behind me. And then I'll come back to our home and tell him.

"Thank you, Duke, really." I quickly drink down some of the orange cocktail, letting it soothe the new batch of nerves filling me up. The ones that make me feel giddy. Because I'm going to confess my love to Wyatt Hensley. "You're a wise friend. How is it that you don't have anyone?"

"Ah…" He presses his lips together, barely forming a smile. "There's a few rules in the way of what I want."

Rules? I go to probe but he clears his throat and quickly adds on, "Anyway, I've said enough. Go sort your boy out." He jerks his head and waves me off as I jump out the booth, squeezing his shoulder with gratitude as I pass.

Once I settle into the driver's seat of my truck, I feel my phone vibrate. Maybe it's Wyatt finally giving in after getting nothing from Duke. I should probably text him, actually.

But a groan rumbles out of me when I pull out my phone and the screen lights up with the message:

> **Jake:** Flight's been delayed, doesn't say how long for. Maybe we can go get dinner and get that closure after all?

THIRTY-SEVEN

Wyatt

I just need some space right now.

I used to be a big fan of space. I've spent the last four years spending pretty much every Sunday night and Monday morning alone. But now, the silence is deafening. The absence of her warm, sweet body tucked within mine, has gutted me.

Everything feels empty. The shadows cast over my bedroom walls seem darker, creeping closer towards where I lie as faint rays of the pale sunrise bleed between the curtains. Like they're readying to encompass me, to drag me back down to the depths of the darker world I used to live in. To remind me that her light was only a temporary flicker in the storm that is my life.

Because nothing lasts forever.

And I was an idiot for thinking otherwise.

Every time I think of that lone tear cutting down her cheek, ripping through her innocent sunshine, I feel my heart shatter even more. Because I know that her mind would've been overflowing with thoughts trying to tear down the confidence and strength she's built back up over the last two months.

The thought of Aurora even questioning whether she's enough for me makes me want to punch another hole through my wall. But I've already bruised my knuckles doing it once after Holly left.

If it took running away to another continent to get over what happened with Jake, what will it take for her to feel better about this? We might have only known each other for a couple of months, but there's no denying what we have is soul deep.

If it were the other way around, I'd be destroyed.

I should've never let Holly in.

I'll come find you when I'm ready. I promise.

But there's still no message on my phone. No missed calls. Her truck came back yesterday and disappeared again, to take Jake to the airport. It's been parked outside the house since last night, yet I've still heard nothing. I'm not sure how much more space I can take.

I just have to trust that she believes me. That's what I'd say to her if it were the other way around, to wait and know that what we have will bring her back. That maybe, I might be the luckiest man alive, and she loves me back. She just needs to give herself one of those little pep talks and then she'll come find me. And I'll be here, arms open, ready to help prop up her world again.

I'd do anything to be her anchor at the bottom of the ocean, sat there for eternity, just so her ship could stay afloat.

Finally dragging myself out of bed, because I still have a ranch to run, I begrudgingly get dressed. I don't even bother eating, knowing I'll feel better once I'm out in the fields, on the back of Dusty.

But as I turn from locking up my front door, I catch Aurora's truck speeding off up the road ahead, towards town, dust clouds in its wake. The sun's barely even up yet. Where is she going?

Then I notice Flynn heading towards me, from the direction of the main house. He waves, attempting a brief smile, but if anything, it's more of a grimace. I keep flicking my eyes between him and the truck disappearing in the distance, barely a dot now within the hazy morning light, small drops of panic starting to feed into my bloodstream.

Something feels off.

"Hey," I call over, jogging up to Flynn. "Did you just speak to Aurora? Is she okay?"

"Yeah, um…" Flynn scratches his head, his eyes lined with shadows. "I don't really know. She seemed super flustered, was babbling on. But she told me to tell you that she's heading to the airport to sort things out with Jake or something and to say goodbye?"

No, this can't be goodbye.

She wouldn't try to patch things up with Jake.

She's *my* future, not his.

She's the middle of my fucking vision board. The thing I want most in life.

But… that's what always happens to me, isn't it?

When I finally let myself indulge in my dreams, the universe comes swooping in and takes something away. I might have managed to beat the universe by stopping Aurora from selling off my ranch, but it would still find a way to get the best of me. It would let me fall crazy in love with Aurora, let myself be completely undone by her, think I might finally be able to have everything I want—and then it would snatch her from me. Rip her from my clutches.

I claw my fingers through my hair, laughing. If I'd just left her crying that night. If I'd just ignored my feelings for her. If I'd never kissed her and let her sweet lips steal my heart—

Actually, fuck that.

I don't regret a single one of those decisions. Aurora Jones might just be the best thing that's ever happened to me, and I'll be damned if I'm just going to let her walk away.

I'm going to fight for what I want this time. Because *she* made me realise that I deserve everything I could dream of and more. There's no way in hell that her coming to Sunset Ranch and igniting my life with her fiery radiance was for nothing.

She's meant to be mine.

She *is* mine.

"Did she say anything more?" I demand, but Flynn shakes his head, mouth twisting into a frown. Spinning on my heel, I barely hear myself over the blood rushing in my ears as I shout back to Flynn, "You're in charge of the ranch today. Don't fuck this up!"

The speed in which I'm running back into the house to grab the paper I need to show her, then jumping into my truck and racing along the road feels superhuman. But she only left a few minutes ago, so I could still catch her.

The whole drive is a blur. My heart feels like wild horses galloping in my chest. I'm honestly shocked I haven't crashed yet when I've been frantically scanning the roads for her truck. But I haven't found her yet, even though I've been speeding the whole time. Surely I should've caught up with her by now?

Pulling into the nearest parking lot, I can only hope that maybe I've overtaken her, and if I stand near the entrance, I can stop her from leaving. Running, I scan the cars around me, hoping I don't spot—

Fuck. That's her truck.

The muscles in my legs scream as I sprint towards the airport, trying to summon the kind of speed I had back in high school, hoping to catch that football in the final game I played. The kind of catch that led to the touchdown that had everyone rushing onto the field and hugging me, making me feel like I was as high as the stars.

But even that feeling doesn't compare to being with Aurora.

To hearing her laugh, all chiming silver bells and bright joy.

"Aurora!" I'm hollering her name through the entrance once I'm inside, dodging between groups of people, seeking out those colourful copper waves. But all I can see are dull shades of grey, dim faces staring at me.

"Aurora Jones!" I try again, now spinning around on the spot, hands to my head as I slowly feel my chance with her trickling away.

How am I supposed to see if her light isn't shining for me?

What about the ranch? The retreat? Surely everything we've worked on together hasn't been for nothing.

Please tell me I'm not too late.

This isn't how it was supposed to end—

"Wyatt?" A sweet voice chimes.

I shoot around, letting go of the painful breath I'd been holding when I finally spot her.

God, she's so fucking magnificent. Light shines down on her, dewy cheeks glowing beneath wide hazel eyes as she stands in the parting of the bumbling crowd. Just gaping at me.

"What are you doing here?"

Her brows draw in when I march towards her, unfurling the rolled up paper I'd crumpled in my tight fist when I'd been running. I present it to her, watching her gaze flick about the collage of pictures that I messily taped down—nowhere near as perfectly curated as the vision board she made.

But it's still motivating as hell, surrounded with photos of Sunset Ranch, Willow Ridge, warm embraces by bonfires and entangled hands. Everything I want for us. It might look exactly like how we spend our days already, but that's the point. I don't want to live a life where I'm not waking up to Aurora or cuddling her while we watch the sunset by the bonfire, where I don't enjoy working on the ranch that little bit more because I know it's as much of a part of her as it is me now.

And right in the middle of it all is the selfie she took of us in the car after she kissed me. The exact moment I knew that there was no option but to devote myself entirely to her existence.

My hands are trembling, making the paper rattle.

"Wh-what is this?" Aurora questions, strawberry lips still hanging open. She keeps blinking, shiny eyes darting between me, my shaking hands, and the pictures.

"It's our future, Aurora." I have to bring the paper to my chest, just to rest my hands against something, to keep the vision board still. "The moment you set foot on Sunset Ranch, I started seeing in colours I'd never experienced before. You showed me how to let the light into my world, to start dreaming beyond the greys my life had been painted with. You showed me that I was worthy of having what I wanted, that I was worthy of *being* wanted. You showed me what love should be like."

Aurora's eyes flash at the word *love*, silver starting to rim their edges. She sucks in a shaky breath, then swallows.

"And this," I hold up the vision board again, "is what I want. You, Aurora, are my home. This ranch was made for *us*."

"Wyatt, I—"

"No, please," I take a step forward, snatching up the distance between us, eyes wide and pleading. Aurora's lip quivers and I drop one hand from the paper to weave my fingers through hers.

"Just let me say this. Just trust in me blindly, for a moment. I know that we haven't had long together, and that I'm asking a lot of you, when you have a whole life back in England. But I don't think you were meant to come here just to find some inspiration to write and then leave again. I think the universe knew we needed each other, that we belong together. And I think Grace did too."

I bite down on my lip, thinking about all the time I've wasted lamenting over what I've lost. But now I realise, it was all to make space for someone as bright as her.

"I've never really let myself dream too far into the future, unsure if forever even exists. But if there is such a thing as forever in this crazy world, then I know that it has to be you. You make me so unbelievably happy, it's actually scary. You're so goddamn beautiful and perfect and funny and... God, I would give *anything* to just have a fraction of your light grace my life."

I lift my hand to wipe away the tear rolling down her freckled cheek with my thumb. Aurora leans into my touch, lashes fluttering down, copper waves falling over one side of her face.

"Because, well, I love you, Aurora Jones."

A wobbly, earth-shattering smile appears.

"I love you too, Wyatt Hensley," Aurora chokes out, glossy hazel eyes sparkling.

Then her arms fold around me, squeezing my core, like she can't get close enough. I nestle her into me, letting her heat imprint into my bones, resting my head against hers so I can breathe in as much of her bright, zesty scent. The one that makes me feel so alive.

I've hugged Aurora before. I've felt and tasted, every inch of her body. I know every one of her curves like the back of my hand. But this embrace feels different. It feels like all the unspoken words and longing we've tried to hide away these two months. It feels like all the promises I've ever wanted to make to her, that I'll give her a life where she never has to question her worth again. And maybe she'd give me that back too.

If I could stay in this one moment for eternity, I would. Just me and her, together. Nothing else matters, because I love her, and she loves me. This right here, is my forever. This is all I want to live for.

"I didn't kiss Holly, I promise," I whisper into her hair, followed by a flurry of kisses against her parting, letting myself get immersed into the fiery red waves I adore so much. The words come out unsteadily, but I need to make sure she knows.

She nods beneath me, arms tightening more than I thought possible, fingers stroking over where my Icarus tattoo lies. I'm going to have to find a new meaning for that now.

I might have flown too close to the golden sun, and I might have fallen, but turns out the depths of the ocean that caught me were more glorious than I could've ever imagined. I fell, but it was in love.

"I know," Aurora whimpers. "I'm sorry for not listening to you. I trust you. I really do."

"Please don't go."

Her body stiffens. She tugs herself back to stare up at me, then admits almost half-laughing, "I was never going anywhere, Wyatt."

Though every one of my muscles seems to relax from her words, the admission pouring hope into all my unhealed wounds, I look at Aurora with twisted confusion. "But Flynn said you were leaving with Jake. To say goodbye to me."

With a shake of her head, hands still gripping my ribs, Aurora counters, "*No*, I told Flynn to tell you I needed to go to the airport to sort out Jake—his flight got cancelled yesterday and we couldn't get him on another until this morning. I was saying goodbye to *him*. I was going to come back to tell you that I loved you, once we were finally alone."

My mouth drops open, but no words come out.

Safe to say Flynn will be shovelling horseshit for the next year.

"Didn't you wonder why I had no suitcases? Besides, why would I drive my own truck and leave it in the car park if I was never coming back to Colorado?"

"Those are some good questions..." I suck my teeth, loosing my hand from the small of her back to rub my forehead. The curls around my hairline are damp from where I'd been running, sticking to my skin.

"You're such an idiot," she chuckles, the beautiful sound ringing right through me, shivers running down my spine.

Aurora stretches onto her tip toes and wraps her hands around my neck, tugging me down until our lips collide.

I hadn't realised how much I'd needed this, to kiss her once more, when I'd bolted over here thinking I might never experience the starfall that came with tasting her lips ever again. My blood sings at the feel of her in my hands, pumping harder when I grab her hips and pin them against me. I've kissed her hundreds of times now, yet every single time still makes me feel like I've been starved up until then. That there will never be enough Aurora Jones for me to drink up.

Aurora pulls away first, barely leaving a gap between our lips. She rests her forehead against mine, peering up into my eyes, two pools of glorious, promising hazel searching mine. She'd looked at me like this before, almost two months ago, and I'd been worried that I might not be able to give her what she wanted. But the way her face softens this time, I know she's found it.

She's found me.

"I love you," she whispers, hot breath against my lips. "I've never been more certain of anything in my life. There's no one's arms I'd rather have holding me up, Hensley."

"I love you too, Princess." I wrap my arm around her shoulders, keeping her close, as we walk out of the airport. I don't want to go another second without feeling her against me.

Once we're outside, she chuckles softly again. "I can't believe *you* made a vision board."

I shoot her a narrowed look. "I'd rather we didn't share that with others."

"Oh, I'm telling *everyone.*" This time she lets out a full blown, mischievous cackle, shoulders bouncing under my arm. "I might even frame it, you know?"

"Don't make me turn around and put you on a plane," I tease, failing to school my features into anything serious when she bites her lip, grinning. Fuck, I am completely undone by this woman.

"Quick question—what's Priya done with that video of me?"

Aurora giggles, waving me off. "Don't worry, she promised she deleted it. And no one's going to say anything about what happened, I think they were all secretly cheering you on anyway."

Relief sweeps through me as Aurora reaches into her bag, the sound of keys jingling when she pulls them out. I snatch them away, shoving them straight into my back pocket. Her eyes flare, copper waves flailing as she spins around to me, ready to protest. I'll be making good use of that fieriness later when she's screaming out how much she loves me with my face between her legs. And probably a couple more times after that.

"I'll pick up your truck later, but there's no way in hell I'm driving home without you by my side. Not after I thought I'd never get a chance to be with you again."

"Home," Aurora repeats, rolling her strawberry lips. But it barely hides the way her grin stretches out, the kind of smile that creeps up on you when your happiness just can't be contained.

Arm still around her shoulders, I tuck her in closer to me, relishing in the way she slots perfectly against my body. I always knew she was made for me, every inch of her perfectly created to be the final piece of the puzzle that has been my life.

"Yes, Princess, *our* home."

Epilogue

Wyatt

Aurora's grasp tightens in my curls, pulling as her breathing gets deeper, longer, with each stroke of my tongue and fingers. Toned, golden legs begin to shake, slung over my shoulders, exactly where they were designed to be. It's moments like these, wrapped in nothing but devotion and pleasure with Aurora, that I wonder if some sort of higher power really does exist. Because there's no way two people could be made so perfectly in harmony with each other just by coincidence.

And when she calls out my name, the sound a goddamn melody as tremors of ecstasy caress her body, I'm wholly convinced.

After lapping up the last few whimpers of her orgasm, I prop myself beside Aurora, pulling her into me, her leg resting on my hip. It's taking every bit of self-control I have to not start grinding against her or roll her over so she's fully straddling me. But I know we don't have time today—well, not the amount of time I want to spend tangled up in the sheets with her.

"Did that help you feel less nervous, Princess?" I ask, rather enjoying the dazed glow in her fluttering eyes. Sunshine glitters through the crack in the curtains, a slice of morning light pouring over Aurora, making her skin glisten. So goddamn angelic.

She's barely caught her breath back but offers me a blissful smile. "I think that might just do the trick."

"Good," I announce, smacking a kiss on her forehead before jumping out bed. "Because you need to get your ass up, otherwise your folks are gonna be waiting for us at the airport."

Aurora groans, trying to pull the covers up around her face. I rip them away, revealing her crumpled face, and have to take a second to just bask in the gratitude that she is mine. But I can also still see the small glisten of worry in her eyes.

"Hey," I whisper, brushing my lips against her freckled jaw. "They're gonna love what we've done with Sunset Ranch, okay? They're so proud of you and this business you've built, just like I am."

Aurora's soft smile and nod send a shot of warmth into my chest. Proud doesn't cut how I feel about how hard she's worked—constantly in awe might be a better way to describe it.

Setting up the retreat hasn't been easy, especially as we've had to navigate how we'll keep the place running during colder seasons, when having guests here just won't work. But we've managed to adapt the activities to suit the weather and time of the year when we can, and when the spring hit, we were already fully booked. It's been a roller-coaster since then, meeting so many new people, and even having to hire a couple more employees to help as we've expanded. Especially now we're building a communal kitchen and dining area for guests.

But I get where her nerves have come from. Her family might know about everything we've been working on this past year, but this will be the first time they've seen it in person. Everything she chose to stay for, instead of returning home like planned.

And if anyone understands the fear of your parents not approving your decisions, it's me. So, I sat for thirty minutes, holding her hand as we did a meditation together, knowing that sometimes she just needs someone to see her and how she feels without judgement. Then I peeled off her silky pyjamas and told her exactly how proud I am of her with my tongue.

As much as I hate to admit it, I do always feel better after doing a meditation with her. A year ago, I would've been appalled at the things Aurora's managed to rope me into doing. I just didn't realise how much more I'd care about loving her than what people thought of me back then. Which is good because I've been forced into far too many of her Instagram posts now. Somehow she even coerced me into going on her friend's podcast with her.

I press another kiss to her neck, running my teeth along the sensitive skin. "Besides, your parents love me, so even if they're not fans of the retreat, they'll still be proud you managed to bag such a catch."

Aurora snorts, pushing me away with a giggle as she finally climbs out the bed. "You have far too much confidence now. I think I preferred you when you were moody and self-deprecating."

"Ah," I say, not hiding the way I'm drinking in every inch of her bare body as she saunters over to the bedroom door, unhooking her satin robe from the back. "The good old days."

Aurora opens the door before checking over her shoulder with a gleaming smile. "Nowhere as good as it is now."

Once she's in the bathroom doing her makeup, I finally let out the long sigh I've been holding all morning. Because if anyone should be nervous today, it's *me*.

I'm the one who's barely slept all night, running over all the things I need to say to her dad if I'm going to convince him to give me her hand. He's only met me once properly when we travelled to England for the holidays, but I feel like we hit it off relatively well. We bonded over sports mostly, but also how little we enjoyed *Love Actually* while Aurora and her mum and sister tried to convince us to watch it for the third time.

I think Aurora's family coming here and seeing how alive she feels on Sunset Ranch will help my case. That I'm where she needs to be. Where she thrives.

Though, I don't think it's really her dad I need to worry about saying yes—after finally quitting her teaching job, Sofia is flying out with the rest of the Jones family to visit. From our conversations during her video calls with Aurora, she's already made it clear that I'll have to go through her as well before I propose. Which, given how much she cares for our little redhead, I know is going to take a lot of ass-kissing.

But I can't wait any longer to ask.

Aurora is my home and there's no way I'm ever letting her go.

My whole body feels jittery. Usually this would call for a ride around on Dusty, but I don't have time for that, and Aurora will just ask questions. Either way, I can't just stand here in the bedroom. I need some fresh air at least.

Once I'm dressed and downstairs, I do a quick check in my inside jacket pocket for the ring box, a shot of relief hitting my heart when I feel it. I swing open the front door of not just the main house, but *our* house, yet I halt at the massive cardboard box waiting on the porch.

She's always getting random packages sent to her from all the brands she works with, so I'm used to finding piles of boxes and bags on our front porch, but this one is huge.

"Did you order something?" I yell up the stairs and grab my keys to slice open the box. Just as I crouch down beside it, Aurora's footsteps tumble down behind me.

"Oh! I think that's my books!" she squeals, hopping past me to inspect the box and giving me a great view of her perfect ass in the tight purple leggings she's wearing.

I love that I don't ever have to pretend I'm not staring now. Because, God, does she look incredible. Wearing that purple gym set she wore when I first saw her. Every inch of her freckled, golden skin glowing under the sun. And that beautiful waterfall of copper waves that always look so good wrapped around my hand.

How I ever managed to stop myself from kissing her for all that time when we first met, I'll never understand. Wyatt Hensley was delusional back then, that's all I'll say.

Aurora holds out her hand in silent request for the keys, which I pass over, and she uses the sharpest to slice open the box, another high-pitched noise of excitement ringing from her as her face lights up. I lean over, hoping to get a look at the front cover of the book she's worked so hard on for the last year, that I've read over countless pages of for her, yet she still won't tell me the title.

But now the release date is quickly approaching, Aurora's ordered a bunch of copies to keep in the guesthouses, including my old place which we've converted so even more guests can stay at the retreat, especially now the summer's hit.

I fold back the cardboard to get a better look. Aurora's silvery giggle erupts from her strawberry lips as she nudges me, clearly having noticed my sigh of disbelief and the shake of my head.

"You've got to be fucking kidding me," I laugh as I spy the three large words sprawled in pink across the cover.

Aurora kisses my shoulder, then leans her head against it, the warmth of her pure, unadulterated happiness radiating into me. "Three things that make for a beautiful, successful life—living every day to its fullest, ranching, and loving as deeply as possible."

Live, Ranch, Love.

About the Author

Emma Lucy is a romance author based in London who loves writing books that will make you swoon, blush, and hopefully learn to believe in yourself a little more. When she's not writing, she's usually reading, listening to whatever new country music artist she's obsessed with, or trying to convince her boyfriend to go to a bookstore with her. *Live, Ranch, Love* is Emma's debut novel. You can find her on Instagram and TikTok at @emmalucyauthor.

Acknowledgements

Whenever I read the acknowledgments pages in books, I normally get super emotional. I think it's such a beautiful opportunity to thank all the wonderful people who help to make an author's dreams come true. I've always dreamed about being able to write my own one day, and today, I finally get to.

To my wonderful parents and step-parents for being the best family I could ever ask for. To Mum, for teaching me to believe in myself and for always caring for me so fiercely. And to Dad, for always being so enthusiastic about my passions and cheering me on from the moment I spoke about writing a book (it's your turn to write one next!)

To my sister, for being my best friend and being there for me whenever I've needed you.

To my amazing friends—Izzy, Gina, Jenny, and Clare—your undying support of my writing means so much to me, and there's never a dull day when I'm with you guys.

To Dave, for being a real-life example of a book boyfriend. You've supported me through every up and down with this book, listening to all of my worries, and celebrating every win, no matter how big or small.

To my amazing beta readers—Alison, Andrea, Cat, Charlotte, Holly, Jagoda, Kayla, Taylor, and Rebecca—thank you so much for helping me to shape Wyatt and Rory's story into the best it could possibly be, and for your continued support.

To Kayla, I am incredibly grateful for your editing, and for you picking out all the English phrases/words that aren't used in America so that Wyatt's chapters felt more genuine. And to Andrea, for not only helping me to perfect *Live, Ranch, Love*'s plot, but also for your thorough editorial expertise.

To my sensitivity reader, Kat Lewis, for helping me to make sure Wyatt's background was presented authentically and respectfully.

To the incredibly talented Sam and Mel at Ink and Velvet Designs for the most beautiful cover ever. In all honesty, I owe a big deal of my sanity to you—you guys pulled this cover out of the bag with such a small time frame, and I will forever be grateful for how you gifted me a cover that brings me so much joy (and continues to fuel my obsession with pink).

A massive shout out to my gorgeous Street Team who, before even reading *Live, Ranch, Love,* have been championing this book. Your constant kind messages and excitement for *Live, Ranch, Love* makes every day worth it.

To all the beautiful bookish and author friends I've made through social media—thanks for all the support, advice, and passion you have shared with me on this journey. Some of you have been with me since my bookstagram days, and without you I might not have ever shared my love of writing with the world.

To younger me, for never letting your wildly vivid imagination stagnate. For working on yourself, building up your confidence, and reconnecting with what truly brings you joy, so that you could finally become the author you always wanted to be. And thanks for running with that random little idea for a cowboy romance you had, because it turned out to be pretty damn big.

And finally, to you, reader. For taking a chance on a debut author like me and giving your time to *Live, Ranch, Love*. Without you, Rory and Wyatt would not be able to come to life, so I thank you for choosing *Live, Ranch, Love*, and hope it brings you joy.

Leave a Review!

Thank you so much for reading *Live, Ranch, Love*! If you enjoyed *Live, Ranch, Love*, then it would mean the absolute world to me if you left me a review. Scan the QR code below to leave a review on Goodreads:

You can also leave a review on Amazon!

Sign Up to My Newsletter!

Do you want to keep up to date with Rory, Wyatt, and the rest of the gang in Willow Ridge? Scan the QR code below to sign up to my newsletter, where I'll be sharing exclusive updates on the Willow Ridge series, including a bonus epilogue from Wyatt and Rory:

Printed in Great Britain
by Amazon

44056729R00209